The Rancher
and the Rock Star

The Rancher and the Rock Star

LIZBETH SELVIG

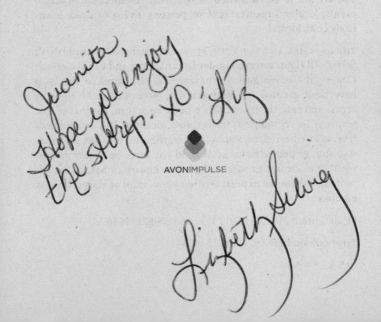

Juanita,
Hope you enjoy
the story. XO, Liz

AVON IMPULSE

Lizbeth Selvig

This is a work of fiction. Names, characters, places, and incidents are products of the author's imagination or are used fictitiously and are not to be construed as real. Any resemblance to actual events, locales, organizations, or persons, living or dead, is entirely coincidental.

EPub Edition MARCH 2012 ISBN: 9780062134646

Print Edition ISBN: 9780062134653

10 9 8 7 6 5 4 3

This book is dedicated to
Jennifer—who fell in love with her favorite singer without
apology, even when he wasn't cool to her friends and who,
in the most wonderful mother-daughter moment, gave
me an idea for a "what if" story. Here it is, sweetheart.

All my love to
Adam—who patiently keeps his mother up to-
date with popular music and recording techniques,
and to my hero, Jan, who's never in all these years
needed lessons on how to be a White Knight.

Thanks to
Carolyn (who thinks this book is half hers), Gretchen,
Jenny, Tami, DeNise, and the AKRWA critters who
started this book with me. And to Laramie, Nancy, and
Ellen, who finished it. Finally, to my wonderful and
tenacious agent, Elizabeth Winick Rubinstein, who kept
after me until this story was its best, and my editor, Tessa
Woodward, who just kept saying the nicest things—
and got me to put the cherry on top of the sundae!

Chapter One

FATE WAS A nasty flirt.

Gray Covey dropped his forehead to the steering wheel of his rented Chevy Malibu and sighed, a plaintive release of breath, like a balloon with a pinhole leak. He had no idea what he'd done to her, but Fate had been after him for months. After this last wrong turn in her twisted maze, he knew she'd finally trapped him.

The long, pitted road before him wasn't described in the useless directions scribbled on the slip of paper in his hand. Neither were the two branches fanning left and right fifty yards away. And being lost wasn't enough. Oh-ho, no. On top of everything, Fate had hung an angry, bruise-colored sky about to unleash enough water to terrify Noah.

He lifted his eyes, rubbing the creases above his brow. As he prepared to admit defeat, the edge of a small sign to the left caught his eye, and his first small hope sparked.

Inching the Malibu over the washboard road, he pulled up to the hand-lettered sign he'd been told to look for. Hope flared into gratitude.

Hallelujah. *Jabberwicki Ranch*.

Still unable to believe someone would give a piece of property such a stupid-ass name, he stopped short of laughing. Half an hour ago, a dour attendant named Dewey at the only gas station in Kennison Falls, Minnesota, had made it clear nobody in the town of eight hundred souls laughed at anything Abby Stadtler–related. The woman Gray sought was no less than revered.

And yet . . .

The saintly Abby Stadtler was harboring a missing child.

His.

He rolled past the Jibberjabber sign, stopping at side-by-side black mailboxes. *A. Stadtler—Jabberwicki* and *E. Mertz*. Ethel Mertz. What?

Alice in Wonderland meets *I Love Lucy*?

"You've got to be kidding me." He spoke out loud without meaning to. Out of habit he checked over his shoulder to make sure he hadn't been followed and overheard.

This explained why Dawson had been so hard to find—he'd fallen down a friggin' rabbit hole. The sophomoric humor helped him remember he was only half serious about throttling his runaway son to within an inch of his life. And it kept him distanced from emotions that had been scraped raw in the past weeks. His current jinxed concert tour aside, between his mother's worsening illness, moving her to the care facility, and Dawson's disappearance within days of that, life lately had been sorely lacking in humor.

Except, maybe, for Ariel. In his ex-wife's case, all he could do was laugh. "They've found Dawson," she'd announced on the phone the night before in her clipped British accent. "But unless you want the authorities to fetch him, you'll have to pick him up, darling. I can't leave Europe with the baby."

Of course not. After all, only six weeks had passed since their son's disappearance—nobody could make arrangements for a two-year-old on such short notice.

Gray had not been about to let the police "fetch" his son, nor had he wanted to alert Dawson and send the boy running again. So here he was in Jabbitybobbits, Minnesota, despite the monumental nightmare he'd caused by leaving his manager, his baffled band members, and eighteen thousand fans in the lurch.

Well, what the hell? It was just Fate adding another hilarious disaster to the worst tour in rock history. Refocusing, he looked left toward a homey log house, then right into a thick stand of pine and oak. Which fork led to Ethel Mertz and which to The Jabberwock's ranch?

Eeny, meeny, miny . . . He couldn't get lost if he stayed right. Slowly he drove toward the trees and didn't see the diminutive, elderly woman staring at him until he'd drawn even with where she stood in an opulent flower garden near the road. For a moment he considered stopping, but her assessing glower and the stern set to her square-jowled face convinced him to settle for an impersonal wave and continue around the gentle curve through the woods. He hoped the dour watchwoman wasn't the much-adored Abby Stadtler.

The house he *hoped* belonged to Jabberwocket . . . *Ranch?* didn't appear until he was in its front yard—an old, two-story farmhouse painted non-traditional Guinness brown with windows and doors trimmed in blue and white. A disheveled patch of shaggy, colorful wildflowers, much less immaculate than the garden he'd just passed, stretched along one side.

The growl of thunder greeted Gray as he exited the car, and he looked with concern at smoke-bellied thunderheads piling high. The end-of-May breeze smelled wet and thick. In front of a small garage stood an older, red Explorer, and on his left a short stone path led to a porch wrapping two sides of the house.

After mounting two loose steps, he faced a pair of dusty saddles, the kind with big, sturdy horns in front, sitting on sawhorses, and several flowerpots in various stages of being planted. A small square of black electrical tape covered the doorbell. He knocked, got no answer, then knocked again. Several minutes later he returned to the driveway, searching his surroundings. Down another gravel slope, a couple hundred yards away, stood a vintage barn, its white paint worn and the haymow window boarded-up from the inside. He sighed and climbed back into his car.

Heady scents of hay, sawdust, and animals hung in the heavy air when he left the Malibu once again. To his delight, a golden retriever loped toward him with lolling tongue and giant doggy smile. "Hey fella." Gray scratched the dog's ears. "Got a boss around here somewhere?"

A muffled *thunk* answered. Ahead, backed up against the open door of the barn, stood a flatbed trailer loaded high with spring-green hay. The golden led him to the wagon front, and a pair of small, gloved hands emerged from inside the barn, grabbed the twine on one bale, and yanked it out of sight. Intrigued, he watched until the owner of the hands popped from the dim barn interior. She placed her palms on the flatbed and, in one graceful movement, hoisted her long-legged body to a stand. Reaching for a top-tier bale, she dragged on it, toppling the entire stack. Gray's brows lifted in appreciation.

"Afternoon," he called.

Her startled cry rang more like a bell than a screech of fear, but she stared at him with her mouth in a pretty *oh* and her chest heaving. "Jeez Louise!" she said at last. "You scared me half to death!"

Flawless skin was flushed with exertion, and her round, bright eyes flashed uncertainty. A thick, soft pile of chestnut made a haphazard bun atop her head, but long wisps of hair had escaped and swung to her shoulders. Her face stopped Gray's thoughts dead. It was not the toughened visage he'd have expected of a woman who chucked hay bales like a longshoreman. The elegant, doe-eyed face belonged in a magazine, not a barn.

"I'm really sorry," he said.

A rumpled, hay-flecked, flannel shirt hung loose over body-hugging, faded jeans that had suffered one nicely-placed rip across her left thigh. He braced for the inevitable squeal of recognition.

"Can I help you with something?" She squinted at

him for a few seconds, but rather than squeal, she shook her head and pulled down another stack of hay.

"Are you Abby Stadtler?"

"Yes." She continued dragging bales, and he sighed in relief.

"I'm looking for my son."

That stopped her. "Son?" Her eyes took on a glint of protectiveness. "Who are you?"

That stopped him. For an instant his vanity stung, but the freedom of unaccustomed anonymity hit, and he allowed a private grin. "David Graham." He used his official alias. "Pleased to meet you."

"Likewise," she said. "Excuse my rudeness, but this hay has to get in that barn before the storm hits. I can't help you with your son. I don't know anybody named Graham."

Abby Stadtler hopped to the ground. The plaid shirt swung open to reveal a bright blue tank top hugging a curvy hip. "My boy isn't Graham," he said, meeting her eyes, which were unlike anything he'd ever seen. Greenish? Blue-ish? "He's Dawson. Dawson Covey."

"I know a Dawson. His last name is Cooper."

He tamped down a flicker of irritation, as she grabbed twine, swung a bale, and took two steps to dump it in the barn. There was not a single sound of exertion—or any hint she was taking him seriously.

"Yes, that would be my devious son." He held onto a pleasant tone. "Cooper is his grandmother's name."

"And why would he use a different name?"

As she turned the interrogation on him, a rope of tension twisting down his neck knotted between his shoulder blades and threatened to stiffen him top to toe. He willed his fingers to uncurl, one-by-one "Because he's sixteen years old, he's pissed off at his mother and is hiding from me. He's also sharp as a knife blade, so it's taken us a while to find him. You've obviously never had teenagers."

An immediate illusion of height accompanied the steeling of her spine, and the soft, nameless color of her eyes turned to stormy aquamarine. "You shouldn't make assumptions." She tossed another hay bale, and Gray took a step backward.

"I apologize. I only meant you don't look old enough to have teenagers." That was true.

"If that was an attempt at getting yourself off the hook, it was smooth but ineffective." The sharpest prickles left her voice.

Finally, she stopped tossing and crossed her arms. The rolled-up sleeves on her overshirt exposed slender forearms with sexy lines of definition curved along the muscle.

Gray produced his best version of a devilish grin. "Dang. I usually have better luck with a silver tongue."

"I'll just bet. Look, Mr. Graham." She hesitated. "Wait a minute. Did you say sixteen?"

"Yup. My Dawson is sixteen. How old is yours?"

She didn't respond to the humor. "Eighteen. We definitely have some confusion here. I hired a young man six weeks ago to help around the farm. He'll be leaving for home in another month. Colorado."

Gray snorted. "He'll be leaving for Colorado over my dead body."

"Mr. Graham." Her voice flashed with annoyance to

match her eyes. "I think you have the wrong Dawson. People must have mixed up the information they gave you."

"I do not have the wrong Dawson." Slamming his palm on the wooden bed of the hay wagon hard enough to cause flakes of alfalfa, and Abby Stadtler, to jump, the humor Gray had been using so desperately as a shield disintegrated. His make-nice smiles hardened into anger lines he could feel. "Look, Madam Jabberingwickets, or whatever the hell this place is called. You've got my son." He jabbed his fingers into a back pocket, yanked out his wallet, and flipped through the three pictures that were part of its meager contents. "Tell me this isn't the little con artist you call Dawson Cooper."

The photo was two years old, but it did the trick. Abby leaned over it with skepticism, and then her shoulders sagged. "Oh no."

"Oh yes."

"I, I'm sorry."

He gave her points for the apology, although she looked for all the world as if she didn't want to give it. "It's all right." He calmed his voice. "All I want is to find my son."

"I've never heard Dawson mention a father. He's talked about his mother in New York."

In a stinging sort of way that made sense, Dawson wouldn't want to mention his dad's notoriety. He jammed the wallet back into his pocket. "She's not in New York. They live in London, and he packed up and left his private school just after Easter last month. Didn't you check him out before letting him move in?"

Anger flared in her face again. For some reason, Gray found the rising and falling storms in her seawater eyes knee-weakening. "You *really* need to stop making judgments. What you just said was condescending and insulting."

She turned her back and grabbed another hay bale, tossing it willy-nilly into a pile along with the others already in the barn. This one went a fair distance with the steam of her anger behind it. He couldn't help but grin in admiration. Abby Stadtler was soft and enticing as a chocolate éclair on the outside, with TNT instead of custard beneath the surface.

"Look, I don't know you . . ."

"That's right." Her fuse obviously still sparked, she clambered onto the wagon again. "For your information, your son had a New York driver's license, references from a past employer, and a personal reference. No, I didn't do an FBI background check on him. Up until now, I've had no reason to suspect I needed to. I don't know where you come from, but around here we try our hardest to believe the best of people."

Gray scarcely heard beyond the fact Dawson had come up with faked reference documents. He didn't know whether to be horrified or impressed as hell.

"I . . . That's amazing." He tried finding some amusement in her face, but she kept yanking hay bales from the pile, her back flexing, captivating him. He wondered where Mr. Stadtler was. "Abby . . . Mrs. Stadtler." He struggled not to anger her again. "I told you my son is smart. I forgot how smart. He's pulled off a professional-level scam here, and I can't tell you how grateful I am he came to a safe place like this."

She threw a glance over her shoulder, her eyes no longer sizzling. "He's a good boy, Mr. Graham, even now that I know the truth. Not that he won't get a proper lecture."

The very first hint of humor tinged her voice, and Gray grinned back, relief sweet in his chest. "You'd be justified. So, where is he?" Realization struck him. "Why isn't he helping?"

"He isn't here."

His attention snapped back to her. "Excuse me?"

"He and Kim are gone for the weekend."

"Gone! Gone?" Gray balled his fists and wanted to hurl a hay bale across the barn himself. "Gone where? And who the—" He took a deep breath. "Who is Kim?"

"The teenager you thought it obvious I never had." This time her eyes danced with a hint of laughter, and if her newfound cheerfulness hadn't come at his expense he'd have found the crinkled corners of her eyes appealing.

"When will he be back from wherever he went? With your teenage daughter." He forced his voice to stay modulated and pleasant.

"They've been on a retreat with the church youth group all week. They'll be back tomorrow late morning."

"Tomorrow?" *Another day?* Gray lost his hold on calm. "Damn it!"

He stalked from the hay wagon. The cloying air pressed

heavier with every step, and the clouds encroached, purple and black. Thunder reverberated, close, angry. He had another show in Chicago tomorrow night. No way could he miss it, too. What would Chris do when he found out tonight's gig hadn't needed to be canceled at all?

Slipping his hand into the pocket of his leather blazer, he fumbled for a pack of cigarettes. He hated them. He was down to half a pack a day, but times like this he despaired of ever kicking the habit. With automatic skill he drew one out, flicked his lighter flame against the end of the cigarette, and took a drag.

The idea of Chris Boyle on a rant made Gray swear under his breath again. Everything came down to money for his manager. Sometimes Gray felt like no more than a wind-up monkey who waddled onstage, banged its cymbals together, made the crowd screech, and raked in the dough. He dug his fingers through his hair and started a vicious second drag—

Thwack!

The cigarette flew from his lips as if a bullwhip had snatched it, and he choked on air and smoke.

"Are you really this phenomenally stupid?" Abby, her face florid, her posture like a boxer ready to jab, ground her boot toe into the smoldering cigarette until shattered pulp remained.

"What the . . . ?" He stared at the ruins then into her furious eyes.

"This is a barn. Fifty feet away is a wagon loaded with hay. Do you have any idea what a gust of wind could do with one of your stupid ashes?"

"Oh, damn, Abby, Mrs. . . . Abby. I'm sorry." Contrition twisted his gut.

He *hadn't* considered the danger before lighting up. Her gaze drilled into his, and regret gave way to a slow roll of deep, unexpected attraction. Earlier they'd been separated by hay and irritation, but now they were separated by nothing but five inches of steamy, sultry air. An asinine string of thoughts ran through his brain: how smooth her cheek was up close; how the middle of her pupil was soft and calm like the eye of a hurricane; how much he wished he had a breath mint.

"It won't happen again."

Along with his sudden, inappropriate desire came an image of Fate laughing as he got pummeled by Mr. Abby Stadtler—who probably always carried breath mints. Then, without warning, Abby's face drained of color. Slowly, she covered her mouth with one slender hand.

ABBY PRESSED SO hard against her lips she could almost feel pulses in her fingertips—ten runaway jackhammers. Every clue, every suspicion, crashed over her as she stared at the earnest-eyed man before her. How in the world had she missed it? What was he doing in her farmyard?

When he said, "It won't happen again," his thick brows furrowed in honest apology, his rich baritone was suddenly, obviously, as familiar as her daughter's voice. And his pale blue eyes were ones she'd seen as many times as she'd entered her child's bedroom, only this time they mesmerized in person, not from a dozen posters on Kim's walls.

He'd given it away himself. "Dawson Covey."

Oh, Lord, she'd slapped a cigarette from Gray Covey's mouth.

Strangled laughter caught at her throat. This was far from the meeting fantasized by ten thousand adoring women at any given time. What did you say to a rock legend after you'd called him a liar? She dropped her hands from her mouth. "You—"

His face changed. The instant before she'd recognized him, he'd shown honest contrition. Now his mouth slipped into a strange, plastic smile, automatic, a little self-satisfied. Her annoyance sparked. It reminded her why, despite his knee-weakening looks, he'd irritated her with his assumptions and attitude. All at once, she didn't want to give him the satisfaction of fawning over his identity.

"Sorry." She forced herself to spin away and pull off a fib. "I just got a mental picture of my barn going up in flames. I accept your apology. But know this. If it *does* happen again, I won't be knocking the cigarette out of your mouth. I'll be drowning it with you attached."

Ignoring his celebrity left her uplifted, as if she was going against nature—something her practical streak rarely allowed. She half-expected him to protest with wounded pride but, in fact, he remained silent until she was back at the hay wagon.

"You're funny even when you're mad," he said. "I guess I consider myself lucky."

"My daughter wouldn't say I'm funny." She half-grinned, although her back was to him.

"Speaking of your daughter and, by association it seems, my son. I don't suppose there's any way of getting them home early? I was hoping to take him with me tonight."

Irritation seized her again, and she glared over her shoulder. Her breath caught now that she recognized who he was, but she shook it off. "Dawson's been living here for almost six weeks. Won't it be kinder to give him time to adjust?"

"You do understand he's a runaway, right?" His voice lifted a notch in irritation. "You have no claim to him. Not to mention, a lot of people have been put out by your . . . employee."

"Put out? How about worried? Has anyone been worried in all the time it took to locate him?" Immediately Abby regretted the thoughtless words. Gray's features stilled, and his eyes iced. "I'm sorry. That was rude of me . . ."

The first plop of rain hit her dead on the nose, followed by a second on her head. Her heart sank. She'd let herself get distracted, and now she risked losing the eighty bales of hay still on the rack if they got soaked.

"Crap, crap, crap." For half a second she waffled between Gray and the hay wagon. She groaned and chose the hay. "I'm sorry. Can you finish this discussion from the barn?"

Two more fat drops left splotches on her shoulders, and she hoisted herself back up onto the wagon. Normally, she didn't mind stacking hay. It taxed her body while anesthetizing her brain. But even if she threw as hard as she could she wouldn't beat this storm.

"I worried about him." Gray's voice held as much promise of thunder as the storm.

"I didn't mean that." She pulled two stacks of bales into heaps with one movement, and they banged into her legs, nearly knocking her off balance. More rain splashed her cheeks. "At least, I didn't mean it to sound so harsh."

"Let's just call us even for assumptions. The point is, I flew from Chicago and am missing work to be here. I'm sure this will sound even crasser to you, but I have appointments I can't miss. My job involves more than just me and a boss."

Two bales. Three. Four.

"So you thought you'd simply grab your son and, what, take him to work with you?"

"As a matter of fact, that's exactly what I thought. I'm his father. I have considered what's best for him."

Five. Six. Seven. Abby heaved the hay just far enough to get it into the barn door. She could stack it later. Her arms started to sting from their exaggerated motions, but she knew how to ignore the discomfort.

"I'm sure that's true." She grunted with exertion. "But wouldn't you like to know why he ran away in the first place, before you haul him off again?"

"Lady." His taut voice caused her to look into his angry face. "I don't know if you think you're some sort of pop psychiatrist, but I'm not the sixteen-year-old here. I know why my son ran and, frankly, I don't blame him.

But, it's not your business, and I don't have the freedom to hang around waiting for him to come back."

The drops fell faster, and the breeze picked up. An eerie twilight settled over the farm.

"Seems to me you do what you have to do where your children are concerned "Sacrifice. Ask yourself what your priorities are." She tossed harder. The tender alfalfa leaves in the fragrant bundles glistened with moisture. In ten minutes the bales would be soaked deep. The rain saturated her shirt, and the tendrils escaping her loose chignon clung to her cheeks.

"You're something, you know that? You warn me about making assumptions then tell me my priorities are screwed up. Who the hell do you think you are? "

The knife-blade edge to his voice made her stop and blink. She'd concentrated so hard on fighting the rain that she'd forgotten her actual fight with the person next to her. Lecture mode always seemed to slip out when she multi-tasked, but Gray's glare of unequivocal anger told her she'd stepped over the line. Although the water beating into her hay made her cringe, she looked him in the eye.

"I'm sorry," she began, but something fluttered in her chest, and she caught her breath in surprise. He didn't look exactly like any picture of him she'd ever seen— and Kim had scrapbooks full of clippings and magazine photos. Three dimensions served him incredibly well. "You're right." She reined in her emotions. "I've grown fond of your son, Mr. . . . Graham. But I don't have the right to be protective of him."

The anger drained from his eyes, but his body remained a study of sculpted seriousness. Cocoa-colored hair feathered back from his forehead and framed his high cheekbones with thick locks that kissed his collar. A chiseled Adam's apple bobbed when he swallowed, and Abby's stomach fluttered again. If the rock-and-roll lifestyle was supposed to ravage a body, Gray Covey's hadn't paid attention to the rule.

Unable to ignore her hay any longer, she pulled her gaze from Gray's, jumped off the wagon, and began dragging bales. This time her back muscles whined with every surge.

"I don't suppose you could wait to finish until this passes?" he asked. He held up his palm to show he knew the answer. The rain on the old barn roof drummed like the backbeat on one of his songs. A flash of lightning slashed the dark sky, and thunder followed mere seconds later. He shucked off his leather jacket. "Aw, hell."

Chapter Two

His fitted, denim-colored T-shirt read "Dashboard Confessional," but it wasn't the band name that unhinged her jaw. Who would have known a singer could sport biceps and pecs like— She snapped her mouth shut. *Get a grip, Abigail. You sound like Kim.*

On second thought, no way did Abby want her daughter thinking what she was thinking.

"Forget it." She meant her refusal sincerely. "You'll just get wet, too. I can handle this."

"You can't come close to finishing all those bales alone, and I can't stand here any longer watching a damsel in distress."

Her flash of defensive pride had no time to grow. Two seconds later they were both soaked to the skin. After they each had a stack safely inside, Abby took a moment to rummage in a corner for a pair of canvas work gloves.

He thanked her with a silly smile, and she realized what a ridiculous situation she was in. His fame aside, they'd known each other fifteen minutes, and here he was in a downpour, ruining expensive-looking leather shoes and a perfectly good pair of jeans, and doing some serious atonement for lighting his cigarette in the process.

As they fell into a quick, efficient rhythm, there was no missing that Gray Covey's pecs and deltoids were not merely for show. He didn't need to get off the trailer and lug bales into the barn. Instead, he hoisted cube after bristly cube and launched them like javelins through the door. For every four bales she heaved, Gray tossed eight. His biceps contracted over and over, smooth and firm, and his hips twisted in fluid perfection with no wasted movement.

By the time they were three-quarters finished, she'd changed her mind—or lost it. He wasn't ruining his jeans. He could have sold the sucked-on denim for a thousand bucks to any woman who saw it. She let herself imagine what a phenomenal photo she could take. It had been a long time since she'd seen anything finer than Gray Covey/David Graham with his thick, rain-darkened hair slicked back to his collar and rivulets of water streaming from his cheeks.

They continued without words. Once in a while, when a bale flew well, she heard a guttural "oof" from his throat that gave her more chills than the rain did. She refused to dwell on the errant thoughts—they were so foreign she barely recognized them as hers. But even in the driving rain, with lightning crackling every half a minute and thunder following much too closely, Abby didn't think she'd ever enjoyed any job on her farm as much.

In ten minutes they had every bale under the roof. She stood beside Gray in the deluge staring at the barn floor, which looked like the aftermath of the Big Bad Wolf versus the first Little Pig's house.

"Woo hoo!" He uttered his first syllables since climbing onto the wagon. Blowing out a deep sigh, he bent and braced his hands on his thighs. He peered up at her and grinned. "Here I thought I'd have to miss the gym today. You were going to do this all yourself, Mrs. Stadtler? I'm damn impressed."

The compliment pleased her ridiculously.

He straightened and held up his palm for her to slap. Their gloves made a pitiful, slurping smack, and Abby giggled, although embarrassment picked at the edges of her gratitude.

"I don't know how to thank you. This defines above and beyond."

He tilted his head back and opened his mouth to the sky. His Adam's apple convulsed, and Abby's throat went so dry she could have been standing in a desert rather than a monsoon.

"Not what I expected when I left Chicago this morning. But it's been a very long time since I've played in a full-blown thunderstorm." He winked and licked the water from his lips.

"I'm a little worried about you if you think you've been playing." She didn't tell him that for over ten minutes she hadn't once considered this work either.

He laughed. "C'mon. A celebratory dance before we get you inside."

"Dance?"

He linked their elbows and pulled her into a hoe-down spin on the wagon bed. To her astonishment, he started in on a pretty song she'd never heard on any disc in Kim's collection.

"A storm-eyed girl took my hand one day,
and said, 'Follow me, boy, I know the way.'
I went with open heart and soul,
till the rain came down and she had to go."

He drew her into a waltz hold and hummed more of the beautiful tune. *"Mmm, mmmm, thought this was our dance. And she said . . ."* He hesitated, then shrugged and grinned. *" 'No, no, no, I'm off to France.'"*

Abby managed a snort at the song's goofy degeneration, but after Gray spun her beneath his arm and let her go, he bowed. She couldn't draw enough breath to make another sound. He jumped off the wagon, reached for her waist, and took her weight to lift her down. She'd never been touched in such a downright sexy way.

Once under shelter she surveyed the hay chaff coating her drenched pant legs. Gray's thousand-dollar Levi's—button front she noticed now—had fared no better.

"What was that song?" she asked to distract herself.

A slight flush darkened his cheeks, followed by an-other shrug. "Let's call it 'Dance in France' and just say you've heard its first and last performance. Sorry, sometimes things just pop out of my mouth." He copied her and looked down his legs. "Wow. Is this Minnesota's equivalent to tarring and feathering?"

"I'm sorry." Unwelcome flutters plagued her as he brushed at the dust and watched it turn to soupy slop on his T-shirt. "I shouldn't have let—"

"Hey?" A firm gaze caught hers. "I offered, so stop being sorry." He burst into laughter. "But we are nasty. What now?"

"The rain is bound to let up. I'll see if I can find some clean towels, and at least we can dry our hair. I'll be right back."

She hurried for the tack room in the corner of the barn, feeling guilty for leaving him alone, but needing time to tame her unruly thoughts. His song infiltrated her mind along with the memory of his powerful body guiding hers through the fanciful dance, and a combination of heat from her face and cold from her wet clothing undulated through her like fever chills.

After peeling off her sodden, flannel shirt, she grabbed a handful of clean towels normally used on the horses. Scanning the room, she spied an old, oversized sweatshirt on the ancient washing machine in the corner. Gray could at least try it.

When she returned, he was no longer alone but squatting beside a wiggling, face-licking, very soggy golden retriever. For a moment she stared as Gray fawned and chuckled over her dog in a classic, heart-warming moment. "Roscoe," she called, breaking her own spell. "Stop it, and leave him alone now."

Gray let the dog smooch him a last time and stood. "It's okay. I used to have a golden just like him when I was a kid. Roscoe, 'eh? Great name."

"He's a lover, but a big baby in storms. This one must be almost done for him to have surfaced. Here." She handed him two towels. "For your hair. And I don't know about this, but you're welcome to try it." She held up the light-blue sweatshirt. "It's a little girlie, but warm."

He took it dubiously. "Thanks. What about you?"

"I keep stuff lying all around. I'll find something."

After toweling his head vigorously, he finger-combed his hair until the little curls at the ends no longer dripped. For a moment he studied the sweatshirt, and anticipation hitched her breath. To her juvenile disappointment, he grinned and disappeared into a stall. Abby pulled the elastic band from her hair, letting it fall to her neck in a soggy clump and drop congealed alfalfa mush between her shoulder blades. She screeched and whipped the towel over one shoulder.

"What? What happened?" Gray popped up from the stall, eyes concerned, in glorious naked-torso-ness.

Abby forgot the gunk slipping down her back and stared at the perfect vee of dark hair across his chest. She spun away, embarrassed as a pioneer schoolmarm, choking on laughter to hide her discomfort. "Nothing. Creepy-crawly mush down my back, that's all." She squeezed her shoulder blades together.

"Here." In three steps he stood behind her and pushed a towel up the back of her tank top. The slimy itching stopped, but his fingers on her upper arm replaced the itch with tremors. "The same thing happened to me. I think I've got wet slime halfway down my shorts."

"Ahem." A cough sounded from the open barn door. Abby leapt free of Gray's touch. Her heartbeat raced for her throat. "Everything okay? Or are we interrupting something?"

EVEN FROM BEHIND, Gray caught the bright flush creeping up the side of Abby's face as she stiffened beneath his touch.

"Ed! Sylvia!" Pure chagrin shook her voice.

Gray lifted his gaze to the wide barn door, and there, backlit by a brightening sky, stood some sort of ancient mariner along with a shorter, female sidekick. Gray winced. His shirtless state couldn't look good.

"Sylvia here said she saw a stranger drive down but never return." The two figures stepped out of the dwindling storm, the man's yellow slicker and sou'wester hat streaming, the woman's familiar square face coming into view as she lowered a flowered umbrella. "Thought maybe you were interviewin' for the barn-help job, Sonny," the man said.

Sonny? He hadn't been "Sonny" since he'd stolen apples from the neighbor's tree as a kid. Dark eyes bored into Gray's even as amusement played on the lined face.

"Just what kind of barn help did you t'ink she was looking for?" The woman spoke, her accent charmingly Fargo-ish. "I knew we needed to come check on you, Abigail."

"Oh, Sylvia. Ed. I'm sorry." Abby apologized as if to parents. "This must look awful."

"I dunno." The man pulled off his hat to reveal a stiff white crew cut and ran a hand over his grizzled chin. "Pretty girl, handsome stranger, a little hay."

"Edward Mertz." The woman admonished him with a laser glare that would have cowed a lesser man, Gray was sure.

He grinned. So these were the Mertzes. Maybe not Fred and Ethel, but endearing just the same, in a fusty way. "I'll get my shirt and we'll explain our compromising situation," he said.

He touched Abby's shoulder. Her eyes had lost their soft mistiness and were once again no-nonsense pools of clear aquamarine. Not without regret, he knew their unexpected, intimate time-freeze was over. More distance would be safer. Still, he'd thoroughly enjoyed watching a sexy little sprite peek out from Abby's tough-mom exterior.

He forced her sweatshirt over his head. It fit a little like spray paint but was warmer than his bare skin. A grimace tightened his lips when he looked down. To call the saying on his chest "girlie" was an understatement, and, although he wasn't too concerned about Ed or even Sylvia, he prayed to heaven his bandmates would never, ever, *ever* hear it had been on his body.

He'd greatly underestimated Ed.

"Pleased to make your acquaintance, your Barn Goddess-ness." The old man read the phrase "Barn Goddess" on the sweatshirt with obvious relish. "Since she gave you the uniform, I guess she gave you the job?"

"What's all this about a job?" Gray turned clueless eyes on Abby.

Sylvia's eyebrows knotted in concern. "Abby, tell me the truth. Are you all right?"

Abby laughed. "Dear Sylvia, thank you, I'm fine." She stepped forward and pecked the woman's cheek. "He isn't here for a job, but he did work much harder than he needed to." She indicated the hay. "Ed, Sylvia, this is David Graham. He's Dawson's father. David, these are my neighbors and guardian angels, Ed and Sylvia Mertz."

"Dawson?" Ed asked. "That so?"

"Yes, sir." Gray reached to take the firm grip he offered. "Pleasure."

"Dawson's been a help around here this spring. He didn't say you were coming to visit. If we'd have known it was you, we wouldn't have worried about Abby so."

"He doesn't know I'm here. It's . . . it will be a surprise."

"Ah, well, fair enough." A quarter-smile quirked the corner of Ed's mouth as he waved a finger at the sweatshirt. "Color suits you. It's a little snug."

Gray folded his arms. "I'd be careful about provoking the Barn Goddess."

Abby giggled and Ed gazed at the mess of hay on the floor. "I like you. I came to kick you out, but I'll wait until the rain lets up."

Gray shook a leg, scowling at the slime. "Hey, I appreciate it."

"Me, I'll just watch you till the rain lets up." Sylvia eyed him with bland skepticism.

Smiling came easily to Gray—a honed business skill. He offered Sylvia one of his best: quick, broad, subtly dimpled, a poster-quality smile. It had, on occasion, made women swoon, but Gray doubted that Sylvia, in her hyper-protective state, would swoon for Valentino.

He was right. She carefully brushed hay goop from Abby's shoulder, shielding her like a miniature mother bear.

"We should stack this." Ed regarded the hay again.

"No." Abby waved away the offer. "It can stay until the kids get home. I'm just going to bring the horses in the back door and take Mr. Graham up to get dry."

She was? He smiled but she ignored it.

"Well," Ed glanced outside and removed his yellow slicker, dropping it into a corner. "It's near done raining. You and Sylvie go get 'em. The Goddess and I will neaten this up."

"I assumed from your mailbox your name would be Ethel." Gray shot him a benign smile.

"Just so you know," Ed replied without missing a beat, "I'm seventy-six years old and you ain't remotely the first one to come up with that."

"Darn."

As they shoved bales closer to the wall, the barn filled with the sweet green scent of fresh alfalfa, as thick and intoxicating as a drug. The rain stopped tattooing on the roof, but new sounds took its place. Doors sliding, horses snorting, Abby's soft voice, and hooved feet clomping on wood. The not-unpleasant odor of horses mingled with the alfalfa. Working beside Ed, harder than he had in months, Gray hadn't felt this relaxed in as long as he could remember.

"Horses are in. You guys did a lot." Abby returned wearing a zipped hoodie, her face pink, her countenance changed, filled with contentment. The sweatshirt's zipper tab stopped inches above her breasts, and it was clear she'd doffed everything underneath. The gray fleece caressed her curves intimately enough to make any male jealous, and Gray mentally declared the shapeless garment as entrancing as her skimpier tank top.

"It was kind of satisfying." He looked around at the more-organized piles of hay and grinned. "Like the Cat in the Hat came along and cleaned up his mess."

"You're a very strange man." Her assessing gaze rose from his ankles to his eyes, and inner warmth overrode the clamminess from his jeans.

"Well, the fun and the rain are over," Ed said. "Sylvie, let's head home. Let these two alone. Nice meetin' you, Goddess. You stack a mean hay bale."

"What are your plans while you wait for your boy to return?" Sylvia cut off Gray's reply with a pointed demand, not quite as ready as Ed to offer her trust.

Gray had pushed that question far to the back of his mind. With a jolt, the reality of his trip rushed back. "Playing it by ear," he said honestly. "I have a hotel room up by the airport."

"Fine, then." She turned, her scowl slightly less intense. "Abby, you come for dinner if you like. I don't want you skimping just 'cause dose kids aren't home."

"Thank you, Sylvia. But I promise, I have a nice pasta meal all planned."

"Hmmpf."

"You might have trouble getting your car out of here now." Ed nodded at Gray. "Call if you need a pull. Don't let that Dawson leave without saying good-bye."

Once they'd gone, it was clear the tension between Gray and Abby had blinked one awakening-dragon eye at the mention of Dawson. Gray wasn't eager to poke the monster into full consciousness, but he fought fresh irritation. It was his son. He wasn't going to walk on eggshells.

Abby grabbed a push broom from beside a wall and stroked at the loose hay on the wooden floor with purposeful efficiency. "This'll only take a second." She didn't look up. "I'll just toss this loose stuff into a few stalls."

He sighed. He needed to stop playing on the farm and . . . and what? Call Chris to hear him yell? Call the band to tell them he still didn't have his kid? What he needed was Abby Stadtler on his side. A cool, wet nose nudged his hand. He stooped to pat Roscoe, which made him want to forget his manager and his rotten tour and stay right here. "Let me help."

"Look." To his relief a glimmer of soft light shone in Abby's eyes. "I feel guilty enough about all you've done, although it's very much appreciated. You don't need to help."

"C'mon, tell me what to do." He grinned. "When we're done we can discuss a plan for the immediate future. Helping will give me a chance to think of one. A plan that is." Was that a smile? The giddy reaction in his belly unnerved him.

She struggled a moment longer, then gave in. "Fine. Grab the wheelbarrow."

They loaded it with the loose hay, and Gray followed her down the barn aisle helping distribute a portion to each stall, chatty as she talked about the horses they were feeding.

"Six are ours, two we board," she said. "Horses have always been part of my life. I used to compete; now I teach a few lessons, and Kim has the show bug. How 'bout you? Have you ever ridden?"

"At a dude ranch. Once," he admitted. "You can write my horse knowledge on your little fingernail."

"Ooh, not impressive." She grinned. "C'mon, there's someone I want you to meet."

A conversation about horses? Regret pricked his conscience. He wasn't the only one affected by tonight's unnecessary concert cancellation. Five others shared the stage with him each performance, and there were sound-and-lighting techs, stage hands, and equipment people. Every one of them was stranded while he was playing in the country.

He pushed his guilt aside with effort. Sometimes being responsible for all those careers exhausted him. Had he really dreamed of living like this all those smoky, dinky bars ago? He should have become the concert pianist of his mother's dreams.

"Here he is. Hey, gorgeous." Abby interrupted his thoughts with a lilt he hadn't heard before. "This is Gucci."

The horse in the stall before them looked his name—like perfectly conditioned, expensive leather. With a snort he shuffled to the bars covering the top half of his box and pressed his forehead against them for Abby to scratch. Every ounce of her careful reserve disappeared. Gray was mesmerized and envious all at once as Abby leaned forward to whisper nonsense. In an instant, she transformed into a different woman.

"He's my pathetic weakness in life." She stepped back with a cute, embarrassed smile. "He's not great outside in thunderstorms, so he's been inside nice and dry. Would you mind if I took a minute to let him out for a quick run around his paddock?"

Gray shook his head. He knew nothing about horses, but as he stood back while Abby snapped a lead rope on this one, he knew it was one of the prettiest animals he'd ever seen. Regal. Bunched-but-supple muscles. A dark brown body with jet black mane and tail and huge, brown eyes. He looked powerful, and explosive enough to scare the hell out of him.

Outside, a paddock with solid posts and four cross boards awaited the horse. Abby pulled his leather halter off and let him go. He snorted again, dashed four strides then planted his feet in a dead stop. With a devilish eye, he buckled his knees.

"Oh, yeah, thanks so much, you big dork," Abby called.

Gucci sank onto the muddy ground and rolled in abandon. Ten seconds later he heaved to his feet, his spit and polish a thing of the past, and took off bucking across the paddock.

"He looks like a street-corner knock-off now, doesn't he?" Gray asked.

She giggled. "Good one. Hear that, Gooch?" she called and latched the metal gate. "He's definitely my guy. I rescued him eight years ago when police found him in an abandoned herd and couldn't place him because he was a stallion."

"Is being a stallion such a bad thing?" Gray stared at the horse, avoiding her eyes.

"They're generally harder to handle. Too much testosterone." She leaned on the top of the gate and hid a smile in her arms. "I should have gelded him but I couldn't. Besides, he's turned out to be a gentleman. He's a German breed called a Trakehner and he's got great personality and bloodlines. It took a while to track his registry, but I did, and he's made a lot of very pretty babies."

"Lucky fella. You obviously treat him well."

Gucci stopped bucking and returned to the gate, nickering for fresh attention.

"Horse people have no perspective." She stroked the horse, her words suddenly clipped with defensiveness. It befuddled him. She was full of magic one moment, matter-of-fact the next. "All right, that's all he needs, he can go back inside. Time to figure out what to do about your wet jeans."

"Does Dawson like the horses?" When Gucci was safe in his stall, the question escaped before Gray thought better of it. He'd been avoiding the subject, but curiosity burned about what his son was doing here.

"He does. He's very sweet with them, and he's not a

bad rider. He hates mucking stalls, though." Her smile was fond.

"I told you my son was bright."

"He doesn't take any crap." Pleasure with her joke lit her lovely eyes. "I like that about him."

"We used to call that stubborn," Gray said. "Sounds like he's got you hoodwinked."

"Maybe you don't know your son as well as you think you do."

He touched her upper arm to stop her, and his voice remained calm with effort. "I don't have to negotiate terms with you, Abby. I owe you all the gratitude in the world, but he isn't another rescued horse. He has people who love him."

"People he ran away from," she said, almost under her breath.

"Now look . . ." His temper almost got the better of him, but she put up her hand first.

"I'm sorry. Until two hours ago I believed he was a nearly-grown kid making his way around the country as a big adventure. I've enjoyed him, and I hoped he'd find some roots here."

"He has roots with his family." Gray breathed out his anger. "Look. I am not here to read him the riot act. Strangle him perhaps . . ."

"I'm a parent, too," she conceded. "I guess I can understand the desire to murder him."

"With my bare hands."

He grabbed his soaked T-shirt and leather jacket and followed Abby out the barn door. Once in the rain-freshened air, they both eyed his car with doubt. The barnyard was half-a-foot deep in slippery mud.

"I'd let it sit here for now," Abby said. "Ed was right. Non-farm vehicles get stuck easily after a rain. Let things dry while we talk and get something to eat."

He shrugged in agreement. Roscoe trotted ahead of them toward the house, his presence a warm memory of childhood, softening the tension between them. "You don't have to feed me, you know."

"Yeah, well . . ." Finally she smiled. "Don't be too impressed. That pasta I mentioned to Sylvia? It's a can of Beefaroni."

He laughed. After endless weeks of room service and junk food, a can of Beefaroni didn't sound half bad. They reached the house and Abby opened the back door. "Roscoe, you have to stay out until you get cleaned. But you . . ." She pointed at Gray and, for the briefest moment, despite their tension, the little sprite he'd seen earlier peeked out again. "Let's take you inside and get you out of those pants."

Chapter Three

GRAY'S VOICE FADED as he prowled the living room talking on his phone in hushed tones. Abby's guilt flared. Hiding the fact that she knew who he was felt dishonest, yet she dreaded telling him. David Graham was simply Dawson's dad, frustrating to argue with but easy to have temporarily in her life. Gray Covey was a celebrity with the proven power to wreak havoc on her senses and trample through her world like a circus elephant through a family picnic.

Besides, since he hadn't come clean, either, anonymity seemed equally important to him.

Nerves darted through her stomach when she heard him say good-bye, but all her apprehension vanished when he appeared in the kitchen doorway. "Phone call finished?" She managed to hold back full-fledged laughter, but one playful sputter refused to stay contained.

"Don't start." He pointed at her, a warning in his eyes.

"Start what?" She feigned innocence. "It's adorable."

Because his overnight bag sat in a hotel room two hours away and his jeans and T-shirt were now in her dryer, Gray stood wrapped in the only item of clothing they'd found big enough to cover him. The shabby, terrycloth, wrap robe—whose vintage even Abby couldn't recall—might have been sensational, showcasing his extraordinary calves and tapered ankles as it did. The trouble lay in its mint-green color and the chorus line of embroidered, jumping frogs circling it from one front edge to the other.

"You swore, not a word. The Barn Goddess comments were bad enough."

Their disagreements might not be over, but no way could she discuss them with a phenomenally attractive man in a frog bathrobe. Absolutely not with her stomach cavorting at the tease of chest hair between the robe's lapels. She remembered full well what he looked like sans frogs.

"Fine." She hid her wayward thoughts. "Supper will take your mind off the humiliation."

She led him to the small dining room off her kitchen where Gray's forehead lost its furrows, and his rich laughter rolled through the room, fanning the flutter in her stomach.

"Too damn funny, Abby. I've never seen a sarcastic dinner table before."

"You did order Beefaroni."

He had—nixing all other suggestions she'd made for their early supper. So, she'd set the table with a juvenile assortment of tableware, left over from when the kids had been little. Boats and cars graced the placemats, bucking horses and cowboys decorated the bowls, and giraffe and monkey cups with neck and tail for handles, respectively.

"Go ahead, pick whichever place you like. Sorry I didn't have a frog cup."

"I know you think you're funny." He sent her a glare made up mostly of laugh lines.

It had been ages since she'd done something so frivolous. During the absurd meal prep, Abby hadn't once considered cost, or time and effort, or whether he'd think her insane. It was so out of the cautious character she'd become, she hardly believed they were in her house. And after a leisurely meal seasoned with breezy laughter, she hardly believed she was with Dawson's prickly father.

"THIS WAS FUN," she said when they both put their spoons down for the last time. "I'm sorry you had to miss your appointment; I just couldn't see how to get to the airport on time."

"It was fun, thank you. And you said the kids are due home before noon tomorrow. As long as I'm back by tomorrow night all will be forgiven."

"David." She used the name softly. "Dawson could stay. Truly. Maybe it would be easier."

With exaggerated calm, he met her eyes. "I don't understand. He lied to you and to your teenage daughter. Why do you want him here?"

"He's a vulnerable kid who ran from something."

"Yeah, a stuffy English boarding school. Wouldn't you?" His eyes flashed into stormy blue and frustration tightened the planes of his sculpted face. His skin tone deepened, accentuating the shadow sprouting on his cheeks. He was back to being an attractive, *angry* man, and her pulse pounded in places that should have embarrassed her.

"I'd want to find out exactly why he ran."

He leaned forward. "You think I'm not goddamned gonna ask him?"

His heated curse broke her spell-like fascination. She matched him, leaning into his face. "In this house, if you swear, you leave God out of it. And I'm sure you *will* ask your son all the pertinent questions—in that tone of voice. How lucky he is to have such an understanding father."

For a moment she couldn't tell if he was reloading for another volley or was simply shell-shocked that he'd been yelled at. Again. But he surprised her with a quieter voice. "I'm sorry, but I'm not going to argue about my son. He isn't up for adoption."

He was right. She wasn't sure why she wanted so badly for Dawson to stay, but she had no right to argue with his father. "I'm sorry, too." She looked away to gather composure.

"I should be glad you've taken a liking to my son, and I am." His voice, laced with humor once again, drew her back. "You're stubborn, Abby Stadtler, but you're a very captivating woman when you're on the warpath."

Abby hadn't fielded an honest compliment in so long her most intelligent response was the heat rising in her face. "How about a truce?" she asked, finally. "I'll make dessert. My secret chocolate potion."

"Secret chocolate can't be anything but good." He grinned. "Here's to truces."

She checked on their clothes first and returned to find him peering out a window in an eerily darkened living room "How are the old jeans?" he asked. "I should head back to the hotel when they're dry. After the chocolate, of course." He smiled, scanning the outdoors. "I did check in already and there's work I could do there."

"The jeans are still damp around the edges, but whenever you need to go . . ." The reluctance in her words surprised her. "We'll see if you can drive out of the mud. I admit the whole area down by the barn is pretty awful after it rains."

"Speaking of rain." He squinted at the sky. "I think there's another whopper brewing."

She joined him and assessed the rapidly gathering new clouds. "Wow, you're—"

With no warning, a jagged arrow lit the yard from heavens to grass. The violent crack that followed all but blasted them away from the window, and the house went dark. A yowl like a banshee on the kill pierced the crackling air.

"Holy sh— crap!" Gray grabbed her upper arms and pulled her into the safety of his embrace. He still smelled of alfalfa, now mingling with fresh soap-on-skin, and she had no idea if her heart pounded from the crash, his arms compressing her breasts into the mint-green terry, or his breath pulsing against her cheek.

"What was that? Freddy Kruger?" His laughter caught in his throat.

"No," she choked. "Just Bird. My cat."

"Abby, please. Please tell me you don't have a cat named Bird."

Her oversized, orange wuss-of-a-tabby glided into the room, blinking regally as if he hadn't just hollered for his life. "Oh, but I do. Meet the Bird."

He stared. "This place *is* a rabbit hole. You've even got the friggin' Cheshire Cat."

"Huh?"

"Muahaha, Alice. The mushroom is working."

She frowned at him, utterly confused. "I say again, you are very weird."

Gray chose not to explain. He doubted she'd appreciate the unflattering humor. He brushed it aside and helped light candles. She left once more to bring their clothes up from the now non-functioning dryer. When she'd gone, Gray was free for the first time to do more than glance at the accoutrements of her life. While Bird stalked him, he roamed the room, which flickered in candlelight. Abby had her old farmhouse nicely decorated, with thick blue and red rugs on the wood floors, a mix of worn, traditional furniture, and shelves and tables filled with books and knick-knacks. The artwork, however, was what piqued his interest.

Several large, professional photographs adorned the

walls, each graphic-like, with dramatic lighting and, in his opinion, bleak subjects: a leafless tree, an advancing thunderstorm—almost like today; an empty swing set beside an apple tree.

They were unquestionably good, but they startled him. In the few hours he'd known her, he hadn't seen such austerity in Abby's personality. Firmness. Stubbornness. She was definitely opinionated. But she was as far from cold as the pictures were from warm.

He moved across the room to a small, side alcove where an old Kohler and Campbell upright piano stood. He sat on the bench, stroking the instrument's carved, oak finish. When he lifted the hinged lid, he exposed original, ivory keys, and a ripple of professional appreciation led him to run an arpeggio across the keyboard. The chords held a hint of old-string twang but still resounded with rich, mellow tones in a testament to the piano's craftsmanship.

It sounded just like his mother's old piano. Memories threatened to depress his mood, until a soft cat body twined through his legs and the sorrow dissipated. He bent to scratch Bird's head, grateful. It sapped too much energy to think about his mother. Dealing with Dawson was enough for now.

The tiny alcove held more photos. He spied three grouped on a side wall and, drawn to the black-and-white pictures, Gray's brow knotted. These were the opposites to those in the main room, possessing a soft-focused, precious quality the bigger pictures lacked: a chubby fist grasping the slender stem of a fuzzy dandelion; a very young child's profile, cheeks puffed and lips pursed to blow; a close-up of long, pretty eyelashes resting against a gently curved cheek. Their simple story compelled him. He would have put these in a more public spot and tucked away the skeletal tree.

The focal picture in the space was a family portrait atop the piano. Abby, with a few fewer laugh lines, sat beside a square-jawed, all-American man with serious brown eyes. Before them sat two children—a sandy-haired girl of two or three and a tow-headed boy perhaps five.

There was a Mr. Abby. Or had been.

Flickering candlelight animated the picture, accentuating the man's face and highlighting that of the boy—a miniature replica of the beach-blond man. Abby had never mentioned a son. Gray studied the faces, mystified.

"My husband." Her quiet voice behind him held a pensive note. A shiver of unwelcome dread traced down Gray's spine. He knew that tone of voice all too well—the one preceding a story nobody wanted to hear. "And my son Will."

He held his breath without meaning to. "But?" He turned and met eyes tinged with old sorrow.

"They were killed in a car accident almost twelve years ago."

His stomach dropped despite having expected bad news. "Oh, hell, Abby, I'm so sorry."

"Thank you. But don't be. It's a safe subject most of the time, I promise."

He couldn't stop himself from tucking an errant

strand of hair behind her ear. They both started at the touch and he swallowed. "So, tell me your story, Abby Stadtler."

"His name was Jack." She smiled, and yet there was a sheen in her eyes and an almost-imperceptible deepening of her voice. "We were married seven years, and he was a wonderful, gentle man. Will was a little rabble-rouser and smart as a whip but, of course, I'm eternally prejudiced." Her chin lifted a fraction in protectiveness. "He was five, two years older than Kim. She says she remembers him, although I'm not sure how much. But they were inseparable."

"Were you and Kim part of the accident?"

"No. It happened on a simple drive to the grocery store. Someone made a wrong turn."

"I've never experienced something that traumatic." His dull pain seemed insignificant.

"I'm glad if that's true." She let her lip quirk in skepticism. "I'm not sure I believe you, though. Everyone has sorrows. And don't be sad for me. Birthdays are tough, the anniversary of the accident a little tougher, and once in a while it feels like it's been five minutes. But, eleven years is a long time."

"It's only been five minutes for me."

For an instant she stared as if she had no idea what to say. "Wow." She finally spoke. "Did estrogen from my sweatshirt seep into you, or are you naturally a sensitive man?"

He laughed and stepped away. "The more you talk, the more I can see why Dawson might like it here."

Her eyes misted. "I . . . People hear my story and tell me how strong I am. But, I'm not. I get strength from God, and, for many reasons, your son has been a gift from Him. I'll miss Dawson, but your words mean a lot. Thank you."

"Nothing to thank me for."

And there wasn't. He understood now why Abby was enamored with Dawson, but he still had to take him. The boy had used to beg to hang with the band. If anything, Abby's story made Gray want more than ever to have that happen.

"Hey! It's time to celebrate almost an hour without an argument." A grin signaled the end of Abby's melancholy. "Ready for dessert? I actually have a little propane stove I can cook on."

"Since it's raining Birds and Roscoes at the moment, I can't think of anything better. Or, nothing appropriate." He waggled teasing brows. "What do you think about my jeans?"

"Still pretty damp in the seams." She looked like she wanted to say far more but let her gaze shift instead to a blatant and unapologetic perusal of his calves. "You certainly don't have to hurry on my account."

In light of what she'd just shared, Gray was sure he had to be misreading her tone, but the slow suggestion and the deepening of her voice were unmistakable. Heat that had been bubbling beneath his emotions since the moment he'd met her turned into shivers, and sweats, and unadulterated, unsolicited lust. Her baggy, cotton, drawstring pants and clingy pink knit top were suddenly as sexy as black lace. Ignoring his guilt, he lifted her chin, and she tilted toward him. He brushed her lips with a kiss that assuaged nothing but set his nerves jangling. Soft and willing, she kissed him back, tasting of sweet mint.

"No. I'm afraid hurrying is a very good idea," he said. He took his jeans and she stepped back, pointing to a flight of stairs at the end of the living room.

"Use the upstairs bathroom. The one you used down here earlier has no window. It's the second door left, right up the stairs."

When he'd disappeared, Abby hugged herself as squadrons of butterflies swooped across the whole of her belly. What on Earth was she thinking? Her lips tingled like a schoolgirl's. Kiss her? She'd let him kiss her?

Back in the kitchen, her hands trembled as she opened a narrow cupboard beside the refrigerator that hid a secret, exorbitant stash of ingredients for making mind-blowing and artery-clogging hot chocolate: chocolate bars, and a variety of cocoas, marshmallows, and a few choice spices. Sensuous smells drifted to her like exotic oils. Her plan had been to seduce Gray with chocolate into spilling his secret—the one she already knew. Instead, she'd lost her mind and kissed him back. She used him to keep the sting of the past at bay. Now she paid for the indiscretion with a heart that refused to settle into its normal beat.

A gentle pop and the beep of the kitchen phone heralded the return of power, and her kitchen flooded with brightness. She raised her eyes in silent thanks and let the light bring rational thought. Her mind calmed. Gray had been gone quite a while when the sensation of being watched made her turn. As her pulse headed for its upper limits again, she examined his face. Everything was different.

With one hip cocked against the doorframe, he held his arms rigid across his chest. His pale blue eyes held glacial flecks, and a question rode his brows.

"Jeans still fit?" she joked. Oh boy did they. But he didn't lift an eyebrow.

"Of course."

"David? Is something . . ."

"You're good at remembering to call me that." His voice was not angry; nonetheless a chill zigzagged down her spine. "Isn't that right? You know."

"Know what?" Regret heated her cheeks.

"Oh, come on." He straightened and stepped into the room. "I think we're *close* enough now we owe each other the truth. How long have you known?"

"David, I . . . Fine. Gray." It was a relief to say it. "Since I slapped away the cigarette."

The incredulity on his face was unmistakable. "You've known all along who I am?"

"I assumed you had a reason for not telling me yourself."

"I did. I didn't want to freak you out."

"Umm, you seem a lot more freaked than I am."

"Was it kind of fun? To see the famous guy in his skivvies? In your robe? To know you'd kissed the man on the posters?"

She reeled as if struck. "What kind of cruel questions

are those? Who kissed whom, poster man? And wait a doggone minute. You're the one who kept the secret in the first place."

"It was mine to keep, not yours."

"That doesn't even make sense." Disbelief curled through her stomach. "I knew you'd tell me in your own time. How the heck did you figure it out anyway?"

He steeled his gaze. "I couldn't remember which way I was supposed to turn upstairs. Imagine my surprise when I wandered into the second door on the right and flipped the switch out of habit. Not only were there lights, but I scared myself to death."

Kimmy's room.

Abby closed her eyes. If Gray hadn't been so miffed, and her butterfly squadron hadn't started crashing and burning, she might have laughed. A tiny part of her wished she'd been there to see his face.

"Have to say, I didn't expect to see myself as wallpaper in what I expected to be a bathroom."

"Gray, I'm sorry. Kim . . . she's one of your biggest fans. That's not an excuse, but I haven't even begun to process the sheer coincidence of all this. Dawson never said a word. He rags on Kim constantly about her hero worship of you, which makes a lot more sense now. Why does this bother you?"

"Because I know how fame works. People lie and cheat to get close to me. And I should have known better than to think it could be any different here. Being selfish tripped me up."

"That's ridiculous. We had a new start on some

great . . ." she said, flushing, ". . . chemistry. I've got my hot chocolate ready to brew. What has to change?"

As if something she'd said flipped a switch, his body relaxed little by little. A smile formed into the practiced curve she'd seen in the farmyard. "You're right, Abby. You're right. I'm overreacting. So, what's this about hot chocolate?"

His voice lacked several degrees of warmth. When his eyes met hers, his gaze penetrated only color deep. She wanted to cry. Fortunately, she'd learned long ago how to swallow useless tears.

"My specialty." Her voice fell flat. "Wait till you try it."

Chapter Four

ABBY PARKED NEXT to her dilapidated garage and fought the mix of anxiety and excitement in her stomach. Gray had not gone to his hotel the night before but spent it in Dawson's room, with rain pounding until dawn and his car mired in the mud. But to say the tension between her and Gray had eased would be an outright lie. Why she should feel fluttery to see him was beyond understanding. His one accidental kiss had been the last warm moment between them.

"Whose car is that?" Kim, beside her in their twelve-year-old Explorer, squinted at Gray's Malibu stuck in front of the barn where it had sunk four inches into giant skid marks.

"Well, I have news. Someone's here to see Dawson." She spoke carefully, heeding, just in case, Gray's fear that his son might run again if he knew he'd been found.

"Me?" Dawson straightened in the back seat, his normally genial face on high alert.

"Yes." Abby drew a deep breath. "Is there anything you two would like to tell me before we head inside?"

"Like what?" he asked warily.

"Like a little mix-up you might have had on your birthdate?"

"Mom, now wait . . ." Kim began her protest, but Dawson stopped her.

"You already know." The sullenness in his voice was the first Abby had ever heard. "Why bother to ask?"

"It's your word against this man's. I'm giving you a fair chance."

"Fine, then. I lied about my age."

"We can explain," Kim implored. "He had to leave home. His parents are crazy. His dad is never around; he just travels making money at odd jobs. The only thing he ever did was teach Dawson to play the guitar. And his mom just threw him in this private school and left him there."

Kim had met Dawson online, and they'd been friends for two years. Her invitation had brought him there, and now her explanation rushed out, an obvious paraphrase of the story Dawson had fed her. The twisted truths were priceless.

Her daughter was a beauty. Abby thought so without apology every time she looked at her. Caramel-colored, straight-as-sixties hair hung to her lower back, and she had Jack's luminous, hazel eyes. She smoothed Kim's long tresses. "Trust me, you'll have plenty of chance to explain. I'm just disappointed you didn't tell me the truth."

"Oh, it's the truth." Dawson slumped into a resigned heap in his seat and crossed his arms. "Who's here anyway? Did Mom send old Tattling Timothy the butler?"

"Hmmm. I think you'll be pleasantly surprised." Abby wasn't angry, but the kids couldn't know that. What Dawson had done was dangerous, and although his actions had turned out all right for now, Abby wanted him to face Gray with more than disgust and Kim to face him with more than awe. "C'mon. This guy isn't here to get you in trouble."

In truth, she had no idea what Gray was going to do. He had every right, just as he'd said, to take Dawson away, but the thought still made Abby sad. The child was about to be uprooted again, and nobody seemed to know why he'd run away in the first place. They trooped into the kitchen, an odd little parade, Dawson in the lead, Kim in the rear—

Abby had no idea what her daughter would do either. Gray filled arenas three times over in every city on his tours, but his core audience was older—adults who'd grown up with Jon Bon Jovi, maybe Billy Joel. Fans Kim's age were uncommon, yet she'd always been the living definition of "Gray Covey Fanatic." It didn't help that she shared his birthday and played clarinet, Gray's first instrument. But Kim had never met as much as a semi-famous person.

Gray's back was to them when they entered the living room. Abby drew a breath in a vain attempt to calm her thrumming pulse. "Mr. Covey?"

He turned slowly as if he, too, was afraid of what he'd find.

Kim's fingers twisted in a fistful of Abby's T-shirt. A half-sob bubbled from her throat. Abby didn't know where to look first, at Kim's bugged-out eyes or Dawson's jaw on his chest.

"Dad?"

"Hey, buddy. Sorry I couldn't get here any faster. I, ah, didn't know where you were."

"Dad?" Kim's word came out a strangled hiss, like an old steam radiator coughing past a clog, and she stared at Dawson. "This is your father?" To Abby's astonishment, a tear welled in each of Kim's eyes, and, with the hem of Abby's shirt still fisted in her hand, she took a half-step behind her mother. "Gray," she whispered. "Mom, it's Gray."

"I know, sweetie. It's okay, I promise." Abby gave Kim's forearm a squeeze.

"What are you doing here?" Dawson's voice trembled. "How did you find me?"

Abby studied the pair—Peter Pan and his shadow. Dawson stood just shy of his father's six-foot height, a slender replica just starting to fill out. Both took the same wide-legged stance. Both had the same crook to their elbows, although Dawson's arms curved in a protective shield over his chest, and Gray stuck one hand in his pocket. The other he lifted to rub the back of his neck. Gone was the cool, practiced superstar.

"We followed your trail, through Heathrow and the Port Authority in New York. It took us a while to find Abby."

"He calls you Abby?" Kim's whisper squeaked in Abby's ear.

"It's my name."

"I didn't ask you to come." Dawson drew his line in the sand.

The light blue of Gray's eyes blanched, and he swallowed as if he'd been punched. "Kids who run away generally don't send announcements." His voice held a false brightness.

Abby's heart went out to him. She sensed him struggling to strike the right tone between disciplinarian and friend. She also watched Dawson stiffen and search desperately for a way out of the trap that had just sprung on him. "Your mom and I have both been worried about you."

"Mom is skiing with Klaus. She's not worried about me."

Dawson's coldness stunned Abby and roused her interest more than a little.

"Your mom is who she is, Dawson. She loves you."

"She loves Danielle, too. But our nannies worry more than she does."

Gray pursed his lips sympathetically. "There is me, Daw. I've been worried."

"Yeah, I could tell. How's the tour going?"

"Worst ever. Inspired me and Spark to write a song about overflowing toilets last week, and they're the best lyrics I've managed in months."

If Abby hadn't known Dawson she never would have seen the tic at the corner of his mouth. So, there was a connection there. Weak but alive.

"I'm sorry you came all this way for nothing. I'm not going back to Heighton to live in cold dorms with blazer-wearing geeks. And I'm not spending the holidays with Klaus the Priss."

"You can spend the holidays with me."

"Oh joy."

At Dawson's insult, Gray Covey the dad disappeared. The plastic shield lowered over his eyes, and his stance solidified as if he prepared to make a sale any way he could. "You know," a smile of feigned confidence appeared on his face, "we've got a little over five weeks left in this tour. The guys want you to hang out on the road and join us onstage for a few shows. It'll be an honor to have you with me."

Kim's sudden weight was going to drag her to the floor.

"I'll bet it would be." Dawson's voice held derision and a note of hurt. "The fans would just go ape-shit over seeing the baby boy, huh, Dad?"

"I think you'd better come up with more appropriate language in front of the ladies."

So smooth, so calm. Abby wanted to cry. He was a pop-star Jekyll and Hyde. *Shake him, Gray. Or better yet, hug him. He doesn't want the singer, he's begging for you.* Dawson backed up, starting to put distance between him and his father. "Sor-ry."

"Don't try to run away from this. I know you're mad at your mom, I know you think she doesn't pay enough attention to you."

"You don't have a clue what I think," Dawson shouted. "How could you?"

The practiced smile faltered, and, for the first time, Gray's eyes met Abby's across the room. He looked lost, and she smiled, trying to send him courage. Unfortunately, little as she knew about him, she did know he'd led with his ace, and his son had a built-in strategy to beat it. He was unimpressed.

"I think I do know." Gray's voice held less confidence. "Your mom sticks you in a private school without asking your opinion and pulls you away from your friends. Then she marries Klaus, has Danielle, and expects you to like it."

"Way to go, Dad." Dawson tapped his temple with a finger. "You've got it all figured out. You think I'm mad at Mom? You're right. But, of course, I have you. Always around. I can't get rid of you you're so in my face."

Gray's stricken eyes widened, and his lips parted wordlessly. Some might have considered Dawson's tone disrespectful, but he was being dead honest. It was just painfully clear Gray hadn't seen these blows coming.

"You have no idea how hard we worked to find you these past six weeks. I canceled a show the instant your mother called to say they knew where you were."

"You did?"

Hope sparked in his eyes. "Of course."

"Wow, how much did that cost you?"

"Oh, for God's sake." The cover blew off Gray's schmoozing, pop-star façade. "What difference does it make? I'm here. You're coming with me, but I'm trying to tell you I *want* you to come. Don't insinuate I don't care about you."

"You care?" Dawson asked. "Which do you care about most? Twenty million fans and all their money and adoration, or the son you'd rather hide away in a British boarding school?" He turned in blank fury and stalked toward Abby and Kim, leaving Gray immobilized.

On the one hand, she could see why she'd believed the boy to be eighteen. He made an erudite argument. On the other hand, his was a little boy's cry. She squeezed Kim's shoulders, hurt for her daughter as well. This was hardly a glamorous way to meet her biggest hero.

Dawson stopped just in front of them. "Why did you let him know I was here?"

"He's your father, I can't keep him away."

Out of the blue, Kim's fist shot from behind Abby's back, and Dawson reeled from a sharp blow to his upper arm. "Ow! What the heck was that for?" He took a confused step backward, rubbing his bicep.

"You're evil and twisted, Dawson. He's your *dad*?" Kim's voice was a stifled whisper, and she sent a furtive glance in Gray's direction. "How could you keep something like that from me all this time, and laugh at me behind my back?"

Abby had learned to love Dawson's ability to deal with Kim as well as any big brother would. He could tease her out of a bad mood or annoy her into one, but their camaraderie had grown strong. This time—for the first time—he dropped her flat.

"You've just seen why," he said, his voice cold. "The guy is a class-A fraud."

"I know you're mad at me." Gray's eyes held no certainty, though his voice remained firm. "But you are coming with me. You have an hour and a half to get packed up."

"What?" Dawson spun, fists doubled, breathing like a stabbed bull.

"I have a show at eight thirty in Chicago, and I cannot miss this one, too. Our plane leaves at five."

"Are you kidding me? You can't just show up and drag me off with no warning."

"And you can't just walk off your school campus and board a plane for a different country with no warning, yet, somehow, here we are. I *can* just take you, Son. It's come with me or you're on the next flight to Heathrow."

Dawson threw a pleading look at Abby. She couldn't help but be impressed with both of them. "Gray, don't you think—"

"No." He pointed at her. "This is not up for discussion. There's no time."

"But is it really best for him to hang out with a rock band?"

"Yes." He closed the discussion with a tight-lipped stare.

"Dad, you're just being a jerk now."

"You don't get to talk to your father that way," Abby chastised him gently.

"But he gets to dictate my life when I haven't seen him in four months?"

"I'm afraid so, kiddo."

"This is bogus." He turned and marched from the room.

Kim stared after him. Gray blew out his breath and looked at the ceiling. Abby searched the archives of her brain for any smidge of an idea that would help and found zilch. "I guess you surprised him." Her lame humor fell flat.

"I don't blame him for being angry. I'll go talk to him in a few minutes." Gray rubbed his cheeks and, just like that, the performer slipped back into place. "Meanwhile, I haven't had a chance to meet Kim yet. I'm very sorry we started off like this."

Kim met the eyes of her hero for the first time. He smiled, but Abby saw the hollowness behind them, the panic building as he realized there was something wrong he'd never suspected. But he was nothing if not a consummate performer.

"I hear I have you to thank for offering Dawson a safe haven. I'm very happy to meet you." He started across the room.

"I look like a dweeb," Kim whispered in despair and looked at her camp-dirty jeans.

Abby urged her toward Gray. "You're beautiful."

He took Kim's hand, sending her cheek color straight to crimson. "I . . . I've always wanted to . . . it's *really* nice to meet you." Under any other circumstances, Kim would have pulled off something more poised.

"Your mom tells me you're a fan." Gray smiled in pleasure. "That's a huge compliment from someone of your generation with all the great music that's out there these days."

Wow, Abby thought. He is good.

"There's nothing as great as yours." Kim gushed for the first time. "I love every song."

Before Gray could reply, Kim blushed to a darker rose, and her hands flew to her face. "It's so amazing to meet you." She looked like she was about to lose her dinner. "I'm sorry. I've got to go. Get something. For a minute. Sorry."

She fled past Abby and pounded up the steps. Abby turned back to Gray, whose face had turned a bit Kermit-colored.

"Gee, Abby," he said. "That worked out just swell."

To an untrained eye, Gray Covey's elaborate stage at Chicago's new Marvel Arena might have looked like a productive beehive. To Elliott St. Vincent's highly-trained eye, however, the meandering techs looked like mechanics wandering a garage in search of something to fix.

Elliott sprawled in a chair cradling his Nikon D3X like a gunslinger protecting his Colt. "I knew there was no way our boy had laryngitis," he said to Gray's agitated manager, although Chris Boyle didn't bother to look at him.

"You don't get to talk now, St. Vincent."

Elliott ignored him. "Gray's too anal with his perfect pitch and his need for control to stay away just because he couldn't talk." Besides, Gray's band was tighter than jeans on a streetwalker—the Lunatics, they unofficially called themselves. Covey wouldn't be MIA during a tour under any normal circumstance. "Where is he? You're full of secrets the past few days."

This time Chris spared him a glare. "Your ass is in one big sling, photography man." He snatched a tabloid paper off a table and flung it Frisbee-style into Elliott's lap. "So sit quietly in your corner, or I'll kick you out." Elliott stroked his thick mustache with an unworried smile.

Before he could speak, new voices filled the air and Gray's band filed onstage, laughing, obviously not the least distressed over missing a gig the night before. Spark Jackson, Gray's lead guitarist for twenty-five years, led the way, and Boyle's eyes shone with relief.

"Did you reach him, Spark?"

"Yeah, he'll be back tonight." As always, Spark spoke with quiet, even words. He leaned on a section of floor riser not yet in place, arms crossed loosely over his chest. "He's got Dawson and says they'll be here on time."

"Dawson?" Elliott snapped to full attention. "He found Dawson?"

The pair ignored him.

Micky Wolff, the group's talented drummer, and Miles Dixon, the percussionist, each shrugged at Elliott as they passed him to check their instruments. They looked like Laurel and Hardy—Micky slight, short, and long-haired, Miles handsome as a young Sidney Poitier but larger than a left tackle. Behind them, bass player Max Hoffmann with his maroon-framed glasses had been with

Gray as long as Spark had and looked his quiet, bookish part. Gorgeous Misty Donahue, the only member who hadn't spent half a lifetime with the band, could sing as mellow as Norah Jones or soar like Mariah Carey. None of them paid Elliott more than a sour glance except for Dan Wickersham, the keyboardist. His lean runner's body matched Elliott's, and they were good friends.

"Heard you were in the time-out corner." Wickersham ambled toward him with a wry smile. "What the hell were you thinking?"

"C'mon, Wick." Elliott dragged him out of earshot. "You know I wouldn't do this." He held up the paper.

They'd all seen the photo, but Wick snorted. "It's funny, give you that."

Elliott regretted taking the picture: Gray, seated in an armchair with surprise—or was it the shock of pleasure?—on his face, and record industry insider Jillian Harper's head buried face-first in his crotch. The picture spoke for itself. Except that it lied. Stupid party, Gray's date, hilarious laughs when she'd tripped and landed in the compromising position. Elliott took celebrity photos for a living. He'd merely snapped the shutter in reflex.

"Funny in private. I didn't sell it to the *Star*."

Wick handed the paper back. "You gotta admit, this is hard evidence. And it had to be worth a few pesos."

"I don't need a few pesos."

"Yeah, richer than Gates." Wick slapped him on the shoulder blade. "Hey, I know Chris isn't seeing any humor in this, but maybe Gray will."

"I'm not worried about Gray; he's my ticket out of hot

water. But do me a favor and keep Boyle away from me. I'm ready to murder him. So, what's up with Dawson? Why didn't I hear about this?"

Spark turned his head. "Because you'd have found a way to follow him, and that wasn't going to happen." He punctuated his reply with an eloquent shrug.

For the first time, Elliott felt a sting. He'd been friends, good friends, with Gray and the band for fifteen years, and they had always trusted him with anything publicity-related. He provided everything from photos for advance promotions to the band members' eight-by-ten glossies. He had access to backstage dramas and personal celebrations. He knew the workings of the Covey Empire as well as anyone did, because he paid very close attention. Nobody questioned the tidy sum Chris Boyle paid him to keep Gray's image in front of the public.

He made money on the side as a paparazzo, it was true. He was good at it. But he was fair, and celebrities generally liked him. Nobody had ever questioned that part of his life, either. Until now.

"Thanks for the vote of confidence." He glowered at Sparks. "So, where did he find Dawson?" Elliott liked Gray's son. The kid was funny and sharp. He figured Dawson liked him well enough, and he'd been as worried as anyone when the boy had disappeared.

"Gray can tell you if he comes back." Spark sidestepped the question and grinned. "With things the way they've been, I wouldn't blame him for staying."

"Bite your damn tongue." Chris glared at the guitar man. "And you, St. Vincent, will lay low with him. Gray's trusted you all these years, so don't chase him, or make excuses for yourself, or give him any reason to leave here again. Keep your lenses out of his business until this goes away."

"Now look here." Elliott stood and beseeched Spark with his hands. "I haven't done anything. I'm telling you, this was somebody's idea of a joke."

Chris held up a hand. "You've had four, or is it five, unflattering pictures from this tour show up in your favorite rags the past two months. We've looked past your sick sense of humor because you make us laugh, and because the pictures actually generated interest. But jeopardizing your friend's career and that of an innocent woman? That's more than taking advantage of a friend, St. Vincent. This time you've gone too far."

Anger burned straight to Elliott's gut, but he didn't voice it. He was tried and convicted until Gray returned. The band members, supposedly his best friends, stood like silent gawkers at a mugging, and, for the first time, the taste of worry left him speechless.

Chapter Five

THE MAROON MASSEY Ferguson, almost as weathered as its driver, chugged up the driveway after making short work of the mud, and Ed raised his arm in farewell from the tractor seat without looking back. Gray watched him, reluctant to face the three people gathered behind him around the newly-freed Malibu. His son, for one, had lost all semblance of manners or good grace. Abby still thought him a rotten parent for kidnapping his own son. And Kim's sweet, blue eyes followed him like a moony kitten's, yet she'd spoken at most a paragraph's worth of words.

When he had no choice, he turned with forced cheer. "Great! We can be on our way."

"Fantastic." Dawson hid near-tears with sarcasm.

"Hey." Abby put her arms around him, and, although he didn't reciprocate, he didn't pull away either. "You're welcome here anytime. You and your dad. You know that?"

"Yeah. Right. Thanks."

"We can talk online, okay?" Kim held out a tentative olive branch.

"I thought you hated me now." Dawson gave a half-hearted grin and shrugged from Abby's hold.

"I do. I'll just yell on IM."

"Go for it." He held out a fist and Kim bumped it, averting her eyes.

"Abby." Gray's smile turned genuine. "You kept him safe. How can I thank you?"

"You could still think about what I said. About what's best for him." Her voice might have been gentle, but she meant every word.

"C'mon." He sighed. "Don't say good-bye like that."

Her features softened reluctantly. "You're right. I'm still being selfish." She ran a fingertip down Dawson's nose and smiled when he glowered. "I enjoyed having a man around for a while even if he had the wool pulled over my eyes."

The boy smiled for the first time. "I did have you fooled."

"Well, don't think you can do it again," Abby warned. "It'll bite you in the behind one day, young man."

"Yeah, yeah."

"Kim." Gray turned to Abby's daughter, a pretty carbon-copy of her mother. "I'm sorry we didn't have more time together. It was wonderful to meet you."

"I . . ." She glanced at her mother. "We have tickets to your concert in St. Paul at the end of July. I'll wave."

"You have?" He looked at Abby, and she nodded. "Then maybe we have to figure something out so we can meet again."

"Really? That would be totally great!" Kim's sudden, goofy smile showed more animation than anyone had in an hour.

"It would be." The hope of seeing Abby again caused a flare of hard excitement. Gray held her eyes with his until she flushed a deep rose color. With a chuckle, he offered Kim a quick hug then held his arms open for Abby. To his surprise, she came willingly into his arms. Her strong, slender body felt so right against his that it startled him.

"Thank you again. I know you're not happy with me, but I'm in your debt."

"I'm *not* happy with you," she agreed. "But you don't owe me thanks. Bringing him here was the Good Lord's idea, and we may never know why. But I got to slap you— more or less. I'm good with that."

Laughter got the better of him, easing his inner tension. "I think you're serious."

"Dead serious." She leaned close again and lifted her lips to his ear. "He liked it here. He felt safe. Call if I can ever help, Gray."

"Thank you. I will. But, if I know my kid, once he gets a guitar in his hand, he'll like it with me, too."

"You may be right." She stepped back, her smile turning wistful. "I hope you're right."

THREE HOURS LATER, the drone of the Boeing 737 failed to lull Gray into sleep as it usually did. Beside him, Dawson stared like a cyborg, tethered to his iPod by earphones he'd worn since leaving the Stadtlers' driveway. Not two dozen words had passed between them, and Gray decided enough was enough. He beckoned with two fingers by his ears. "Take 'em off please."

Dawson complied with a scowl and stared straight ahead. "Fine. They're off."

"I understand the silent treatment. You're mad at me." Dawson's sideways glance was as sarcastic as words. "Okay, really mad," Gray amended. "But we're half an hour from Chicago, and we need to get a few things sorted out."

"Just tell me what I'm supposed to do, and I'll do it."

"I'd like to do this together."

"We're together already. What more do you want?"

"A little enthusiasm?"

"For?"

"Okay, I'll settle for a little less lip."

"Yes, sir."

Gray sighed, lost and confused. To say he hadn't expected this was an understatement. He had no idea what to do. It was like they'd never met.

"Do you want to tell me why you ran away? You don't want your mother. You don't want me. What did you want?"

"I wanted to stay with Grandma."

The words were a slug to the gut. Honest and raw with

emotion, Dawson's eyes finally lifted. Their threatening tears almost undid Gray.

"Grandma Covey?" His rhetorical question made Dawson roll his brimming eyes again.

"Thanks for telling me she's not home anymore. Thanks for telling me why she stopped answering when I called her."

"I'm sorry, Daw." Gray barely found his voice. "I know how close you two are, and I didn't know how to tell you. She only moved six weeks ago, and you disappeared just a few days later."

"Yeah, because nobody, not even her nurse, would tell me why I couldn't talk to her. And nobody can find *you* when you're on tour."

"You can't have tried very hard. Did you leave messages? Try Spark?"

"Whatever, Dad."

He chose to ignore that issue. "You managed to get a ticket so you could come and find your grandmother?" Dawson nodded. "And?"

"Pauline told me she was in a nursing home." The threatening tears had been replaced by righteous anger. "But she wouldn't say which one. Said you or Mom had to bring me."

Pauline was his mother's personal helper. "You were in Virginia? You went to Grandma's house?" The news astounded him. How the hell far had this kid traveled?

"I told you I did." His lips firmed into an exasperated line.

"Dawson, I mean it. I'm sorry. It was time to move her.

Grandma fell and got very confused after that. She can't stay at home, at least for a while. The Alzheimer's is progressing more quickly than they believed it would, even though she's not all that old. I wanted to tell you when I knew more about how she was doing."

"Great. I'm not old enough to handle anything, am I? Not staying home, because there's a baby around. Not deciding where I want to go to school. Not hearing about my grandmother when she's sick. So Grandma got stuffed away, too, huh? Put where somebody can watch her because nobody has time for her. Is that just what you do, Dad?"

This slam was a roundhouse kick to the heart. Gray had no idea if the heavy burning in his chest was hurt or fury. "Just what the hell was that supposed to mean? It's a pretty immature thing to say, I might add."

"Truth hurts, huh?"

"That's enough." Gray lost it as quietly as he could. There was a fair amount of privacy in first class, but not enough to hide the full-blown anger he wanted to unleash.

"Why? You have more money than God. And Mom has more money than God's wife. We're so rich you could probably cure Alzheimer's if you wanted, but you just keep touring, and you put Grandma in a home and me in the stupidest school on the planet."

"I am not going to apologize for my job." Gray forced calm into his words. "I admit I let your mother walk all over me about the school. I tried."

"Can't have been very hard," he mimicked.

"Dawson, how many times can I say I'm sorry? I can talk to your mother about school. But your grandma is sick. I'm not a doctor. What the hell would you have me do?"

"Use your money to fix her." Once again tears beaded in his gray-blue eyes. For the first time he looked honestly sad, defiance replaced by immaturity and confusion.

"Don't you think I would if I could? I miss my mom, too."

"Then do something for her. The whole world listens to you."

Gray snorted. "Hardly."

"All you have to do is hold some supermodel's hand and there's a picture. Do something good instead. Get a hundred nurses and let Grandma stay at home. Hire some doctor to live with her and do research. Hire a *hundred* doctors. I don't know. But even old farts like Elton John and Bono do stuff with their money."

Gray leaned back in his seat and closed his eyes, fighting a sudden pain in his gut that hurt like hell. Somewhere along the line his son had learned how to argue like a prosecutor and hit below the belt like a brawling street fighter.

"Life is simple for you isn't it?" Gray asked.

"Sure, because everyone tells me what to do."

"I hate to tell you, you might as well get used to that. Some things never change."

"Yeah? Then what's the point?" he mumbled.

"The point is, it's hell being a kid, and it's hell being an adult. You make the best of it, and if you're lucky you have some fun along the way." Gray firmed his voice. "So, suck it up and give this a chance. We're going right to the arena because there's no time to stop at the hotel first. But everyone's waiting to see you. And eventually," he patted Dawson's leg, "we'll figure out school and your other problems. Okay?"

"I'm not going back to Heighton no matter how much sucking-it-up you say I have to do."

"I'll keep that in mind." Gray tried to smile, but all he could manage was a sick-feeling grimace.

The first thing in his head ninety minutes later when he led Dawson onstage at the Marvel Center was Abby Stadtler's farm and how calm it was, compared with the raucous atmosphere of his world. The incongruous thought surprised him, and the flash of melancholy that followed it disturbed him.

"Lawd a'mighty, if the wanderers ain't done returned!" Miles popped his head up from adjusting a bongo stand and reached Gray in three huge strides. "Hey, man, welcome back."

His big, black hand thrust forward like a bear paw, and Gray clasped it, his brief moment of blues vanishing. "Hey. Good to be back."

"And my man, Dawson. Welcome home, too."

Dawson allowed the first smile Gray had seen. Greetings piled on after that, each band member welcoming Dawson with equal enthusiasm. Micky handed Gray a beer. Wick brought Dawson a Coke. They asked questions like a flock of Larry Kings.

"About time you showed up." Spark's voice cut through

the banal chatter, and Gray felt the full relief of being back. Spark's calm always smoothed the waters. Abby had reminded Gray of Spark, he realized, although he couldn't imagine why since they'd argued like nine-year-olds. "Successful trip, I see."

"On the surface." Gray shook away Abby's memory. "He's not here willingly."

Spark shook his head. "Kids." He tapped Dawson on the shoulder. "Hey you, juvenile delinquent, good to see you."

"Spark!"

With a twinge of envy, Gray watched the embrace between his son and his best friend. They hadn't seen each other in over a year, but in the early days Dawson had spent a great deal of time at the Jackson home with Spark, his three kids, and his wife, Lindsey. At the moment, Gray was the bad guy, but Spark wasn't.

"Hot dang, you've grown a foot," Spark said.

"You sound like a grandma."

"I'm just old. So, you gonna hang around and play with us?"

"I dunno. I guess." Dawson's smile dimmed again, but Gray took heart that it didn't disappear.

A camera shutter whirred at close range and Gray found himself staring into Elliott's Nikon. He laughed, but then the first strange thing of the reunion wiped the laughter away. Chris strode to the photographer and grasped the camera by its wide, expensive lens.

"I told you to put that goddamn thing away."

"Just doin' my job." Elliott smiled. "Welcome home to the crazy farm, Gray. Things fall apart when you leave."

"Oh? What's going on?"

"My, my. I didn't realize it was bring-your-child-to-work day." Chris ignored the question and turned raised brows on Dawson. "Hi, kid. How's my favorite reason to cancel a concert?"

"Good." Dawson paused only a moment. "Came to wreck one in person."

A smattering of laughter punctuated his cheeky response. Once again his quickness surprised Gray.

"Nice boy." Chris winked, but Gray caught the sarcasm. Chris had never been a kid person. Never been a marriage person or even much of a dating person. He was, in truth, slightly humorless, but he was a hell of a businessman.

"Now back to my question." Gray studied the abnormal wariness in Elliott's eyes and patted his cheek. "Am I sensing a wittle bitty tiff between friends?"

"You're an ass," Elliott growled.

A chuckle escaped from Dawson, who offered the photographer a high-five. "Hey, Elliott," he said, his eyes lighting up once more.

"Hi Dawson!"

"And you're an ass, you ass." Gray ignored their greetings. "Talk to me."

"You were right, it's just a tiff." Chris stepped between them. "You don't have time now; we're pushing this a little close."

"It's only six thirty. We have time." Gray stood firm. He didn't like dissension in his ranks, and joking hadn't eased the tension wafting through the room. Gray stared down his band members, his manager, and Elliott. "I was gone one friggin' day."

Spark rummaged in a pile of papers behind an amplifier and returned with a folded tabloid. "Make of it what you will, but you are in the news."

"What now? Can't be any worse than the stupid pratfall pictures and embarrassing moments that have been appearing—" He saw the picture and flicked his eyes to Elliott. "What the hell?"

"I didn't send it to them."

Gray had been friends with Elliott St. Vincent since they'd met at a New York hot dog stand probably fifteen years before. Elliott had actually negotiated a candid photo with Gray, impressing the hell out of him. If Elliott wasn't now an official paid staff member, he was close. He'd always been a nice guy, and as close to an ethical paparazzo as one could get. Along with that, he was responsible for a lot of great publicity. Lately, everyone knew he'd been taking advantage of his close ties to the band, but pictures sent to the rags so far had been harmless, embarrassing moments from the doomed tour. He'd claimed to have sent one, an innocuous trip onstage captured by every contraband camera at that show. Four others had been tension-breakers more than anything. But this . . .

"Bullshit." Chris jumped in. "Who else could send it? It's your picture."

"It is. Everybody knows that. I'm telling you, I didn't send it anywhere."

"So, what's your story?" Gray asked. "You must have proof if you're this adamant."

"Of course I don't have proof." Elliott spat the words. "Whoever's doing this has covered his bases well."

Dawson grabbed the newspaper from him and stared at the picture of the girl with her head in his father's lap. He began to giggle. "Wow, Dad, a public blow job. This almost makes you look cool."

The uncensored declaration brought shocked silence. Spark sputtered his disbelief first and whipped the paper away from Dawson. "You're a sick kid."

"Aw, come on." Dawson laughed. "It has to be a fake."

"Well, thanks for that, anyway." Gray let out his breath. "The public won't care, though. This could be a disaster."

"It's already a disaster." Chris pinched the bridge of his nose. "It's all over the Internet."

"Man, what were you thinking?" Gray pleaded with Elliott.

"Are you listening to me?" Elliott raised his voice for the first time. "I did not do this."

"Can't you see Gray's not buying your bull either?" Chris turned. "The worst of it is what happened this morning. Since the picture went viral, it cost Jillian Harper her job. She worked with Ron Revers, and you know we've been trying to get him to produce Gray's next record for over a year now. This makes it look like there are very sleazy favors being given in exchange for special treatment. Truth makes no difference—a record label can't afford misperceptions."

"Fired? Are you kidding me?" Gray forgot about his son, forgot about the show he had to do in less than two hours. He saw only the mercenary betrayal of a friend. Chris kept such a tight rein on this kind of thing, he'd know the truth. Elliott was the only one allowed into the Lunatics' inner circle. They'd all seen this shot a month ago when it had been an accidental—and hilarious—joke. It wasn't hilarious now. "You can't do this to me, Elliott. There's too much other crap going on in my life. None of us needs this."

"You don't believe me." Elliott's eyes filled with shock. "After all we've been through, you just . . . automatically side against me? Chris has no proof I sent the damn picture."

"Oh, my friend, it happens I do." Triumph shone in Chris's eyes. "I checked with the paper. They told me the file came from one Elliott St. Vincent. They have the e-mail. They have the date stamp on it. You might as well quit lying. Your ass is toast."

"You are so far off the mark." Elliott stood his ground. "If I even wanted to do this, tell me why I'd be stupid enough to use a picture you all knew I'd taken and then send it from somewhere that could be traced to me?"

"Because it would look like a perfect cover—just like what you're asking us to believe right now," Spark replied.

For only a moment Gray waffled, his natural sympathy kicking in. But his resolve hardened. It hurt, but in his world this wouldn't be the first time he'd been sold out by a friend.

"I think you should leave," he said quietly. "This is already screwing with the vibes before the show. We'll finalize things later, but I have to tell you, ruining someone's career in the name of money is not all right."

"You're joking, right?" Elliott seemed frozen in disbelief.

"Dad?!" Dawson tugged hard on Gray's sleeve.

"This is none of your business, Son."

"What are you doing? Elliott's one of the good guys."

"We'll talk about it later."

Dawson glared, but what else was new? Elliott gathered his camera bag and vest from where they'd been heaped on the floor. Flinging the bag strap over one shoulder, he stopped inches from Gray. Fury crackled between them.

"Your sixteen-year-old son has more sense than you do." Elliott's words were pinched. "I figured friendship meant something to you, Gray." He took one angry step then looked back. "Don't ever accuse me of doing this for money again. Not until you take a look at the path you're on."

He pushed past the stunned band members. Only Wick followed, but when Dawson tried to do the same Gray caught his arm and shook his head.

"But, Dad . . . Jeez, you just fired a guy you've known forever."

"I didn't fire him. He doesn't work for me. And I have only an hour to get ready. You're staying with me."

"Why? So I can see you put on one of those lame se-quined shirts? You look like some loser who got lost on the way to Las Vegas."

Gray had given up being wounded by his son. Besides, his nerves were numb enough that someone could have dropped a piano on his head and he wouldn't have felt it. "You don't like anything I do. I get that. I'm your worst nightmare. Fine. You're coming with me anyway. And when it's time for me to go on, you can sit with Chris right in front."

"Front row seats to a Gray Covey concert? Dude, how'd I get so lucky?"

"My son, glowering at me for two hours in the front row. How'd I get so lucky?"

For half a heartbeat Dawson fought a smile. It was half a heartbeat long enough to burn away Gray's annoyance.

"Do I have to sit with Chris? Can't I watch from in back with the techs?"

"Dawson!" In a moment of perfect timing, Corky Hotchkiss, the head sound technician, passed on his way to check the miles of cable under his care. Lanky for a man of medium height, with saggy-seated jeans and ear-phones hanging around his neck like a stethoscope, he looked like a middle-aged guy lost in a dorm room, not a brilliant sound engineer. He clapped Dawson on the shoulder. "I heard you were visiting. Good to see you!"

"Hey Corky. Yeah, you, too."

"Did I hear you say you're looking for a place to watch your dad?"

"More than anything." Gray didn't miss the hundredth, long-suffering eye roll of the day.

"How 'bout you come sit with us at the mixer board? I could maybe find a job for you since one of my guys is sick. You can come now."

"Please, can he take me now?" Dawson seemed disbelieving at his luck.

Gray clapped his hands together and stared up. "Hallelujah. Go. Just stay in the arena."

"I will." He turned to follow Corky. "Oh, Dad?"

"Yeah?"

"Whatever you do, don't wear the silver. You always look like a disco ball."

Chapter Six

"They're always beautiful, aren't they?"

The cool iron of the safety railing pressed into Abby's torso, and a faint mist spritzed her cheeks. Kim leaned forward to look over the frothing pool below Kennison Falls, the thundering treasure for which their small town was named. Hidden in Butte Glen State Park, just a mile from town center, the thirty-five foot falls were as wide as they were high. They were also a huge tourist draw, but, despite regular crowds, the site was always peaceful. Abby closed her eyes and opened them as soon as Gray Covey's image invaded the darkness behind her eyelids.

The picture was now familiar. As was the act of pushing it away.

"Yup, they are." Kim straightened.

"Ready to head back? We can grab some ice cream."

"Okay."

They walked the two-mile round trip often, but tonight tension hung in the air as it had for the twenty-four hours since Gray and Dawson had driven away. Abby knew Kim felt bereft. How could she not? Abby's life had fallen into a black hole, too, after six weeks of light from Dawson's presence. And the lone, meteorite-bright day his father had spent in their lives.

Gray.

Their ridiculous arguments hung word-for-word in her memory. His tiny, stolen kiss still burned her lips if she let the thought simmer too long. She was a grown woman, but the whole surreal experience and her lingering reactions left her both regretful and embarrassed. Kim's twenty-four hour sulk hadn't helped.

"So," Abby said after they'd made a quarter-mile of progress in the first-day-of-June twilight. "How about you explain why you're still mad at me?"

"I'm not."

"You haven't said this few words to me since you were a year old and couldn't talk." She teased but didn't push, as Kim clearly concentrated on what she wanted to say.

"You scared him away." After that first reluctant admission, her words finally tumbled free. "It was Gray, Mom! That was my chance to really meet him, but I couldn't, because every time I tried to talk to him you were arguing about Dawson."

"I scared him *away*? Kimmy, I couldn't make him stay. The truth is he doesn't belong in our world." Her heart gave an unhappy thump.

"But, if you'd just been nicer to him."

"In some ways we both could have been nicer." Abby

partially conceded the point. She regretted constantly questioning his plans for his son and letting her emotions rule her words. But he hadn't always been a model of sweetness and light either. "We weren't angry all the time, though, and I tried to talk Gray into letting Dawson stay. He just couldn't. It's that simple."

"But, it was my dream-come-true. Maybe he might even have liked me."

Ahhh, the real truth. It didn't matter to a fifteen-year-old if her love—not to be confused with a mere crush—was twenty-nine years older than she was. Love was love. Abby had squashed it.

"He's pretty good-looking in person, isn't he?" She gave her daughter a hug. At this point, she could afford a little sympathy and a short, shared fan-girl moment. Maybe it would help them both.

"Oh, Mo-om." Kim buried her face in Abby's shoulder as they walked. "He's gorgeous. Gorgeous! And he hugged me and held my hand and everything. He's amazing."

And he kissed me and everything . . . Abby kept that fan-girl moment to herself, laughing instead at Kim's theatrics.

"Yes, darling, he did. You got to meet him, and he was very nice." *And stubborn. And clueless about his son.*

"He should have stayed. Or let Dawson stay." Kim pouted like a pretty princess.

"I admit, I thought that could have been a good solution, but he is Dawson's dad."

"That's just weird and creepy." The princess disappeared. "I can't believe he didn't tell me. Even when he saw Gray's pictures were all over my walls."

"I'm sure he thought it was pretty creepy you find his father sexy."

"Mom!" Kim hid her face again, clinging to Abby's bicep and giggling. "I suppose it did gross him out. That's so cool."

"Young people are cruel." Abby tugged on her pony tail.

"I'm not cruel. I just wanted a chance. I almost had it."

"You have a strong friendship with Dawson, and Gray knows you now. He won't forget you."

"You think?"

"I'm sure. There's a reason God put Dawson, and Gray, in our lives. Even for a short time. He'll remember us."

The first shops of Main Street came into view. The May evening was unseasonably warm and already smelled of dogwood and linden blossoms. Ed had told her the *Farmer's Almanac* was predicting a hot, stormy summer, and that was fine. Abby loved weather. Thunderstorms were her favorites. *A storm-eyed girl took my hand one day, and said, "Follow me, boy . . ."* The song, tune and all, popped into her head. The memory of warm, drenching rain, a slick hay wagon, and strong hands at her waist followed.

"Mom?"

She shook her head, and her cheeks heated. "Sorry, what?"

"I said it would be cool if Gray came back and he and I and you and Dewey went on a date."

"Ummm . . ." This was taking the daydream a little over the top. "I don't think so. That's kind of creepy to *me*, Kimmy. Besides, I don't date Dewey anymore."

She could see where the conversation had originated. They passed the one service station in town, a combination gas station and repair shop, which Dewey Mitchell had made the most successful in the area. Behind it was the farmer's co-op Dewey co-owned. Local boy made good. The former football jock—and most eligible divorced male in Faribault County—had made it clear Abby was his choice for a permanent date, and she'd tried. But any feelings on her part carried the heat level of a sister for a brother. "Dewey's a nice guy. Not my type."

Kennison Falls opened up before them, and familiar warmth spread through Abby. She and Jack had moved here thirteen years before with their babies, hoping it would be a good place to raise them. Jack and Will hadn't made it two years, but now it was her home. The eight hundred ten residents all knew each other. During the turmoil after Jack's death and the problems she'd had with his parents, the town had cared for her and Kim as if they'd been native-born.

She loved Kennison Falls's pretty main street lined with simple, old-fashioned, iron lampposts. Friendly blue-and-white welcome banners hung on the posts most of the year, flags took their places on the Fourth of July, followed by festoons of garland and white lights at Christmas. Beautiful, mature maples were staggered in the boulevards, shading the angled parking spots along the street.

Flo's bakery always smelled fabulous from a block away in either direction. Majestic carved lions decorated the tiny library's front door, and the two newest structures, the post office and the water tower, made modern splashes in the quaint town. They arrived at the Body Arts Shop with its new-age star on a hanging sign beside its door, and Kim tugged Abby to the window to start a familiar conversation.

"Can I get a tattoo? Just a little horse head or a dolphin or something?"

"If you get a tattoo before you're thirty, I'll disown you," Abby laughed.

"You could get one, too, a peace symbol or a kangaroo."

"A kangaroo?"

"It would make you even cooler."

"Sucking up will not help you. But, hey, you're saying I'm cool?"

"For an old mom."

"You're so kind."

Abby tried to keep the jovial feelings flowing. She didn't want their reconciliation ruined by her mercurial moods. Was thirty-seven an "old mom"? Did it matter that she didn't want to be fixed-up with the one man in town who would take her in a heartbeat? And who could ensure more financial stability? She had a good life, fashioned in her own way. She'd vigilantly proven for eleven years—in many ways was still proving—to her late husband's parents that she could care perfectly well for their only grandchild. They never believed her capable of such a feat. Not a woman who'd lured their son to some backward, hinterland town where he'd been taken from them. Not a woman who refused to get a real job. Abby shuddered, as she always did at thoughts of her in-laws. True, things weren't financially wonderful these days, but two part-time jobs and the regular riding lessons she taught kept her and Kim more or less afloat. It was things like the shavings, the feed, and the fencing that she never told her in-laws about. Marrying someone like Dewey . . . She shivered again.

"Mom!" Kim yanked on her shirt sleeve, startling her out of her reverie.

"Sorry, sorry. No dolphins. No kangaroos."

"Then how about ice cream?" Kim inclined her head.

They stood in front of the Loon Feather, Kennison Falls's most beloved café. Its bright purple door and rustic wood gabled roof faced the corner. The rest of the building stretched along the sidewalk, its siding painted with a mural of cattails and a lake filled with loons.

"Of course. Ice cream is the plan."

"I know I promised not to tell friends and stuff about Gray yet, but could we tell Karla?"

Karla Baxter was Abby's best friend. Music teacher by school year, Loon Feather waitress by spring and summer. "She doesn't work Sunday nights," Abby said.

"Oh right. Bummer." Kim faked a pout.

Reality reared its head again. "Maybe we should wait to tell her, too."

"Not say anything to anyone? About the coolest thing that's ever happened?" Kim's eyes flashed—pretty blue neon signs of disbelief.

"I know, but think about it. We don't want anyone asking questions about Dawson yet. Or hanging around because they think Gray might come back. Give it a couple of weeks."

"Aw, jeez, Mrs. Buzz Killington."

Abby laughed out loud and kissed her daughter's head. "Yeah, I'm sorry I'm so lame. I'm just so dang good at it."

"HA! I TOLD you not to mess with me. I'm too dang good at this." Gray swept the stack of blue and red poker chips from the middle of the table, his ostentatious gesture garnering a bevy of groans and card slaps as Spark, Miles, Misty, and Micky threw their cards on the low table. The makeshift lounge in the backstage area of the Madison arena smelled and sounded like a cheap pool hall.

"Good since when?" Miles groused. "Dawson, man, are you handing him cheatin' signs or are you just some freaky good-luck charm?"

"Take your pick."

Dawson, hunched in a corner chair, held Gray's acoustic guitar and plucked absently, the same kid-at-the-elderly-aunt's-house-for-tea look on his face that had been there for seven days. The mindless background music he created was nice to have around, actually comforting, but Gray hadn't found the key to dispelling his son's resentment.

"Deal again," Micky ordered. "I'm winning back some of my pot from Covey if it's the last thing I do."

"You've got a show to play long before that happens." Gray rubbed his palms together.

"Dad? You said you'd come listen to something before you had to change for the show. You gonna have time?"

"Yeah, of course. One more hand?"

"Whatever."

"What song am I coming to hear?" Gray picked up his cards as Micky dealt the hand.

"One for Grandma."

"Really?" Gray looked up, but Dawson's head remained bowed over the guitar. "That's great, Daw. Why don't you play it here?"

"Yeah, go for it, kid," Miles said. "We're a good audience."

"It isn't *for* everyone yet." Dawson lifted his head and stared point-blank at Gray, mild accusation in his steel-colored irises.

Gray offered a smile. "I get that."

"You sure you don't want to join us onstage tonight?" Spark looked up from scowling at his poker hand. "I heard you playing a couple of the riffs earlier. You'd do great."

"Nah. I'll stick with Corky at the board. It's pretty cool."

"You like it there?" Spark asked. "Corky says you have an ear for the sound. Do you have perfect pitch like your dad?"

"Nope." A half-smile from a corner of his mouth indicated Dawson appreciated the compliments, but a tic at

the corner of a narrowed eye indicated he didn't appreciate being lumped with his father in any category.

"Just remember, you're welcome to play any time,"
Gray said. "I promise I wouldn't make a big deal out it."

"It's okay."

"Just want you to feel at home."

"Dad!" Dawson popped to his feet, dangling the guitar
by the narrowest section of its neck. "Would you chill
already? I'm *not* at home. I'm in Saint Tiddlywinks nowhere. I don't want to go onstage. I'd rather muck a stall
than go onstage. I'm okay hanging around with Corky, so
why can't you just quit harassing me about playing?" He
shifted his grip on the guitar and let his glare slip to the
floor. "I'm going back to the dressing rooms. When you're
done gambling for geezers let me know if you want to
hear that song. It's not that good. It's not that important."

"Dawson, come on . . ." Gray's voice trailed off as
Dawson left the room. Digging one thumb and forefinger
into the bridge of his nose, he pressed against the dull
tension headache that rarely left him. He couldn't win.
He'd actually been enjoying the quiet time with Dawson,
and suddenly he was the bad guy yet again. He stood
to head after him, but Spark held him back. "Give him
a minute to cool off. He'll think you're just after him to
argue. Finish your hand, just like you said, and then go."

Micky chuckled. "Saint Tiddlywinks nowhere. You
used to say that."

"What the hell is wrong with him?" Gray sighed. "I'm
trying my best."

"No you aren't." Spark sat back and laid his cards face down on the table. The others copied him, obviously unconcerned with the rest of the poker game. "You're trying, yes, but the kid's been in two hotels, a plane, a limousine, and three dressing rooms in a week. He's bored. You need to try harder to let him be who he is."

"Who is that? He's a kid I don't know." Gray threw his cards down, too.

"Precisely. So get to know him."

His stomach knotted as he realized he'd been avoiding listening to Dawson. He was afraid. Afraid if the kid was no good it would just be another wedge between them. His son had asked him yesterday if he had time to listen to this song of his, but there'd been a sound check and then a quick local radio interview followed by a requisite meet-and-greet with some winners of a contest. Perfect excuses.

"I have no clue what to say half the time. It was nice just having him next to me, playing that guitar. He's got this great vibe, you know? Calming. He reminds me of my mother. But I can't do anything right."

"He's sixteen. You're supposed to seem like a Neanderthal to him. But he'll get over it. He's an incredibly smart kid. Talks like a thirty-year-old half the time. He's got good ideas, too."

"He said something when we were on the way to Chicago I haven't been able to stop thinking about."

"Yeah?"

"Told me I should use my money to make his grandmother well. I can't do that, of course, but why not something to help find a cure in the future? I'm going to run some ideas past Chris."

"Run what ideas past me, Covey?"

Chris entered the small space like a reigning emperor, leaving an entourage of half a dozen twenty-something young women at the door, gawking and covering squeals with their hands over their mouths. Annoyed, Gray glanced down at his worn jeans and favorite holey T-shirt. They all looked like evictees from a homeless camp. The only good thing was that Elliott wasn't around to memorialize such meetings with his camera. Everyone in the band had agreed he probably shouldn't cover the rest of the tour, and he wasn't allowed backstage.

"Philanthropy, Christopher. I've been thinking of doing some Alzheimer's work on behalf of my mother. Maybe starting a new foundation?"

"Hmmm, good idea, Gray. Hold on, ladies," he said to his group. "Let me make some room in here."

"I'm serious." Gray lowered his voice as Chris moved a couple of chairs and pushed aside a second table. "I've been talking with Dawson and thinking a lot the past week about getting involved in something outside the rock world. I'd like to talk about it."

"Look." Chris patted his arm and captured him with a serious eye. "I think it's a fantastic aspiration. And, yeah, let's talk. But remember, you're at the top of the game, man, and your market isn't Alzheimer's patients. I say, in five or ten years, when they're selling your CDs at card shops, that'll be the perfect time to sock money into a project. You'll have the time and you'll need the good PR."

His manager wasn't always the warmest guy, but he made a strong case. Gray wasn't ready to give up a good idea, but he'd wait until Chris didn't have a bevy of visitors to schmooze.

"You've got a point. But I still want to talk later."

"Smart man, of course I have a point, I always do. So, now I need to introduce you to a great group of gals. They're singers with a . . ."

Gray knew his rock-star manners. They'd been drilled into him after years of just such surprise visits. But he didn't hear much else once Chris ushered the girls into the lounge. This band here, that girl-group there, the president of this city's fan club everywhere.

"I can't wait to hear more about you, ladies." Gray shook hands all around, causing another ripple of tittering. "But I need to leave you in the hands of my band for just a sec. I was about to meet with my son, and I need to tell him I'll be late. I'll be right back."

"Nonsense!" Chris grasped Gray by the shoulder, turned him away from the door and into the group of women. "We'll get Miles to occupy Dawson. You—greet your fans."

"Chris, I promised to talk to him, I need to . . ."

"We'll talk to him. You can go in just a few minutes."

Gray sent a silent plea to Miles and inclined his head toward the door, receiving a nod from his bandmate. He turned back to Chris and the girls, digging deep to find his schmoozy-best smile and aching for a cigarette.

The picture of angry aquamarine eyes filled his mind. A booted toe crushing a glowing cigarette into the dirt. The fear of a barn going up in flames . . .

Ah, Abby. What I'd give for a lecture from you right now. It'd beat this conversation I'm not paying attention to all to hell. Heck. Abby Stadtler would say *heck*. She was not an *all-to-hell* kind of woman.

A small crash—the door banging open—interrupted Gray's musings, and he looked over his shoulder. Dawson stood in the door frame, eyes bright with bitterness. Miles set a hand on the boy's shoulder. "Hey, he'll be outta there soon. Come on with me for now."

Gray caught the full-force of his son's wounded anger, and his heart slid to the bottom of his ribcage, its beat erratic as a faulty watch. For an eternal second they stared at each other.

"Thanks, Dad." He handed the guitar to Miles and sprinted down the hall as if he couldn't leave fast enough. Gray started after him, but Chris grasped his shoulder. When Miles pointed at himself and then down the hall, Gray nodded, but a gut full of dread told him it was a bad decision.

MORNINGS CAME SOMETIME after noon on post-concert days. The band's warped sense of day and night took weeks to straighten out once a tour had finished. Gray blinked awake at the noise in his weird dream—he was pounding nails into Abby Stadtler's front porch, making sure the big saddles stayed nailed to the floor.

The pounding rang again. This time at his hotel room door. "What the—?"

Scratching his hair just above his forehead and running his tongue over fuzzy teeth, he yanked open the door.

"Just making sure your son is here." Spark stood in the hall, far too wide awake for 9 a.m. Beside him, Corky Hotchkiss looked like a guilty man dragged before a judge.

Gray glanced to the second bed in the room, empty and untouched as he'd expected. Even when he slept in their room it wasn't unusual for Dawson to be out before Gray arose. The kid functioned on sixteen minutes of sleep a night. But he'd told his angry son he could sleep in Miles's room, and Miles had given the plan a thumbs-up.

"He's in Miles's room. He was still mad at me late last night, and Miles told him he could bunk there."

"Yeah. Miles said Dawson claimed you'd given permission for him to stay with Wick instead, because they were going to work on Dawson's song. Dawson told Wick he was staying with Miles. They both thought he was with the other. What did he say to you last night?" Spark pushed into the room. Gray opened the door wider for Corky. His chest had begun to constrict as if something awful was about to happen and he couldn't stop it.

He'd seen Dawson at the break before the band's last encore. "He wasn't speaking to me much. He said, 'Good show,' but I doubted he meant it. He said he wasn't coming to the after-party; he was going to bed early because he wanted to get up early."

"He left the sound booth just before the encore and never came back." Corky held his arms tightly across his chest, his face as worried as Gray felt. "But everyone I asked told me he was up here in bed."

Gray's legs suddenly lost strength, and he sank onto the bed, rubbing the back of his head. The unease in his chest moved toward pain. Dawson had navigated an entire cross-Atlantic trip. Whatever he'd done this time was hardly likely to be more dangerous than that, but worry clawed at Gray like a fast-growing cancer. What the hell kind of father was he? He'd allowed Dawson his space last night, trusting him to be safe with his band members, but because he hadn't double-checked for himself, here they all were, evidently caught in a classic Dawson Covey sleight of hand.

"We'll find him." Spark squeezed his shoulder. "He can't be far."

Gray's heart rose to his throat and dread flooded his gut. "Damn it all. Yes he can."

Adrenaline pushed him to his feet, and he strode around a corner of the big suite to the dressing area. This time his heart plummeted back down into his stricken chest. "Shit!"

"What?" Spark stood beside him.

"His duffel bag is gone."

Chapter Seven

ABBY COULDN'T REALLY afford dinner out, but Friday had been a very long time arriving. She was tired of hamburger and rice, she missed the fun of Dawson's helpful presence around the farm, and she wanted a treat. When she and Kim stepped into the Loon Feather for the second time that week, Lester's cheery wolf whistle was just the boost she craved.

"Lester!" Kim skipped to a large cage where a pair of cockatiels puffed their chests expectantly. Abby joined her, and gray-and-white Lester hopped across his perch when Abby wiggled her index finger between two bars. He pecked at her fingernail and repeated his whistled compliment.

"Hi to you too handsome," she murmured.

Next to Lester sat his mate, pearly-white Cotton. "Howdy, stranger," Kim cooed.

Both birds boasted stunning, rouge-red cheeks and saffron crests, but while Lester preened and clucked for attention, Cotton channeled an owl. "How-dee stran-jer." Kim enunciated.

None of the Loon's regulars worried for half a second about birds in a restaurant. Everyone considered the cockatiels family, and helping teach Cotton to speak was part and parcel of a visit. Still, after a year, the customers' diligence in trying to teach her "Howdy, stranger" had produced only unintelligible grousing from the baleful bird.

Except from one person.

"Come on, Cotton. You'd almost say it for Dawson, but he's not here. I'm sorry, but you remember. Come on, girl. Howdy, stranger."

"Dawson sure had a way with that bird." Abby let Lester have one more soft nibble and removed her finger. "He had a way with most animals, didn't he?"

"I wonder how he's doing." Kim turned from Cotton, too. "I haven't heard from him since Tuesday. He said they were leaving Chicago and going to Kansas City and Madison. He said it all sucked, but I don't know any more than that."

"He's probably grumping but really having a great time."

"Abbs!" From across the cozy café, Karla Baxter, with coffee pot in hand, beckoned them toward the Loon's pride and joy, a booth crafted from local birch logs. The benches and table were nestled into a corner, the spot coveted by every teenage couple in town.

A mishmash of worn Quaker tables set with napkins and tablecloths made from every color and pattern of calico imaginable made for Grandma's-kitchen coziness. Knotty pine wainscoting warmed the walls, and a narrow shelf rimming the room near the ceiling held the owner Effie Jorgenson's enormous collection of bird statues and antique coffee cans.

One other feature made the Loon Feather a special place for Abby. Along one entry wall hung a series of ten photographs—her photographs. Effie and her husband, Bud, had bought them from her before Jack and Will's accident at the town's summer art fair. In those days, Abby had seriously considered taking up photography as more than a hobby. Now several immortalized residents and the town's most well-known icons formed her only tiny art gallery.

She and Kim crossed the spotless blue linoleum to their booth, accompanied by an enthusiastic avian rendition of the "Colonel Bogey March." Lester, unlike his mate, had an actual repertoire of three selections if you counted the theme song from *Andy Griffith* and the chauvinistic wolf whistle. His cheery melody and the rich aroma of baked bread and cinnamon added up to a happy conviction she'd made the right dinner plans.

"How are my girls?" Karla gave Kim a careful hug, holding the coffee pot well away. "Hey, where's Dawson?"

Abby gave a heartfelt pout. "Dawson's gone."

"What?" Karla pushed up on the bridge of her thick, black-framed glasses.

"His parents found him. His father picked him up a week ago."

"But? I thought he was eighteen."

"Mmm hmm." Abby fingered her napkin and straightened her silverware. "So did I."

"But?"

"Try, he's sixteen, a runaway, not from New York but from London."

Karla's hand jerked in surprise, sloshing coffee over the rim of Abby's cup. "Boy, there's a story worth hearing."

Kim pleaded silently with Abby, her eyes pathetic like a dog begging for steak. She'd agreed to keep Gray's visit a secret until after his concert in six weeks, in case they all got to meet again, but she obviously regretted her part in the bargain. Abby didn't blame her. It was a hard secret to keep. "He ran away from boarding school!" Kim settled for imparting that news.

Abby nodded. "He got here on a fake ID and his real passport."

"You're kidding? So, what? He went back to England?"

"His father took him, he's . . . a musician. I'm not sure what their final plans are. I tried to talk him into letting Dawson stay for the summer, but no go."

"And here I thought Dawson was such a good kid."

"He is a good kid, Karla." Abby's defensiveness surprised her just as it had when she'd let it flare in front of Gray. "Maybe he lied about his age, but he never gave a moment's trouble in the time he was with us. He's polite and hard-working. I got the impression he felt ignored and was looking for attention from his parents. I hope he gets what he needs, but I do miss him."

Her friend's look was a little too knowing. Too sympathetic. At least she didn't state the obvious: Will would have been Dawson's age. Abby refused the idea. That wasn't what the Dawson thing was about.

"Well." Karla sopped up her spilled coffee with a towel from her back jeans pocket. "Guess you had your summer adventure before summer even got started." She adopted her teacher's voice for Kim. "Now you won't let your practicing go by the wayside having another kid in the house. You can spend the summer getting ready for music camp."

"Yeah, okay."

"Hey now, a little more enthusiasm please." Karla tapped her on the head.

"You gave me a really hard piece for the contest."

"Because you're good enough to handle it."

"Are things looking better for the funding?" Abby asked.

"Who knows?" A careless shrug loosened a strand of hair from Karla's dark brown pony tail. Her pretty, round face took on the shadow of determination.

The Kennison Falls summer music camp was Karla Baxter's beloved annual project. For ten years, the week-long combination of lessons, activities, and a solo-and-ensemble competition had attracted high school kids from around the state. This year, funding for the camp was in jeopardy, along with the entire school music program.

"I'll do something no matter what happens. We'll have a chopped-down version, and I can always get a couple of judges to donate time." She dragged the black glasses down her nose. "So, you keep that clarinet hot and smokin', my girl."

"Yes, ma'am."

Abby laughed. It was a blessing and a curse to be friends with your teacher.

"Enough digression." Karla grabbed a pad from another pocket. "What can I get you two for supper?"

An hour later, stuffed with the Loon's homemade potpie and decadent strudel, Abby pulled into her driveway. Kim's frustration over keeping Gray a secret had turned into a giggly mother-daughter secret that had wiped away Abby's blues and served to keep her memories of Gray Covey alive and warm. Whether that was a good thing or not she didn't know—the warmth was a little too warm, and the memories were a little too alive—but, really, what could it hurt?

"Mom!" Kim grabbed Abby's wrist, her whisper a frightened squeak. "Someone's on the porch."

Sure enough, even in the eight o'clock dusk there was plenty of light to make out someone slouched against the porch rail facing the front door. A trill of fear raced across Abby's shoulders, and yet she assumed a person wanting to harm them would not be sitting in full view. Adrenaline pumped courage into her protective mama bear's veins.

"Hello? Who's there?" She took an aggressive step forward and almost lost her breath when the owner of the body unfolded and turned, a sheepish hunch to his shoulders.

"Dawson?!" Kim pushed from behind Abby and bounded toward him, stopping at the bottom porch step. "What are you doing here? Is your dad here, too?"

Abby looked behind the boy, then chastised herself for falling prey to hope of her own.

"I'm pretty sure the answer to that is no." She stroked his arm. "The real question is, does your dad know you're here?"

Dawson shook his head. His pocketed cargo shorts were wrinkled from travel as was the white, patterned, button-down shirt whose tails hung long over his hips. "He won't care." No anger couched his words. The child was serious, and Abby's heart broke for him.

"I'm sure that's not true."

"He doesn't want me there. I hate being there. Abby, please let me stay with you. You don't have to tell him where I am."

"Dawson, sweetie, you know this is the first place he'll check now. I won't lie to him."

"Then tell him I'm staying. Tell him you won't let me go." Actual tears formed in tough, young Dawson's eyes. Abby mounted the steps and pulled him into a hug.

"We'll figure it out, okay? I'm not about to promise you anything I can't deliver. And I'm furious at you for running away again. That was stupid. But I am glad you came here and didn't disappear."

She released him, and he spoke to the porch deck. "I like it here. Even when you're furious."

Taking her turn to sigh—a great, sad release of concern—Abby closed her eyes. Something deep inside warned her to hang on. Maybe for dear life.

HEADING BACK DOWN the rabbit hole to Jamawonky Ranch. This was just brilliant.

Gray pictured his reunion with Abby and swallowed against the knots twisting in his gut. He glanced at the bouquet on the seat beside him. Flowers? They were too easy and cliché. The mark of a desperate man. What he needed was a bouquet of miracles.

He pulled into Abby's driveway in a drab brown Outback—a four-wheel-drive vehicle this time, to assure he wouldn't be seeing the back of Ed or his archaic Massey Ferguson again. The warm evening air calmed him only slightly when he exited into the yard. He had no idea what he was going to say to the woman who kept winding up with his son. He'd been monumentally arrogant about Dawson, and a rock-and-roll prima donna to Abby. She'd paid him back by being nothing but kind last night on the phone, when he'd called praying Dawson had gone back to her. The lame flowers were all he had as a peace offering. Unless he counted the even lamer bar of chocolate.

Roscoe lay outside the familiar back door and thumped his tail as Gray approached. It was a completely different kind of day from the last time he'd arrived. No storm clouds, no thunder. He inhaled the fragrance of grass, dirt, sun, and fresh breeze. Why did Minnesota smell like freedom? Roscoe shifted his eyebrows and hoisted himself to his feet. The simple act of squatting to touch the golden's velvety head soothed Gray from fingertips to nervous heart.

"How is everyone, buddy?" he asked. "Are they all mad at me?" Roscoe nosed his hand, stood, and led him to the door.

ABBY HEARD THE knock at 6:33. Not that she'd been checking the clock. She'd kept herself from looking out the window, however, and now her heart raced until she felt like it might reach the door before her legs did.

Such nerves were hardly called for. She had no reason to expect anyone at her doorstep but a suave celebrity with, perhaps, a dash of annoyed father. The trouble was, the person she'd dwelled on for eight days was not the celebrity or the father. It was the soaking-wet Gray Covey tossing hay bales as if they'd been toys, and the handsome, caring Gray Covey who'd left a soft, unexpected kiss on her lips.

She reached for the knob, promising herself she would not be hurt by his mannequin smile or his smooth confidence. She'd just call his son from upstairs and let the fireworks go off.

He held flowers in his hands.

And had the farthest thing from a mannequin's smile she could imagine on his face. He looked miserable. A tremor spread outward from her stomach, found her toes, raced for her cheeks as a flush of pure attraction, and settled in her core as unexpected desire.

"Hey," he said, his voice devoid of bravado but sexy and rich.

"Hey."

"I'm with the lame gift society. Are you interested in seeing anything in our line today?"

She clapped her hand over her mouth to stifle a laugh then removed it to speak. "I don't know. There's a real trick to good lame gifts. I'm kind of picky."

"Roses, daisies, fake blue carnations, and some green stuff. Very unimaginative. Doesn't come close to apologizing for being an ass."

"I think you've failed miserably." She got a strange sense of power from watching his eyes fill with distress. "In fact, I don't think you have a very good sense at all of what makes a lame gift. That bouquet has pink roses in it."

The relief on his face was so touching it wrenched her heart. She wondered what it would be like to kiss away his discomfiture, but banished the thought.

"I guess it's remedial gift school for me."

"Why don't you come in and tell me what else you've got?"

She ushered him into the kitchen. Bird appeared and astounded Abby with a cliché cat-act, rubbing and purring against Gray's ankles. Gray bent and stroked the big cat from head to tip of tail.

"He doesn't like people," she said, bemused.

"I hate to think what that says about me." He straightened and handed her the bouquet. "I did think these were pretty unoriginal."

"There's a reason they're unoriginal. They always work." She sniffed the perfectly perfumed roses.

"I have one other attempt at lame."

"Let's see."

He reached into his pocket—not the leather jacket this time, but a brown, suede blazer that draped from his shoulders. "For the next batch of hot chocolate," he explained, and handed her a candy bar. It wasn't fancy, just a Hershey's Symphony bar, available in any grocery store in the country. Abby's mouth went slack.

"But . . ."

"I think my arteries are still running slow from the cream in that hot chocolate drink you gave me. This won't equal the expensive stuff you used, but it's my pathetic favorite. I couldn't stop wondering what it would taste like made into your magic potion. Sometime when you try it, you can think of me wearing your bathrobe."

It was the most ridiculous thing to weep over Abby could imagine, but a tear rolled down her cheek and she pinched back more with her fingers.

"Aw, Abby. I told you it was lame."

"I didn't think you'd even noticed. The chocolate I mean."

"Oh, I noticed."

She drummed up the courage to perform half her fantasy and closed the distance between them. Rising on her toes to bridge the half-foot gap in their heights, she placed a kiss on his cheek. "You lose—this isn't lame either. But I'd like to keep it anyway."

"In any other place but the land of Jumbawonka, it would be lame."

He'd butchered the farm name several times, and she had no idea why it didn't irritate the heck out of her. She was defensive about the name. "You have to stop making fun of my farm name."

"I don't think that's possible."

Above her head a floorboard creaked and Gray looked up the same time she did. Their reunion atmosphere immediately turned tense.

"Does he know I'm here?"

She nodded.

"And he didn't run?"

"He doesn't want to run. He wants you to find him and notice him."

"Damn it, Abby. I did. I . . . I enjoyed having him with me. It was really pretty great. I don't know what else to do for him."

"Does he know you think it was pretty great?"

"What's that supposed to mean?"

"Don't get irritated right off the bat. That won't help."

"Don't get . . . ?" His gaze turned incredulous. "You bet I'm irritated. I've followed him here twice now, and I don't have time for this."

"Then leave him here until you do have time." Her annoyance matched his. Couldn't he see that his son was shouting for attention?

"What gives you the right to keep telling me what to do?"

"I didn't suggest Dawson run away again, but he did. He could have gone anywhere, but he didn't. Your son came to my house, and now he officially affects me, too. *That's* what gives me the right." She shouldn't be irritated, but his stubbornness was maddening. Still, the steel in his eye sent a shaft of desire through her body, giving her the ridiculous longing to grab him and kiss his anger away rather than fight. Unnerved, she put a step between his sexy anger and her continual, annoying, lust-filled reaction to it.

"For crying out—" He cut himself off. The hardness melted from his face, leaving exhaustion in its place. "Oh, Abby, I'm sorry. I came here with gifts in hand hoping to beg for your help. You seem to be right about him. I don't know why he ran away again."

"Then you should ask him. Is that really so hard?"

"Hell yes, it's hard. I'm his father. I should know things about my son."

"Under the best of circumstances it's hard to understand teenagers." She curled her fingers around his bicep, remembering the solid bulge from their dance on the hay wagon over a week before. "Come on. I'll put these in water quick, and then I'll call Dawson. He's upstairs."

"I don't know what's going to happen." He clasped both her hands around the flowers, and a silver-flash of excitement numbed her fingers when he squeezed. "I haven't said it, and I should have. Thank you. For everything."

"You're welcome." She smiled, and gently withdrew her hands, her cheeks heating at his touch. "We'll figure this out. I promise."

The scene as the two teenagers entered the living room this time couldn't have been more different from the week before. Kim descended the stairs first with a bright smile in place. Rather than rumpled camping clothes, she'd encased her slim legs in a favorite pair of low-cut jeans with studded rhinestones and embroidered pink flowers winding up one leg. She'd topped it with a sucked-to-her-body white-and-pink knit top, its scooped neck just high enough to keep Abby from hauling her little butt right back up the stairs.

Dawson followed, shoulders tight, eyes downcast, hiding his pained combination of embarrassment and defiance.

"Hi, Gray." Kim had found her fifteen-year-old confidence. They were in for teenage-trouble with her, too, Abby had no doubt.

"Hey, Kim. It's great to see you again."

She beamed.

"Hello, Son."

Dawson's scowl deepened. "Hey."

"Nice of you to make finding your whereabouts easier this time. On the other hand, I had to put your mother off this morning when she called to talk to you. You'd be on a plane to England with armed guards if she'd learned you'd run off again."

"Why don't you just tell her and let her do it? That would make your life a lot easier."

"Not fair."

"No? You could play poker all you liked. You could do whatever Chris asked you to do and not have to worry about sending a babysitter after me. I wouldn't embarrass you in front of your girl-*fans*." He glared at Kim who rolled her eyes and sneered right back.

"I *never* looked at it that way," Gray said. "You aren't in my way. It was nice to have you with me, Dawson. I was kind of proud to show you my life."

"Oh yeah? All I ever saw you do was fire a nice guy, follow a jerky guy, suck up to gushing women, and wear shiny clothes while people screamed for you. All I did was sit around, learn a few guitar parts from your songs, and talk to Spark."

"I'm sorry my life is such a wasted disappointment to you. Maybe Heighton doesn't sound that awful anymore."

Abby's heart went out to Gray. Dawson had inappropriately hit below the belt, but somehow they had to get to the heart of the issue, or he'd just keep running away. She held her tongue with difficulty.

"It's not that," Dawson shuffled restlessly for the first time. "It's just—it's *your* life, and you don't have time for mine. You didn't even know I'd left. All I had to do was tell three people I was going to a different hotel room, and that was it. You didn't care. You promised to come, and you didn't. It's that simple."

"You're right. I messed up. Come back with me, and I'll get it right. I care that we get it right. I wouldn't be here if I didn't."

The child disappeared, and a resolute lawyer took his place. "You're here because it would look bad if you weren't. If you care so bloody much then prove it. Prove I'm more important than seven girl-fans who show up on

Chris's arm. Miss work more than a day to stick around and see what real life is like for me." His eyes glowed as if he'd just found the secret to the universe.

"Now look . . ."

"I tried it your way, Dad. I'm not going back on tour."

"Then what, exactly, is it you think you are you going to do?"

For the first time, Dawson's eyes met Abby's. Her heart sank. She'd talked a big story, but did she really want the responsibility of having the boy around when his mother and father had other plans for him?

"I'll stay here and work for Abby."

"Dawson, I . . ." she began.

"Think again." Gray interrupted her protest. "You can't impose on someone like that."

Dawson's frustration blew the calm off his reasonable persona. He glared at his father, glared at Abby, and shot unfair darts at Kim, who watched the exchange like a witness to an accident. "Then you figure it out." His voice doubled in volume. "When you three make it all happy and fine for you, tell me, and I'll get used to it. It doesn't matter what I want. It never has."

He stomped away before Abby, or anyone, could react to his petulance. She knew there were clues to his unhappiness in his tantrum, but the child was Jekyll and Hyde—hard to find fault with one minute and running away the next. Dawson was a kid who'd never learned to handle his emotions, and she had no idea how Gray was going to help him learn.

Chapter Eight

TWILIGHT STEEPED THE living room alcove in blue-gray shadows, and its one, tall window magnified a last spray of neon pink sunset. Gray parked himself on the bench in front of Abby's piano. She and Kim, who'd chattered her fill with him about her favorite songs, had gone to feed horses. God knew where Dawson was. The quiet taunted him.

He stared at the keys, so precise, so symmetric. He knew their secrets and how to unlock them as well as he knew how to put one foot in front of the other and take a step. Normally, he could stare like this and, without touching a single ivory, have a melody rush at him like wild mountain water through a gully. The deluge would flow over the rocks and boulders of rhythm and structure until, finally, lyrics—the final touch of sunlight on the water—would come. But as had been the case for six weeks, with exception of a freak stanza written in the rain, there was no rush of creativity, and he was filled with an ache rather than inspiration.

The ache grew from the idea of accepting responsibility for his son's anger. An immature desire to pound out his frustrations on the poor piano gripped him. He'd been self-righteous, certain of Dawson's joy at seeing his dad ride in to rescue him. Turned out—and how could he have missed this?—he was a sanctimonious, self-centered bastard.

The thought cut him to the quick. It wasn't true.

Was it?

Admittedly, he hadn't been around for every one of Dawson's milestones. By sheer virtue of his notoriety he couldn't be a typical T-ball dad or go on Scout camping trips. His very presence would have overshadowed anything Dawson did. But he'd seen his son's first step. He'd played catch at home. He'd taught him to play music.

To exacerbate the problem, Ariel hadn't been a T-ball, Scout-camp kind of mom either. The impact on Dawson of having two jet-setting parents had never dawned on Gray.

Prove it, Dad.

A rare memory dredged itself from the depths of Gray's past. A picture, with only the dregs of childhood bewilderment attached to it, of Roy Cooper's face floating above his bed in a night-shadowed room. "Good night, my man, you're going to grow up big and strong someday."

Gray hadn't been quite four when his biological father had come in that night. According to his mother's story,

Roy had packed up, left the next morning, and she'd never seen him again, either. Gray would never know why, since five years later, Roy Cooper had died in a hunting accident. Now, the only reason the man held any significance was because he'd given Gray life. He didn't matter, because his departure had allowed Neil Covey into his and his mother's lives.

Neil. Dad. If a model for fatherhood existed, it was the man who'd been what was called on paper a stepfather. Not only had Neil never missed a school concert or performance while Gray had been growing up, but he'd flown himself and Gray's mother up the east coast countless times to see performances all through Gray's years at Juilliard.

He placed his fingers on the piano keys, cooling his desire to pound on them, and eased into the intro riff of "Piano Man." How many countless times had his dad joked to the world it was his favorite song? The day Gray had been able to introduce Neil Covey to Billy Joel was one of his proudest.

All the things a father should teach, Neil had taught to a son without a strand of his DNA. Gray's fingers slipped from the ivories.

"Dad, don't let her take me to England! Jeez you can't get your driver's license there until you're eighteen."

Dawson still didn't have even a learner's permit.

Gray spun on the bench, pinching the bridge of his nose with his fingers. Where was Neil's influence now? He was more like the man who'd walked away from fatherhood all those years ago. The alcove had lost its sunset glow, and the darkened shadows, purple now, magnified his remorse.

"Shit." The word, spoken aloud, echoed as purple as the light. His language didn't fit in this place. But, then again, neither did he. What he was contemplating would, with his lack of parenting skills, likely turn out to be the worst thing for Dawson. He already knew it was for himself. Even so, with dread for the conversation he was about to have, he pulled his phone out of his pocket and moved slowly toward the back door. Suddenly, there wasn't enough air indoors for what he planned to do.

ABBY PLACED HER hand on Dawson's shoulder as they neared the house. She'd found him in the barn shining his favorite horse's coat to a high gloss, and now, as his steps slowed, she pushed aside the thought that Will might have looked like this and tried to tamp down her sympathy. Before she could promise him everything would work out, Gray's strident baritone carried from the other side of the yard.

"I'm not asking your opinion, the decision is made. What I need is for you to make it happen." Dawson stopped to listen, his brow puckering in confusion. "Chris. Chris! Tell them I'm dying of dysentery, or cholera. Make up whatever you need to, for God's sake." Gray's voice tightened a notch with each word, and they found him pacing around Abby's favorite maple tree, phone to his ear. He acknowledged them with a hapless shrug. "I know you think this is your worst nightmare, but I've banked a little good will over the years. You'll manage it."

The roiling in her stomach and the dryness in her throat told Abby something major had just happened, but when she tried to back away to give him privacy, Gray held up one finger and pulled the phone out from his ear, his face pained, like a kid who'd heard his father's lecture a thousand times before. Through the phone's speaker came an agitated garble.

"If you pop a blood vessel, Boyle, there's nobody around to save you." The first hint of humor laced Gray's voice. "Stop yelling. I'll call you in the morning after I talk to Spark. Yeah, yeah, I know I'm a dickhead." He listened another second and turned serious again. "I do know it's a big deal. I'm sorry. Good night. And Chris? Thanks."

With dread and awe, Abby peered at him, afraid she knew what had happened.

"What's going on?" Dawson's voice, thin as rainwater, barely made it across the distance to his father.

Gray's words, when they came, were measured and unsteady. "You were partly right, Dawson. You tried my way, so I'll try yours. I've taken that vacation you asked for. You have two and a half weeks."

Abby feared the boy might faint dead away. His face turned moon-colored, and his slender body went rigid. All that moved was his nut-sized larynx.

"Hey, where is everyone?" Kim, still in spangled jeans and tight shirt, slipped around the corner.

Abby struggled to corral her escaping sanity. Before her stood a teenage girl whose outfit had been chosen under the influence of raging hormones, and a man who'd just canceled hundreds of thousands of dollars' worth of work at the petulant request of a boy who, in turn, was about to keel over. There wasn't enough chocolate in the house to fix this group.

"What's up?" Kim asked.

"Aliens just abducted my father," Dawson replied, and headed once more for the barn.

Gray started after him, but Abby caught his arm. "No, be patient. I just got finished telling him all the reasons this couldn't happen. Let him process it."

"Aw, Abby." He took her breath away by spinning in place and wrapping his arms around her like a man sinking in quicksand. "What the hell did I just do?"

He trembled in her arms, and her pulse took off on some crazy, made-up beat. "I don't know. Maybe you just gave your son an incredible gift."

Their embrace lasted only seconds, but by then it was Abby's turn to tremble, overcome by his spice-and-musk aftershave and his hard physical touch. She hadn't had a man hold her that close in more years than she cared to remember.

"I'm sorry, Abby." Calm returned to his face, if not her heart. "I'm in way over my head here."

"Trust me, that feeling never goes away. He'll come back when he's ready. You can spend another night here while you figure out what to do, and I'll go make us all some cocoa."

"Is that the cure-all for everything?" He searched the yard with distracted eyes.

She linked elbows with him on one side and her shell-shocked daughter on the other. "The recipe was my grandmother's. Heat of July or dead of winter, it was her drug of choice. Now it's mine."

She dug out her ingredients after that, had Kim help melt Gray's Symphony bar, butter, and vanilla in a pan, then topped it off with rich, decadent cream. When the mixture was hot and thick, she handed a mug to her daughter, added a liberal splash of schnapps to Gray's, then set the pair on the couch and admonished both to drink, like a parent dosing sick children.

With a brave grin, Gray lifted his mug toward Kim and shook his head. "Guess it's you and me, darlin', until my child gets over his mad. Cheers?"

"Cheers!" She clunked mugs with him, an adoring shine in her eyes.

"I don't have many true fans your age," he told her. "How'd I get lucky with you?"

The unintentional double entendre wasn't missed, and Abby chewed her lip to keep from smiling. "We have a lot in common." Kim's voice took on an affected note of maturity.

"Oh?"

"I have the same birthday you do."

"July eighth? We're birthday twins?"

Kim sparkled and beamed like a little bejeweled star. She was too cute for words—despite sitting on the cusp of being too big for her embroidered britches. "And, I play clarinet."

"You do?" His smile broke into genuine interest. "I

started on the clarinet, and the piano." Kim nodded that she knew. "I detested it at first because I was the only boy in the clarinet section, but my mother made me stick it out, and when my dad found music by all kinds of guys who played clarinet I fell in love. How 'bout you."

"I like it. I'm not good like you, but I love classical music. I think it's cool you went to Juilliard."

"Juilliard was . . . great. Hard. Taught me I didn't want to be a concert pianist. I broke my mother's heart when I let Spark turn me to the dark side."

"Did he go to Juilliard, too?"

Gray laughed out loud. "Not in a million years. He's a self-taught musician all the way. His brother was my roommate, though, and when he introduced me to Spark, we were immediate friends. I'm very picky about my music, and he's a free spirit. We're perfect for each other."

Abby had an impossible time seeing Gray as a famous person sitting in her living room. Instead, his patient indulgence with her daughter, and his unexpected self-sacrifice for his son, were wearing away at the first impressions she'd had of his high-handed celebrity.

"What's your favorite song?" Gray stood and motioned for Kim to follow him. "C'mon, sit at the piano with me."

Panic and excitement vied for top emotion in her daughter's eyes, and she bounced to the bench where she sat hip-to-hip with him. "Umm. I think 'Forever,'" she told him.

If Abby hadn't been staring at him, she wouldn't have seen the second's worth of pain that blitzed through his eyes. He covered it instantaneously with a smile. "I don't get that one very often."

"I like how it's about so many levels of love."

He leaned back and stared. "That's very astute. Okay then, do you know the words?"

Abby could almost feel Kimmy's stomach somersaulting in excitement as Gray started the slow, melodic song. To her shock, Abby found her heart flipping right along. Unadorned and unamplified, Gray had one of the smoothest baritones she'd ever heard. Like an old-fashioned crooner.

"That was beautiful," Kim said when they'd finished, her voice tremulous after finding courage enough to sing with him. "You should do it simple like that sometime."

"I haven't sung that song in concert." His voice was thoughtful. "Only the biggest fans know it." He winked, which set Kim to blushing. "It's a little personal for huge crowds anyway."

"Personal?"

"I wrote it for a special girl." His voice trailed off as if he seemed to think better of what he'd revealed.

"Ariel?"

"My mother."

Abby had no time to dwell on his quiet sadness. The back door hinges protested, and a moment later Dawson stood in the living room doorway. He eyed his father, then Kim, and stuck his hands in his pockets.

"Were you serious? You actually told Chris to cancel six shows?"

"Yes."

"What's the catch?"

Gray stood and patted Kim's shoulder before moving toward Dawson. "The catch is, if it gets out that you had anything to do with this, all the hate mail will come to you."

Once again, Abby saw the faint tic of a smile at the corner of Dawson's lip, but he masked it perfectly. "What are you going to tell Mom?"

"That you're safe, and you're with me."

"She'll want me to go back."

"Maybe."

"What will you do if she says I can't stay?"

"Dawson." Gray grasped his son's shoulder, his fingers squeezing just a little too quickly, and vertical creases weaving his brows into a single, frustrated line. "I don't know what's going to happen five minutes from now. Can't we take it one step at a time?"

That stopped Dawson's flow of questions. He turned to Abby, a flicker of hope in his eyes. She wondered how she'd ever thought him eighteen. He looked young and vulnerable.

"We'll stay here then?"

"For tonight. Abby's very kindly invited us. Then I thought we could go to the penthouse in L.A. Hang out in the city."

"No way." He renewed his adamant tone. "Half the band hangs out there, too. Plus, I have work to finish for Abby."

Panic flushed her face and sent blood buzzing into her ears, so she scarcely heard Kim's whoop of agreement. It was one thing to have a teenage boy here, and it was easy enough to entertain his father for an extra day or two. But longer than that?

What about her crazy job schedule? Her minimal budget for anything extra? The financial negotiations she was facing this week with one neighbor for hay and Dewey Mitchell for stall shavings? She could hide all that from Dawson. But no way could she fake the realities of her life for someone like Gray.

Not to mention that his lifestyle scared her to death. She and Kim lived quietly in a quiet place. What if someone found out he was here? She glanced at the three faces, and Gray's features softened in understanding.

"No," he said to Dawson. "That's too much of a burden on Abby. It's not fair to subject her and Kim to my life. You know what can happen."

Stubborn-Dawson surfaced again with all his devil horns and pride. "Yeah, I do know. Better than most. But, it's really safer here than in L.A., unless Chris tells where you are."

"He'd better damn well not. Sorry." Gray glanced at Abby, then at Kim. "People will ferret us out all on their own."

It had always seemed glamorous to be famous. Now that the reality of it was in her face, Abby saw how wrong the notion was. Dawson's words struck a chord of sympathy. "So, if you and Dawson hid here, just for a little while, until you've had some time together, *would* you be safer?" The question was reluctant down to her core, and she forced her smile.

"I won't ask you to do that, Abby. It's too much."

"Abby, you advertised for barn help. Let Dad be your handy man."

The idea of hiring help had been a pipe dream from months ago—one not based in reality to begin with. The idea had died for good when the cost of hay had started rising over the winter. She'd kept up the sham of looking for help in order to hide the full extent of her financial woes from Ed and Sylvia. They tried to help her too much as it was.

"He doesn't have to be my barn help, Dawson. You're both welcome to stay. There's still an empty guest room upstairs, although it's no penthouse."

"Oh, good grief." Gray scowled at her. "Are you sure?"

No. "Of course." Abby fixed Dawson with a stern look when he all but preened. "Don't get cocky, mister. You said you had work to do? You're right. That's part of this deal."

"Yes ma'am."

An uneasy silence enveloped them. Abby checked her watch, which read nine thirty. Her brain raced through a litany of the things, in addition to negotiating for hay and shavings, she had on her list for the week. Go to work, teach a half-dozen riding lessons, manufacture meals for four out of thin air . . .

"Hey?" A gentle voice startled her from behind, and Gray's hands lit on her shoulders. "Are you okay? You really don't have to do this."

She blinked, as if she'd just awoken. Kim and Dawson had moved to the corner and chatted a mile a minute, heads together, friends again. Abby's smile came slowly, like it had to surface through thirty feet of water. "I'm fine, and I'm very sincere about the invitation. Of course the idea of a fan invasion scares me a little, I can't lie, but I think Dawson is right, this could be quieter and safer for a while. But how about you? You did, well, a pretty rash thing."

"I guess." His shoulders drooped almost imperceptibly.

"Is it going to be all right?"

For a moment his bottom lip caught in his teeth. "It'll have to be," he said finally. "Here's the hell of it. I've just put about two hundred people on forced vacation. So what if they get paid? We don't ever miss concerts and this'll make six. But I don't feel guilty. What's wrong with me?"

His eyes didn't quite match the words. There was guilt deep behind the smiling blue, but his rich-timbre voice was sincere. His fingers trailed from her shoulders, leaving her tingling.

"You gave your son a lot of power tonight."

"Yes. I'm afraid of that. I could have dragged him with me again, and he'd have run again. I could have left him here and proved he's right—my career comes first. Or, I could try," he spread his hands helplessly, "this. Maybe Chris is right. I'll win Dawson and lose the fans."

"Or maybe you're just doing something you're supposed to do." Her fingers itched to stroke his arm, soothe him. "Sorry, that was dumb. You really are so famous that it matters."

A self-deprecating snort passed for a laugh. "Abby,

Abby. How'd your daughter get to be such a fan, and you didn't?"

He touched her nose with his finger. Her heart stumbled as her gaze caught on the shallow dimples that dotted each corner of his mouth when he smiled. She stared at his prominent cheekbones and triangular nose. Got lost in eyes as pale blue as a clearing sky.

"Because you're only my third-favorite singer?" She tore her gaze away and studied her fingernails.

"Third?"

"Paul McCartney. Raised on him by an aunt. Old but still handsome. Great music."

"Super guy. But, yeah, old. Old enough to be your grandfather."

"Billy Joel."

Surprise flashed like heat lightning in his eyes. "What is it with him? You and my dad. So, fine, another great guy—still, way too old."

"That leaves you, Number Three. I bet you don't think you're too old."

"Well, three's always been my lucky number, but you're wrong. The past few weeks I've felt ancient."

"You aren't! Forty-five on July eighth. I know because, well, you said it, Kim's a fan."

"Whatever. I'm pretty sure I'm terrified about what I did tonight, but all I feel is rebellious excitement. I'd call that a middle-age crisis."

"It will all work out as it should. God has His ways of taking care of things."

"I doubt He's much interested in giving me any free rides."

Such an insane indictment of himself nearly took away her speech.

"I don't know why you said that, Mr. Number Three. But I don't believe it for a second."

"Sweet Abby, you aren't a fan are you? After the life I've led, I can't tell you how lucky I am to get a clean slate with you."

"I don't want to be a fan." She gave in and touched him, skimming the soft black hair on his sculpted forearm. "I could try to be a friend."

"What did I say?" His smile didn't quite make it to his tired eyes. "Three is my lucky number."

Chapter Nine

THE SCENE IN Abby's warm, eclectic kitchen the next morning was a mini-carnival of milling animals, pot clattering, the smell of bacon, and the bickering of teenagers—unbelievably different from Gray's usual noon-delivered, room-service breakfasts. The closest he ever came to such cozy domesticity was when he had a rare morning to himself with his own box of Lucky Charms.

"About time you got out of bed," Dawson called. "We've been up over an hour."

"It's eight-flipping-o'clock." Gray's lips twitched into a grimace. "What's the matter with you people?"

"Horses to feed, stalls to clean." Abby turned from the stove and grinned.

"Is it a requirement here to be cheerful in the morning?"

"Yup." She handed him a steaming mug. "Maybe this'll help. Do you drink it?"

"Coffee?" Gray took a stimulating sniff. "Where's the needle?"

"How many eggs?"

The question threw him. He never had to think about something as mundane as egg math. "Uh, two?"

She laughed. "Uh, two it is. Go, sit. Toast?"

"Sure. I didn't mean for you to have to wait on us, Abby." He sat and sent a tentative smile to Kim. She and Dawson scribbled on a piece of paper covered with a penciled-in grid.

"Once I tell you my schedule for the day, you might not feel so apologetic. Lunch is on your watch, since I'll be at work. I come home, teach two riding lessons, and dinner will be late."

"As the resident interloper, I wouldn't think to complain." He squinted at the two kids. "Some sort of weird breakfast game?"

"Trading chores," Dawson replied. "Kim likes cleaning the stalls. I hate it, but we both hate cleaning the bathrooms, so we're splitting it up."

"We do this Monday mornings now, or I have to listen to them harp on each other all week."

"I don't like cleaning bathrooms either."

"Good." Kim beamed at him. "Since you're the new guy, you get the creepiest tasks."

The fact that she'd escaped her fan nerves pleased him. But the strange, familial atmosphere was unnerving.

"No chores for Gray." Abby shook her head firmly. "He gets a tour and the low-down on the schedule around here. That'll be enough for the first day."

"No fair. You made me cut the grass my first day." Dawson curled his lip.

"You are a child." Abby set a platter of eggs and bacon and a small plate piled with toast on the table. Gray's mouth watered. "Children were put on this earth to torture."

"No lie." Dawson scoffed.

Once Abby joined them at the table, Gray reached for the salt shaker, but Dawson caught him with a covert glance and gave a microscopic shake of his head before bowing it. Kim followed, then Abby. Gray blinked, lost for a moment, then forced his eyes closed.

"Lord," she began, "thank You for this food. Thank You, too, that You've brought Dawson and his father together. Please watch over Gray and all the people in his business while he can't be with them. Keep us in your care today. Amen."

Kim and Dawson echoed her, and Gray mumbled "Amen," waiting for the fidgety, embarrassed feeling he'd gotten as a boy when his grandmother had prayed for him like a fervent evangelist. But no fidgets came.

"Dig in." Pleasant chatter picked up where it had left off, as if they'd merely stopped to say hello to a neighbor. Abby smiled at him as she handed over a plate of toast.

Breakfast tasted as if it had been prepared in a five-star kitchen, but he ate in half a fog, feeling like a sightseer on another planet trying to relax and pretend he understood the horse and farm jargon. Before he knew it, Kim and Dawson were finished, had bussed their dishes to the sink, and were out the door. Dazed, he looked helplessly at Abby.

"I don't fit in here even a little. I just had breakfast on Jupiter's red spot."

"Welcome to life with teenagers. It's a gas, what can I say?"

"It's foreign."

Abby leaned back and traced the inside of her coffee mug handle with a forefinger. "How often do you see Dawson?"

"A few times a year. He makes one trip here for two weeks, usually when I'm not on tour. I go to England once or twice for a couple weeks. We e-mail." He sighed. "I was blind enough to think that was working. He always seemed willing to talk. I heard a lot about how frustrated he was being in England and how much he dislikes his stepfather."

"And there's a baby, did I hear?"

"Danielle. She's two. He's mostly neutral about her."

"And he doesn't get along with his mother?"

"I wouldn't say that. He's as angry with her as he is me right now. Ariel can be overbearing, and lately she seems to have no moral authority with him. But she loves her son and spoils him—as long as he stays where she puts him and doesn't cramp her style."

"Doesn't that bother you?"

"Of course it does." He shoved a hand through his hair and straightened in his chair. Defensiveness rose in his chest at her questioning, and their easy rapport turned brittle. "Legal custody is hers until he's eighteen. I have unrestricted visitation, and although I can't take him away from her, I think I can talk her into letting him stay with me through the summer. I'm betting on her appreciating more time with Danielle. And the model."

"Is he really?"

"They're a hot couple." He steeled for more interrogation.

"We all parent how we parent." She spun her mug like a top, looking into it as if it helped her concentrate. "And I can tell you, whatever you do, you'll find a way to feel guilty about it. Trust me, I'm all over that emotion."

His defensiveness dissipated. "You? Feel guilty? You're a natural."

"I am definitely not a natural. I need to try and keep order or I lose control."

He could see the hyper-organizer in her. His mother had possessed the same quality, and sometimes he missed it in his frenetic life. He let go of his annoyance fully, wishing they could get through an entire conversation without ticking each other off.

"You look like a natural to me, Abby Stadtler. C'mon. Let me help you with these dishes, and when they're orderly you can show me the ranch."

By ten Gray was mentally exhausted. Walking Abby's forty-acre place with its horses, chickens, dog, and hand-erected fences was exhilarating, but thinking about how she'd carved out her independence made touring with a rock band seem like eating cake every day.

"Sounds like you can wield a chainsaw as easily as you crack a velvet whip." He enjoyed causing the flush that radiated from her skin.

They stood beside the farthest paddock, and he admired the sturdily patched top rail. She built fences, rode horses, taught a few riding lessons each week. The juxtaposition of an elegant horsewoman carving up wood with a chainsaw and whacking fence posts with hammers . . . He leaned his chin on his fists and stared into a paddock filled with three of her eight horses, hiding a grin.

"Working outdoors makes up for the twenty hours a week I'm stuck in the office." She thumped like Tarzan on her chest. "Loud, scary chainsaw make girl feel like tomboy."

She needed to stop putting sexy-tomboy-with-ripped-jeans images in his head. "So." He swallowed, straightening. "You teach, you work at an architect's office, you help out at the grocery store in town every other weekend. Busy lady."

"I have an accounting degree, but I've always wanted to be around when Kim came home from school, so I never took a career. My mother-in-law has never thought I make enough to care for Kim the way I should." Her face twisted in some private memory he couldn't read. Then she brightened. "Ed and Sylvia have been godsends, always willing to keep an eye on Kim. I don't need to worry about her any more, but letting her become independent is a slow process."

"It seems to be working."

"That's a nice compliment for a mother. Thank you." Her pleasure warmed him through to the core. Maybe they *could* get through a conversation.

The place wasn't perfect. A hodgepodge of solid structures and faltering outbuildings dotted the acreage. But even the old pieces were tidy. Fascinated, Gray hoarded information about her like a magpie collecting shiny things. Back at the house he took in the whole picture.

"It's beautiful here."

The deep-seated truth in his statement worried him. Standing in the warm summer breeze with the smell of green earth and horses around him, he was gripped, again, by a desperate longing to forget that his band and his fans existed.

"I'm lucky. I thank God every day for this place. And there's always something new."

"My son sure seems to think so. Fun times at Jumbawumba." He wiggled his brows to show he was teasing.

"I warned you not to make fun of my name." She laughed. He couldn't tell if it was faked or forced.

"Tell me why you picked it. *Maybe* I'll stop."

"A combo of our names." She didn't hesitate, and he almost missed the skin tensing around her eyes. "Jack, Abby, Will and Kim. Jabberwicki. We dreamed of a small, working, Midwestern ranch with about ten horses, some dairy goats, and our own hay crop. I'd teach riding lessons. Jack would sell boutique milk and cheese. The kids would grow up away from big-city problems. Obviously, some of that never came to pass."

Gray's heart dropped, as if it had been tossed across all forty of Jabberwicki's acres. He'd probably just set a record for the amount of time a man could exist with his foot in his mouth. "I'm sorry, Abby. I've been rude."

"No. It was always a silly name. I used to be a silly person."

"You don't think you are anymore?"

"I have fun. I'm not silly."

"Maybe I should take you to hang out with a rock band." He bared his teeth in a teasing grin, and elicited a Kim-like giggle. "I am very sorry about what I've said about the name. Really. No more making fun."

For long minutes they stared at each other—the first time he'd really assessed her since the day on the hay wagon. The longer he stood, the heavier his body grew until a dull, pleasant throbbing started low in a place he definitely didn't want her to notice. They hadn't annoyed each other in an hour, but her sunny fragrance and her aquamarine eyes were bothering the hell out him right now.

"It's all right." Her voice held the perfect amount of breathlessness to bother him even further. "I thought you were kind of cute." She colored.

The urge to repeat his one, unprotested kiss from a week ago hit so strongly he nearly obeyed it, but he'd already created enough complications where she was concerned.

"I know you need to get to work." He cleared his throat and stepped back. "Thanks for the tour. I, ah, should call Spark. My band . . . guitarist." He stammered like an idiot.

"I know who Spark is." Her smile was indulgent, the kind you'd give a peculiar relative. "Go. Call. I'll see you later."

She turned to enter the house, and Gray rolled his

eyes to the sky-blue heavens. This was an alien world all right. That, or he really was an idiot.

ABBY AND KIM finally left the barn at seven thirty that night. Despite feeling guilty that Gray's first dinner would be so late, Abby's mood flirted with contentment. Her riding students were gone, and the horses were fed. The strength and purpose she got from her animals filled her with satisfaction. This was the part of her cobbled-together days she liked best.

The aroma of food confused her as they entered the kitchen. All day she'd tried to figure out what she had in the freezer that would make a quick, acceptable dinner for four, but the smell of roasting meat, and the grins from Gray and Dawson, rendered plans for her favorite hot dish moot.

"Yum," said Kim. "Who's cooking?"

"Men cook." Gray thumped his chest like a caveman bragging about his mammoth kill.

Abby couldn't believe it. Even in Jack's day those words had never rung from her kitchen. "This is a surprise."

"Consider it a thank-you for putting up with us." Gray's dark stubble and pale blue eyes were beautiful but incongruous in her familiar space.

Whatever was cooking, it hadn't come from her larder. Her freezer contained two pounds of hamburger and three frozen TV dinners. She'd been staving off shopping day.

"Where'd you get food?" She made herself sound pleasant. "I haven't had time to go shopping for a while—we were pretty depleted."

"I had a couple of ideas, so I enlisted Ed and Dawson to go to the store."

Abby hovered between gratitude and beyond-words humiliation. She edged to the stove and looked into a pot of boiling potatoes.

"You know how to cook?"

"Who'd guess, right?" Gray laughed and pushed Roscoe away from the range with a pat. "My mama taught me a few things, and an aborted scouting career taught me a couple more. My repertoire makes me an impressive date for a five-day week, and then I get boring super fast."

"My, this is awfully nice." Her voice emerged a little cooler than she intended. "It wasn't necessary."

"I know." He shocked her by placing his hands on her shoulders. "I wanted to do something to help, and stuffed pork chops are part of my repertoire. Sylvia sent Ed down to double check I hadn't axed you overnight, and we got to talking. It's that simple."

His explanation at least proved he knew she was uncomfortable.

"Pork chops?" She softened her voice and received a broad smile. Lord, he had fantastic teeth.

Okay, admiring his teeth was going too far.

"Big ol' thick ones. With Granny Covey's famous jerk sauce and corn stuffing."

"I think I'm in love with Granny Covey."

"As well you should be. Go wash up, you two. This'll be ready in ten."

SCRUMPTIOUS. ABBY COULDN'T think of a more appropriate word, nor could she have ordered better food in a gourmet establishment. The pork melted in her mouth, and the heat of peppers and allspice dazzled her tongue. She had no idea how to thank either Dawson or Gray when she stood from the table once the meal had been demolished.

"It's been a long time since someone took care of us girls without asking."

"Remember that, Son." Gray winked at the boy. "Make 'em believe you've never heard the word chauvinist."

"I'll remember."

"You guys go ahead," Abby said. "Kim and I can clean up."

"Naw, let the kids go. I'll finish what I started."

Once they were alone, unexpected nerves assailed Abby full force. She was used to being in control, and lately, even before Gray's appearance in her life, control had been slipping from her grasp. This perfect man was not helping. Today he shared far too many traits with a fantasy Prince Charming she'd created long ago. She couldn't afford fantasies, much less a living, breathing reality.

"If you're trying to impress me, it's working," she admitted.

"Good."

"I hope you don't feel like you have to keep trying so hard."

"What makes you think this was hard?"

"I just mean you and Dawson are welcome here, Gray. I don't need you to pay your way." She swallowed against the specter of reality, but letting him be anything more than a guest was unthinkable.

He cocked his head and studied her. "I don't feel obligated. I want to help."

"I appreciate it. But I . . ." She got no more of her protest out.

"Mom! Gray! Come see this!"

At the urgency in Kim's voice, Abby and Gray exchanged quizzical looks and trotted for the living room. Kim perched on the edge of a couch cushion, her eyes glued to the full-screen visage of a popular TV entertainment-show host. Dawson sat in the neighboring armchair, his face a shuttered window.

"Officials at the Scottrade Center in St. Louis say their information was not detailed," said the host into a microphone. "Gray Covey's manager, Christopher Boyle, called the cancellations necessary because of a serious family emergency and promised the concerts would be rescheduled. No word as to when. Meanwhile, sources hint two more concerts scheduled for Phoenix and two after that for Kansas City have also been cancelled, but that is still unofficial."

As he continued, a disturbing picture filled the screen. Abby peered hard to see if she really was seeing what she thought she was: Gray, arching out of a chair, wearing a smile of surprise, his hands splayed on the back of a woman's head buried in his lap. She turned to the living, breathing Gray beside her.

"It isn't what it looks like." His voice, dull and rough, sounded defeated.

"There is speculation that Covey, who has dealt with drug-related issues in the past," the reporter continued, "is once again facing substance abuse issues due to a difficult road trip. Pictures such as this now-viral shot of the singer ostensibly caught in a compromising position with the fiancée of legendary producer Ron Revers have been appearing in tabloids. Covey's manager insists the picture is a fake designed to embarrass the singer. Other sources say the photo was taken at a party earlier this month.

"Fiancée?" Abby raised her brows.

"Fiancée?" Gray asked at the same moment. "I never . . ."

The picture disappeared, replaced by side-by-side portraits of two beautiful women, both blond and fashionista slender. "Amanda Rogers, the ex-Victoria's Secret model who's been seen with Gray most recently, had no information about the sudden cancellations or Covey's mental or physical state. His ex-wife, Ariel Wyatt, who lives in England with the couple's teenage son, could not be reached for comment.

"What the f—?" Gray choked off his vulgar expletive, his color deepening.

"Christopher Boyle refused to disclose Covey's whereabouts, asking that the public respect his privacy at this time. We'll keep you up-to-date right here."

"Great, just unbelievable." Gray pressed his palms into his eye sockets. "I said Chris could tell them what he wanted, but this? They harassed your mom?" He blinked at Dawson.

Stunned, Abby glanced around the room. Shiny-eyed Kim was the only one who seemed unruffled. Dawson looked as if he'd been kicked in the stomach. For a moment, she couldn't get the dreadful picture out of her mind. What kind of man was he? Juxtaposed with the red flags and alarms going off in her mind was the humiliating fact that the mention of a Victoria's Secret model had shot her last shred of self-confidence. "Is that . . . that picture really a fake?"

"She tripped." His voice held such heaviness. Even so, his stooped shoulders warred with an angry fire in his eyes. Was this how he lived? In a nightmare, having his life invaded without being able to defend himself? "We all laughed ourselves silly over the stupid, accidental picture. Now it's proof that I'm drugged out? And she's no fiancée of Ron Revers. She works for him."

"They'll all be embarrassed when they find out the truth," Kim said firmly.

"Those few who want to believe the truth. As far as half the population is concerned, I'm a cheating SOB back in rehab. For them, any story that comes out now is just a cover-up."

"But that's stupid." Kim set her jaw. "So you did rehab twenty years ago. All your fans know you're, like, totally anti-drug now."

A spot of color returned to Gray's face. He purposefully walked to Kim and planted a kiss on the top of her head. "Thank you, sweetheart. For the kindest thing you could have said."

Kim grinned, but Dawson still hadn't said a word.

"Abby." Gray turned his eyes to hers. "You asked if the picture was faked. No. It wasn't even planned. I can't make you believe me, but—"

"I hardly know you," she sighed. "But, of course I believe you."

Did she?

"Thank you. I don't know what else to say." He took a resigned breath. "I need to make some phone calls. I'm sure Chris is being molested. I'll have to give some sort of response."

"Why?" Dawson finally looked up, his face as defiant as his father's was tired. "This is what they do to you. They run your life and backstab people like you and Elliott. They tell you how to feel and what to think and say."

"That's enough!"

Abby started at the thunder in Gray's voice. He turned on his son and pointed. "I'm not upset about what I decided to do for you, but don't you for one minute take it for granted, my boy. You think there are people running my life? You bet there are. There are such things as commitments in this world, not to mention contracts. I broke several of both yesterday and barely blinked an eye, so, whether you approve or not, I have to pay for what I did."

"What about your commitment to me?" Dawson shot to his feet.

"That's a card you can play one too many times. Watch it."

For several seconds Dawson stared his father down. When Gray refused to soften his stony anger, Dawson turned and left the room.

"He does that a lot, doesn't he? Run away." Vestiges of anger lingered in Gray's voice. He looked at Abby, then at Kim. For the first time since she'd met him, he'd lost the easy-going smile that always surfaced no matter what. "I think I'll go and make those phone calls."

"Gray?" Abby's chest hurt with confusion. "It's all going to be okay."

"Things usually work out," he agreed. He passed her and stopped once more in front of Kim. Her eyes were now shell-shock bright, and Abby felt sorry for her, too. A little shine had certainly been scuffed from her hero's armor. But Gray offered her an apologetic smile that she returned without hesitation. "You were the bright penny in the room tonight, Miss Kim. Thanks for sticking up for me."

Her eyes cleared in an instant. "Anytime!"

Holy cow, Abby thought. If she hadn't just seen him rescue his reputation in ten seconds, she'd never have believed it.

She left him alone for an hour, even though she knew Gray was the kind of man she should leave alone for good. His was a life she couldn't come close to understanding. One she had no desire to understand. After seeing the TV report, she feared the chaos and the people surrounding him more than ever.

To top it off, she'd let herself overlook his past. Drugs? Rehab? Victoria's Secret models? Potential sex scandals? What had she expected? He was a rock star, made from the same cloth as every burnt-out, groupie-loving, famous rocker since Elvis. She'd given him her vote of confidence, but she honestly didn't know what to believe. Her worst nightmare was really that the truth lay somewhere between the sensational report and Gray's earnest protestations that he was innocent. Wasn't there a kernel of truth at the heart of every rumor?

Stay out of his life, Abigail. Put the pretty man down and walk away.

It was the very best of advice from her wise and trusted inner self, and yet she still headed out the door to find him.

Chapter Ten

GRAY OPENED HIS eyes in the cozy yellow-and-brown guest room that had become familiar over three days. He closed them quickly against the pain of morning and tried to recapture the simple dream he'd been enjoying far too well. Sleep had come more easily the past two nights even though his system was still off, cycling on a concert tour time zone. Except for the daily doses of haranguing from Chris, life had settled into a quiet pattern of marking time.

Dawson's attitude had stayed civil, if awkward. Adorable Kim flirted her fifteen-wishing-she-were-twenty-five heart out. And Abby . . .

Thinking of her finally brought back the dream—Abby, in a clinging blue dress designed by his imagination, stroking his cheek, over and over. The vision held nothing erotic, nothing that should have affected him, yet his body grew heavier—and harder in the most male of ways.

He groaned, hung over with frat-boy desire, embarrassed, albeit pleasurably, by his body's reaction to the remnants of his fantasy. Not that he didn't cling to it selfishly, ready to stay wrapped in the soft homemade quilt and crisp sheets and fight his hard-on all day. But his window stood open, letting in a cool breeze scented like the mornings of his childhood, calming his body in spite of his wishes, bringing him to his senses. He glanced at the clock radio on the small stand beside him and groaned for a different reason. Ten o'clock? Dang, he was late. The days around here started right after midnight.

He threw on a pair of jeans and padded down the hall, but his son's room was empty. As was Kim's. As was Abby's. It didn't surprise him, then, that the kitchen was also devoid of activity. He followed his nose to the coffeemaker, and only after his first slug did he realize that, although the room was empty, something wasn't right. Breakfast dishes sat in an untidy stack on the counter, two crumpled napkins swam in a puddle of coffee in the sink, a small carton of half-and-half sat open on the table. Most curious of all, Abby's mug sat beside the cream still three-quarters full.

Gray had lived in Abby's house only four days, but a few things were already ingrained as The Standard. Abby was meticulous and organized—her kitchen most of all. The kids made their own chore charts for crying out loud, and she cleaned the kitchen thoroughly and without fuss after every meal, despite the fact that the dishwasher was broken and she hadn't gotten around to fixing it yet. The disarray this morning was almost shockingly out of character.

He'd have talked himself into believing it was a simple anomaly, but then he found the note. "Kim, Dawson, Gray. All I care about today is the horses. Feed them, let them out. Take the day off. Don't know for sure when I'll be home—dinner when I get there."

Day off? Don't know when I'll be home? Concern lapped at Gray's mind, even though he didn't honestly know Abby well enough to worry.

But what he did know was that he found her more beautiful and sexier by the day in a no-nonsense way. She was so different from women in his real life that his fantasies were starting to overshadow appropriate thoughts. Case in point, his state upon waking this morning. Whether she had on shorts, a suit for work, or riding breeches and a dirt smudge on her cheek, she was, in a simple, unavoidable word, hot.

The flap of a breeze-blown curtain was the only sound as he sat with his coffee and his thoughts. The kids normally had specific tasks every morning, leaving them little time to goof off until after lunch. The tight ship kept her from worrying and asking too many "what have you been doing" questions when she got home. He supposed her over-concern was understandable considering what she'd lost in her life.

His heart still stuttered over the idea of losing a spouse and a child in one violent instant. Abby acted matter-of-fact about the past, but that only made reading her true emotions a fascinating challenge, and made the departure from her careful control this morning all the more worrisome. The strains of Rachmaninoff from his iPhone made him cringe, knowing it had to be Chris with another dose of guilt.

Only, it wasn't. Gray stared at the caller ID until the phone nearly stopped ringing before he slid the phone's "on" bar. "Why, Ariel," he said, adopting a pleasant tone. "What a shock."

"My, such a warm greeting. I don't know why it's a shock given the circumstances."

"How are you?"

"Let's say I sound calmer than I feel." Her tight Sussex accent never failed to make him squirm, as if she planned every syllable to force a reaction. To think he'd once found that British purr sexy as hell.

"Why, what's happening?"

"For one thing, there are photographers hounding my every step. I'm calling to ask where the devil you really are."

"Photographers?" Gray's underlying annoyance gave way to a fresh wave of guilt. "The press found you? I'm sorry, Ariel, I am."

"It isn't completely them, darling, although they are exasperating. But they seem convinced you're in some sort of rehabilitation center. You didn't lie about being with Dawson?"

"For crying out loud, why would I do that?" He stood to pace the kitchen floor, combing his hair with frustrated fingers. "You've talked to Dawson. I trusted you with where we are."

There was such a long silence Gray thought he'd either lost her or she'd hung up. "Yes, Gray, you did." Her voice finally came out subdued. "I couldn't resist baiting you. I'm sorry."

What the hell? Ariel pulling a punch? "Thanks."

"You really did cancel six shows to stay at some widow woman's farm?" She said *widow woman* as if she imagined the witch from *Hansel and Gretel*. Gray didn't bother correcting whatever it was his ex-wife was picturing.

"I really did. Where are you?"

"Still Switzerland. I called to make sure Dawson was all right. I don't know where these vultures get their stories."

"Out of their ass—" He cut off the vulgarity that didn't belong in Abby's sunny kitchen.

Then, as if in response to a silent cue, the back door opened, admitting a shuffling Dawson. When he realized he wasn't alone, his eyebrows puckered, and Gray mouthed the word Mom.

"Look," he said into the phone. "You *know* where reporters get their lies."

Her purr turned into an appreciative, kitten-like snort. "All right, darling. So, when do you think you'll need to send Dawson back?" She sounded as if she cared about the answer, but whether she wanted him back, or was calculating how long she had left to play, he wasn't sure.

"He can stay as long as he likes as far as I'm concerned."

Dawson's eyes lit with delight.

"Now that's bloody brilliant, Gray, so like you. Just *where* would he stay, may I ask?"

"With me."

She laughed with no hesitation. "That's ridiculous. School starts in August, and he should be back early enough to settle in."

Gray's stomach recoiled. August was only six weeks away, and the thought of sending Dawson to England suddenly made him desperately sad. "Hold on. You have to know he hates that school. Why do you think he ran off?"

"Dawson is a child, Gray." Her tone would have sounded imperious if hadn't been typical. "We don't expect him to know what's best for himself. Heighton Academy is a fantastic school, and he can live with Mother if he really dislikes the dormitories."

"What? Dad, what's she saying?" Dawson pushed closer, his features twisted in anticipation. Gray held up a finger.

"C'mon, Ariel, that makes *me* want to run screaming."

"Very funny," she replied. "Dawson needs to come back soon. We'll sort it here."

"We are not deciding this now," Gray said, the slightest touch of newfound conviction in his voice. "I'll talk to him about it. I want you to plan on him staying here through July—"

"July?!" Dawson shook his head vehemently. This time, Gray raised a forefinger to his lips.

"You and Klaus will get more time alone with Danielle. I'll get my turn for . . ." he said, glancing at Dawson, ". . . a little time with our son."

"Let me talk to her." Dawson reached for the phone.

"Wait," he whispered.

"You've lost him once already. Why should I trust he'll stay with you?"

"I think we're pretty even on that score." He tamped the hackles on the back of his neck down, wishing he dared say more, but Dawson stood with his hand still out for the phone.

Silence came across the line once more. Finally Ariel sighed. "Fine. He's yours through July. Will that make you happy?"

"Yes. Yes, for now, but . . ."

"There's always a *but* isn't there?"

"I was simply going to ask you if you'd consider keeping our whereabouts a secret."

"Oh. Well. For goodness' sake, I'm not an idiot."

"It's not for me. This is a nice family he's with. I'd hate to see her—their—privacy invaded before we can leave."

"Well, if that doesn't sound perfectly intriguing, my darling!" Her laugh, amused and knowing, broke the tension. "Okay, must run. Kiss my baby for me. I'll talk to him and see him in August."

He opened his mouth and closed it again. There was no point in arguing. She'd made a huge concession—it was all he'd get in one shot.

"We'll discuss it. Ariel? Thanks . . . for the discretion."

"He's my son, too. Good-bye, darling. Oh, and do see if you can manage to get rid of the lions at the door won't you?"

The line went dead. Gray pushed the off button and stared at the pile of breakfast dishes in the sink.

"Why didn't you let me talk to her?" Dawson demanded.

"Trust me. She was in martyr mode and you'd have wasted perfectly good arguments on her."

"Just like always, I'm not old enough to find that out for myself."

"Knock it off." Gray turned, irritated. "I'm pretty tired of that argument myself. She wanted you home in six days, and I got you six weeks. I'm on your side here."

"Whatever. Not like I should get to say hi to my mother or anything."

Well he was right about that, Gray thought, although wanting to talk to Ariel would be a first. So, fine, let him nurse his anger. God knew he felt pretty petulant himself at the moment. "Where's Kim?"

"Probably on her way from the barn."

"Good. When she gets here, you guys can clean up this kitchen."

"But Abby said we can have the day off."

"Abby's not here, I am. She doesn't need to come home to this mess."

"Why don't you help, then?"

"Because I'm famous, and I don't have to."

Dawson's eyes went wide, but then a wry twist of his lips gave away his reluctant amusement. "Guess I know what I want to be when I grow up."

"Darn right. Nothing but perks. I'm going to see what needs to be done outside." He left before Dawson could get another *whatever* out of his mouth.

Bird slipped into the yard with him, rubbed once

around and his ankles, and disappeared into the wildflowers. Gray longed to follow him. He was so tired of
his life being full of turmoil and guilt. If the paparazzi
were so hungry they were gunning for Ariel, how long
before they doped out where he was? He tried to picture the tranquility of Abby's secluded farm shattered
by shouts from money-grubbing photographers and the
locust-like clicking of their shutters. The thought of careless feet tramping through the wildflower garden turned
his stomach. He had no business being here.

He couldn't talk to his kid. He couldn't keep anyone
happy. He reached to his back pocket for his pack of cigarettes and shook one out without thinking. As he put the
slender tube to his lips, however, the memory of Abby
slapping one like it from his mouth loomed like a specter, followed by his waking nightmare of her classic barn
engulfed in a ball of fire. Nauseated, Gray snapped the
cigarette in two.

"Damn it, Abby," he mumbled.

How many times had his mother tried cajoling, lecturing, shaming him into quitting? Abby Stadtler, in one
livid-eyed moment, had come up with all-too-effective
aversion therapy.

"Don't do it," he warned himself out loud. "Don't
make reasons to get close. You should be getting your ass
out of Dodge."

Tonight would have been the first Kansas City concert. Gray's fingers itched for the cigarette pack again,
and again his stomach made a queasy roll. Were he not
here, he'd have slept until one with no guilt, and, after

waking, he wouldn't have had the aggravating talk with Ariel; he'd have ordered room service and taken Wick and one of the security guys to the nearest park for a quick run. He took a deep breath of the clean morning air. A run . . .

He'd never thought of it here, but . . . Why the hell not? His restlessness stilled for the first time. He wouldn't need bodyguards on the country roads. Could peace really be as close as the time it would take to change his clothes? He stole into the house, not willing to engage Dawson again. Five minutes later he'd donned a pair of blue running shorts always in his bag and an old black T-shirt, along with a New York Mets cap pulled low over his eyes.

"Hey," he said when he returned to the kitchen. "Will you tell Kim I'm going running and I'll help when I get back?"

"Sure." Dawson turned his head slightly and called out. "Hey, Kim! Dad's going running."

Kim, wearing cut-off jeans, a ratty sweatshirt, and ankle-high, lace-up boots with dusty pink socks, appeared in the kitchen from the living room as if she'd been shot from a circus cannon. Her eyes scoured him, wide and interested as always.

"You run?" she asked.

"Now and again." He sneered at Dawson and granted Kim a smile-and-a-wink, and she flushed to match her socks.

"Do you ever have to run for your life? From fans and things?"

"Nah," he laughed. "I'm not exactly Beatles popular."

"Oh, yes you are." She smiled eagerly.

"Hey." Dawson looked fully over his shoulder. "I have an idea. You should dry these dishes."

"Hey, I have an idea. You should get some Nice pills next time you go to the store."

Dawson let out an exasperated sigh. "Girls."

"If you two decide to murder each other in the next hour, finish the dishes first and then go outside so the gory mess is easy to clean up, okay?" Gray slipped him a wink too, got an incredulous stare, and left before the boy could reply or Kim could gush again.

Roscoe led him ecstatically past the house and up the driveway toward the Mertzes' log house. The dog's carefree joy, tongue flapping and ears streaming behind him, infected Gray and turned his earlier melancholy into relief. He usually got to run several times a week, but while on tour it took slightly less planning than a presidential motorcade. Here he ran with abandon, unconcerned with the public, relishing Roscoe's companionship and the way he checked back periodically to make sure Gray was still with him.

After forty-five minutes of winding down multiple back roads, basking in the heat and sweat and in the pure scents of grass and gravel, he guessed he'd gone almost five miles, although they'd passed like two. By the time he got back to Ed and Sylvia's he was far more invigorated than out of breath, and restlessness had been ditched along with any nicotine cravings from an hour before.

When he slowed to a walk, he spotted Sylvia, kneeling on a foam pad beside the same flower garden where he'd first seen her. He hadn't met or spoken to her since their meeting in the barn. He cowered at the thought of doing it now.

She lifted her head, and Roscoe, drooling like a St. Bernard, galloped toward her, forcing her to stand or be knocked over.

"Mangy mutt." She gave the golden a firm scratch, not a hint of annoyance in her words.

"Sorry." Gray stepped onto her perfect lawn.

"He lives here half the time." She pushed the dog aside. "Guess I should say welcome back." Gray flinched beneath her laser stare.

"My son and I are building a questionable reputation around here, aren't we?"

"That scalawag. So which one of you has the right name?" She got lithely to her feet.

"Neither." He extended his hand, and she clasped and released it with no ceremony. "I'm Gray Covey, Mrs. Mertz. I'm sure Abby's told you Dawson is a Covey as well. It's a long story, but it's nice to make our introduction official."

Her strong, Scandinavian face remained implacable. He was under a scrupulous assessment of some kind, but he had no idea how to pass muster. "You might as well call me Sylvia. Your boy does. As long as our Abby is all right, I'm willing to keep my eye on you without fussing. So far she seems all right."

"You're very close to her, aren't you?"

"Ever since she and Jack bought the farm from us, we love her like she's our own."

Ahhh. That explained the relationship and the Mertzes' new, modern home. "I'm learning she inspires that love in a lot of people."

Sylvia's eyes bored into his. "Just remember that if you have a single thought of looking for it yourself, you'd better earn it."

His eyebrows shot up, and he studied her right back. Her piercing gaze held a strange combination of warning and challenge. "I won't be taking advantage of her hospitality for long, Mrs. . . . Sylvia." He acknowledged her with as sincere a smile as he could muster. "In the meantime, I won't hurt her."

"No." She ended the conversation by turning back to her weeding. "Because if you do, you'll answer to me."

Chapter Eleven

EVERY MOVEMENT OF a horse had its sound. A snort. A soft stomp. The shake of a large head causing metal halter fittings to clink against snaps. The sounds soothed as always. Abby allowed her shoulders to lower away from her ears. Finally, her mind calmed as she swept a soft body brush along Gucci's sleek sides.

Although it was still light in early June at eight o'clock, it was late to be saddling up. But she was better off here than in the house. From the dire rumors that had circulated at work all week, to the knowledge that tomorrow would be no more than a day to survive, life pressed in like heavy weights tonight, and she needed a haven. The house was far too full to provide it.

Far too full of one person.

"Hey, there you are." At the sound of his voice, she leaned into Gucci's mane, hiding her face, expecting the turmoil he always carried in his wake. "Abby, is everything okay?"

Instead of causing her heartbeat to speed up, however, Gray's appearance brought an unexpected calm. Unlike the house, the barn seemed big enough to hold her emotions and him at the same time. She looked up and found it easy to smile. "Everything's always fine in a barn."

"But things weren't fine before?" Gray stopped on Gucci's far side and stroked the stallion's neck.

Abby sighed. She hadn't meant to give away any part of her mood, but the concern in his eyes was genuine. "Some days the office is just too stressful a place," she admitted. "Gucci is my therapy." She hoped her generic answer would suffice. To her relief, his lips eased into a warm smile.

"You have a wonderful home, and a good life. I'm messing with that, and I'm sorry."

"Oh, Gray, please don't think that. You and Dawson are model guests. In fact, you're hardly guests anymore. You've been working like slaves."

He'd mowed the lawn the day before, mended two broken gates the day before that, and helped muck stalls every morning. She'd never have bet a pampered celebrity would be so handy.

"It's hardly enough payment for the generosity you're showing. I appreciate it more than I can say. But I know this is wearing on you, Abby. It's hard having strangers in your house. It's hard knowing the world could invade at any moment. I met Sylvia today, and I know she's concerned—you're lucky to have her and Ed nearby. But, Dawson and I need to think about making our way home so you and Kim stay safe here."

She stiffened and kept her face calm with monumental effort. The fact that he was right—about everything—didn't stop panic from rising in her chest at the thought of him leaving.

"And strand me without my summer help?" She smiled and swallowed her misgivings as she always did. "I love Sylvia and Ed, and I love that they guard me like I employed them to do it. But I'm a big girl, and I made a deal with your son, remember? Besides, can't you see this set-up has been working pretty well for you and Dawson? Maybe it isn't the most comfortable for either of us, Gray, but I believe you're supposed to stay. If I didn't, I'd send you packing."

His pale blue eyes caught hers over Gucci's crested neck, and she might as well have turned her face to the sun. His lean fingers rested on her horse's mane, and as they played slowly through the wiry, black hairs, a hard shiver shimmied through her belly. "I just . . . don't know how to say thank you. I didn't mean to bother you. I'll go and let you finish de-stressing."

"Or not." She lowered her eyes, inexplicably shy—something she'd never been around him.

"Are you going for a ride?"

"Want to pull out another horse and come with me?" Her heart rose at the thought.

"Oh-ho, no!" He lifted both hands away from the horse. "I'm nobody's cowboy."

"Hey, almost anyone can learn to ride." She mixed a fun little taunt into her voice. "Long as he ain't sceerd."

"Oh, I ain't scared." His mock defiance gave her the chance to laugh. "I'd simply rather watch you do it right."

"Suit yourself, lily-liver."

There was something sensual about having him watch her ride. For the next half-hour, Abby couldn't shake her awareness of his sculpted body draped against the arena fence, and she put Gucci through his sexiest movements—a half-pass that took him sideways across the arena, a passage that floated him around the fence line in a slow-motion trot, and showy, single tempi changes that made him look like he skipped across the sand. Gucci performed like the ham he was. When she finished and dismounted, her legs were steady as licorice sticks. She faced Gray as if facing a judge.

"How do you *do* that? It's beautiful," he said. "See why I'm glad I didn't try?"

"You'd have been fine." They walked Gucci into the barn side-by-side, and Gray's subtle spice filled her senses more powerfully than the pungent barn smell she loved. "Besides, I hear you've been running lately. You should have nice, strong legs for riding."

"I don't think so. Watching you made me pretty certain riding and running are not the same."

"I don't know. Great leg muscles are great leg . . . muscles."

They halted simultaneously, and he stared so deeply she feared their gazes would fuse. For an instant she imagined his head lowering, and for a longer instant she imagined herself lighter-than-air as she lifted onto her toes. Then an adamant shove from Gucci's muzzle sent her rocking into Gray's torso. He caught her firmly and sent shocks surfing through her body. She tried to push away, but his hold remained locked. He winked.

He smelled like Irish Spring and coffee. Her throat constricted.

"Guess he's ready to get undressed." His smooth baritone rumbled against her breasts.

Her groan nearly made it past her lips.

"You have to promise me something." She forced herself to ignore the innuendo and the new, heavy ache of desire. "Before you do leave, you'll let me take you on one trail ride. I guarantee we can give you enough riding skill for that." She extracted herself, slowly.

His second wink left behind a smolder. "I promise."

THE NEXT MORNING, Gray awoke to a repeat of the day before. The dishes sat unwashed, Abby's mug sat on the table half-full, her daily list of chores was anemic, and when Gray asked Kim if her mom was all right, the quiet "she's fine" said otherwise. More concerned than ever, he offered to clean the stalls by himself, unwilling to try hiding his tumultuous thoughts from either teen. The day drizzled from high, sullen clouds, and Gray took Roscoe for company. He needed to see if he could take in some of the calming barn atmosphere Abby talked about.

It might have worked, except she was everywhere in the space.

A new craving, far stronger than his old one for cigarettes, had him reliving their close call last night. Raw desire for Abby now replaced simple attraction. He'd come awfully damn close to kissing her, and he was pretty sure she'd come just as close to letting him.

He couldn't allow it. Not a kiss, not whatever else desire might entail.

What's wrong with you, Covey? She's a beautiful woman. Why couldn't he just grab a chance at being normal? A chance with a woman who liked him for himself and not his fame?

Because he could never have normal. Nor had he known many women he would call normal. He'd definitely never known a woman who could settle his soul one second and send it twistering off to Oz the next like Abby Stadtler did. Somewhere along his path to superstardom, Gray had made a deal with the devils of rock 'n roll. Those demons would warp Abby's life into the furthest thing from normal she could imagine, and judging from her behavior the past two days, he was afraid they'd already begun the job.

An engine, too low and lumbering to be a car, growled its way down the driveway, interrupting his thoughts. Gray stepped outside, thrust his hands in his pockets, and watched a white, one-ton pickup rattle to the door, its bed loaded with wood shavings and covered ineffectively with a flapping blue tarp.

The driver was perhaps mid-thirties and somehow familiar. His square face sprouted high, hamster cheeks, an offensive lineman's forehead, and a neat auburn mustache. Once stopped, he rolled down his window, a suspicious question in his eyes.

"Mornin' hey." He leaned a thickly muscled forearm out the window. "I'm lookin' for Abby."

"She's working in town today." Gray stepped toward the truck.

"I see." The driver looked like he definitely didn't see.

"Can I help you with something?"

"I have a load 'a shavings for her. She wasn't expecting me till tomorrow, but I won't be able to make it then. Didn't want her to have to wait. Who are you?"

Gray pulled his hands from his pockets. "David Graham." He offered a shake, hoping the distrustful, Bunyan-esque delivery guy would stop eyeing him like a boxing opponent—especially since he had no idea why the man seemed to instantly dislike him. "I've been helping Abby the past couple of weeks."

"Helping, huh?" The driver gave Gray a skeptical once-over before his giant hand emerged from the truck like a reluctant diplomatic flag. "Name's Dewey Mitchell. I'll just back the truck into the barn, then."

The light went on in Gray's memory. Dewey. He'd provided directions to Abby's on Gray's first trip—and he'd been equally suspicious back then. He backed his truck expertly through the wide door and nudged up to the double stall where Abby kept the shavings. When he stepped from the truck and rolled back the tarp, he took up half the barn.

"Got two scoop shovels in the back." Dewey showed his teeth in a crafty smile. "With two of us, would be . . . yeah, well a snap to unload."

"A snap, huh?" Gray mimicked the man's earlier words and snatched one of the shovels, feeling strangely as if he'd been called out.

It was an ugly job—as Dewey had known it would be. Turned out a "snap" translated in Dewey's Minnesotan to thirty minutes of an undeclared shoveling contest, during which it grew perfectly clear he didn't like Gray's presence on the farm. Still, when he tossed his shovel into the empty truck bed, and Gray followed suit, Dewey begrudgingly held out his hand. Gray slapped his palms against his thighs, finding the denim caked in coarse, sandpapery grit. He smelled like a sawmill.

"Quick as spittin'." Dewey shook hands. "As they say."

"Do they?" He grimaced. "Minnesotans definitely have their own way of keeping time."

" 'Bout right." He sounded downright cheerful.

After the tarp was folded and shoved into the cab's back seat, Dewey dug into the breast pocket of his navy-blue T-shirt. For the first time, he looked uncomfortable "So, I have to get this to Abby." He pulled out a folded white slip of paper.

"I'll be glad to give it to her."

"It's none'a your business." Dewey held his gaze like he'd hooked a fighting fish. "I should bring it to her, but I'm already behind for the day, and we need for her to see it."

"Despite what you think, you can trust me to give it to her." Gray smiled easily. Dewey's discomfiture was Gray's upper hand.

"I don't trust you far as I can throw you. Just you be careful here. Abby's good people."

"Yes, yes she is. Wait. Is this the bill?"

"For this load and the last two." Dewey wrinkled his brow as if trying to figure Gray's angle.

A lump formed in Gray's stomach, and a multitude

of signs he'd seen in the past week suddenly made sense. He'd known Abby wasn't wealthy, but Dewey was hinting, unintentionally, that her financial issues were pressing.

He surreptitiously unfolded a corner of the paper. Three hundred and thirty dollars.

"I'm glad I thought to ask," he said, faking nonchalance. "Abby mentioned in passing there'd be deliveries in the next few days, and I just put that together with you." His audacity churned inside like a carnival ride, but he had money in his suitcase. It was the least he could do.

Five minutes later, a still-skeptical Dewey drove off with three crisp hundreds and three tens in his wallet, and Gray breathed easier. As he headed for the shower, satisfaction engulfed him for one of the first times in weeks. Abby had refused to let him pay room and board. She felt guilty if he cooked for her. Maybe this would make her life the smallest bit easier. And it was probably more practical than pork chops.

"A storm-eyed girl took my hand one day, and said, 'Follow me, boy, I know the way' . . ."

The song that had come to him in the rain two weeks ago flowed along with the shower water streaming down his face, and Gray added to the verse as he lathered the shavings dust out of his hair. Maybe he would test the song on Abby one of these days—see if she remembered it. He hummed into the water. It felt good to give back, ease things for her—especially since he was causing some of the burden.

Chapter Twelve

SMILING, BARELY, ABBY set her forehead against the wire cage in the Loon Feather's foyer and wrinkled her nose. "Howdy Stranger," she cooed. Lester whistled, but Cotton ruffled her feathers and harrumphed away. "Trust me, I get it, girl." Abby touched a fingertip kiss to the slender bars.

"Hey, Abbs." Karla waved, her face filled with understanding sympathy. But she only knew half the story today.

Abby cemented her shallow smile into place, unslumped her shoulders, and wished the blended aromas of savory chicken soup, sweet apple pie, and strong coffee were remotely enticing. She hadn't come in to eat; she'd come to avoid going home. To hide out. Fortunately, in the mid-afternoon lull, only the predictably unremarkable Sisters, on their daily visit, occupied the café.

"You look beat." Karla's eyes offered empathy, and

she led Abby to her booth. A cup brimming with coffee-slash-furniture-stripper appeared on the table. "Sit. I'll be right back. The last pie is due out of the oven." She waggled her slender brows. "Want a piece?"

"How 'bout the whole pie?" Abby's smile was still mostly unsuccessful.

"Yeah, I figured." She wrapped Abby in a protective hug. "Happy Will's birthday. I'm sorry."

"Thank you." Abby squeezed her hard and pushed her back to work, pointing at the coffee. "I'm just here for this. Go. There's no hurry."

Karla nodded. "Be right back."

Abby really had no right to sit and not hurry. Gray had been stuck alone with the kids and animals for several days now. Folding her arms on the tabletop, she dropped her head and tried to bury the dull ache lodged at the base of her skull. Few people knew her son's birthdate, but Karla would always remember, and it was nice to have one good friend who didn't get maudlin. But, then, there was the rest of today's disaster. The "Colonel Bogey March" started over again. If only her life could be as uncomplicated as Lester's.

"So." Karla's sage-green eyes captured Abby's as she plopped a pie tin and two forks onto the tablecloth patterned with flying Canada geese. "How 'bout you tell me what else is bothering you today. You look particularly upset even for this date."

She hadn't brought the hot pie, but a solid two-thirds of this one remained, thick with pale, sugar-glazed apples spilling from the double crust. She set no plates but simply handed Abby a fork and slid her curvy figure into the bench across from her. Karla was far from fat; still, the fact she was willing to sabotage her latest dieting effort in the name of solidarity filled Abby with gratitude. "You guys just holler if you need something, okay?" Karla called to the Sisters, and then leaned forward. "What gives?"

"Just a very long day at work."

Abby dug into the heart of the pie. The luscious filling melted against her tongue in a tart-sweet explosion, and she closed her eyes as her shoulders finally gave up their tension.

"Long? Or bad?"

After sucking the cinnamon-laced sugar from her lips, Abby sighed. "Okay, it was pretty much as bad as it gets."

"Oh, honey. What happened?"

"Mitch is closing the office in Faribault."

"What? When?"

The fresh shock in Karla's eyes was gratifying. Her friend knew how much she relied on the twenty-hour-a-week administrative assistant's job with Mitch Wagner's small architectural firm. The job wasn't rocket science, but it paid good money for part-time work.

"In four weeks."

"Holy cow, that's crazy! And today of all days. Abby, I'm sorry." At thirty-nine, Karla was two years Abby's senior, a native Kennison Falls girl who'd left to attend college and travel Europe before returning to marry her Kennison Falls high school sweetheart.

"How many times have I threatened to quit that stupid

job and not really meant it?" Abby asked, miserable. "I mean, a trained monkey could do it some days, but my zookeeper was paying me twenty bucks an hour to be that monkey. It's the kiss of death to lose that salary."

She'd kept tears of panic at bay during her drive from work, but they pressed hard behind her eyelids now. She almost lost control when Karla covered her hands briefly and didn't tell her automatically that everything would be all right.

"You work your little tush off, Abbs, and I know you're struggling. You're sure Mitch isn't just being a diva—going through male menopause or something?"

Abby laughed, despite the ache in her stomach, and shook her head.

Karla chewed a fingernail, her eyes scrunched in thought. Finally she shrugged, too. "How 'bout I get you a slug from the cooking sherry?"

"I'd love it. Unfortunately, I can't sit here long enough for it to wear off."

"Stay as long as you need to. Kim will be fine."

"Yeah, that. So, I have more news for you." She hesitated, considering what she could safely tell. "Dawson's back. He ran away from his dad again and came back here. He refused to leave, so his dad is staying."

"Abby?!" Karla lunged forward to grab her wrists.

"I know, I know."

"Is he cute?"

"Karla!"

"Wait, what am I thinking?" She sat back, smirking. "I suppose he's married."

"Divorced."

"Abby!!" She grabbed for another vise grip.

"Will you stop that?" She twisted free and flicked her friend on the knuckle with a middle fingernail, which only elicited a giggle. "Having an extra body in the house to feed is the issue here. Doesn't matter what he looks like."

"How the heck long is he staying?"

"Maybe a couple of weeks. It's complicated." She hedged her answer. "Dawson would have to go back to England if he left. His dad usually . . . travels a lot."

"I dunno. Sounds a little crazy. "

Abby flexed the tension from her shoulders. "You have no idea how crazy. But," she took a fortifying breath. "Dad *is* cute."

Much more than cute.

A naughty spark dawned in Karla's eyes. "You like him."

"He wouldn't be there if I didn't." That admission was easy enough.

"This is sweet, Abigail."

"Don't start—"

Lester let out another wolf whistle. Karla looked toward the café door. A male voice followed. "Howdy, stranger."

"It's Dewey."

"Oh, great." Abby's stomach dropped in dread, and she buried her head in her arms again. "I owe him for shavings, and I simply haven't had the money to pay him. Don't tell him I'm here." Abby rolled her eyes. "Jeez, listen to me. What am I, thirteen?"

"Let me see what he wants." Karla patted her arm and slipped from the booth.

Bereft of her friend's stabilizing presence, Abby's mind whirled, desperate ideas for replacing her job mixing with images of opening cans of Beefaroni for Gray and Dawson every day for the next month. How long *was* Gray going to stay? How long could she hide the fact that gas prices, broken fencing, and wood shavings were limiting the choices she could offer for dinner?

"Hey Abby, how's it going?" Dewey called out and ambled past Karla, clearly ignoring her attempt to seat him nearer the door. She followed, mouthing a heartfelt "I'm sorry." When he reached her, Dewey leaned comfortably against the side of the bench. "Saw you and had to stop over."

"Nice to see you," Abby fibbed.

His real name was Duane, but few people ever remembered. Working at the station and co-owning the feed mill gave him double access to as much town gossip as any old woman. Fortunately, he was nice enough that he rarely used it. In fact, the appealing, teen-jock smile he wore signaled this as a be-ultra-nice-to-Abby moment. It wasn't necessarily a welcome sign.

"Wanted to tell you I was out at your place a coupla hours ago. I dropped off the shavings." His handsome, auburn mustache lifted.

"You did?" Abby lowered her voice. "Oh, Dewey, thank you. I know you're waiting for the last two payments."

"Well, no. You're paid in full now. Your new . . ." his smile faded, ". . . barn help? Remembered to give me the payment you left."

"What? Who?" Suspicion sprouted in her stomach.

"Yeah. David isn't it? Kinda familiar looking. It isn't really all that safe to leave your place and money in the care of a stranger, Abby. He seems a little possessive already. Still, he handed me the cash you left."

"Uh . . ." Suspicion turned to sick certainty. "So, it's paid—the whole bill?"

"Three hundred thirty dollars. Left the receipt with him, although I didn't want to."

"I appreciate your concern. I do," she forced herself to say. "But you don't need to worry. He's a good guy."

"Well, maybe you and I can go to dinner again sometime soon? It's been a while."

"Oh, Dewey, thanks. Maybe sometime." She never knew quite what to say when he asked her out. She didn't want to hurt him, and they had to live in the same tiny town.

Impassive, Midwest affability took over his wide features, and he nodded. "Just you let me know if you need anything out there at your place. Wish I'da known you needed help." He gave a regretful nod and headed back to a table in the front of the restaurant.

Karla leaned toward Abby with wide eyes. "Wow! I think you found a white knight."

"White knight?" Abby glared, Dewey forgotten, her heart heading for arrhythmia, her breath nearly choking her. "This is the most arrogant thing I've ever heard. How dare he?"

She grabbed for her purse on the seat beside her and

yanked on the zipper. A moment later, wallet in hand, she dug for cash while Karla protested.

"What's the matter? Isn't this a godsend, Abby?"

"No, it isn't a godsend. He has no business knowing about my outstanding bills, and he has no business paying that much money without asking me. Godsend?" Her voice squeaked. "It's showing off!"

"Sounds like he can afford to show off a little. And he's not Jack's father. This doesn't have to be a threat."

"That," Abby slapped a five dollar bill onto the table, "is entirely beside the point. Thanks for the pie, and the ear."

"Keep the money, Abbs, you didn't order the pie, it was just left over from this morning."

"What's this, charity for Abby Stadtler day?" Her harshness was unfair, but the day had just fully imploded. "I can afford a piece of pie. I don't need you paying for things, too."

To her credit, Karla only smiled. "Fine. Go get 'im, girlfriend. Just don't be too hasty. White knights are hard to come by."

Abby wheeled into the driveway eight minutes later and threw the Explorer's shift lever into park hard enough that the red SUV lurched to its halt. There was no sign of life except the annoying drizzle. Her trip from The Loon had given her eight minutes to settle down, but she needed eight more. Or maybe eighty more. In fact, eighty more days might not be enough. She exited the car and searched her yard. It would be far wiser to calm her emotions before hunting him down and opening her mouth, but in truth she wished Gray was right in front of her so she could blast him.

How dare he? People's bills were private matters, and casually paying one for somebody defied common sense. She'd give him a piece of her— A series of muffled crunches on the gravel made her turn. Gray, flushed and soggy from running, pulled up beside her. A pair of lightweight, navy-blue running shorts had molded to his planed hips. Her mouth went dry mid-swallow.

Damn. She raised her eyes. *Sorry Lord.*

The shorts hung to mid-thigh, leaving the rest of his upper leg and long, muscular calves free for her to . . . enjoy? There was a joke. Not even anger could penetrate her enjoyment.

"Hey there!" A joint-weakening grin didn't help—or quench the drought in her throat. "I waved, but you were leaving too big a mud tail to see me. Welcome home."

She'd missed him? Looking like this? In her own driveway? A dark vee of sweat stained the front of a faded, red T-shirt, the anemic rain had wet his wide shoulders, and moisture clung to the little spiked ends of his dark curls. His splattered white shoes bore a familiar black swish. She'd heard he was a runner, but not that he was this incredibly *attractive* a runner.

"The kids helped Sylvia in her yard all afternoon, and because it was wet, nasty work she's feeding them pizza. I told her I'd feed us. And, I just had the best run of my life." His Peter Pan smile spoke volumes. "Didn't see a soul for five miles. You have no idea how cool that is. How can I thank you?"

He was breathing harder than normal between his chopped-up news reports. Her eyes fixed on the pulse ticking beside his throat, and she struggled again to swallow when he braced sinewy hands on his thighs and bent forward for a deep breath. Why she should be surprised by the perfectly proportioned legs when she'd seen them before . . .

Oh, no. You don't get out of it this easily. "You can thank me by keeping your nose out of my finances." She winced at her own brusqueness.

His gaze rolled up first, and a quizzical knot formed above his nose as he straightened. "Excuse me?"

"You paid the shavings bill. Of all the presumptuous . . ."

"Wait, I—"

". . . things to do. That's not your business."

"Abby, for crying out loud, hang on." He reached to touch her upper arm, and she stepped deftly out of range.

"What? You think you have something to say?"

"I . . ." He puffed in exasperation. "Yeah, I do. I . . ." He stopped, cocking his head like Roscoe did when he was trying to figure something out. "How did you know?"

"This is a small town, Gray. Not Hollywood, or New York, or, or Nashville."

"Nashville?" A side-sparkle of mirth lanced his confused eyes.

"What*ever*." As quickly as her roiling anger spiked, it

was sucked from her body like the tide rushing out after a tsunami. An embarrassing urge to weep swept over her, and, mortified that he'd see the tears forming behind her lids, she spun away. "I'll pay you back."

"No, Abby, this was nothing. I didn't mean—"

"Nothing?" Her anger sparked anew. She held up one warning hand. "I will pay you back, Gray. Just act like the welcome guest you are, all right? Do not try to help with things that are my business."

Staying anywhere in his immediate vicinity was no longer an option, and Abby left him stammering behind her.

"For God's sake, Abby." His voice faded, so she knew he wasn't following her. "This is just not a big deal. I only wanted to help . . . you . . ." He paused. "You do know Nashville is *country* music?"

The ridiculous, bewildered question tugged at her, made her want to turn and run back. The farther she walked, the more solidly anger spun itself into embarrassment and settled like lead in her stomach. It wasn't having Gray pay the bill that actually annoyed her. It was the fact that the payment, obviously easy for him to make, had been exactly the godsend Karla suggested it was. She was supposed to be strong, a survivor, even on what would have been her son's seventeenth birthday. Twelve years ago, she'd gone to court to prove she didn't need help from anyone to care for her daughter.

When had her life plan shattered beyond the point of being fixable?

Chapter Thirteen

THE OLD FARMHOUSE was big, but Gray wouldn't have thought a person could actually get lost in it. He'd kept out of Abby's way for half an hour after her tirade, but when he finally went to apologize, she'd vanished. He'd struck an angry nerve by paying her shavings bill. That much he got. Still, this was an unfair attack. If she'd let him explain, or explained her own anger . . .

"Aw, hell," he groused on his way back from searching the barn. When did a woman explain anything? In the cobwebbed recesses of his once-married brain was a memory. He was supposed to figure things out from clues. Or maybe it was thin air. Either way, he'd never been good at it.

He prowled through the kitchen, living room, basement, and both bathrooms. When he took the liberty of peeking into her bedroom, concern lapped at his mind. Dusky light faded the flowers on her wallpaper into muted grays and blues. Prim lace covered her plump featherbed. But no Abby, sad or mad, occupied the silent room. Only a soothing hint of mint tinged with orange infused the air, and Gray stood motionless inside the doorway, intoxicated.

The way he always was around her—even when she was angry.

Back in the living room Roscoe, stretched like a lazy amber rug in front of the sofa, thumped his tail rhythmically.

"Where's your mistress, fella?" The dog opened one eye wider than the other as if seriously debating whether to answer. Gray laughed. "Roscoe, where's Abby? Find Abby, boy."

To his astonishment, the golden heaved himself to his feet and wandered into the kitchen, stopping in front of what Gray knew was a walk-in pantry.

"Right." Gray opened the door, finding it empty as he'd expected. "Good dog," he said. "Confused, but good."

Roscoe cocked the furry skin over one eye in a frighteningly human way and padded forward, followed by Gray's scowl. Abby clearly wasn't here, but Roscoe stopped at the end of the tiny space and flopped his rear down in front of the end wall. Gray had paid no attention to it before, but now a set of small, painted hinges on one side popped into view.

"Are you kidding me?" He bent over the dog whose luminous eyes said "I told you so" as clearly as a human voice.

Before he could lose the nerve, he rapped firmly on the door. Nothing happened. He shot Roscoe a skeptical look, and then a sliding lock clicked and a knob turned. Seconds later, Abby stood in the half-opened door. The light behind her glowed eerie-red, like a movie version of the guts of a submarine.

"Traitor." She scowled at Roscoe, who only let his tongue fall out of his mouth and whacked his tail on the floor.

Gray waited, nervous as a kid at the principal's office door. When her eyes finally met his, he saw only melancholy, not anger. His heart hiccupped in concern, but his relief soared.

"Good hiding place," he said. "But we found you, so tag, you're it."

"I don't suppose you'd just go away?"

He made a show of looking over her head into the room. "I would. But you know, finding your hidey-hole is like hearing a punch line. Now I really want to know the whole joke."

"Maybe I'm not a clever enough comedian to tell jokes."

"Hey. I'm a clever enough audience. I laugh at pretty much everything."

He couldn't resist reaching out to lift her chin with his forefinger. The smallest glint of laughter in her huge, aqua eyes ignited a burn of excitement around his heart.

"No dogs allowed." She opened the door a few inches wider. "Meddling men allowed only when their lines are smooth enough."

She closed the door behind him.

"Yeah," he said. "About the meddling. I am sorry if I overstepped the bounds."

"You did." A conciliatory note graced her voice, but when he faced her in the weird, red hue, the puffiness around her lower eyelids stood out clearly. Guilt for his part in causing it pinched deep in his belly.

"The last thing I want to do is make your life tougher, Abby. My motive was truly just the opposite."

He thought her shoulders sagged as she turned. "I know that. It was a long day, and you stepped into the crap left over from it. That's all."

"As long as I didn't cause the crap." He grinned at the back of her head and was rewarded when she looked back at him over her shoulder.

"Only one scoopful."

"Can I make up for it by letting you talk about your long day?"

"No. You can make up for it by taking The Oath."

"That sounds ominous."

She led him from the small entry into a large, square room lined with tables, a sink, and counters covered with pictures. An acrid-sweet odor gave away its purpose. A darkroom? Images of the photographs Gray had seen in the living room flashed into his mind.

"This is quite a hideaway, Mrs. Stadtler."

"That's why there's an oath. There are, maybe, five or six people who know of this place, and all of them are sworn to secrecy. One is your son. Are you as trustworthy as he is?"

The sharp tingle of photo chemicals swirled pleasantly in his nostrils. He lifted his right hand, stiffening the middle three fingers. "I do solemnly swear, as the sixth or seventh person to be granted access here, that the existence and location of your sanctum will forever remain secret within the confines of my brain—puny as that space is."

"Do you have to make a joke of everything?" Her chestnut hair shimmered bronze beneath the darkroom lights. In a thick curtain, it hung past her shoulders, and Gray wished with every accelerating heartbeat that he dared to reach out and sift the silk through his fingers.

"Yeah," he replied. "Otherwise I get too serious." He waggled his brows Groucho-style. "But, I am serious about keeping your secret. Can I ask just one question?"

"Is it impertinent?" Her eyes narrowed like a Siamese cat's.

"Oh, I'm sure it is. My questions seem to end up that way."

"Then ask, but I may or may not answer." Her cat eyes morphed back into gorgeous, aquamarine mirrors, and their lids fluttered in a tease.

"Why, Abby? Why hide this? I think I've seen the art that comes out of this room, and it feels to me like you're not hiding the place as much as you're hiding yourself."

She wandered across the twelve-foot space toward a wooden stool. "Just the opposite. I come in here to find myself."

"Do you lose yourself very often?" He followed her.

"No. And I don't like it when I do. Like tonight in the

driveway." Her smile was only half-strength. "Justified as I was, I don't usually get that hot."

He didn't know about that. He'd seen several flare-ups the past week, but they were moments of passion and conviction he admired. The kinds of things others might hold back because of who he was.

"You weren't that hot. Under the collar, I mean." A flush warmed his face, because he badly wanted to tell her she was very hot.

"Thank you." Her deep breath was visible, as if she had to gather resolution for her next words. "And thank you for the gesture today. For paying Dewey. But I will pay you back."

Gray's own resolution hardened. "Abby, I don't want you to." He held up his hand as she parted her lips to speak. "You won't let me pay you anything for the privilege of staying here, and the shavings bill was something that fell into my lap. I thought taking care of it was a way I could contribute for both Dawson and me. Please, it wasn't planned. It was no more than one of those random acts of kindness."

A blush crawled onto her cheeks. "I was embarrassed enough that I got behind with him. I'm mortified that you paid my bill for me."

"Do *not* be. Good gosh, Abby. Who doesn't have to prioritize bills? Stuff happens and eventually we take care of things."

"Water heaters die. Feed prices go up." Her voice was small. "Dewey was next on the list."

He cupped the deceptively delicate curve of her shoulder. It hid so much strength. A buzz of electricity penetrated his guitar string–toughened fingertips. "Let me cross him off the list this one time." He massaged her shoulder gently. "It's no big deal for me."

"I can't tell you how much that pisses me off." At last she lifted her gaze. Color still stained her cheeks. "Don't you dare make a habit of this. But . . . thank you."

He stared for longer than he intended, and the pink in her face turned a beautiful rose under the warm, red lights. A tug low in his groin forced him to drop his hand and breathe again.

"You're welcome."

She reached back to gather her thick hair and sweep it behind her shoulders. The pretty bulge of her feminine bicep and the swell of her breast beneath her pale-green tank top set more desire wheeling through him. He would have stuffed his hands in his pockets but there were none in his running shorts. He settled for clearing his throat.

"So, show me the magic in this room that helps a stressed-out mom find herself."

He had a hard time thinking of her as anyone's mother at the moment. Vulnerability mingled with strength left her looking soft, youthful, different from any woman he'd been close to physically or . . . Or nothing. Hell, there hadn't been anything more than the shallow and physical in so long he hardly remembered.

"Jack always said he built this room for me, but it was his studio." She led Gray to the far end of the darkroom, where two file cabinets and a wide cupboard with nine shallow drawers stood. "He created so much beauty in here. We both poured our hearts into our work, but he was the master. When I come in here it isn't sad or nostalgic, it just makes me remember how worthwhile it is to work hard for your goals."

She pulled open one of the shallow drawers to reveal a stack of poster-sized enlargements. Gray recognized the stark, melancholy lines. "Jack's work?" he asked. She nodded. "Where's yours?"

"Mine? I have stacks of old crap filed away. I rarely look at any of this."

"Let me then."

"Gray, I . . ."

"C'mon Abby." He pleaded, eliciting another laugh. "One artist to another."

"One artist . . . right." A scoffing little snort escaped from behind a curled lip, but she pulled open a file cabinet drawer packed with colored folders. With a sweeping gesture, she stepped back. "Knock yourself out."

Several minutes later, forty or fifty black-and-white prints papered the counters, and Gray stared, star-struck in love with the array before him. "Who did you say was the master?"

He held up an eleven-by-fourteen print of a young child spying from behind the wide trunk of a tree, while a large, black dog circled the front, searching. Simple, funny, a whole story in one image.

"Pictures of my kids." Her right shoulder hunched, blowing off the work.

"Animals, sunsets, landscapes . . ." He flipped picture edges one at a time. "Abby. These are incredible."

"Thanks."

He shook his head at her. "Seriously. Wonderful. One artist to another."

"Oh, Gray, that's nice of you." Pensively, she stroked one of the pictures. "I like them. I'm proud of them. But Jack did the spectacular stuff."

"Jack did the depressing stuff."

"Huh?" Genuine confusion pulled her face into a tight question mark.

"His stuff is polished, yeah, and I hope I'm not dishonoring his memory, but every picture is empty. Full of lines and contrasts. Yours are full of life, Abby. Every picture tells a story. Each one is a song."

"That's a huge compliment coming from you. But it's a lot harder to write a song than snap a shutter."

"It's got nothing to do with hard or easy. It's about something inside a person that comes out in a way nobody else can imitate. I couldn't take these pictures. And it's obvious to me that Jack couldn't either."

"Jack's pictures sold well. Mine didn't."

"What do you mean?"

"We met in a photography class my first year of college and his last. I was in a little over my head. Jack had already been featured in a small gallery exhibition. He turned out to be a better teacher than the teacher, and one thing led to another. " Abby smiled, but there was neither sadness nor joy in it. "I married young, but we planned to make the photography a joint effort. We did two shows together—a little arrogantly on my part, because I wasn't really ready. Jack had the commercial success. Some interior designer bought a whole series of prints for a couple of office buildings. That gave us the down payment for this place. I sold half a dozen little prints over the years. I have a couple at a little restaurant in town, for example. But . . ."

"Why did you give up trying?"

Incomprehension clouded her eyes. "There wasn't anything to try. I was sort of left without a partner."

"Did you ever consider that, maybe, the main partner was not the one who died?"

She actually laughed, despite the blunt words. "You're sweet, but no."

Biting thoughtfully on the inside of his lip, Gray assessed the room. Wide trays sat next to the sink. Neat rows of taut wire stretched over the far counter with little clips ready to hold negatives or prints. A set of metal canisters were lined neatly on a center island, and two enlargers sat beside them. Gray had been in darkrooms enough to know this one wasn't all that far from being useable.

"When's the last time you used this? As a darkroom I mean?"

"Gosh, a couple of years maybe. Digital photography is faster. This is time-consuming and expensive. There's no point."

"I think there's a big point. This is special."

"You seem to have *developed*," she grinned, "a prejudice for your landlady."

"You have no idea."

Their eyes and smiles held for another long second

before Gray tore his gaze away. "So, you don't develop film here, yet you have the low light on, and I see bottles of chemicals on the shelves."

"It truly is ambience. If I do look at pictures, there's something elemental about seeing them under this light. They look just as they did when they were emerging from the developer."

"Like playing a song with my acoustic guitar. No frills; just the way you created it."

She turned back to him, her brows arched with delicate wonder. "Exactly."

"What did you take these with?" He pointed at the photos.

She moved to another cabinet and opened one of its double doors to an army of cameras and lenses. Gray let loose a low whistle. She reached for a spare-bodied, silver-and-black camera and handed it to him. It was heavy like a little tank.

"My ancient Minolta," she said. "Has no auto anything. Can't find them anymore."

Did she have a clue how rich the timbre of her voice had become? Almost as if she spoke of a lover. There was more wistfulness for the camera than for Jack.

"Is there film in this?" He handed the sturdy camera back to her.

"Old film," she acknowledged.

With slender fingers she stroked the rectangular body, reminding him of the way he touched piano keys or coaxed a melody from his old clarinet. A wayward fantasy of those fingers combing his hair slithered through his imagination. When he pushed it aside, an actual un-selfish thought followed it.

"Take some pictures," he said. "For me."

"Now? But it's dark in here."

"There's a lamp right there. I want to prove you can make anything look good through a camera lens, even in very low light."

Her genuine laugh, warm and easy, sent a shiver through his belly, like someone tickling him gently. "I think you're actually proud of being crazy."

"Don't argue with a crazy man. Just take pictures."

She wanted to argue, he could see it in her reluctant eyes, but something inside of her was stronger than what-ever tried to hold it back. He reached to switch on the work lamp, and after a moment Abby hefted the Minolta to her eye and set the stops and shutter speed. The sibi-lant click of the shutter filled the space. Two more clicks followed. He had no idea what she was shooting, but he smiled to himself.

"I don't know what you think this is proving," she said from behind the lens. "We can't see these pictures to test your theory."

"We can if you develop them."

"Right." She aimed the camera at his face and clicked. "How silly of me."

"No fair." He stuck out his tongue, and she clicked again, and then again when he puffed out his cheeks.

"Could I make a fortune if I sold these?" A giggle es-caped her.

A flash-thought of Elliott caused a moment of panic. He ignored it. "If you were that kind of girl."

"You have no idea what kind of girl I am."

She was more than right. From behind the camera, she revealed a side he'd had no idea existed. Flirty, free. After she'd snapped four or five more shots, he darted his hand out and stole the camera. "You've proven you belong behind the viewfinder; now let's see you work it for the photographer."

"No way! Give that back." She shrieked in protest when he snapped the shutter. "Gray!"

"C'mere." He grabbed her shoulders and pulled her to his side, then held the camera at arm's length, facing them. "You're in a photo booth. One, two, three, cheese." He snapped again and Abby sputtered.

"These won't work. Your hand isn't being nearly steady enough, and I have the shutter speed at one-fifteenth and the f-stop at one point four."

"I have no idea what that means, but if it means we'll look blurry and mysterious so much the better." He wound the film and held the camera out again, pulling her close. "Ready?"

"No."

He snapped. Her protests stopped, and Gray grinned. "See how easy it is to unwind after a hard day at the office? Why isn't this camera always within reach, Abby? I'm a dense man and I can see this is who you are." Without warning, she was weeping. His heart plummeted to his toes. "Sweetheart, what? I'm ... God, Abby, what's wrong?"

He set the camera on the counter and turned helplessly. To his astonishment, she wrapped her arms around him and burrowed her face against his chest. With no words, he gathered her close and let her cling as her slender shoulders shook. He searched his brain desperately for what he'd said to make a laughing woman burst into tears.

At last, a shallow snuffle marked the end of her crying jag, and she pulled away. Gray let her go, although he liked the feel of her in his arms more than he'd imagined he would. It had little to do with the shape of her body or his thoughts from earlier. He couldn't remember the last time he'd wanted to protect something this desperately.

"I am sorry." She wiped her face with both hands, pressing her pretty index fingers into the corners of her eyes.

"Tell me, Abby. What did I say?"

"Oh, no! It wasn't you." She squeezed his forearm with warm, certain fingers, and he saw as he had once before when she'd first told him about Jack, the telltale signs explaining her true sadness. "It's a bunch of ridiculous stuff all put together. It's the day. It's this room."

His heart sank.

"This was a room with a specific purpose. Nothing as irreverent as wasting film by playing photo booth ever happened."

"I'm sorry if I wasted film."

"Will you stop? This isn't about you." Finally, the corners of her mouth twitched, and when she wiped her eyes a last time she left the smallest sparkle behind. Still, there was the tiny, protective lift of her chin, and a tight, low quality to her voice. "I'm trying to tell you, very inadequately, that I needed to hear you liked my pictures. I needed to laugh tonight."

"It's a sad day today, isn't it?" An inner heaviness had disappeared, however briefly, from her eyes and face while they'd played with the camera. It was back now, masked by her smile. "Something with your husband? Your son?"

She gaped at him and swiped her nose with the back of one hand. "Why would you guess that? I don't tell anybody." She scrubbed self-consciously at the legs of her jeans. Those wonderful jeans with the rip in the thigh.

"I've been paying attention." He wrinkled his nose. "You're strong, but not the last two days. Today I see it in your face and hear it in your voice."

"Are you for real?" She touched his cheek tenderly and sighed. "It's Will's birthday."

"Abby, I'm sorry." There was nothing else to say. He couldn't tell her he really understood.

"Time helps. Hugs help. I know, because yours did."

"Maybe you've needed a hug for a while."

The atmosphere in the dark red room changed in a heartbeat. Tension eased. Comfort swirled in like a misty cocoon and tightened like an electrical force to bind them together. Electricity and mist. Locked eyes and elevated pulse rates. Gray spanned her slender waist with his hands. She yielded, her spine rolled softly inward, and her hips rocked against his.

"Hugs I can do," He murmured the promise into the earthy-sweet smell of her hair.

She melted against his torso and sent her hands up his back in a slow expedition. Each inch of progress sent a chill careening along his spine. He slid his hand beneath her fall of hair and closed his eyes to play in the chestnut silk. It was everything he'd imagined, like stroking a mink or sifting through down feathers. Her sigh vibrated against his throat.

"You do them well. Hugs."

Gray arched back and drew his hand around her cheek, until his thumb rested on corner of her mouth. Banishing caution, he lowered his lips to hers, intending the shortest of tastes, the briefest of comforts. But her lips surrendered beneath his, her mouth opened the tiniest fraction and then closed on his bottom lip. A soft tug set off a deep internal reaction that enflamed and weakened him.

"Abby," he whispered against her mouth.

"A hug," she replied. "And a kiss."

He sealed their mouths while her hands went on roaming his back. Her tongue pulsed against his thumb resting on the corner of her mouth, just before its sweet, warm tip penetrated his lips. A rainstorm of shivers raced through his belly. His hand slipped to her rounded bottom, where he cupped one cheek and tugged, eliciting a mewl that swirled its way into their kiss.

He knew exactly how to kiss her, when to draw back and when to seek more, as if he'd done it a hundred times. He lost breath, he lost time. A soul-deep tranquility that he'd never known was there to find filled him to overflowing.

Backing up two steps, taking her effortlessly along, he braced against a counter and spread his legs. Abandoning all restraint, he pulled her close, swiftly with no apology, and dragged her pelvis into his new hardness, reveling in the shot of heat. When she raised her right leg and curled it up around his knees, he had no power to stop his own groan.

Their kiss grew sloppy as it lengthened, with perfect wetness, perfect friction. Gray slid his fingers from her bottom, down the leg wrapped around him, and met the rip in the denim on her thigh. Eagerly, mindlessly, he pressed his fingers through the hole and stroked the soft skin. Soft as her hair, soft as her mouth—up under the fabric he reached, learning that tiny bit of her until her breathing hitched and unlocked the kiss.

He withdrew his fingers and their bodies relaxed. He pushed back an errant strand of hair, and she smiled shyly. But she didn't back away. The aquamarine irises held no regret.

"I thought you were the one who needed a kiss," he said, surprised at how unsteady his voice came out.

"Oh, I did."

"I've never kissed anyone in a darkroom. I guess it, um, got to me."

"It happened once or twice." She fell back against him, turning her head against his chest and resting her cheek like a contented child. "But never like that, Gray. Never, ever like that."

Chapter Fourteen

ABBY SMILED AGAINST the soft, textured lace of her pillow sham and shivered with hot, residual pleasure. Little electric bolts chased through her body, playing tag with her emotions, and memories held her like Gray's arms. The kiss changed nothing. But the kiss changed everything.

She would still lose her job in a month. She still had to feed two extra people. Yet girlish giddiness shimmied through her stomach, carrying with it a faint hope. She had no business indulging in hope sparked by a man like Gray Covey. It was just . . . Hope had been such a rare commodity lately.

Her eyes closed, and she floated, relaxed. She jumped when Gray entered the room. He didn't speak, just held out a piece of chocolate and popped one like it into his sensual, moist mouth. A Symphony bar. The mattress sank beneath his weight. "Abby, share it with me." With that, he pressed his chocolate-slick tongue against hers, and the Symphony became more than candy. When he pulled from her kiss, his rich voice rumbled like thunder into her ear. "This isn't enough. I want more, Abby. More of you. All of you. I want to be all the way inside of you . . ."

Her eyes flew open and she started, squeaking the mattress which cradled her body safely—and alone. She clutched her pillow like a teddy bear and held it over her eyes with an embarrassed groan. How could his voice have sounded so real? He'd never said such words to her. They'd come from an unknown place deep inside herself. What did that mean about her state of mind?

She'd spent the past eleven years of her life learning to become an independent woman. With one delve of his finger into a hole in her jeans, Gray had given her a taste of how good it felt to connect with another person who could make her brave and bold, be it with a camera or a kiss. Since Jack's death, there hadn't been anyone who'd made her consider loosening her stranglehold on survival.

But why this man? This unreachable, unavailable man who belonged so much more to the public than he ever could to one person. He came from a world she didn't want. One in which she could never live.

"Damn it all to hell, he's gone too far this time!"

Her breath froze in her chest as Gray's real voice pierced the silence. Tossing the pillow aside, she swung her legs to the floor and ran four steps to the bright light of the hallway. Another low curse wafted from downstairs.

"Dad, it's okay."

"It's bloody not okay!"

Her pulse skyrocketed as she dashed into the middle of a motionless tableau. Tension filled the room like smoke. Gray stood like a steel girder in front of the couch, arms welded to his sides, fists tight as knotted cables. She followed his furious glare to the television, surprised the screen wasn't a fizzling heap of wires and glass. Dawson stood beside him, by far the calmer of the two. Kim huddled in the big leather chair, wide eyes fixed on Gray, knees drawn up.

"What happened? Gray? Dawson? Is everything all right?"

A drizzle of incongruous excitement fluttered through her stomach when she caught his eyes. For the briefest of seconds his anger remained pooled there, but when she offered a tentative smile his body relaxed.

"Abby, I'm sorry. I didn't mean to disturb you."

"You didn't, I was just . . . freshening up."

She reached his side and, to her astonishment, he wrapped an arm around her shoulders and pointed at the TV.

"I still think it's not that big a deal." Dawson's voice held a brittle bravado. "It's just a picture. She looks fine."

"Who is that?" Abby stared at Gray's taut mouth knowing this was serious and she shouldn't be remembering how soft the lips could be.

"My mother."

The TV pictured a lovely woman, with dark hair, a kind smile, and Gray's jawline. Abby gasped. A reporter's voice supplied more than she needed to hear.

"Covey's manager, Chris Boyle, admitted today that while Gray is neither in rehab nor with his mother, he *is* in an undisclosed location with his sixteen-year-old son, Dawson, who is the one having personal problems. Staff members at Bridgeport Care Complex insist Mrs. Covey does not know the whereabouts of her son or her grandson."

"That son of a bitch!" The words blasted from Gray's lips and hung with no apology. He dropped his arm from Abby's shoulder and spun on his son. "Still think this is no big deal?"

Dawson stared at the television as if it had popped out an alien. Anger flowed from Gray like heat waves. Abby ran her forefinger soothingly along his cheek. The memory of their darkroom kiss danced between them.

"I'm going to turn off the TV now," she said. "And you're going to sit down and tell us what's wrong."

It was a relief having a problem to solve that wasn't hers. Only after the TV was dark did Abby notice Kim's silent, rigid gaze flicking from her, to Gray, then back. Jealousy? Abby nearly burst into laughter, the emotion was so incongruous with the moment. But she had no time for teenage hormones so ignored her daughter.

"Now," she said to Gray. "We're not much, but we're all the family you have, so out with it. What's happening with your mother? And why is it upsetting you so much?"

He rubbed his hand across his eyes. "Elliott St. Vincent happened. He took that stupid picture and has started a chain reaction."

"I thought that was taken care of."

"Welcome to the world of cutthroat celebrity." Sarcasm turned his voice bitter. "Where nothing is ever really taken care of."

"You're saying Elliott has been to visit your mother?"

"So it would seem." Gray ground out the words and took a breath. "But we haven't told you about her yet. I don't know why, because in a way she's the reason we're mooching off of you." He looked to Dawson who only glowered. "Dawson wanted to come to the States and stay with her, but she's ill. My mother has Alzheimer's, and I recently had to place her in a care facility."

"You mean hide her there," Dawson mumbled under his breath.

Gray's face iced, but he didn't respond. "Ironically, my mother loved Elliott St. Vincent. I don't know why he'd use her this way. He was a good friend. Even for a mercenary, this is cold."

"You don't even know for sure he did it, Dad."

"I know you've always liked Elliott, and this is hard for you to believe, but after what's happened with the other picture, I don't know who else it would be. And I won't tolerate him using my family. They can lie about me, but you and Grandma are off-limits."

"It's okay. Nobody knows me."

Abby thought Gray's chin might drop clean off. He stared and, without preamble, wrapped his son in a massive hug. "I wish people did know you," he said. "And I'm going to make sure this gets fixed."

Tears beaded in Abby's eyes at this first physical display Gray had shown. Dawson withstood the maudlin moment with the high color of a boy who was embarrassed but didn't want to be. Even Kim lost her pique and patted Dawson's back when Gray released him.

"How old is your mom?" Abby asked.

"Sixty-three."

"She's so young!" Abby's heart broke for him.

"Eighteen when I was born. My biological father left when I was three, and she married Neil Covey when I was five."

"They were cool." Dawson said. "Grandpa took me fishing, and he built stuff out of wood. He made me a scooter once out of an old crate and some ancient roller skates. But Grandma showed me how to use it."

Both he and Gray laughed.

"My mother is the nicest but most stubborn woman I've ever known. There was no telling her what to do once she made up her mind. And there was no quitting once you'd agreed to do something. Take piano lessons? Then you practice, young man. Quit Juilliard for a rock-and-roll band? Not on your ever-lovin' life, buster. Then she turns into the band's biggest groupie. There were plenty of times I was pure mad at her and she knew it. Now I'd give heaven and earth to have that bossy woman back in my face."

Silence reigned for long, hard seconds. Kim reached forward and patted him shyly on the shoulder. Abby took his hand. "It sucks, Gray. I won't tell you otherwise."

A wan smile formed on his face. "Thank you." He wrapped Abby in a hug, and his sigh filled her ear. "She has moments of clarity. I told her once we were looking for Dawson in Minnesota. If she happened to remember that, it won't take Elliott long to find us. And when he does, the world does. As bad as that would be, it's worse that everyone knows about Mom."

"There's no shame in her condition, Gray." Abby touched his arm.

"Of course not. But she's not an ordinary mother, for which I couldn't be sorrier. Now that they know where she is, reporters, and even more photographers like Elliott, will start hounding her, or at least go after the staff where she's living. I have no idea what made him hate me this much."

"Who could hate you?" Kim thrust her first, indignant words into the fray and garnered a genuine smile from her hero.

He sought Abby's eyes. "Who could?" she echoed softly. "Maybe it's strictly money, not hate. There's probably a big check waiting for the person who solves the canceled-concerts mystery. Money is powerful."

The touch of his fingers on her cheek warmed her to her toes. She wished she could erase the sadness in his eyes.

"You're absolutely right. And if Elliott St. Vincent is successful, you'll be up to your quiet country neck in reporters and photographers."

Gray's words sliced into Abby's heart like knife blades. Since the magical-but-rash kiss, she'd been downplaying worries about her lost job, her fragile finances, and her fears, but reality battered her peaceful fairy tale like hailstones. What was she thinking? She wanted no part of media or rumors or back-stabbing paparazzi. Losing her safe solitude and disrupting her efforts to keep things running on her fraying farm was not worth hanging onto a white knight, no matter how well he could validate her. Or how thrillingly he could kiss.

Resolutely she stood. Gray clung to her hand, sadness changing to concern in his eyes.

"Abby, I'm sorry. Don't leave."

"It's okay," she lied. "I just think, maybe, it's time for cocoa. It has been almost a week since I made any." It sounded lame even to her, but at the moment it was any port in a storm.

She half-hoped Gray would follow her to the kitchen, although his company was probably the last she should have. With a smidgen of disappointment, she heard the high-tech warble of Rachmaninoff's Prelude in C-sharp Minor, signaling his iPhone ringing. Her body tingled when his low, sexy voice answered, even though he wasn't talking to her.

With effort she shut the sound out. There was nothing she wanted to hear. No more she wanted to know. Helping Gray was a task so far out of her league that the hot cocoa fix was an exercise in sheer ridiculousness. Nonetheless, she started her chocolate to melting.

"That was Chris."

She spun from the pan on the stove in surprise, her wooden spoon shedding a glob of chocolate onto the floor. Deep lines of distress marked his brow, and his thick hair had been raked back from his forehead.

"And?" She placed the spoon back into her pan and moved it from the heat, ignoring the drops at her feet.

"He called the Bridgeport Center where Mom is. They confirmed that Elliott signed in several days ago. Assho— Sorry." The last came out a whisper.

"Want me to go beat him up for you?" Her heart hurt for him.

"Would you?"

"Sure."

Before she realized he'd moved, he pulled her into his arms. Had there been time to think she might have dodged him, but his hold was needy and persuasive. Kim and Dawson's proximity be danged— she wanted him to kiss her again. And that was dangerous. "If you want your chocolate, you have to let me go." Her argument was weak; his arms tightened.

"You're like a living fantasy in the middle of a nightmare, and I hope you know I wish I could hold you like this forever."

"But . . . ?"

"But that picture Elliott took could happen again in a heartbeat. I'll tell you again, Dawson and I have to go. Leave you and Kim so you don't end up on Entertainment TV."

His words shoved her heart right off the Grand Canyon. "I understand, I do." She swallowed against a lump of fear, larger than the one the night before. "But think, Gray. They'll expect this to flush you out. The more often you travel, the more likely it is you'll be spotted.

Nobody knows you're here yet. Let it all settle down. For you and your mom."

He said nothing, and Abby kicked herself mentally. Hard. What was she doing? He was a thousand percent right. And he was offering to leave. Giving her space. Her life back.

"Sweet Abby. I opened myself up to hurt the day I decided to make this my living. My skin is tough. But this isn't fair to you."

"Yeah, if you were so tough, you wouldn't want to run away."

"Don't start lecturing me, woman. I'm mean when I'm mad, remember?" He ran one finger through the hair around her ear.

"Oddly enough, I've always found that weirdly attractive." She extracted herself reluctantly from his hold, relieved he hadn't kissed her. Although, if he had she'd at least have a temporary insanity defense for what she was about to say. "I think leaving is a bad idea. You need to stay put just as we planned. You should help me finish the cocoa, we should stay up watching a stupid movie, and I'll go in late tomorrow. Just forget about Elliott for now."

She released his hand and turned to the stove, shivering when he set his chin on her shoulder to watch her add the cream to her decadent chocolate mix. His breath sent a scalding line of fire down her shoulder.

"Life is simple for you, Abby Stadtler. You're right. I needed to find you."

Simple? "Sure." She closed her eyes and squeezed them tight to keep from weeping.

THE NEXT MORNING Gray's immediate world was back in order. The dishes sparkled in the drying rack, the chore list was plenty long to last all morning, and the coffee was fresh and hot, his mug waiting for him to fill it. But not even the return to normalcy cured his feeling of being the holiday relative who wouldn't leave.

The world had him over a barrel. The PR spin was all in Chris's hands, Gray could move his mother to a new, unknown location but to what purpose? Confuse her further? He could prosecute Elliott, but to what end? More publicity for him?

He could change the whole paradigm by going back for his next two concerts. Had he not canceled in the first place, he wouldn't be in this situation. But changing his mind now would only stomp on the extremely fragile bond he'd built with Dawson. And fragile was describing it optimistically.

He sat on the back door stoop with Roscoe at his feet, his brain in turmoil while his body basked guiltily in paradise. The hot, June air, filled with sweet grass and wildflowers, smelled like Mother Nature's dressing table.

After failing to solve his troubles after ten minutes, he entered the relative cool of the house and made his way upstairs. He could at least take what had become his daily morning run. So far, they'd come closest to bringing calm to chaos. When he passed Dawson's open door, he found his son plugged, as he usually was after chores, into his computer. Dawson's head popped up when Gray stopped in the doorway and, slowly, he dragged off a pair of huge earphones.

"Hey, Daw." He hoped his son wasn't still cringing at the memory of the unmanly hug from last night. He didn't seem like a particularly demonstrative kid.

"Hey."

"Some heavy duty earphones you got there."

"Bose noise reduction."

"Impressive. Abby pays you well." He was teasing, but Bose equipment was far from cheap.

"I wish. Mom bought these when I threw a fit about going to Heighton."

"You? Throw a fit?"

Dawson glared at him and Gray held up his hands. "Kidding, kidding. I don't blame you. I'm sorry I didn't stand up for you. Not that you're supposed to whine to get what you want."

"It worked on you."

For one instant, shock at his child's impertinence stopped Gray's thoughts, then their eyes met for a furtive second and he caught a flash of shy humor. His heart swelled a tiny bit.

"Don't be a smart ass, kid." He eased his way into the room. "What are you working on? Or am I interrupting something private?"

Dawson shrugged and pushed his chair back slightly from his desk in invitation. Gray leaned over the keyboard and studied the frequency lines and slider bars of a well-known music mixing program. "What's this, ProTools?"

"Yeah." Dawson nodded. "Asked for it with the headphones."

"You're smart as well as manipulative anyway." Gray took a chance and patted his son's shoulder. He didn't flinch. "You're into this?"

"I guess."

"This isn't beginner stuff. How did you learn it?"

"A guy I met at school messed around with it in his room and taught me. The only good thing that ever happened at Heighton. I tried it because one time at a recording session with you I remembered thinking the control booth was cooler than making the music . . ." He trailed off as if he realized he'd spoken heresy.

"It's okay. This is where a lot of the magic happens, I know."

Dawson leaned forward, moved several sliders, adjusted a couple of bars and then clicked play. Wordlessly, he offered Gray the headphones. Gray settled them over his ears, surprised but curious. Ambient sound disappeared and an upbeat guitar melody flowed through the earpieces. Gray had heard it once, right after finding Dawson back here at Abby's. The melody was catchy, starting low then rising until it wove seamlessly into a rocking harmony with a second guitar. Forty-five seconds into the piece, the thumping backbeat from a tom-tom lifted the song into a full rock rhythm. It ended abruptly.

"Whoa!" Gray pulled off the headset. "This is your song. The one for Grandma." He'd ended up giving a cursory listen-to it the night Dawson had run from the tour.

"You said I should finish it. Haven't laid down the lyrics yet, just two guitars."

"But when did you do this much?"

"This week. I'm pretty slow. Now I'm adding percussion and I'd like to record some bass, but there's no way to do that here. It's nothing, just messing around."

"It sure *isn't* nothing. It rocks. You bet you have to finish it." He stared thoughtfully at the screen. "I've always liked the production side of things, but I'm not nearly as strong at it as I am at the performance part." Gray shrugged. "I've always gotten good technical people to make up for it."

"Yeah. Well . . ."

The question suddenly burning in him was one he really didn't want to ask. "So, did you . . ." he said, scratching the top of his head self-consciously, ". . . ever listen to the newest? CD?"

"Yours?" With an uncannily adult look, Dawson grinned at him. "C'mon, Dad, I only hate *you*; I don't avoid the music."

"Nice, kid. Real polite."

Such flashes of camaraderie were unfamiliar and delicate as eggshells. Gray knew at any moment he could, and probably would, blow it.

"You're talking about *Luck of the Draw*?" Dawson named Gray's latest album. "Yeah. I listened to it. You're singing the title song on tour. I know that one."

Now what? How did he handle the role reversal, looking for approval from his son? Did he really want to know what Dawson thought?

"It's fine, Dad."

Gray slid further into embarrassment. "A ringing endorsement."

"Look." Dawson squirmed. "What can I say? You're good at what you do. You are, and you can play anything. You're kind of stuck in a time warp, that's all."

Aging-rock-star syndrome. He knew *Luck* had stalled on the charts. Number, what, fifteen, Chris had said? Respectable. Disappointing. His lowest showing in years. Still, it stung stupidly to have his son nail him on the reality.

"I'm no Green Day, is what you're saying?"

"You're not Green Day. You're not Sledg."

"Sledg? Shit, who the . . . Sorry."

Dawson grinned, and Gray was now on a Bad Parents list somewhere, he had no doubt.

"I'll play you some of their stuff . . . sometime."

"Things look grim for the old man?"

"They don't have to. It wouldn't be that hard to make something tolerable of your songs." Dawson's eyes stayed riveted to the computer screen. A barely discernible tic lifted one corner of his mouth.

"If that's really true, maybe I should have my people call your people."

"Sure."

"So, show me what you're doing?"

Within three minutes Gray was rapt and amazed at the amount of expertise Dawson had gathered. He was sitting on the corner of the bed, pointing at the screen over Dawson's shoulder, when they both jumped at a deep, humor-filled voice.

"Lookee here, found the boys' club. Kim said you'd both be around, so I broke into the house."

Ed stood in the doorway, gray twill pants low on his hips, a blue-striped dress shirt tucked in neatly, and gray elastic suspenders holding it all together. He carried a battered ball cap in his hands, and his monk's fringe of gray hair stuck out slightly on one side.

"It's Ethel Mertz!" Gray grinned.

"I hated that show," Dawson said.

"Me too," Ed replied. "I was looking for you, Goddess. Thought I could borrow your muscles."

"Goddess?" Dawson looked up for the first time with a full, floppy grin.

Ed smirked. "Ask your papa here about his favorite shirt. The one he found in the barn."

"Just never you two mind. What do you want my muscles for?"

Pleasure drizzled through Gray like refreshing rain. He got asked for donations, for appearances, and autographs. Getting asked for plain old favors was rare.

"Sylvie's got it in her head I should make up a fancy tack trunk thing for Kim's birthday next month, and I need several big pieces of wood. Thought mebbe you'd ride along to the lumberyard and help load it."

Gray's delight turned to an acid lump in his gut. He didn't dare leave the farm. If anyone recognized him . . .

"I'd be happy to help you, Ed, you know that. I . . . don't know if it's smart to take me into public."

"You got some sort of communicable disease? You spit at people uncontrollably? What?"

Laughter spilled from Dawson like frogs and marbles from a little boy's pockets. Gray fixed him with his best parental glare and was ignored. "Look, Ed, I love that you and Sylvia don't know who I am—"

"I know who you are. Kimmy came and used our computer two, three months ago when her Internet was down to order tickets to see you. I guess she don't need them anymore, heh?"

Gray didn't know which surprised him most. That Ed knew exactly who he was or that the Mertzes had a computer. "Your computer?"

"Yeah, yeah. Abby says it keeps us young. Hah. Look, you can sit in the truck while I buy the lumber. I need your strength for five minutes to load it up."

"You could take Dawson . . ." Gray cut short another sigh. He wanted to go, damn it.

"Scrawny kid like him?"

"Hey!"

For a long moment, the three generations poised in silence. "Oh, fine." Gray ruffled his son's hair, and Dawson ducked away. "C'mon hot shot, let's go. You can cover me. What can go wrong?"

Chapter Fifteen

"WHAT KIND OF wood are you after?" Gray asked forty-five minutes later, as Ed drove through rows of stacked lumber, and Dawson took in the surroundings with reluctant curiosity.

"Birch. Be finer-grained for sanding, and it'll look a little lighter than oak. There." He pointed to a stack of pale boards and stopped his truck.

Out of habit, Gray glanced warily out the windshield. A handful of people shuffled down the aisle, but they weren't paying attention to Ed's ten-year-old Dodge pickup. Gray wore an unadorned white T-shirt and jeans, and a UCLA baseball cap pulled low over his brows. He dug a pair of empty, Clark Kent glasses frames from his pocket and settled them over his nose.

The cords of Ed's neck stood out from the effort of holding back laughter. "Where's the fake mustache, Mr. Bond?"

Dawson sputtered like a choking engine. "Not all that funny. Dude, he actually used to have one."

"Don't knock it." Gray adjusted the fake glasses. "In a crowd, it comes in handy."

"Yah, and I'm sure it's real handsome," Ed said. Dawson snickered again.

"You two are getting far too much enjoyment out of each other." Gray yanked the handle and flung the door wide, ignoring the residual laughter as they all climbed out.

Under Ed's tutelage, Gray and Dawson sorted through a dozen four-by-eight sheets of wood. After friendly debates and plenty of random laughter, five sheets meeting Ed's exacting standards were loaded into the truck bed. Gray had forgotten all about fake glasses and mustaches until a voice startled them all from behind.

"That you, Ed?"

Gray turned involuntarily with the others and his heart hit his toes at the sight of linebacker thighs and curled ginger hair. Mr. Lucky Charms himself.

"Yah, Dewey," Ed replied.

"Hey, Dawson." Dewey spoke but super-glued his gaze to Gray's. "This is your dad?"

"Yeah. Bummer, huh?"

Dawson took a subtle step toward Gray, and he caught a glint of steel in his son's eye. A wave of gratitude rippled through his surprised heart.

"David, isn't it?" Dewey put his hand out, but a challenge rode his gaze, once again as if he were about to suggest pistols at dawn.

"Right." He caught a glimpse of Ed's amused eyes and accepted Dewey's handshake, a crushing grip full of blatant aggression.

"Still at Abby's?"

"She's still putting up with us," Gray acknowledged.

"'At's right, Dewey," Ed's voice soothed. "And Sylvia and me are watchin' closely."

Dewey's brows folded into one feathery line. "You've seemed familiar all along."

"He gets that a lot. It's the pits." Dawson curled his lip.

Ed clapped Gray on the back and turned him toward the lumber stack. "It was good to see you, Dewey. We gotta get home before the wimmenfolk know we're gone. Come on. Quit yakkin' and shut that tailgate."

"Nice to see you again . . ." Dewey's eyes narrowed to green slits. "You sure I haven't seen you somewhere? Other than Abby's?"

"Pretty sure," Gray nodded.

Nervousness jogged down his spine. He'd spoofed his way through enough situations to know when a ruse had worked and when it hadn't. Dewey wasn't buying this for long. When the large man ambled off, a leprechaun on steroids, Gray didn't breathe much easier.

"Thanks for the cover," he said to Dawson.

"It's why you brought me."

Gray slammed the tailgate, and once they were all back in the truck Ed snorted. "You're more fun than a car of clowns, Goddess. Fake name too?"

"Official alias. Thanks for not blowing it."

"You really need all this cloak-and-dagger stuff?"

A sigh of frustration escaped Gray's lips. "I don't know. It works sometimes. The problem is, Dewey's on the right track. I'd never forgive myself if Abby was hurt by me being here. If the media catches wind, she'll be plastered all over the tabloids."

"Mebbe that wouldn't be all bad." Ed spoke almost to himself, dismissing the comment with a shrug.

They headed for the exit and drew up behind Dewey, striding with much more determination than when he'd sauntered off moments before. Gray avoided looking at him, but a sharp stomp on the brakes jerked him forward into his seatbelt.

"Dewey, what the—?" Ed called.

Dewey stood, hands-on-hips, directly in front of the truck. Now he was an *angry* leprechaun on steroids.

"I know who you are." Dewey slapped the hood, literally jumped around to the door, and met Gray's eyes with blazing accusation. "You're that singer on the lam. Covey. Gray Covey. They said you were in rehab."

"Covey?" Even to his own ears Gray's forced laugh sounded desperate. "Hell, no. I hate that guy." *He's not buying this for a second.*

"I might come from a small town, but I can put two and two together as well as any hot shot singer. Kennison Falls doesn't need any trouble, man."

Dropping his head forward, Gray removed the glasses. "You're right, Mr. Mitchell. You're right. That's more important to me than you know."

To his astonishment, the Dodge jerked again as Ed slammed the shift lever into park. A second later his new old friend was out his door and onto Dewey like metal to a magnet. Not-so-gently, he took the big man's arm and urged him half a dozen steps away from the truck. His words were inaudible, but his jaw thrust in and out at Dewey like a fencer's blade.

"Go, Ed!" Dawson cheered.

"No, no." Gray held his pounding temples in his hands. "This is a disaster."

Two minutes later, Ed slipped back into the cab, as calm as if he'd never left. They passed Dewey, who rubbed his chin with a hooded stare. Once Ed handed his paid slip to the attendant at the lumberyard gate, they were on the road back to Kennison Falls.

"I'm sorry." Gray's voice echoed dully in his own head. "I knew this was a bad idea."

"Give it up," Ed admonished. "You're a free man. You got a right to go where you like."

"What did you say to him?" Dawson asked.

"I told him if he cares for Abby, and you should know he does, by the way, he'll keep his mouth shut for the next few weeks. I think he saw my point."

Gray had stopped listening. Ed had just explained a whole lot about Dewey's attitude. "He and Abby have something . . . together?"

"No, but not for lack of effort on his part. Folks say he'd marry her tomorrow if she'd look twice at him. I don't listen to that sort of talk." He winked at a smiling Dawson.

"I'm serious. If there's anything between them, I shouldn't be out there with her."

His heart's nervous riff angered him. Maybe he shouldn't have kissed Abby yesterday, since more than a few complications had risen from that selfish act. But she certainly hadn't kissed him as if there'd been anybody else. A latent thrill detonated deep and low at the memory.

"Weren't you listening?" Ed asked. "Dewey Mitchell's not a problem."

"Fine." Gray mashed on his throbbing temples. "But those sound like famous last words to me."

"WHAT THE HELL are you doing here?" Chris Boyle's stunned tone and his wide, caught-in-the-gun-sight eyes brought Elliott a deep satisfaction.

"I could ask the same," he replied. "What's a big-shot manager doing in an empty dressing room? Finding a dramatic place to slash your wrists over the money your golden goose is costing you?"

A folding chair flew unexpectedly through the air, landing three feet from Elliott's boot and shattering the quiet with a metallic screech. Chris rushed him, a tan-cashmere-sweatered grizzly advancing on fresh meat.

"Where is he, Boyle?" Elliott held his ground, unperturbed. "Or, have you lost control of him?"

Chris grabbed a fistful of Elliott's T-shirt and hyperventilated half-a-dozen garlicky breaths straight up his nostrils. "You ballsy little bastard." Then, as if catching himself, he released Elliott's shirt with a five-finger flick, as if throwing off a distasteful bug.

"Ballsy? Maybe, but I'll never have the stones to be a good manager. That takes, how should I put it? Creativity. Framing me for that picture, for example? Very creative. And now we all know he suspects I took the one of his mother. Once again, I think that was a hundred percent your genius."

"I had nothing to do with it. You're getting desperate to find a way out of this, Elliott."

"Me? You're a very rich man because of Gray Covey, and you're the one who's desperate to keep it that way. I believe you'll do just about anything to keep him in the news, including pull something cruel like that stunt with his mother." Elliott curled his lip in distaste. "It was supposed to bring him running back here, but it didn't work, did it? He's playing hooky with his son, and I know there's a woman involved. What if I sort of let something like that slip?"

"I'd say you don't have your facts right, and I could prove it." An anxious tic at Chris's temple gave Elliott the first sign that the manager's words were bluster.

"What if I simply planted more and more very big questions about Gray's character in peoples' minds? The public will only take so much spin before its skepticism kicks in and you have a bona fide scandal. Gray blowing off concerts and lying to his fans because he's pissed over his worst chart position in twenty years? His loyal peeps won't like that. Tell me where he is, and maybe I'll keep my mouth shut."

Chris's pasty, businessman's complexion deepened in color like a marshmallow held to the fire, even as his voice took on a false tone of camaraderie. "What do you want, Elliott? I'm sure we can figure this out."

"You know? I'm sure we can. Tell me where he is, and give me exclusive rights to his story."

"I can't do that, and you know it. It's not my right to decide those things."

"That's bullshit. You've been deciding these things for twenty years. You know full well all I have to do is print something, anything, and all hell breaks loose. For the tiny price I'm asking, I'll lead the media on a wild golden goose chase as long as I can, and that could be valuable since I'm hardly the only one digging for information. Gray's the hottest quarry out there right now."

Chris's lips twitched. "Why should I believe you?"

"Gray tossed me out of the band's life without a trial. I owe him no loyalty, but I want to be the one who deals with him. I want my moment before the vultures swoop. Then you can spin it however you like."

He withstood one more, long, angry assessment before Chris capitulated.

"Fine. I'll tell you where he is, but here's my deal. I see any story you write, any picture you take, before it goes to press. If new pictures turn up anywhere before that, a kitten-killer will have a better reputation in this town than you do."

Elliott snorted. "I have no doubt someone's reputation will end up on the chopping block, Chris. No doubt at all."

It DIDN'T MATTER what control Ed thought he had over Dewey Mitchell; now that a jealous suitor knew Gray was here, the world was only moments behind. That the safe time left was limited Gray had no doubt.

He powered his last wheelbarrow full of reeking shavings and mounded horse turds out the barn door. Ribbons of sweat bound his T-shirt to his back, and dust-tinged grit freckled his skin. He grunted and wondered how he'd come to such a lower-than-sewer-water task. And, more remarkably, how come that task had become more soothing than an arena full of adoration. He should have felt tired. He should have been cussing at the flies and the sweat smeared across his forehead from wiping it with his shoulder. Instead, the pungent horse-tailings were all that kept him from punching frustrated holes in the stall walls. He'd cleaned all eight stalls since returning from the lumberyard. He wished he had eight more.

His band would be gobsmacked, his mother . . . an-noyingly delighted.

His mother. He wondered if he'd be in this position at all were she well . . .

"Hi." A soft voice interrupted his sightless musings over the manure pile. "What's wrong?"

He lifted his eyes to find Kim, in short jean shorts, snug yellow tank top bearing a regal, full-sized horsehead, and rubber muck boots, eyeing him from the barn door. His heart scrambled into panic. Time and again he'd shown he had no skill for handling Kimmy's out-of-control crush, and the teasing little smile she wore now, one reserved strictly for him, proved he hadn't made a dent in her teenage infatuation.

"Nothing's wrong." He smiled. "Enjoying the view."

"Very weird."

"Hmmm, your mother says that about me."

She frowned at the mention of her mother but curbed it as she sidled closer. "Weird is fine by me."

"What do you have there?" He distracted her by pointing to a slender, rolled-up magazine under her arm.

"A tack catalog. Hey, can I show you what I'm saving for?"

"Sure."

She opened to a page filled with pictures of saddles. They all looked the same to Gray, but Kim pointed very specifically. "There."

"A new saddle."

"Yeah, a dressage saddle. See, I have a jumping saddle with these short, curved side flaps, but the dressage saddles have long, straight flaps. They keep your legs in the right position when you're not jumping." She pointed out the differences and explained, with excitement Gray found blessedly lacking in flirtatiousness, why she'd chosen the one she wanted.

But he'd never have guessed a slab of leather could cost thousands—as much as a high-end Les Paul guitar. "Big goal," he said. "How's it looking?"

"I get paid for teaching a few lessons, and for extra work around here. Sylvia pays me for helping in her garden. It might take years, but I'll get it eventually."

Gray could detect no complaint in her voice. In fact,

she shrugged with a resigned smile. She really was a good kid. Unselfish and kind. Like her mother. "Times are tough all over," he teased, "especially for a couple of single women trying to feed eight horsey mouths."

Kim's smile blinded him like a spotlight. "Too bad horses can't eat soup and soda crackers, Mom says."

"You and your mom work hard. It must be a bigger struggle than it looks, keeping up a place like this."

"There's always something to pay for." Kim shrugged. "She jokes about selling horses, but she never will. I think she'd starve us before losing them."

"She'd never starve a great kid like you."

He hadn't realized a teenager could make her eyes smolder. Or pout like a baby Marlene Dietrich. "I'm not a kid," she said slowly.

"Oh, yes you are." His brain raced while he called himself every kind of idiot for letting her corner him. With high cowardice, he grabbed the wheelbarrow handles and nodded toward the barn. "I'm done here. What are you up to now?"

She harrumphed with cute disappointment. "I came to help you. It's too hot to ride until later."

"Well . . ." He grasped for something, anything. "You told me when we first met you play clarinet. How come I've never heard you practice?"

Her sultry pout disappeared. "I'd never practice in front of you."

"That's silly. Tell me when you want to practice, and I'll come outside."

She shook her head. "The only reason to practice

would be for music camp in August, but that might not even happen this year."

"Camp?" His interest was honestly piqued. "Tell me about that."

"Four days of lessons with guest instructors and a contest where we play solos for a judge. At the end there's an all-day concert. Like Woodstock. Our band teacher, Mrs. Baxter, calls it Kabbagestock."

"Ummm?" He laughed. "I don't get it."

"It's part of the Kabbage Festival. That's our town celebration. Lame, I know."

"No." He scratched his head. "Got it now. Sounds great. Why might it not happen?"

"They say school budget cuts. They won't know until the city council meets the middle of July if we did enough fund-raising to help."

"School budget cuts." He tamped down a familiar anger. "Don't get me started. Well, Kimmy, I think you should prep for it anyway. You're playing something for the contest?"

"Yeah, but it's a stupid-hard piece. Mrs. Baxter is tough."

"I suppose I could help you."

"Seriously?" Her eyes morphed into saucers of delight, no lessening of her hero worship in sight. "Really, seriously?"

"Seriously, but I warn you, I'd make Mrs. Baxter seem like a fairy godmother." Which was perfect, he thought. He needed to be authoritative and unattractive.

She obviously didn't see it that way. "Oh, that's amaz-

ing. Thank you, Gray. Thank you!" She sneaked under his
defenses by wrapping her arms around his waist.

"It's no big deal." He swallowed and peeled her firmly
away, his heart suddenly quailing at what he'd rashly offered. You tell me when you're ready."

"This is absolutely the best idea ever." She nudged in
for another squeeze and then let him go, her eyes glistening with pleasure as she backed away.

He closed his eyes. No. On further thought, this could
turn out to be the worst idea ever.

Chapter Sixteen

ROSCOE RELEASED A rare, sonorous bark of warning as he and Gray rounded the trees in Abby's driveway after their run the next morning. Gray squinted toward the house and made out an unfamiliar, silver SUV next to the lawn as Roscoe took off at a gallop. He winced, still gulping air after his five-mile sprint, but trotted after the dog, concern brewing.

His fears erupted when he reached the vehicle, and Chris appeared from behind the house. Impeccable as ever, his overly jolly face and his authoritative, self-assured demeanor, sent Gray's stomach plunging and his pulse pounding in dismay. Dawson strode behind Chris, storm clouds in his eyes, and Kim followed, *her* eyes bright with excitement.

"My dad won't—" Dawson's vehement objection got cut off.

"And just like that he appears!" Chris clapped his hands together and twisted them like a satisfied Scrooge. "Right on time."

"What are you doing here?" Gray demanded.

Chris waggled his eyebrows, and four more people appeared behind him as if he'd conjured them from the void. Roscoe gave three ecstatic barks at the glut of potential new friends.

"Traitor," Gray muttered.

"If Mohammed won't come to the mountain . . ." Chris shot both forefingers in Gray's direction. "Meet your album cover shoot crew."

"My *what*?" Gray's breathing turned to wheezing. "Are you out of your mind bringing people here?"

"They're on your payroll, and they know it means their jobs if they divulge your whereabouts."

Gray drew a lungful of air and blew it out slowly. "I asked you to reschedule this shoot."

"I did," Chris laughed. "To a new location. And, my God, it's perfect. We've already scoped out two sites. That barn down below is amazing. And that garden behind the house . . . Dawson, you're a genius."

With a warning shake of his head, Gray stopped his son from retorting. "This is a private home, Chris, you can't just barge in with equipment and people. You have to have permission."

"I told 'em you'd kick them out," Dawson said, his voice trembling. "Abby will have cows."

"Yes. She will." That was partly the cause of the ache growing in Gray's gut.

"I don't think that will be a problem." Chris set his hand on Kim's shoulder.

"It'll be awesome, Gray." Kim spoke for the first time. "If a few of the flowers or the barns ends up as your album cover, I'm sure Mom won't mind. I'll talk to her."

"It might not be so awesome in the end, Kimmy." He spoke without looking at her and caught Chris's gaze with unfettered anger. How dare he solicit behind-the-back help from a vulnerable teenager? Of course Kim would think this was a grand idea.

"We're not doing this now," he said.

"But we are." Chris's smile firmed, the jolliness dissipated. "Despite what you think, there are still deadlines to meet. This is an expensive compromise, so just do it, and we'll be out of your hair in a couple of hours."

The deal was clearly done. As Gray watched helplessly, his son fuming beside him, a woman named Penny, who worked in his wardrobe department, pulled two large suit bags from the back of the car and toted them to the house. A make-up artist named June followed with a case large enough to prepare the cast of *Cats*. And the photography duo of John and Tammy hauled bags of tripods and lighting umbrellas across the lawn. Chris dug his way deeper into Kim's heart by sending her scurrying wherever she could be of help, and she eased into the commotion like a seasoned veteran.

"Why are you letting him get away with this?" Dawson whispered angrily.

"Tell me how I could make it any different? You know Chris when he's on his game." Gray looked at his running watch. "We have four and a half hours until Abby comes home. Let's just work on getting them out of here by then."

"Grow a little backbone, Dad, and we wouldn't have to work on anything." Dawson huffed out an exasperated breath. "Fine. I'll go help Kim and see if I can unbrainwash her."

"Covey," Chris snapped as Dawson slipped away. "Get in and take a shower. June will be ready for you in twenty minutes. She'll do your hair."

Gray caught the sleeve of Chris's favorite shirt, a striped, linen Armani. The man was not an advertisement for frugality. "You are going to make these people hurry, do you hear me? I'll be out of the shower in ten."

"Yes, sir." Chris patted his arm consolingly. "Leave it to me."

ABBY EDGED AROUND the corner of her house, following voices she didn't recognize, eyeing the silver Lexus in her driveway. She heard a male laugh. She heard a lilting woman's voice and the words, "This would be stunning if we move the umbrella into the middle here and diffuse that glare." And just as she rounded into full view of an alarming anthill of activity, Gray added, "Damn it, no!"

Curiosity hit her first. Anger replaced it almost immediately. Three people waded through her wildflower garden, two carrying huge, white diffusing umbrellas and lights, and the third a tripod so hefty it could have held a farrier's anvil.

"Excuse me, please." She shouted above the buzz, and

for an instant everyone turned. Gray's eyes were stricken, his face literally a mask. "May I ask just what is going on here? You." She pointed at the man with the tripod. "And you, and you. Get out of my flowers."

"Mom!" Kim raced toward her, hair flying and face brimming with excitement. "Wait till you hear! This is going to be Gray's new album cover."

Abby's stomach turned to lead. She stared at Gray, who only managed a defeated-looking shrug. A slim, handsome man with graying temples, crisply pressed white dress pants, and an expensive-looking, black-and-gray striped shirt rolled at the sleeves headed her way. He stretched out his hand long before he reached her.

"You must be Abby. I'm so happy to meet you. I certainly have heard good things."

"Then I'm afraid you have the advantage," she replied, more coolly than she should have. He seemed too smooth and perfect, his smile like an ad for how white your teeth could be.

"I'm Chris Boyle, Gray's manager."

For a moment she was speechless. This was the god, the magician behind the singer? She cleared her head and took his hand. "Well. Mr. Boyle. To say this is a surprise would be putting it mildly." She lifted her eyes back to her garden. "I'm sorry," she called again. "Was I unclear? I asked you to take that equipment out of my garden."

"We're very nearly finished," Chris said solicitously. "I apologize for intruding. This shoot was scheduled months ago, and rather than make Gray travel, we came to him."

Intruding? Abby stared at the rivers of extension

cords, the small mountain of equipment cases and bags, the three tables set up for holding miscellaneous tools. This was less an intrusion than an enemy occupation.

"Mom, seriously, this has been so cool," Kim broke in. "You should see what they have to do to get Gray ready for this. And John lets me look through the camera lens to see what they're shooting."

"It sounds really fascinating, honey." She barely looked at her daughter. Instead, she focused on Gray, coming toward them like a felon turning himself in.

"Abby, I'm really sorry. I swear I had no idea this was coming."

"I'm sure you didn't."

She clung to her angry resolve even though he was a sight to behold. A pair of jeans even tighter and sexier than his thousand-dollar Levi's skimmed his long legs. A black chambray shirt draped his shoulders, buttons open to his mid chest. His hair had been sprayed and molded to look naturally windblown. But the most distracting thing about him was the mask, courtesy of at least half a dozen bottles-worth of makeup caking his face.

"They'll be out of here in half an hour. I promise."

"That's fine," she said calmly. "But they'll be out of the garden in half a minute. I'm going in to change. If any of my wildflowers are damaged . . ." She smiled and left the threat unspoken. She didn't really have one she could back up, anyway. What was she going to do? Sue Gray Covey's manager?

"Abby." Gray caught her arm as she turned. "I really am sorry."

"Hey." She gently slipped his grasp. "You warned me this was going to happen, didn't you?"

The photographers took closer to half an hour to vacate the garden, and the entire entourage took nearly an hour and a half to leave. Abby never returned to watch the proceedings. She would have said things she couldn't take back. Glancing periodically out the window gave her all the sense she wanted of a photo shoot's painstaking nature. It was probably impressive, but she missed a lot of it because of the red haze fogging her eyes.

Finally, the back door opened and closed. Abby waited at the kitchen sink but the only one who approached her was Dawson. "The dickheads are gone."

For the first time, Abby felt a genuine smile slip into place. She faced Dawson's angry visage, grasped his temples between her palms, and made him bend over so she could kiss him on the crown. "I could tell you were on my side. Thank you. Where's your father?"

"The wimp? He went to wash the gunk out of his hair and take off his drag-queen face."

Abby actually laughed. "Here now, be respectful."

"Why? He was a gigantic jerk."

"Yeah," she nodded. "He kind of was. But, they're all gone now, and that's what I care about. Is Kim in the barn?" He nodded. "She's afraid of me now?" He grinned. "Good. I'm going out to check on my flower garden."

"I'm not sure you want to."

She sighed and stroked his cheek. "Face it head-on, kiddo. That's all I can do."

One obvious path of partially trampled flowers led to the middle of the garden, where someone had made an attempt to revive a small, flattened patch. Upon closer inspection, she found a few broken stems and a couple of gouges in the dirt. Mostly, the delicate anemones and coneflowers, wild bergamot and her favorite purple blazingstar simply lay dazed and bruised. She knelt and tilled the hard soil with her fingers, coaxing slender stems and knowing she shouldn't be angry. She'd asked for this when she'd talked Gray into staying.

"Abby?" His voice actually made her start. "I can't tell you how sorry I am."

She leapt to her feet and spun, her anger bubbling. "Stop saying that."

"Okay." Taken aback, he waited for her to speak again, but she didn't give him the satisfaction. His hair was damp but natural once more, and he'd removed the dreadful make up. Shuffling uncomfortably, he looked over the garden. "Chris showed up without so much as a phone call and with everyone in tow," he said. "There wasn't anything I could do."

Abby caught sight of Dawson, listening by the corner of the house, before she muttered, "Obviously."

"What's that supposed to mean?"

"I mean, Gray, that I asked several times for those people to leave my flowers alone. That's the only thing I asked for in the five minutes I stood here. Your manager blew me off, and so did you."

"I did not."

"You did nothing. Same difference."

"Now wait a minute. I told them no many times. It did no good. They don't listen to me, either."

Color crept up his neck, whether in anger or embarrassment Abby couldn't tell, but for once she didn't care. Watching him struggle, she realized her anger stemmed as much from Gray failing to protect her flowers as it did from feeling invaded.

"Okay. Did you go sit in there and have your picture taken?"

"I had no choice."

"That's the stupidest thing I've ever heard." Her voice raised a notch. "You couldn't have refused? You could have told them to take your picture by the tree, or even next to the garden, but you did it in the one, the *one*, place I asked them not to go. If you can't stand up for that much, how am I supposed to believe you want to protect us from all the bad things you keep saying could happen because you're here?"

"That's not fair," he said. "You sound like my son. I've tried to keep Chris off my back and still on my side, yet when I asked him to reschedule this shoot he came anyway. I'm trying to keep Dawson happy and you and my mother out of the spotlight, yet everything is unraveling the longer I stay. My band thinks I'm crazy. I have a friend turned saboteur. What exactly does everyone expect from me?"

"I expect you to stick to the path you choose. If you want to stay here because it's private, then keep it private—no matter who shows up. You know what? I would have felt like a queen if you'd just stuck up for me about the darn flowers."

"Screw the flowers, Abby." He glared at her now, his pale eyes flashing. "What's this really about?"

"About feeling safe. Just like you're always talking about."

"It's about not being a wimp." Dawson moved from his quiet corner and stood beside Abby. "I think you're afraid of Chris. I think he can tell you something is important for your career, and you'll do it. I'll bet he even told you to put Grandma in a nursing home, so you wouldn't waste so much time taking care of her."

"That does it!" Gray's hold on any kind of calm burst like a broken dam. He pointed at Dawson and stepped to within inches of his face. "You've said one thing too many, and you and I are going to settle this once and for all. I want you to get in the house and start packing your bag. I'll be up to talk to you in five minutes."

"Dad! I, no—"

"*Don't* talk back. You get no say in this decision."

He turned back to Abby, and her heart jumped to her throat. She'd seen him irritated to the point of gruffness and angry at circumstances beyond his control, but this tight, self-righteous fury was new.

"I'm sorry I disappointed you." His eyes still sparked but his voice calmed slightly for her. "I wouldn't hurt you for the world, Abby. You've done more for us than I ever had a right to expect. But it's clear I need to take Dawson on my own before I have to start the tour again. There are some things he needs to understand."

"You're going to uproot him over something like this?"

"*This* is a big deal." He started to reach for her cheek but pulled his finger quickly away. "If anyone tracked Chris, it'll be better for you if I'm not here. And now you know exactly what I mean."

"Oh, Gray, c'mon . . ."

"I'll let you know exactly when we're leaving. I have to make a couple of calls." He turned for the house, but then looked back. "I'm paying for the damage to the flowers, too. And I'll tell you just like I told Dawson, you don't get a say in the decision."

If she'd been ready to forgive him anything, he wiped out her sympathy in that second. Of all the egotistical, unfeeling, pig-headed, cliché rich boy . . . Abby seethed as he headed for his son. He didn't get it. He probably never would.

STANDING IN THE elegant lobby of the Bridgeport Care Complex in Richmond, Virginia, Gray set his hand on a subdued Dawson's shoulder and rubbed against the tension. "Okay?" he asked.

"Grandma has a giant garden. She grows amazing flowers. She has a cool house. Why does she have to live here?" His voice was tiny.

Gray nodded. Laura Covey had been a fiercely strong woman who'd owned her own land long before marrying Neil and had protected it fiercely since his death five years before. For her to be in a place like this, however ritzy, was unjust.

Exotic-wood wainscoting and furniture in blue and burgundy brocade looked like they belonged in a Rockefeller sitting room. Plants abounded. The half-dozen elderly men and women seated in the room were well-dressed and involved in reading, knitting, or quiet discussion.

"It's hard." Gray gave a last squeeze to Dawson's shoulder.

A young woman behind a carved reception desk smiled in practiced welcome, and then her mouth fell open. "Mr. Covey!"

"C'mon, Brenda." He knew all the staff. He'd insisted on meeting them so there'd be no screeching scenes. "You know it's Gray."

"I do. Gray." She flushed. "Your mother will be so happy to see you. She talks about you all the time."

"I'll be happy to see her, too." He took two visitor badges from her and handed one to Dawson. They didn't have to sign in, however. That deal had been struck to keep pages of the register from being stolen. Sometimes he hated his job.

The assisted living wing's hallways were lined with oak doors, many bearing flower wreaths or welcome signs. Most stood partially open as in the case of his mother's. Dawson remained pale and quiet as Gray rapped softly on the door.

"Mom?"

She sat in her favorite blue armchair in front of a sunny picture window, her nimble fingers pushing a needle through fabric in an embroidery hoop. A beautiful bouquet of roses and lilies sat on a nearby table. When he and Dawson stepped into the room, the expectant, quizzical smile, as if she were a child hoping for a gift, broke his heart, as it always did.

"Grandma?" Dawson finally came to life.

"Hello, dear," she said softly. "It's nice to see you."

He grinned, his eyes clearing, and glanced back at Gray. "See? She knows me." He bent to hug her and Gray's heart sank further knowing Dawson couldn't see the confusion in her eyes. "I miss you. I've been trying to come see you for a long time, but I couldn't reach you."

"Goodness." She patted him awkwardly. "I haven't heard that from you in ages. I'm thrilled you had time to take a break from your practicing."

Confusion fueled his son's frown. "Practicing?"

"Oh, no need to hide it, David. I know about your little band." Gray caught her eyes, and his beautiful, sixty-three-year-old mother, with nothing but a few lovely streaks of gray in her dark hair, didn't recognize him in the slightest. "You must be Spark. I've heard a lot about you."

Dawson's jaw dropped, and he staggered back. Gray caught his shoulders and held him.

"Mom, I'm David. This is Dawson. He only looks like me."

Her brow furrowed and she set her embroidery on the table. With a slender hand, she brushed at her light blue slacks. "Dawson?" A smile blossomed. "He's such a good baby. And your name is David, too? My son is David. Davy."

A small sob caught in Dawson's throat. Gray pulled him more tightly against his chest. "I know," he whispered. "Just talk to her. Sometimes she remembers."

"David told me he wants to start a rock band at Juilliard, can you imagine? I told him they'll kick him out." A girlish giggle escaped. "They won't, I know, he's too good, and he'll probably be good at rock 'n roll too. I wish he wanted to be a concert pianist, but . . ."

"He's done pretty well anyway, hasn't he?" Gray asked softly.

Her eyes clouded, and she stroked at her chin in obvious consternation. Then, as quickly as she'd grown agitated, she smiled and reached for Dawson's hand. "He is amazing isn't he?" She looked at him. "Twelve years old and they're letting you play with the high school band. Most mothers can't get their kids to practice at all, and you love it. I'm lucky."

"You always made me practice my guitar, Grandma. Just like you made Dad practice." Dawson's voice quavered, but Gray smiled encouragement. He remembered how awful it had been the first time his mother hadn't known him.

"Mom, look closely," he said. "I brought you a surprise. This is Dawson. Remember, he ran away? I found him and he's okay."

"Dawson?" She sat rigid a moment, her forehead creased in deep thought, but then she lifted her eyes and Gray had to hold back tears. Her green irises had cleared of all confusion.

"He shouldn't be in that school Ariel put him in, but

he shouldn't have run away." She turned. "You shouldn't have run away, young man. You scared me to death."

"Grandma? Grandma, do you know who I am?"

A flicker of sadness crossed her features, but she stroked his cheek when he knelt beside her. "I do, Dawson. Are you all right?"

"I came to see you, but they wouldn't tell me where you were. I went to Minnesota to stay with a friend."

"I knew David would find you." She looked to Gray. "Hi, handsome."

"Hi, beautiful."

"Do not run away again." She kissed Dawson's head.

"I won't, Grandma." He choked back tears and clung to her hand. Gray bent and kissed her temple.

"Minnesota? That's a long way away," she said.

"I was working for my friend's mom. She's really great, right, Dad?"

"She is. Very special." Gray swallowed against the lump in his throat and ignored the hole in his heart.

His mother looked at the pair of them for a long time, and Gray held his breath. There was never any telling how long her moments of lucidity would last. "So? What's wrong?"

"Wrong?" He exchanged looks with his son and let his shoulders slump. "She's quite angry with me at the moment, and I feel badly about it." He could never explain to her what an understatement that was.

"Why is she angry?"

"It's all mixed up with work, Mom."

"What is her name?"

"Abby."

"Abigail. One of my favorites. Work doesn't matter, David. You said she was special, and you don't say that often. That's what's important."

She looked down at Dawson's hand, still clutching hers, and lifted it to her lips.

"Sweet boy," she said. "I adore you, you know. And I always will in here," she touched her heart, "if not here." She did the same to her forehead, and tears finally spilled from Dawson's eyes.

He swiped at them with the back of one hand. "I love you, too, Grandma. Get better so you can go home, and I'll come and help you."

"Pretty flowers, Mom. Who are they from?" Gray tried changing the topic, but her brain didn't follow the new course. He saw it before she even answered.

"Flowers?" She glanced around the room till she found the vase. "Oh, of course. They're from Davy. He was by yesterday."

"No, don't go away yet, Grandma, don't . . ." Dawson buried his head in her lap, and the confusion returned to her eyes.

"Mom," Gray said, forcing his own voice not to break. "We're going to go get you a strawberry milkshake from downstairs. And some French fries, just like you love. C'mon Daw." He pulled the boy to a stand. The tough teen had been reduced to Jell-O and Gray knew he now needed a break. "We'll be right back and have a little party. Then we'll go down and you can show us the birds in the lobby."

"That sounds lovely. I'll get some plates and napkins." She rose with them and headed for her small kitchenette, where she kept paper plates, a few canned goods, and some sodas in the refrigerator.

"It's all right," he said to Dawson, when they'd left the room. "It is."

"It's not," he cried. "It's never going to be all right."

"If there is anywhere she can get help, it's here, Son. I just needed you to know. I didn't stuff her away. Moving Grandma here was the hardest decision I've ever made. But Pauline couldn't take care of her at home anymore. It was just too hard."

To his shock, Dawson threw his arms around Gray's waist and sobbed. Even though he pulled away, embarrassed, after only moments, Gray felt his own eyes well as he thumped his son on the back.

"Please can we go home to Abby's?" Dawson asked.

Gray hadn't made much peace with her before they'd left. He'd set another hundred-dollar bill on Abby's counter this morning before walking out the door, and now the memory of that alone appalled him. It was just another thing she'd asked that he'd ignored. He didn't understand her aversion to help, but he should at least respect it. And he missed her. But he'd cleared out of her life—how could he go back and put her right back in the same position?

"We'll stay here one night and visit Grandma again tomorrow. Then we'll decide what to do, okay?"

For once Dawson didn't argue.

Chapter Seventeen

ABBY GAZED SADLY at her wildflowers standing straight and strong in the steamy sunshine, dancing almost imperceptibly in a tiny, ineffectual breeze. She'd been such an idiot, raging over the garden. These were wildflowers, tough despite their fragile appearances. They sprang back after every frigid Minnesota winter, and they withstood ninety-degree days like this every summer. It was why she loved them.

And why no sign remained of the abuse they'd taken two days ago.

She stroked the heavy camera hanging from its strap around her neck. She hadn't ever really worried about her flowers; they'd been an excuse. An excuse to unload all her fears and hurt on Gray, when he'd been just as upset as she. She was still afraid. All she'd wanted was for him to stick up for her, and it had hurt that Chris and the photographers were more important to him. That's what frightened her—the possessiveness she'd felt after less than two weeks with him. He didn't belong to her; but she'd treated him as though he did.

The flowers swished, and Abby focused back on the garden, lifting the camera and squatting. A moment later Roscoe emerged and Abby snapped her shutter. She duck-walked backward, getting off four quick shots of the advancing doggy nose and drooling grin before he started barking like a maniac and she ran smack dab into a solid mass, toppled onto her butt, and screeched when a pair of hands reached to haul her up.

She scrambled to her feet and stared at the boy, who looked like he'd actually grown in forty-eight hours. "Jeez Louise! Dawson?"

"Hi."

He smiled, but his eyes were dull, his face drawn. "Sweetheart, what's wrong? Are you all right?"

A heartbeat later he'd wrapped his arms around her and laid his head on her shoulder. She held him with all her might, tears beading in her eyes at the emotions and need tensing the wiry, teenage body. She took a quick glance over his shoulder. Her heartbeat somersaulted with joy and relief.

"Hi," Gray echoed. His hesitant smile grew slowly, but his eyes shone more clearly than his son's did.

"I could kiss the pair of you. What happened? Where have you been?"

At the threat of kissing, Dawson pulled away, but his features were still wrapped in pale sorrow. "Grandma.

We went to see her. She mostly doesn't remember us." He chewed his lip at the difficult admission.

"Honey." She pushed at a lock of his caramel-colored hair, and he allowed that fussy gesture without a flinch. "I am so, so sorry. Tell me about it. Did she remember you at all?"

"A couple of times. But she kept thinking I was Dad and Dad was Spark."

"Oh, dear . . ." She trailed her fingers down his cheek, searching for words that would help, when she knew nothing would. "What did she say when she did know who you are?"

"That . . ." His gaze flickered between hers and his father's. ". . . I'm not supposed to run away anymore."

She tried to smile without the ache in her heart showing through. How could she care so much about a family she didn't know? "Then you need to take comfort in knowing your wise grandma isn't gone yet. She's absolutely right." Dawson didn't look at her. Abby touched his cheek again. "Isn't she?"

That got her a nod and, finally, a half-strength smile. "She always was a little bit bossy."

"And you wish she could be bossy all the time, right?"

He rubbed the heel of his palm across his nose as he nodded, like the child he still was pushing back his tears. Abby grabbed him into a hug again even though, this time, he squirmed.

"You don't have to let her go, Dawson," she said. "You don't have to be afraid of being sad. Start writing to her now. All the time. Tell her everything you're doing. We'll take lots of pictures of you so she can remember as long as possible."

"Really?" The whispered word barely made it past the emotion clogging his throat.

"Of course, really." She let him free and held up her camera. "I'll take them myself, okay? Have I told you how awfully glad I am you're back?"

He straightened and took a minute to compose himself. "I talked Dad into coming." He glanced again at Gray, who stood patiently a half-dozen steps away, a mix of confusion and, maybe, wonder on his face. Then Dawson shrugged. "But I didn't have to talk very hard." He stepped back. "I'm gonna go . . . put stuff away and . . ." He shrugged again. "Thanks."

"Sweetheart, nothing to thank me for."

Her heart danced through her chest as the boy passed his father, who laid a hand gently on his shoulder. They nodded almost imperceptibly at one another before Gray let him go and faced her. Her heart pounded in earnest.

She scanned him thoroughly, halting deliberately several times as if he'd disappear again if she finished looking. Instead, when she reached his beautiful, familiar face, the world felt whole once more.

"How do you do it?" he asked.

"What's that?"

"Tell him exactly what he should hear without threatening him. I barely get full sentences out without pissing him off."

"It's easy for me. I'm a neutral party." She wasn't, but

she couldn't yet put that into words. "You did the right thing, taking him, you know. But I'm glad you're back, too."

"I had to come back and get my money."

"Ah. Well, it's right where you left it."

"I'm sorry, Abby." He moved closer. "It was disrespectful to leave it. I was an ass all the way around."

"No, Gray, I was the idiot. I wasn't mad about the flowers, I—"

"You were mad for the same reason I was. Our safe haven was gone." Abby nodded, her eyes burning. "I didn't plan to come back. I wanted you to stay safe from that scene happening again." He stood directly in front of her, and his masculine spice blended with the scent of wild asters and columbine.

"But you had to get your money." A half-smile teased her lips.

The instant he lowered his head, hers lifted automatically, happy surprise surging through her veins like adrenaline. The exact moment he parted his lips in invitation, her tongue knew to slip in and stroke his. Their coolness and warmth swirled like the finest wine in her mouth, and she drank, reveling in the powerful shudders diving for her stomach.

He thrust his powerful tongue deep and then drew it out, pulling the strength from her knees as he bit gently on her lip. Their tongues tangoed again. And a third time. The exploration ended in sync and melded into a succulent kiss. Perfect. Flawless as a choreographed dance, yet unexpected as snow in summer.

"I see you have the old picture-taker out." He adjusted her camera strap like he was straightening a collar, trying to look like he could ignore what had just happened.

"You're a horrible influence. I should be fixing the screen door."

"No, Abby, it's good you were playing. I'm happy you were." He lifted her chin and cut off her protest. "I don't know whether it's wise to stay, or if I'm even welcome to stay, but I promised Dawson to finish out my vacation."

"Oh, all right," she whispered. "I haven't rented out your room yet."

A long, satisfying silence let her take him in again.

"So are you, uh, going to develop that film anytime soon?"

"What's it to you?" Biting softly on her bottom lip, she just barely avoided his eyes. Her stomach ached with desire that was way-too-suddenly out of control, and liquid sluiced to the aching spot between her legs.

"I had a short apprenticeship in a darkroom," he said into her ear. "I'm a fair assistant."

A movement and a flash of reflected light from the trees caught her eye, and her reply lodged in her throat. A creepy, watched sensation sent unpleasant shivers up her spine. "Did you see that?"

He nodded but continued to hold her tightly. "Are you expecting anyone?"

"No, but I'm pretty sure I saw someone or something over in the trees." She pulled back slightly in his arms, her brows creasing. "Let's go find out."

"Stop." He squeezed her shoulders gently and brought her attention back to him. She grinned when he smoothed her forehead with a finger. "You look like a little pit bull. Abby, I had to be told not to smoke around a barn; you need to be told not to go running off after potential people-in-trees."

"It's probably the dog." She nibbled his earlobe, and he groaned.

"Probably. The better part of valor is to—"

"Mom! Mom!! Come quick. Quiiiiick!"

Kim's shrill, panicked shriek sent Abby's heart plummeting to her feet then lurching into her throat. Desire fled. Gray blanched. "Oh, God," he cursed.

She pulled away and dragged the Minolta from her neck, dropping it next to the flower bed. A million unspeakable images sliced through her brain, as she and Gray raced down the driveway. Only when she saw Kim standing at the barn door, beckoning wildly, did the picture of her daughter lying broken on the ground from a fall disappear. But Kim's dusty face was streaked with rivulets of water, her breeches and T-shirt half-soaked.

"Kim, Kim, calm down, sweetie, what's wrong? Who's hurt?"

For an instant Kim froze. "Gray? Gray! You're back!"

"Yes, love, I'm here. But what's going on? You scared the hair off us."

"Ack! It's the hose in the tack room. I can't shut it off."

Abby tamped down a hysterical urge to giggle and then she was running again, past the hay to the tack room door where she stopped so abruptly Gray banged up against her. Together they stared into a Looney Tunes cartoon.

A black rubber hose attached to the old washing machine flailed like a demented snake, hissing water that drenched the floor, walls, ceiling and a half dozen saddles.

"I tried to wedge it in the sink," Kim gasped, her voice squeaky and breathless. "I was going to wash all the saddle pads, but everything went nuts as soon as I turned on the machine. I turned it off again, but the water kept coming."

"Oh, for crying out loud!" Abby rushed forward and grabbed the maniacal tubing, wrestling it safely into the laundry sink. "What would cause pressure like this?"

"The pressure tank still being full," Gray replied. "Where's the water shut off?"

"In the house, but I'll go. I'll never be able to explain where it is. Can you take this?" She transferred hold of the hose to Gray. "Kimmy, wipe the saddles before the leather gets . . ."

A fart-like sputter emanated from the hose, and without further warning it lost all tension. Two more convulsive spurts left it quiet in Gray's hands, its slow stream turning to a steady trickle that petered out as they watched.

"Touch of the master," Gray quipped and offered a smile, but Abby's thoughts flooded with sick horror. "Thank goodness, right?" Gray peered at her

She buried her face in her hands. "No, no, no. No way is this going to be good."

The cartoon theme continued when Dawson wheeled in like Wile E. Coyote chasing the Roadrunner. Abby almost heard the screech of his heels sliding to a stop.

"What's going on?" His chest expanded and contracted like a wheezing concertina.

"The washing machine hose went crazy, and now there's no water." Kim said. "Hi. Welcome home." Dawson gave her a sideways smile.

Gray cranked the knob on the washer and pulled. The machine only buzzed expectantly. Incapacitated with disbelief, Abby searched her mind for a solution and drew a pitiful blank. Gray tested the laundry sink faucets. They were similarly unresponsive.

He let out a grunt. "Yup, there seems to be a problem."

The colossal understatement sent fear through Abby's body, and she clamped her lips tight against the words in her mind. *Yeah, I'll tell you what the problem is, man who can lay a hundred dollars on the table without blinking. No money—that's the problem.*

The unkind thought pulled her up short. He'd already apologized for that, and this was not his fault. But why was she standing here like an imbecile? She handled things. She made decisions. A handsome guy showed back up and she went brain dead?

"Good observation, Dad."

Abby sputtered, and the next second she was sobbing, although, mercifully, her choking did sound like hysterical giggles.

"It's okay, Mom. It's okay." Kimmy put her arms around Abby's shoulders, and it helped. It was the way of things in their tiny family, and suddenly the two men standing around were no longer sapping the strength from her. "It's probably easy to fix."

"Are you sure you can't explain where the pressure tank is?" Gray asked.

"In the basement." She sighed. "You know about wells and pressure tanks?"

He actually looked wounded. "I grew up in rural Virginia. My dad made me learn all kinds of stuff because I might need it someday. I'm not a totally worthless geek."

"Sorry. I didn't mean it that way."

"I'm not promising I can fix anything, but it won't hurt to look."

"I appreciate it, I do. But I have a bad feeling. When you can use 'no water' and 'well' in the same sentence, you're rarely talking about a problem that can be fixed with duct tape."

"We'll for dang sure do our best, 'eh? C'mon Daw. Let's go pretend we're superheroes."

"Who has to pretend?" Dawson didn't crack a smile.

Despite the valiant turning of dials and adjusting of tubing, the Covey Superheroes were unsuccessful as well as smudged and rumpled when they were forced to give up on restoring water. Despite her heart sinking steadily deeper into panic, Abby couldn't help but be enamored of the father/son duo working so hard for her. Deep in the recesses of her heart, she remembered what a family could be. But it was too much to dwell on.

"I'll call Orv at Barrett's Well Service," she said. "I'm sure he'll know exactly what needs to be done." *And how big a loan I'll have to take out from the Bank of Someone Who Doesn't Know Me.*

The weight of Gray's hands on her shoulders almost loosened the hold she'd grasped on her tears. Dirt stained his shoulder, and a dark, wet spot spread down his thigh. His blue eyes offered sympathy in the dim light of the musty old basement.

"Is there a quiet spot in town or nearby, where I can take us all to dinner?" He massaged gently, imperceptibly with his fingers. "We can't cook without water."

"Beefaroni." Her voice dulled even though she intended to joke.

"As much as I love Beefaroni," he smiled at their memory, "I think you need a break."

"I don't know. Are you sure you want to chance it?"

"Yes, to get you away from here for a little while."

"We could go to the Loon Feather," Abby said. "It's mid-week so it should be pretty quiet. I could call Karla and ask for the booth."

"*The* booth?" Gray's grin widened. "This is a big place, then."

"Huge for a town of eight hundred."

"Let's do it." He slapped his thigh and did a ridiculous jig. "C'mon kids we're all going to the big city."

Dawson gaped as if his dad had grown an extra nose, and Kim's slightly horrified stare gave a rare indication that she thought Gray had returned from his trip as the totally un-coolest-dude on Earth.

"Welcome back," Abby said dully. "Don't I know how to throw a homecoming?"

An hour later, at the Loon's door, Abby checked Gray with a hand on his arm.

"We should miss the dinner crowd, but I won't be able to keep you a secret from Karla."

"Listen." Sincerity laced his words. "The only reason I care is because of you and Kim."

A scrabbling of little bird feet, along with Lester's rewarding wolf whistle, greeted them as they entered, and Gray, delighted, bent to the cage. "Hey, now there's a great greeting!" He adopted his best DeNiro. "You talkin' ta me, sweetheart?"

Dawson rolled his eyes. "Will you quit being such a dork?"

"This is Lester," Abby chuckled. "And his mate, Cotton. Howdy Stranger." She cooed at the white bird and explained the rules.

Kim repeated the line, and Cotton stared indifferently. Gray gave a try, and Cotton merely fluffed her feathers.

"Give it up, you losers." Dawson stepped forward with a swagger, and Abby winked at Gray. "Howdy Stranger. Hey Cotton. Howdy Stranger." He sounded ten years younger and paid no attention to his dad's curious stare.

The doleful gaze vanished from the white cockatiel's face, and she opened and closed her beak, jumping a quarter inch forward on her perch. "Ha, Ha," she gurgled.

"Howdy stranger. C'mon, girl, you can say it."

"H, how."

"One of these days, buddy," Abby nodded, feeling strangely proud. "This is the closest anyone gets to enticing her. She took a liking to Dawson right away."

"She thinks he's cu-ute." Kim stuck her tongue out, and Dawson threw an elbow at her.

Abby's heart swelled. The emotional warmth of a squabbling family freed her momentarily from the weight of a broken well. She glanced around the nearly-empty café and led the way across the floor. "Karla's probably in the kitchen. We can go sit."

Lester accompanied them with "Colonel Bogey." Gray turned to stare. By the time they'd reached the booth, Lester was on to "Andy Griffith."

"That's one talented bird."

"See if you think so by the end of dinner." Kim grimaced. "You'll be whistling 'Colonel Bogey' from your padded cell."

Gray laughed out loud. "Funny girl."

Kim giggled and bumped purposely into his side. Abby sighed, wishing her daughter still thought he was dorky.

"Abby!" As she and Gray settled into the booth, backs to the door, Karla bustled out of the kitchen all swinging pony tail and endless smile. "Kim, Dawson, how are you guys?" She reached the table and settled her gaze on Gray. "And this must be Dawson's . . ."

It happened. Karla's smile froze into a distorted comedy mask, her eyes shining with a slightly crazed light of incomprehension. Abby had never seen the live reaction. If she'd imagined it would be cool, it wasn't. Just awkward.

"Dawson's dad." Gray filled the silence. "That's me. And you must be Karla, the mastermind behind Kabbagestock. I'm Gray. Very pleased to meet you."

Dang, he's so good. "Karla, breathe." Abby poked her friend in the hip. "Yes, it's him, so get it over with—whatever you have to do."

"Oh, gosh, I'm sorry." Karla recovered and adjusted her glasses. "This is . . . this is, uh, amazing. Gray, it's a real honor to meet you. I'm a huge fan."

"That means a lot, Karla. I appreciate it. And I'm sorry we've sprung this—me—on you with no warning. I don't like to do that."

"I . . . well, I guess now the great mystery of your whereabouts has been solved." She smiled with false calm at Abby. "You are in serious trouble."

"I'm always in trouble with you." Warm affection filled her as Karla continued to search for equilibrium. "You can see why I couldn't tell you. We really need your help to keep this a secret. At least until he leaves."

"You know I'll do everything I can. But what kind of help?"

"Keep this to yourself. And if anyone comes around looking for Gray, give me a call?"

Karla's giggle was high and girlish. "Unbelievable."

"Yeah, I know. It is."

"Can I ask how long you plan to stay?" Karla focused on Gray with the steadiest look she'd managed so far.

"We're still figuring that out." Abby caught his quick glance in Dawson's direction. "I'm supposed to go back to work next week."

Dawson's reaction was unreadable. They hadn't been back long enough to discuss what came next.

"Aren't you playing a show in St. Paul at the end of July?"

"Yes, ma'am," he said. "I promise you'll be one of the first to know if they blacklist me."

Karla blew out a deep breath, but her wide-eyed smile wouldn't quite disappear. "Tell you what. If you need a change of venue, we'll put you onstage at Kabbagestock in a heartbeat. Don't think that wouldn't get the city council to pony up some bucks." Her cheeks pinkened as she belatedly realized what she'd said and to whom. "Phew, sorry, Gray. I'll put my waitress hat back on and be professional now, okay? I assume you came to order dinner, not have me act like a groupie."

Abby had to give Karla credit. She'd recovered from her fan-shock with a perfect combination of appreciation and self-deprecation.

"Groupies are entirely different from appreciative new friends." Gray's schmoozy smile was appealing when it wasn't aimed at her, Abby thought. "I've heard about this camp you organize every summer. If you weren't working I'd make you sit and tell me how it works."

Karla's embarrassed pink turned to pleased-and-flustered red. "Gosh! Thanks, but you don't want to get me going, much as I'd love the chance." She composed herself with a warm smile. "Now, tell me what I can get you to drink."

When she'd scurried back to the kitchen, Abby caught Gray's eyes. "Whatever kind of fan she was before, she's a lifelong one now, Mr. Covey. You do know how to schmooze."

Gray scrubbed a finger along the crease of his nose, more embarrassed than Karla had been. "Now, there's a skill to be proud of."

Lester let out a brand new wolf whistle and followed it immediately with the theme for Mayberry's finest. He halted mid-song, let fly another whistle, then started Andy's theme anew.

Abby peered around the bench. Dewey stood at the doorway. "Good grief, doesn't he ever work?"

"What's wrong?" Gray asked.

"Don't look around."

She pushed him further into the corner of the booth and squeezed more tightly next to him, hoping Dewey wouldn't see her before he sat down. Dawson leaned out from the table. "It's Dewey," he said unnecessarily. "He already knows Dad is here."

"Excuse me?" Abby glared at him.

All at once some great secret stood between Dawson and speech. Abby turned to Gray. He tossed back a be-atific smile and arched his brows as he fingered the sleeve of her T-shirt. "How *you* doin'?" he asked like a Brooklyn letch.

"What is wrong with you two?" she asked in a strangled whisper. "Where in the world would you have met Dewey Mitchell? You just got back."

Gray squirmed. "One day, while you were working, Ed asked for some help with . . . ah, something. Dewey ran into us."

"Up at Ed's place?"

"Not exactly."

"Tell me exactly."

"Abby, look, I can explain later." Gray stroked her thigh beneath the table. She waited for him to remove his hand; instead he squeezed above her kneecap. Her breath nearly choked her. "Ed had a little chat with Dewey, who promised he wouldn't leak a word."

"Why didn't you tell me? I could have gone and talked to him before now."

Gray's whisper pulsed against her ear, his breath hot, his words inaudible to the kids. "Maybe I didn't want you to go talk to him."

There was a snappy comeback somewhere in the universe, but it floated out of her reach. Her throat seized like hot winds from every desert on the planet had sucked it dry, and insistent soft pressure, just under the hem of her shorts, sent shocks racing the length of her thigh. Her fingers slid into the valleys between his prominent knuckles. Gray flipped his hand beneath hers, laced their fingers together, and gave a squeeze. Abby forced herself not to slip under the table and babble incoherently.

"You'd better hope Ed had big time power over him," she croaked, her voice powerless. Gray only grinned at her, and, to her relief, Dewey sat without seeing them.

They'd all tucked into their meals when Lester's fourth wolf call of the evening made them pop their heads up yet again. Abby froze when she saw Dewey had moved and could now see directly into the booth. He snared her gaze with concern and censure in his eyes. She swiveled her head to see a tall, wiry man with a thick, blond mustache that looked like it weighed more than he did. The newcomer gazed ominously around the restaurant.

For a moment Abby prayed he was just choosing his table, and her heart gave a vain stutter when the man's eyes fixed on her pictures. He studied them for several moments but then went back to scanning the room. When his eyes found Dewey, Abby's would-be suitor bobbed his head once. The Judas gesture sent dread trickling into Abby's stomach.

"Gray?" she whispered as mustache man headed in their direction. "Somebody's here."

Chapter Eighteen

"HELLO, GRAY."

Every visible muscle, sinew, and inch of skin on Gray's frame went rigid when the man stood beside their table. "Abby, let me out please."

At his disquieting tone, she didn't consider questioning him, and he exited the booth so quickly she barely saw him move. She stood back with no idea what to expect. Dawson's features hadn't been this shocked since Gray's arrival, and Kim followed the action in nervous fascination. They all gasped when Gray splayed his right hand on the man's chest and shoved him like a rag doll against the pine wainscoting next to the booth.

"What are you doing here, you son of a bitch? What were you doing photographing my mother?"

"I took no photos of your mother. Take it easy, man. You don't want a scene, especially since there are still very few people who know you're here in Watercan Falls, Minnesota."

Gray let him loose, a tic pulsing in the center of one dimple, his eyes full of ice daggers. "Get out of here, St. Vincent."

"But you asked so nicely why I came."

"I changed my mind."

This was Elliott St. Vincent? Abby's heart plummeted as he deftly side-stepped Gray and offered her an unexpected smile. "You must be Mrs. Stadtler." He held out a slender, sinewy hand, which she ignored. "I'm Elliott St. Vincent, a friend of Gray's."

"No friend of mine, you lying . . ." Gray stopped himself. Abby refrained from replying.

"Are those pictures on the wall with your name on them really yours?"

"Pictures?" Gray turned to her. "This is the restaurant?"

She continued ignoring Elliott's proffered hand and nodded. "I was going to show you."

"Hey, Dawson." Elliott turned. "You doing okay?"

"Hey, Elliott. Sure." The boy lowered his eyes.

Gray's anger returned. "I'm giving you a chance to go and leave my family alone."

"Your *family*? Ahh . . ." He shook his head. "Look, man, we just need to talk. None of this is what it seems. I can help you."

"Help me what?" Gray nearly spit into the other man's face. "You've come as near to ruining things for me as you possibly could, and you did ruin them for Jillian Harper.

Chris has done nothing but spend the last month cleaning up your messes."

From the purplish hue spreading on Elliott's face, Abby could tell Gray had hit a nerve. "Jillian Harper will cause more grief than you know, but that's another story. You're blind, Gray. You follow Chris Boyle like a lemming, and if you don't listen to the truth, he'll lead you right over a cliff."

"There's nothing I want to hear from you. I don't know how you found me, but we're finished talking."

Chagrin boiled beneath Abby's cheeks when she glanced around the restaurant and saw Dewey openly watching the exchange with "I told you so" written like neon in his eyes. "I found you because your beloved manager can be bribed," Elliott said.

"Bribed or blackmailed? You have no idea what's going on."

"Then enlighten me. Or, keep showing me. Your little domestic interlude this afternoon spoke volumes."

"What?" Abby rocketed forward. "That was *you* skulking around my farm?"

"It was, and I apologize, Mrs. Stadtler, I do," Elliott said. "I have no desire to use anything I photograph in Kennison Falls. I just want a chance to prove myself."

"You arrogant SOB." Gray reached once more for the photographer, but Abby rested her fingers on Gray's forearm.

"Don't, Gray. It's not worth it."

He backed down, and behind the cold anger in his

narrowed eyes she finally saw a warm spark for her. "I'm telling you to leave for the last time."

Elliott held up a hand. "I'm going for now, but I'm not leaving. Not until you talk to me."

"I'd buy a house here, then, because you'll be waiting a long time."

"Oh, you'll talk."

Elliott turned to her again. "You seem like a reasonable woman. Ask him to meet me."

"I can't tell him how to run his life," she replied, shocked at his request. "He came here for personal reasons, and I think he and our children deserve their privacy."

"Mrs. Stadtler, there won't be privacy for any of you if Gray doesn't hear me out."

Gray positioned himself between them. Calm was returning to his features, but when he took her hand nobody could see how hard he squeezed. "Don't say anything else, Abby."

"You're making this too goddamned hard for words." Elliott worried his bushy mustache as if searching for something more to say. Unsuccessful, he turned away and a moment later got piped out of the cafe by Lester's cheerful march. For an uncomfortable minute everyone stared.

"So." Karla edged around the corner from the kitchen. "Anyone ready for dessert?"

Gray pulled Abby into a brief hug and kissed the top of her head. "Thanks for saving me," he whispered.

Dewey closed his unused menu, stood, and with a

scathing glare at Lester, who switched to "Andy Griffith," followed Elliott out the door.

AN HOUR LATER, Gray watched Abby watch him like a patient parent from her seat in the living room armchair. "Stop fretting, Gray," she said. "You were ambushed, and I don't blame you for being angry, but it's over."

"Oh-ho, no. It's just starting. You thought Chris's photographers were bad."

He paced the floor in direct contrast to everyone else and scratched in agitation at his rough cheeks. Dawson sat with the rigidity of a rag beside Kim on the sofa, his hands threaded into the cargo pockets of baggy black shorts that hung to his calf. Abby, on the other hand, stretched firm legs, clad in very close-fitting white shorts, onto the ottoman, fueling Gray's distracted thoughts.

"It would be over, Dad, if you went back early."

"Excuse me? Who are you, and what have you done with my son?" Gray stopped prowling, his heart pounding in disappointment.

Disappointment?

"If you want Elliott to leave, you leave. Un-cancel one concert, and you're forgiven."

He'd been handed a get-out-of-jail-free card, and he felt disappointment? Gray studied his son. They'd had a breakthrough in Virginia, but now Dawson was back to being an enigma. Despite his words, he looked like he wanted to take on the world in a cage match. Then there was Kim, who'd reverted to shyness and swung her feet so her heels thumped against the sofa front—rhythmic thuds filling the room. If he'd been playing at the fantasy of living like a family the past two and a half weeks, Elliott had brought reality crashing back.

"I think he might be right," Abby said gently. "It'll be two full weeks tomorrow. I think you've proven a few things to your son. Don't you, Dawson?"

"Whatever. Yeah."

"But I think you should talk to Elliott, too."

"I'm *not* talking to him." His pulse reacted to the very thought. "I am my own man." His voice rose more petulantly than he intended. "Elliott can't dictate to me. And if I were to say I'm not finishing the tour at all, that's how it would be you know."

"Right." Dawson hunched deeper into the sofa. "And Chris's head would spin around like the girl in *The Exorcist*. He knows I forced you to cancel the concerts in the first place. He'll totally find a way to have me hauled back to England."

"He doesn't hold that kind of power," Gray insisted, but a freshly-seared memory stopped him. *You follow that man like a lemming.*

Not true. Where would he be without Chris Boyle's steady guidance?

"Chris holds *all* the power." Dawson's hands appeared from his pockets, and he stood. "You know, maybe you shouldn't go. Maybe I didn't think it through."

He spun to leave, but this time Gray stepped in front of him. "Oh, no you don't. Don't start running away again." The lack of anger in his voice pleased him. He sounded a little like his father. "Leaving is a coward's way out. You stay and talk."

For a moment he didn't think Dawson would listen. Then the boy slumped his shoulders. "What are you going to do with *me* if you go back on the road?"

Gray sighed. Of course Dawson would ask to stay. They'd barely returned as it was. But whatever was occurring between Abby and him, she'd never given him permission to assume he could stay indefinitely. With Elliott hanging around like a bad smell and the rest of the media a mere phone call away, the threat of fans finding the farm was more real than ever. Still, his heart dropped to his stomach at the thought of leaving.

"Two choices, just like before," he said. "Come with me, or go back to your mom."

"Wait, Gray." Abby silenced Dawson with a hand. "I thought we were past that. Let him stay here. Please? The only condition would be that you come back and get him."

How different from the first time she'd all but demanded he leave his child here. This time her eyes smoldered not with indictment, but with suggestive sparks. And he certainly didn't want to fight with her, he wanted to climb up her long legs and lose himself inside of her.

Dawson's entire demeanor went from dejection to disbelief. "You'll let me stay?"

"It's totally up to your dad, but it's all right with me." She caught his eyes. "Your birthday is in two weeks. You don't have any shows that weekend, I know."

"How do you know?"

"I've had a calendar of your concert dates since the beginning." She batted her lashes. "I wanted to know how long you might be here."

"In case you wanted to kick me out?"

"In case I wanted to talk you into staying."

Kim kicked the front of the sofa one last time and stood. With startling boldness, she sidled up to Gray and slipped her arms around his waist to give him an enormous squeeze. "It would be so cool to share our birthday. We can do a party." She tilted her head to smile her frightening baby-Dietrich smile. If he hadn't known better, he'd have said she was sending some possessive signal to her mother. If he hadn't known better, he'd have laughed.

"A party would be good." He extracted her arms from his torso and grinned, popping a kiss onto her crown. "Sharing it with my best fan? Nothing better."

"Hey, I'm more than a fan by now, aren't I?"

"I hope so." He knew immediately he'd fed right into her crush again. He was out of intelligent ideas for dealing with her.

Abby rescued him with barely contained laughter. "After a party, and after you're done touring, you'll have time to make permanent plans—you and Dawson."

"There's one thing." Dawson fidgeted with a knotted cord bracelet around his wrist.

"What?" Gray asked.

"School is supposed to start again just after you get done touring. I'm not going back . . . even if you and Mom never agree."

Gray massaged his brows, grimacing at his own touch. Nothing was ever easy. Ever.

"Let your father and me talk about it." Abby's voice, calm and sweet, bailed him out again.

"Seriously?" Clearly Dawson didn't quite believe it.

Gray sighed in relief. "Yeah, we'll figure it out."

"Well," Abby said. "I think I'll leave the horses outside tonight where they have water, since there won't be any in the barn. It's hot inside anyway. Kimmy, would you and Dawson go check on who needs a fly sheet on please?"

"Sure!" Dawson leapt to the task, clearly happy to leave the conversation where it had ended in his favor.

"Yeah." Kim flashed Gray a last flirty smile and followed outside.

When they were gone, he found Abby's eyes. It only took seconds for him to stride across the floor and grab her unceremoniously into his arms. Her hair tumbled backward, and her lips parted in sweet, breathless surprise. He pulled away, grasping for her cheeks.

"Thank you," he said. "You're my guardian angel. You've protected me from pretty much everything tonight—mostly myself."

"No, Gray. It just turns out we're not a bad team. I'm no angel."

Not a bad team. The words certainly lifted him like wings.

"You're a good person, Abby, and I've rarely been good—until recently. Maybe it's your prayers, the way you're robbing me of all my vices—a little old time religion my mother would have said. It's been a long time

since I've been part of a team . . . like this. With a girl."
He bumped his nose gently into hers, drawing in the taste
of her laughter.

"Girl cooties." Her fingers wriggled into his hair, and
their tips circled his scalp, sliding, massaging down to his
temples as she rose on her tiptoes to kiss him.

"Oh, please, gimme cooties," he whispered into her
mouth.

When they parted again, his blood swished excitement through his body, and he wished desperately he
could figure out how to stay with her. He longed to lose
his bad-boy rock life by taking on hers, to find a way he
could actually fit into a small town like Kennison Falls
with its tiny cafes and singing birds. But he knew better.

"Your daughter thinks *you* give me cooties and she
doesn't like it. She worries me."

"Kim? Why on Earth? She's smitten with you."

"Exactly. And I don't want to make a mistake."

"She's fifteen, Gray. She writes her name next to yours
in secret notebooks. You have fabulous songs and a very
sexy voice. And you're kind of hot, in case you don't
know. Those things get to a fifteen-year-old girl."

"And that comforts me how?"

"They get to thirty-seven-year-old girls, too."

He hauled her hips forward until they could have held
quarters securely between them anywhere from chest to
knee. "I'm not sure that comforts me either."

She tapped her finger on his lip, and the heat growing
between them soldered her gaze to his. "Let her have her
fantasies," she whispered. "You won't make a mistake."

She outlined his upper lip with her finger and drew it out to his cheek, where it bounced along his uneven stubble. "Some night you'll take off your shoes, she'll smell your stinky feet, and the magic will be gone. I promise."

"Really nice. So much for seduction, Abby. Sheesh."

"If seduction is what you want, how about we talk about that apprenticeship in the darkroom? We can meet after the kids go upstairs, forget about teenagers and paparazzi. And having only ten jugs of water. Which I'm going to get from the car."

She disengaged from his hold and backed away, licking her lips. His knees wobbled. "I'm pretty sure I can fit that into my schedule." He swallowed.

"Oh," she added. "Just to let you know? I'm leaving my halo upstairs."

"When they say 'darkroom,' they aren't kidding." Gray's disembodied voice floated to Abby's ears in the darkroom, lightless as a bottle of ink, and his breath set her skin shivering.

"Dark as the inside of a heifer." Her chuckle drifted into the void.

"How would anybody *know* how dark that is?"

"My dad must have. He said it all the time."

"Your dad is funny."

"Was funny."

"There I go again, Abby. I'm . . ."

"Shush." She stretched out a finger, delight dashing all the way to her stomach when she met his lips. "My dad was great. He raised me because my mother left him when I was a baby, but he was already in his late-fifties when I was born. He died of natural causes ten years ago. It was sad, but not tragic."

She cupped his roughened cheeks, running her thumbs past the corners of his mouth to stroke beneath his eyes. The ache deep inside for him was formed of respect and admiration. And mostly, at the moment, of pure lust. She couldn't remember ever feeling safe enough for lust before. Jack had commanded the respect and admiration. And he'd had her love. But not lust. Lust was not for good girls—or even good women. She'd had a solid, respectful marriage.

She initiated the kiss—a decadent, open-mouthed, free-for-all of tongues and murmurs and gooseflesh. When Gray pulled away, his breathing rushed over her in a swift, needy sound, and his fingers tippled at her side, playing beneath the hem of her shirt, generating full-body, shivering heat.

"You kiss better than anyone I've ever known," he said.

She was so drugged by him she believed the hyperbole. But how many women must Gray Covey have kissed in his life? He lowered his mouth again to her parted lips, sucking her tongue into his mouth and engaging it in a sweet, wet wrestling match. The heat in her lower belly radiated downward until sharp desire sprouted full-blown and heavy between her thighs. No slow-sparking burn. No slow build up.

Wide palms and long, dexterous, piano-player's fingers cupped her bottom and lifted until her feet left the floor, and her legs wrapped his hips. When she fit herself against him, he groaned and twisted his mouth free.

"Much more and this could be hard to stop."

The words should have frightened her. In the dim recesses of her incoherent brain, she knew she wasn't ready. It had only been three weeks since he'd walked into her life. She had to tell him before things got out of hand . . . "I trust you." It wasn't what she'd planned to say.

For a moment she was wrapped around a frozen column of a man, and she feared she'd thrown ice water on their fire. But he relaxed back into her, thrusting gently while he tugged her hips tight.

"There's a lot of pressure involved in trust." He sowed kisses across her face like precious seeds. "I don't deserve it."

"I think you do."

Unwinding her legs, she slid to the floor, took hold of his fingers and pressed them to the curve of her lips. "We have to slow down. I'm turning on the light to show you something."

"I liked what you were showing me just fine."

"We'll get back to it."

She opted for the red safe light instead of the overhead fluorescents. When Gray's face appeared, softly illuminated, her breath got stolen all over again. The firm cheekbones she'd been stroking were high and broad. His plush, cocoa hair, as rich to her fingers as the drink was to her tongue, swept back from his forehead and curled around the side of his face, ending in thick waves just below his earlobes. Heavy, handsome eyebrows slashed over his pale eyes, puzzling at the way she stared. She grinned in unabashed pleasure, amazed at how unembarrassed she was around him, at how fun it was to gawk at a male who gawked back.

"All right, then. What was so danged important you interrupted us?"

"I snuck in here a couple of hours ago." She dragged her gaze from his. "I, ah, developed a new roll of film." She reached for a photograph clipped to a drying line and turned it slowly to face him. "This is my favorite."

Gray, stripped to the waist, walking back from the pasture gate, his more-than-decent sixpack glistening in the early morning heat.

"When in the world did you take that?"

"One morning a week ago, before I left for work. You look like an ad for Calvin Klein."

There were seven black and whites of him working in the barn, taken surreptitiously after the first shot, some shadowed, some from unusual quarter angles. None looked like anything ever shown in a fan magazine or tabloid rag. Gray's eyes were unreadable as she let him flip through the prints.

"They said they wanted something suggestive for that album cover, something to make women buy the record for the cover. They should have used this one." He held up her favorite.

"Well, my mouth is watering, and I have the real thing right in front of me."

He came to a wonderful close-up of him with Dawson, laughing. "I like this one."

"I do, too. A lot. It's for you. The others I took for strictly selfish reasons."

"Did you now?" He kissed her ear. "Can I have the other one too?"

"So vain!"

"I want to remember how you think I look."

She laughed through the shivers spreading across her shoulder blades and brushed him away. "Stop that. We're working. Yes, you can have it. Here, what do you think of these?"

He set his chin on her shoulder, his arms around her waist from behind, while they looked at the photos she spread on the counter. Most were mediocre, but a handful had caught the light and shadows just right, and another that should have been silly—a close-up of Roscoe's nose emerging from the wildflower patch—had caught such a wonderful moment of doggy joy that the picture was perfect.

"These are amazing, Abby." His simple statement was a better compliment than any grand superlative.

"You think?"

He spun her in his arms. "You, who are so capable you can run a farm even when there's no working water, need to have as much confidence about what's in here," he tapped softly right over her heart, "as you do about what's in here." He tapped again at her temple.

His affirmations hit as powerfully as his kisses. Had

she truly forgotten what a relationship could be? Or had she never known?

"You're right." She tried to lower her eyes. "That's a forgotten concept."

His hands slid along her jaw until his thumbs rested below her ears. Gently he tilted her head so she had to keep looking at him. "That's your homework while I'm gone—get confident."

"Gone." Stupid sadness welled in her chest, her throat, her eyes. "I hate that you'll be gone. I hated when you were gone for two days."

"I'd think it would be a relief. Get things back to normal."

Hah. Broken wells, busted fencing, lawns to mow. You're leaving me in the lurch, buddy. She ducked from his arms. Once again, in her desire to care for him, she'd let herself get distracted from the issues she wanted to forget. But she couldn't afford to forget. Things like finding a new job so she could pay the well company. Things like worrying every night about creating a dinner that didn't look like yesterday's leftovers. Things like being scared to death of what would happen when the world did find out she was with Gray.

He didn't let her get far from him. Grasping her shoulders, he bent enough to look deep into her eyes. "I'm coming back. For more than a party. Whatever this crazy thing between us is, we have to finish it."

"Finish?"

"Maybe you think this is how I normally conduct

myself. But this is new for me. I want you to trust me to do right by you. Please?"

She honestly didn't know what to say. He'd touched directly on her fears. Crass as it made her feel, she had assumed she'd be just another dalliance in the life of a rock star. With a full measure of pain and longing, she realized she didn't want it to be so. But she didn't want his lifestyle either, and asking Gray Covey to become a farm husband was beyond ludicrous.

"Besides. You're keeping my son."

She banished her worry by cuddling into his embrace. "I'll trust you, then. To come back. For your kid and the hot chocolate. It's all I have to offer."

"Oh, love, that's about the dumbest thing I've ever heard."

He erased all space between them, lowered his head, and kissed away the last thoughts of the real world.

Chapter Nineteen

APPLAUSE, ROLLING LIKE distant Minnesota thunder, punctuated with whistles and calls, propelled the band off-stage. Miles Dixon, with his bear-paw hand, slapped Gray on his sweat-soaked, spangled blue blazer, making him choke on a laugh. "Tell me before I find out I've died and gone to heaven what just happened!" Miles's voice echoed like his bongos.

The roar from the crazed audience continued to fill their ears like ocean breakers.

"That, my friend, was the best friggin' rock concert in history." Gray let a wild high lift him physically off the floor. Or maybe it was Micky grabbing him from behind and hoisting him like a college frat brother. Either way, narcotic-like euphoria brought waves of laughter rolling from every Lunatic. *This* was the point. This was what he did for a living—and what hadn't been happening for the past three months. Hell, the past eighteen months.

"Hot damn that was fine!" Miles hopped with excitement to grab flushed and breathless Misty in a bear hug. Her gauzy skirt flew like wings. "Girl, you done sang like a nightingale."

Gray gave Misty his own massive hug. "An angel, Misty-love. An angel."

"And you sang like a man with a throat transplant," Wick added. "What happened, you get some sort of magic potion at that farm lady's house?"

Abby. Sweet Abby—if only you were here, this would be perfect.

"Yeah, great tonight, man." Spark, laconic as always, offered his highest praise.

The recorded music piped into the arenas before and after their shows swelled while the lights were going up, telling the audience Gray's second encore had been his last. But he would have gone out again—they all would have. Not a single thing had gone wrong with this show—not a broken light, not a malfunction, not a missed lyric.

"*That* is what I call an auspicious return!" Chris met them in the corridor behind the stage and offered high-fives all around. "Gray, I can't tell you how happy you've made my life tonight."

"Then *my* life is nothing but complete." Gray slapped palms with Chris and caught his manager's hand in a full clasp. "I live to please you."

"Damn right. Lady and gents, well done. Sounded great."

"Great? It was freakin' perfect, man!" Miles pounded

Chris on the back. "Where's the cold stuff? We got us some serious celebrating to do."

"Let's get you out of here. The press is rabid. I've got a spread back at the hotel."

The hassles of security lines, limos, lucky fans who'd found the exit route, and camera flashes strobing the night were as familiar as breathing. As Gray ran the gauntlet, his adrenaline began its drop from the post-concert high. The six bandmates shared a white, super-stretch limo, and within minutes, while everyone laughed and cussed and began popping bottle caps, the close air grew redolent with body odor and beer.

Micky and Max found packs of cigarettes in the limo's side pockets, along with lighters, breath mints, and packages of M&Ms left from the ride over.

"You guys are disgusting." Misty shot them a stern warning. "Wait until we're in fresh air to light those death sticks."

Micky ignored her, shook his pack, and offered it to Gray. He stared for a minute, almost reached for one but raised his palms.

"Huh?" Micky's brows hit his hairline. "Turning over a new leaf?"

"Maybe." Gray grinned at Misty. "She's always been right. They are death sticks."

A pleased smiled tugged at his vocalist's pretty lips. "There's something different about you, Gray. I'm still trying to figure out what it is."

"Nah." He sat back and took a drag on a bottle of Pilsner Urquell. "Just had a good vacation."

"You haven't said much about Dawson." Spark relaxed back as well. "He's okay?"

"He's . . ." A sensation of wonder welled in him. "Great. He's great, man. In fact, I want to talk to you about him later. There's a reason I had you send that song file to him."

"Something about him playing with ProTools. You didn't elaborate."

"I think he's got talent for production. I dunno, call it a gut feeling—which is stupid, maybe, considering how little time I've spent with him."

"I'd be surprised as hell if he didn't have some of the old man's chromosomes." Spark took a pull from his bottle.

Understanding in Spark's eyes added to Gray's inner warmth. Spark loved to brag about his three kids—in a loving way that had always left the tiniest hole of envy in Gray's heart.

Miles punched him in the arm. "C'mon, boys, drink up, we got some serious catching up to do. Do you think Chris got us any girls for this party?"

"You have a one-track mind, you pervert." Misty stuck her tongue out, and Miles beamed. It was a regular line of teasing for the pair, and Gray laughed, too, but he also endured a shot of longing just under the surface of his excitement. He looked at his mates, satisfied, knowing he was back doing his duty and they all appreciated it. Still, when he closed his eyes, the sounds blurred, the concert high dissipated, and all he could see was the red glow of Abby's darkroom.

Chris had orchestrated the usual gathering of local press, officials, and wealthy super-fans ready to schmooze at a free buffet in the hotel ballroom. Forty-five minutes later, showered and back in casual clothes, Gray had to sit on his hands to keep from calling Abby to share the post-show high. It was only midnight, but that made it nearly 2 a.m. in Minnesota, and he'd talked to her just before leaving for the arena. He didn't want to hound her. It amazed him that he had someone to think about calling, like a tenth-grader with a new girlfriend.

Girlfriend?

The mayor of Los Angeles was in the room. Several women for Miles to choose from hovered around the hors d'oeuvres. Chris, expansive and ebullient in his roles as mentor and maestro of Gray's career, introduced him to thirty upstanding citizens Gray would not remember in the morning.

The whole scene was familiar and would also take place three more nights here, then in Oakland, then in San Francisco, then in Seattle, before he could fly back to Minnesota. Suddenly he could tolerate it, but only just. It was over an hour before everyone had gotten his or her chance to meet him and get an autograph or a photo, and he finally had a moment to duck aside with Spark.

"You havin' fun, man?" his friend asked.

Gray laughed. "What kind of dumb-ass question is that?"

"Nothin'." Spark brushed it off. "What's up?"

"I wrote a new song."

"Serious?" Genuine surprise and delight lit his friend's face. "That's something I haven't heard in a while."

"Yeah." Gray scratched the back of his head self-consciously.

"So, she's special."

"I . . . yeah. But it's crazy and too new to say much. For now it's between you and me."

"And the song's about her?"

Gray laughed and plied the back of his tired neck with tired fingers. "I'd be hard pressed to deny it once you hear it. I want your input. But I'd also like you onboard with Dawson helping when it comes time to record it."

"Hey, I got no problem with that."

"What's this?" Chris sauntered into their twosome, a glass of whiskey in his palm and a carefree, short-of-boozy grin on his face. "Did I hear Dawson's name? How is my little troublemaker?"

Gray scowled, as his son's words flashed into his memory. *He'll totally find a way to have me hauled back to England.*

"He's not the trouble, Chris. I needed time with my son. It's all good." He smiled.

"Yes, after a shitload of legwork, palm-greasing, and re-scheduling." Chris put his hands theatrically around Gray's neck. "Swear to me, Covey. You'll never do this to me again. I'm too fuckin' old."

"You're a drama queen," Spark said. "The publicity is giving you a permanent hard-on."

A look of pure pleasure colored his manager's face.

Gray slapped him on the shoulder blade. "Spark and I were just discussing something to give you even greater orgasmic pleasure. Imagine the publicity if my son gets involved with the next record. He's a budding sound guy. I'd like to bring him along to the next session."

Chris's face went blank. "Whoa, Gray, I don't know about that."

"Why the hell not?" Defiance and defensiveness gripped Gray.

Chris fidgeted. "Look. I was saving this for a quieter time, didn't want to spoil the mood. You know we had Ron Revers onboard to produce the next record."

Chris had scored Revers nine months before and gloated about it since. The man was difficult and opinionated but the very best in the business and almost guaranteed gold.

"Had?" Spark asked.

"That picture with Jillian Harper has caused more trouble than anyone bargained for," Chris said. "Turns out she wasn't Revers's intern. She's—"

"His fiancée," Gray finished. "I heard that. So? She knows the picture isn't real."

"Yes, but the party was, and she was there as your date. Let's just say Ron is none-too-pleased with either of you."

"How the hell was I supposed to know? She never said a word."

"That's not what she told Revers. Anyway, it doesn't matter. She's left the label to save their face, and I've smoothed it over so that all you have to do is apologize.

You do, and he's still ready to kick ass on the next record."

"Me apologize? She lies, and I'm still the bad guy? Here I was feeling sorry for her."

"Blow it off, Gray. One grovel, and you've got a gold record. The point is, you don't want anything else pissing Revers off. This is not the time to bring in a surly teenager."

"Excuse me?"

"Sorry, sorry. I didn't mean it that way. We just know Dawson's got some issues; you said so yourself. We'll talk about it later, okay? Just remember this is Revers, for God's sake."

Gray bored straight into his manager's know-it-all gaze. "This has gotten insane, Chris. You're right. We'll talk about it along with several other things. Like a different picture for my new album. Here. Abby's work." He reached behind the sofa for a folder he'd stashed earlier and handed over Abby's picture of him.

"Lord in heaven." Spark grinned. "She Photoshopped your body."

Gray grinned. Chris laughed out loud.

"You're a hoot, Covey. The little woman's fantasy 'eh? Black-and-white. A little cliché. But cute, Gray. Very cute." He handed it back.

"I'm serious," Gray said, losing his smile. "We're showing this to the art department."

Chris patted his face twice then slapped it softly. "You're getting cheeky in your old age. Forty-five-year-olds." He winked at Spark. "Can't do a thing with 'em."

"It's hell, man." Spark nodded.

"Enjoy your party tonight, my friend," Chris said. "You've earned it. Tomorrow we'll discuss the rest of the tour. I've got some major interviews lined up during the breaks, and we'll talk about how to maximize the story of what you've been through."

Gray's heart nearly punched a hole through his rib-cage. "There's no story. It's a dead story. One word gets out about where I've been, and there'll be hell to pay."

Nobody was going to make a spectacle out of Abby. Or of Kim and Dawson.

"They want to know something, Gray."

"Then we'll tell them something, and it'll be all they need to know. Gimme a break. I need all the help with this you can give me."

Chris sighed, long-suffering and pathetic. "I don't know what the hell happened to you in the past few weeks. I'll be glad when you have your little hiatus out of your system." He smiled. "You'll feel better after your birthday."

"I sure will." Gray calmed his annoyance. "There's a big party planned back in Minnesota. I told you about the birthday I share with Abby Stadtler's daughter?"

"Fuck, Gray! Don't do this to me. You are not going back there!"

"Chris?" There was no point in reacting further. "Go. Have some more pâté or whatever other fancy food you've ordered for us. Eat, drink, be merry. Stop worrying."

"You're killing me, Covey. I swear to God."

Chris skulked off, and Gray dropped into the sofa next to Spark. "The feeling is mutual."

"Man, don't worry about it. You're his pride and joy, and things have been a little dicey the past eighteen months. He thinks he's protecting you."

A vibration from his back jeans pocket caused Gray to start. He reached to pat his iPhone and it buzzed again. "What the hell?" He pulled the phone free and squinted at the number. Adrenaline from joy and concern pumped into his system. Abby!

"Hey you!"

"Gray?" A timid, quiet voice filled with trembling tears launched his heartbeat into the stratosphere.

"Kimmy? Honey, what's wrong?" He shot Spark a desperate look and stood.

"I'm s . . . sorry to call you."

"It's all right, you know it is. But, honey, it's three in the morning there. What is it? Is it your mom? Is it Dawson?"

"M . . . Mom."

Oh, God. "What happened?"

"She didn't go to work this afternoon, but she left and was gone such a long time. She was so sad when she came home . . ." Kim's voice caught, and she gulped. Gray forced patience, waiting, his fingers ice-cold. "She told me things are really bad with the finances, and there's no money to fix the well. She . . . she . . ." Her crying turned to quiet sobs. "She sold Gucci."

Her words made no sense. Abby loved that horse with a passion. She needed that horse. And in the millisecond it took to remind himself of that, he realized, too, how tied to Gucci he felt himself. The space occupied by his heart suddenly contained a boulder.

"No, Kimmy, she couldn't have."

"I know. I can't believe it. But she says she did. And she went down to the barn late and wouldn't let me or Dawson help clean stalls. She told us she just wanted to be alone for a while, so we didn't bug her. Now she just woke up, and she's crying, and I don't know how to help her. I told her to call you . . ." She hesitated.

"That's good. That's fine," he promised, his voice hoarse, his careening thoughts useless.

"She won't. She said it was her problem to solve."

Gray's boulder-heart cracked painfully. "Well, I'm glad *you* called. Are you okay?"

"N . . . no. I'm scared. I'm sad for her."

"I'll call her, honey, don't worry."

"No! She'll be upset if she knows I called. I don't know why I did. Just, you said . . ."

"Yes, I did, and I meant it. Listen, you go and climb into bed with her, and hug her as tight as you can. Sleep with her all night if you need to. And you tell her everything will be okay. Promise her that, okay? Because it will be."

"I . . . I know."

"Does Dawson know about this?"

"Yeah, I told him. I don't think Mom wants anyone else to know, though."

"Your mom's brave, and she likes to take care of everything. I won't tell her you called."

"Thanks." She sounded calmer.

"I'll be there in ten days for our party, okay? You call me again if you need me. I can be your dad as much as

I'm Dawson's. You mean a lot to me—I don't like that you're sad."

"You mean a lot to me, too." There was a longer pause, a short sniff, and then a sigh. "And to Mom."

He hung up the phone and returned to Spark in a daze. What the hell had he gotten himself into? Why the hell did he have to wait ten more days until he could get back to it?

"Ed? It's Gray."

"Goddess? This is a surprise! How's the spy business?"

Gray laughed into the phone at the crusty old warmth, familiar and comforting. "Great, great. Full of spies."

"What can I do you for?"

"Kim called me last night and said Abby sold Gucci. I'm worried about her, Ed. I realize you don't know me that well, but please believe I've come to care about her and Kim very much. Tell me how bad things are for her— she puts on a brave face when I'm around. Is she all right?"

The extra-long moment of silence told Gray almost all he needed to know. "She struggles," Ed said at last. "Syl and I do the best we can to help her, but, first of all, she don't take help easily. Second, we're too old to have much to give her."

"You're like parents to her, Ed, don't kid yourself." Gray sighed and let his brain click furiously. "Can you do a little James Bonding for me yourself? I know she doesn't like help, but we can't let her lose Gucci. That animal is part of her sanity."

It was true, she wouldn't want his help. But she'd said she'd trust him to do right by her. She'd just have to make good on that promise.

"Do I get to wear a fake mustache?" Ed interrupted Gray's thoughts.

"You're nothing but funny, Ethel, you know that, don't you?" Relief overwhelmed him.

"I don't know why I like you enough to trust you with Abby, but something about you . . . What is it you want me to do?"

"Find out where Gucci went and how much the new owners want to buy him back. I know it means being sneaky with Abby, but she'll stop us otherwise."

"I can be sneaky. How do I get hold of you?"

Gray gave him his number, told him about his schedule, and thanked him—profusely.

"Ain't nothin' to thank me for. Somebody's got to watch out for that girl. Sometimes I think she'd have fought the Alamo without asking Davy Crockett."

Gray's throat tightened, then he swallowed away the emotion. "Ed, I don't know why the hell you like me, either."

"Got a soft spot for James Bond. Besides . . ." he said, hesitating, ". . . the only other time I've seen a girl look at a man the way Abby looks at you was the first time I met Sylvia."

Chapter Twenty

NOTHING COULD DRAIN a body as quickly as oppressive Minnesota heat. Abby shuffled along the winding, wooded park path just above Kennison Falls, hoping to find any relief from the unrelenting sun. The past two days were a nightmarish blur. Yesterday had been the worst since Jack and Will's death, her still-swollen eyes bearing the testament. Selfishly, angrily, she believed that, if not for Kim, she'd have given up a functioning well for the rest of her life if it could have meant not loading Gucci onto that trailer.

It hadn't made things any easier to have Ed and Sylvia there, serene as gurus, promising her everything would be all right. She was breathing, as were her children—no, as was her *child*; when had they both become hers?—so she supposed everything *would* be all right. But she didn't want it to be. She definitely didn't want anyone to tell her it would be.

Except maybe Gray. An unstoppable tear escaped the corner of one eye, and she brushed it away, hugging her Minolta into her stomach. He didn't know about Gucci. How could she tell him she'd sold her best friend to strangers for a pump and three hundred feet of pipe? Him, for whom purchasing several hundred dollars' worth of shavings had been equivalent to buying a new shirt? She missed him, but she didn't want to miss him. Just like she didn't want to miss Gucci. Or Will. Or Jack. Sometimes surviving life was simply too difficult.

"Mrs. Stadtler?"

Abby jumped, staring at the enormous lens on the Nikon in the hands of the man who'd spoken. When she stopped being envious, she remembered to be angry and stared into the steady, hazel eyes of Gray's nemesis.

"Mr. St. Vincent." Her voice frosted the hot air. "What are you doing in town? Gray isn't here."

"I know. I went to his come-back concert. I'm happy to report it was triumphant. Could we talk for just a few minutes?"

"I'm pretty sure that isn't a good idea."

"I disagree. Respectfully, of course." His sandy mustache lifted in an easy smile that held no threat. "I have important information for Gray, but I have to get him to listen. You could help."

Abby glanced over her shoulder as if she expected Gray to appear and catch her cheating. "It's disloyal for me to even talk to you. After that picture you took, and after betraying his mother, why should I trust you?"

Elliott took his camera from around his neck, offered it to Abby and then held out his hand for hers. Confused but fascinated, she complied. "It's common knowledge I took the photo," he said. "But I never sold or sent it to anyone. The file got stolen, and it's taken weeks to figure out who did it and how. As for Laura, I never went to see her." He held the old Minolta to his eye, looked at the settings, and nodded with appreciation.

"So, who *do* you think took it? Or sold it? Or both?" Abby stroked the beautiful Nikon and examined its lens, as Elliott had hers. It was like holding a Stradivarius.

"I'll tell you, if you'll please hear me out. Is it all right to call you Abby? I'm Elliott."

Something in his sincerity told her he wasn't out to hurt her. Still, she respected Gray too much to be gullible. "Elliott," she consented. "I'll listen, but I won't promise to believe."

"Fair enough." He slipped a hand roughly through his hair, looking something other than collected for the first time. "Every day, I download all my picture files to a secure online storage site. Since they're sometimes sensitive, I rarely leave them on my camera. If I lost it, you see . . ." A half-smile finished his sentence. "I never have lost it, and I never leave it out of my sight. It's like a third limb. But someone got into that online site at least three times."

"And you think you know who."

"Chris Boyle."

"Gray's manager?" The allegation appalled her. She wasn't smitten with Chris, but Gray talked about him as if he was God, responsible for every bit of his success. The idea of Chris Boyle backstabbing his star seemed preposterous.

"His very controlling manager."

"Isn't controlling things part of his job?"

"Not to the point of using sabotage as a marketing tool. Here's the honest truth. Chris is worried. Gray is still crazy-popular with people who've followed him all along, but he isn't gaining new fans like he once was. If he stops making money, Chris stops making money. His reputation lives or dies with Gray's."

"So he does things that hurt Gray's career. That makes no sense."

"Chris Boyle is on a weird, misguided mission. For the past two months he's drawn attention to all the negative things that have happened and spun them to generate interest and sympathy. He's sensationalizing Gray, making him look like a victim. The old idea that even negative attention is good attention.

"I'd forgotten that two months ago, I left my computer with Chris for one night when I wasn't going home. He has an assistant who's a techno genius. I'm sure they hacked the access codes to my storage site, because it was after that my pictures started appearing in public."

"Of course they did." Disgusted, Abby tried handing his camera back, but he waved for her to keep it. "That's the stuff of movies, not real life."

"I wish, Abby. I believe Chris took a calculated risk by stealing and selling the Jillian Harper picture. The public got its shock, and then he circulated the story that his boy was framed. The question he put in people's minds pushed Gray's current record from number fifteen to number five in a week."

"That can't be true. Maybe you're just a jerk trying to deflect suspicion from yourself?" She sighed, confused and worn out.

"All of us in the entertainment business are some level of jerk. Gray is when he has to be. Chris is more than one. But Gray and I, and his guitarist, Spark, we're also closet nice guys. Gray's been looking for a way out of the closet for a while now. When I saw him with you and your kids? He was all the way out and a long way from the door."

All she could do was stare. He could be handing her the biggest line since "I am not a crook," but his words exhilarated her. Terrified her. Pleased her. "How do you think I can help?" The question tumbled out unplanned.

"With a sting. Bait Chris by feeding him a picture—one you, not I, took. If he gets it with the right message attached, I think he'll pass it to the press. But I can't have anything to do with it. Nobody would believe I didn't send it to the papers myself and lie. It has to be you."

"I absolutely will not!"

"Think about it, Abby. You wouldn't have to say a word. Either nothing at all would happen, or the picture will appear and we'll all know who sent it."

The pall of intense disloyalty shrouded her like the hot, humid air. How could she possibly know whether Elliott was telling the truth? "I can't decide something like this that quickly."

"I don't expect you to. Talk to Gray first; tell him the idea. If he'd go along, it would be even better. Whatever happens, I owe you one just for hearing me out."

"You know what? Yes, you do." She scowled at him, frustrated that he'd put her in such a position. She didn't want to be part of a world like this.

"What are you taking pictures of?"

The change of subject threw off her thoughts. "I . . . don't know. I never know until I see one to take."

"Perfect answer. You're not shooting digital. I'm impressed as hell. I miss film work."

"Black-and-white."

"Best of all. Having trouble with the weird light in the woods here?"

"I always do."

His words were a trap. She hadn't discussed photography with anyone for so long. Elliott was offering her mental flowers and chocolate. Wooing her. "That's one of the things I'm experimenting with. I thought the shadows would give me a challenge."

"Believe it or not, I do more than take celebrity pictures. Here, look at that patch of wild strawberry over there. See the crazy contrast? Why don't you play with my camera a little?"

She followed him along the path without anywhere near enough caution. At least she hadn't thought about Gucci in fifteen minutes, and for that alone she had to thank him. What harm could come from considering what he'd said? She hadn't agreed to anything. She wouldn't until Gray got home . . . uh, back. Got back. She shook her head to clear it.

Nine days and counting.

ONE NIGHT AND counting.

Abby turned off the car in her driveway and pressed the heels of her hands into her eye sockets. Only a week left of work and no new job. When she looked up again, slashes of sunlight streaked the horizon, but thick clouds filled the overhead sky and six o'clock looked like nine. Ed's *Farmer's Almanac* had accurately predicted the hot, stormy summer. She turned at the soft pat on her shoulder and smiled at her daughter.

"We'll get through it, Mom."

Her beautiful Kim—so naturally wise in the ways of caregiving. Abby grabbed her into a hug. "Have I told you how much I love you? For being my rock the past two weeks?"

Kim smiled. Outside the car, Abby drew a lungful of sweet, rain-laden air and tried to figure out why things didn't feel quite right—aside from today's lack of success. Two job interviews had yielded no promising results. She couldn't afford to miss paychecks.

The world just felt . . . off. To start with, Gray hadn't called for the first time since leaving. And her dog was not there to greet her. "Where's Roscoe, do you suppose?"

Kim shrugged.

Whatever she'd expected upon entering the kitchen,

it wasn't the heavenly smell of garlic and roasting meat bubbling on the stove and live guitar music from the living room. And, at last, Roscoe raced into view, toenails clicking on the kitchen flooring. The music stopped. Five seconds later, the most beautiful man in the world stood in the archway.

"Well," he said. "I've definitely just learned the meaning of *sight for sore eyes*."

Her heart skittered and slipped in her chest like Roscoe on the linoleum. Gray's robin's-egg eyes glistened with enjoyment over his surprise, and she couldn't take him in fast enough. Kim screeched with joy and launched herself across the room. The world righted itself. All she saw was how his thousand-dollar jeans rode his hips like paint on a master's canvas, and how a form-fitted, navy-blue T-shirt hugged his pecs and biceps the way she longed to do. He didn't take his eyes off her until Kim threw her arms around his waist in a bear hug.

"I'm so glad you're back!" she cried.

There was something gratifying in the unabashed greeting, so different from the anxious disbelief the first time Kim had seen Gray. He gave her a squeeze and smooched her crown.

"Hey, Kimmy. It's nice to see you, too." He pushed her to arm's-length and peered up and down at her, giving a wink. "I think you've grown."

"Very funny."

He let her go, and Abby's heartbeat zigzagged. "I wondered why you didn't call. How did you get here so early?"

They remained across the room from each other, and

even though Abby wanted to run to him just as Kim had done the anticipation was somehow more exciting.

"They cancelled tomorrow morning's flight. No way in hell . . . sorry." He glanced at Kim. "No way in heck was I waiting until Saturday. That's our birthday. We finished the last concert, I ignored Chris's temper tantrum, and David Graham rebooked his flight when nobody was looking."

"You know, David is one of my very favorite people."

"I'm going to go change," Kim said. "I've been helping at church all day, and I'm gross."

"Dinner's in forty minutes," Gray told her.

"Okay."

"I think I'm in love." Abby closed her eyes. "A man waiting with dinner ready?"

When she looked again, Gray was craning his neck to make sure Kim was gone. He turned back, and they moved at the same instant, meeting in the middle of the kitchen.

"Abby, Abby," he murmured as his embrace swallowed her. Every sadness of the past two weeks evaporated like a ghost in a bad dream. "Does it make me certifiable that I missed you like a lost hand?"

"If it does, I'm headed to the padded room right along with you."

His mouth covered hers with a kiss as familiar as if she'd always known it. Its soft insistence and sweet succulence nourished her like vital nutrients.

"So," she said against his cheek when they peeled apart. "You've been having fun?"

He dropped a kiss on her neck, another behind her ear. "Not until now."

"You're smooth, Mr. Graham."

He arched back and looked her up and down. "You and I need to talk."

"About . . . ?"

"This. Us." He gripped her upper arms. "I'm old, Abby. I've been through so much junk in my life that I know whatever you and I are developing is not normal. Not for me."

Abby's heart thumped so crazily she was certain it had divided in two and fought itself—one half praying Gray would say something white knight-ish and happily-ever-after-like, the other half scared to death. She was struggling to stay afloat these days, but she wouldn't give up that struggle or the things she'd worked so hard to build. The struggle was not Gray's. She couldn't—she wouldn't—foist it on him or let him feel sorry for her.

"You're right," she agreed. "What's happening is not simple."

"Maybe it could be." He stroked her cheek.

She put a finger against his lips. "It's never been simple for one second."

"Do I need to tell you two to get a room?"

Abby jumped. Gray landed a full two steps away from her in a quarter of a second. She'd forgotten about Dawson, and the boy rolled his eyes, laughing. Wasn't this completely backward, she thought, as he sauntered to the refrigerator.

"Give it up, Dad, it's no secret you kissed her a long time ago."

If Abby hadn't been thoroughly mortified, she would have laughed at the look of panic on Gray's face. "Does Kim know this secret too?" She eked out the question, and Dawson gave a genuine shrug.

"How should I know? Why would we talk about our parents kissing? Dude, no thanks. Just remember, I not only don't want to talk about it, I don't want to see it."

He palmed a can of Mountain Dew from the refrigerator and closed the door, a cute little smirk on his face. He clearly thought he had the upper hand, and Abby couldn't find a way to deny him the moment.

"Hey . . ." Gray took a breath deep enough to find his voice. "Don't wreck your supper."

"Hmmm." Dawson raised his eyebrows. "I'm not sure you're in a position to lecture me, young man."

"Smart-ass kid. Were you raised in a barn?"

"No, an English boarding school. I would think you wouldn't want to send me back after seeing what a bad job they've done."

"Maybe they just aren't finished yet."

He sobered. "I'm kinda trying to be serious here. You've told Mom I don't want to go back, right?"

Gray's features tightened. "I've tried, Daw. She isn't inclined to discuss serious things these days, when I can reach her at all. She's a little PO'd at me because of the media still hounding her."

The moment of Dawson's role-reversal passed, and he

kicked his toe at a scuff mark on the kitchen floor, looking every bit of sixteen.

"I'll call her at the end of the week," Gray promised. "She'll be back in London. There's still time before decisions have to be made."

"The decision has been made, Dad," Dawson said with a little too much eerie calm. "Mine has, anyway."

"If we don't do this by the book, we could both be up crap creek, buddy." Gray's voice was firm yet gentle. "I'll talk to her, but you know it never works to give your mother an ultimatum."

Dawson didn't look appeased. He shrugged with such apathetic eloquence Abby wondered if teenagers would ever be able to make themselves understood were they to lose the ability to lift shoulders to ears.

"What am I supposed to promise, Dawson? There are a lot of problems associated with you changing schools. You don't get to act like you're going to be here. This isn't your home."

"It's more of a home than you've ever given me."

For an instant the room went silent, and the air thickened with palpable tension. Father and son stared in a revival of their original anger, but this time Gray didn't retreat into the fear of making Dawson angrier.

"I know you feel that way. I grant you it's true of the past few years. But it doesn't mean you can stay. It just means we have some stuff to figure out."

"You know what? I heard that line a hundred times when you and Mom split. I think it's been long enough for you to have gotten your shit together."

"That," Gray pointed his finger and took a step forward, "requires an apology. You can have your opinion, but you keep words like that to yourself in company like this."

Dawson stared a second, his defiance warring with his emotions. "Sorry Abby," he said without looking at her. His lip quivered as it curled into an angry sneer. "So, fine. You just let me know when you've figured out my life."

He all but stomped from the room, just barely avoiding five-year-old behavior. Abby almost smiled until she saw the defeat on Gray's face. She turned into his arms instead. "Sucks to be the grown-up doesn't it?"

"What happened? How'd I blow that so fast?"

"Blow it? You did great. He can't always have what he wants, Gray. That's the rotten part of your job. But it's also important. He's good at getting his demands met."

"Like his old man." Gray grabbed her into the hug she'd started. In it she found warmth, security, and mutual need.

"What does his old man want?"

"How 'bout a ride off into the sunset? I've been imagining it for two weeks."

She smiled into his shirt, kneading a long, slow line down his back. "Is that right?" His quiver played through her fingers as she extended her stroke toward the pockets of his jeans. "Let's see how the weather holds. Maybe that could be arranged."

Chapter Twenty-One

THE WEATHER DIDN'T hold.

After they stuffed themselves with Gray's amazing beef stroganoff and cleared the aftermath, the skies opened and there was no sunset to ride off into.

"Stupid, rainy summer," Abby said, fighting childish disappointment. Gray just held her and laughed.

"Don't give up. I've seen these summer storms pass quickly. Meanwhile, I have an idea for normalizing things with my Kimmy-fan. C'mon."

They knocked on Kim's open door, and she greeted them with joy. "Hi," Gray said. "Got a little time?" She nodded. "Do you remember when I offered clarinet lessons?"

"Yeah." The word emerged slowly.

"I'm thinking now's a good time."

"Oh, no I . . ." Her joy turned to panic. "I've hardly practiced."

"Perfect, a fresh start."

"But—"

"Meet me downstairs by the piano in ten. Chop chop!" He didn't give her a choice, and as they walked away, Abby laughed.

"You're tough."

"I'm hoping she'll see me as an authority figure for a change. May not work, but it's worth a shot."

She kissed him on the cheek as they walked. "Good plan, Mr. Covey. Good plan."

Exactly ten minutes later, Gray held Kim's sheet music in his hands. He didn't recognize the piece but played the melody line in his head. Its relative difficulty impressed him. If Karla Baxter thought Kim was capable of this, the girl was talented.

"This is an awesome piece," he said. "Have you played it at all?"

"Yeah, we worked on it the end of this year."

"How often do you practice?"

A rise in her cheek color answered for her. "Do I? Or should I?"

Gray laughed. "I think that answers my question. So, my mother never yelled at me to practice, and I won't yell at you. She always said, 'It has to come from inside, David, or you might as well find something you love better.' Still, she was firm. I had to finish what I started. That's all I'm doing—making you finish what you started."

For the briefest instant she looked properly put-in-place, but then she grinned. "Fine." A minute later she had her clarinet assembled and held a wafer-thin reed in her mouth. While she waited for the wood to soften, Gray took the book to the piano.

"You want me to play the accompaniment?"

Her eyes lit. "Would you? Yeah, sure!"

"Just tell me when you're ready."

She was shaky at first, but her effort impressed him. A clear, mellow tone carried through her nervous wobbles, and her only mistakes were matters of practice. When she finished, Gray turned on the piano bench.

"Not bad, my girl."

"Ach, I blew it."

"You don't know the runs yet, that's all. Eight, ten hours a day till camp. No sweat."

Her expression, as if she'd just been told she had to play in front the world wearing donkey ears, made him laugh. "Aw, Kimmy. You know I'm not serious. Give it an hour, even half an hour a day—you can whip this thing."

"Thanks, give me a heart attack why don't you?" She sobered. "Gray? Would you play it once?" The question was shy but determined. "I want to hear what it should sound like."

"Wow, I . . ." It had been a long time since he'd sight-read clarinet music, but after admonishing her about nerves, fair was fair. "Okay. Hand me a fresh reed and I'll give it a whirl. It won't necessarily be that pretty."

"Oh, it will be."

He popped the new reed into his mouth, and looked past Kim's shoulder, nearly dropping the little sliver of cane from his lips at the sight of Abby in the doorway. She stared at his mouth. "Lucky little reed," she said. "Make sure you suck on it long enough."

His pulse throbbed into his groin. "Ooo-kay, I'm pretty sure this is long enough." Refocusing with difficulty, he reached for the clarinet, propped the reed against the mouthpiece, and tightened the ligature screws. A sense of familiarity soothed the heat inside of him. He lifted the instrument and blew a scale. "What the heck, here goes nothing."

He liked the music. The pretty melody would make the challenges worth practicing. His performance was far from stellar, but he was able to show some of the dynamics he wanted Kim to hear. When he finished, she stared in admiration, but Abby spoke first. "Gosh, I think that's the definition of *blew me away*."

"Thanks." He'd long before been taken down several notches from vanity, but impressing Abby swelled his head and chest just enough to feel good.

"I can't believe how you just did that," Kim pushed close to peer over his shoulder at the music. "You only heard it once."

"I have thirty years of practice on you. You might not have heard all the mistakes, but there were plenty. I've just spent enough time faking on stage that I blow over the gaffes. No judge would have given me good marks. I expect you to do better."

"Yeah, you sound like a mom." She grimaced.

"More like a dad, but yeah. So, consider the whip cracked young lady. Another twenty-five minutes. I'll listen once more if you like." She blinked as if she didn't think she'd heard him right, and he took advantage of her surprise. "Switch the reed back. I'll go get some water."

Kim bent to the task and Gray dragged Abby by the hand into the kitchen, where he spun her into a hard, assuaging kiss that assuaged nothing. "Cruel, Abby," he murmured into her mouth. "No reed jokes when I'm working with your daughter."

She sputtered against his lips. "Couldn't help it, it was the sexiest thing I've seen in a while."

He placed his hands on either side of her hips and leaned forward. "Wait for me?" he whispered.

"Oh, I dunno, you won't even know I've been gone."

The rain spent itself, and the sky lightened to a gorgeous purple-and-pink twilight, as Abby tidied the kitchen and listened contentedly to Kim's clarinet solo grow more confident under Gray's patient teaching. Worries that normally sat just below the surface of her emotions ready to overwhelm her were held in check by the rare calm of the evening, but they were still there. The well had been the tip of an iceberg.

The house roof wasn't far from failing, and, while she had next month's mortgage money in the bank and enough for a half a month of horse and basic people-feed, she couldn't absorb another major disaster.

She'd been sure Maggie Watson at the Faribault Library would take her on part-time until she could find another higher-paying job, but budgets were tight everywhere, and Maggie had no money for another assistant. It had been the same story at the nursing home where Abby had worked ten years before. And three offices who'd advertised for help had already hired.

She watched the sky continue to brighten as the clouds blew away on the breath of a fresh breeze. She opened the chocolate cupboard and allowed ten seconds for her wave of guilt. Yes, she should stop indulging in the extravagant chocolate bars—but she never would. She'd figured out once that about five dollars a month went to her vice. If one day she lost everything because she was sixty dollars short at the end of the year, she'd give up her addiction.

This batch of hot chocolate, she told herself, was to celebrate Gray's return. Engrossed in melting the chocolate, she jumped when a light touch shimmied up her spine.

"What's the occasion—happy or sad?" Gray leaned in behind her, his whisper causing shivers.

"Happy. You're back safely." She giggled and then sighed as his hand stopped at the small of her back. "My magic potion."

"A love potion?"

"I said *magic*. Don't get full of yourself, buster."

He nibbled down her neck to a point just beneath the collar of her polo shirt. First wetting the spot with his tongue, he worried at it gently with his teeth. She groaned and pushed him away. "No hickeys, the kids are home."

"If this were a movie, now would be the time our hero sings to the girl and changes her mind."

"Ooh yeah, like in an Elvis movie." She laughed again. "Hmm, forgot about Elvis. Maybe he's number three, and you're number four."

"Nope. I'm pretty sure I'm moving up the list, not

down." He started humming, and her skin vibrated beneath his breath.

She closed her eyes. "I always wondered where the background music came from."

He straightened and winked. "Be right back."

He returned with his guitar, a flashy Ovation acoustic, slung across his shoulders. At his first chord, a thrill dove for Abby's stomach. Then he sang, for her alone, a slow, gravelly version of the old "Love Potion No. 9." He trailed her around the kitchen, leering as she added the chocolate to the pan on the stove, laughing as she pulled out four mugs. The "gypsy's pad on Thirty-Fourth and Vine," the "turpentine," the "India ink" . . . all the silly, novelty lyrics took on the sultry heat of a jazz love song. His fingers mesmerized her, flexing to form chords. The knuckles slipping beneath his tanned skin were as sexy as the baritone she could no longer resist.

He sang over her shoulder while she stirred her chocolate potion, sang in her face when she backed up, giggling, against a counter, and sang as he finished with an Elvis-worthy pelvis-waggle. Abby had never seen The King move with any more heat in his hips than Gray did when he pulled the Ovation's strap over his head and leaned the guitar against a cabinet.

"Now Elvis kisses the girl," he said.

"Oh." There was barely breath enough in her lungs to speak. "I guess you'd better follow the script."

His mouth devoured hers. In the back of her mind she'd feared the singing would draw Kim's curiosity, but when his fingers formed their chords on the skin beneath her ears, the worry faded. When Gray's tongue slid between her lips and more liquid drizzled into her core, she forgot to care.

He pulled from the kiss, and she moaned in protest.

"Abby, the rain stopped," he whispered.

"Yes, it did."

"It's only nine thirty. I think there's still time for that horseback ride. Now. As it gets dark."

"Are you serious?"

"I want you to myself, for a couple of hours. The darkroom is too close to my son and your daughter. You told me once nighttime rides were fun."

"And dangerous. I mentioned that as well."

"I can promise you this one would be dangerous in more ways than one."

She knew better than to go riding off into danger and, still, her heart soared directly into its path.

WISPS OF SMOKE hissed skyward, while a tiny flame struggled in Abby's makeshift fire pit. Gray smiled at her fussing over the fledgling campfire. She added a few precious dry leaves and pursed her lips to blow. His groin tightened. She was the most beautiful thing he'd ever seen, and he wanted to grab her and beg her to blow on him like that.

He adjusted his seat on one of their two blankets. She turned with a private smile. "It'll come, I promise you."

His groan escaped into the warm night air. "Abby, you did not just say that."

Even in the dark he saw her head dip to hide a grin, and she blew again. He forced down his burgeoning desire as he massaged a saddle-sore point just inside his right knee. He and Abby had all but stolen away, telling the kids that they'd decided to take a spur-of-the-moment ride only after Jackson and Fable were saddled and ready to go.

"Woo hoo!" A gleeful whoop from Abby sent her sinking back on her booted heels.

Flames had engulfed her twig teepee and were licking at the next level of slender wood branches. The campfire had officially taken hold.

"I am impressed, woman." Gray loved her triumphant smile.

"You've been taking care of me all evening. It's my turn to do something nice for you."

"It's been a long time since I've had someone I wanted to take care of."

He eased to a stand, stretched, then sat beside her and ran his hand down her back. She was slim and strong. Her spine curved beneath his palm, and she leaned into his touch like a puppy. Warmth and well-being mingled with his growing desire.

"This is a great spot." He gazed up at the pine trees that guarded their secluded little meadow. There are very few places like this for me. It's a treat."

"I'm sorry." Her earnest eyes lifted to his. "I can't imagine living your life. I hope you feel safe at the farm, too."

"It's why I've grown to love it so quickly. The problem is, I can't hide anywhere for very long. Now that Elliott knows where I am, it's just a matter of time." His gut twisted. Elliott's betrayal still stunned him. Abby's body stiffened beneath his touch. "What's wrong?"

Still squatting, she turned on her toes and placed both soft hands on his cheeks. Her eyes, colorless in the night darkness, held troubled clouds, and even as her thumbs started new little fires inside of him by stroking beside his mouth, he worried. She leaned in and kissed him.

"I can't keep secrets from you," she said, and sat as he did, tailor fashion. "I saw Elliott St. Vincent while you were gone."

"What?" Shocked, he pulled back. "What did he want? Did he harass you?"

"No. No. Truly he didn't, Gray." He searched her face and knew she was telling the truth. "He was very nice. I think he cares a lot about you."

"Bullshit." Gray saw her flinch at his vehemence and grabbed her, hugging her as forcefully as he'd cursed. "I'm sorry, Abby. But that guy's a lying backstabber."

"He says he didn't sell that picture."

"He says a lot of things."

"What if he's right?"

"Abby. He's not right." Elliott St. Vincent was the last person Gray wanted between him and Abby, and he fought to keep his frustration at bay.

"Don't you want to know what he had to say to me?"

The man wasn't worth ruining this incredible night over. "I don't want him here with us tonight, okay? Love, he's charming, but don't be suckered in by him. Please? Let's talk about him later."

She looked as if maybe she wanted to say more. Her eyes dropped to the blanket one instant then lifted back to his with determination. "I won't be suckered. He's not the one I'm falling in love with, Gray. I just didn't want to hide the fact that I'd talked to him."

He couldn't decide whether to crow with joy at her honesty or shout to the heavens. He set his forehead against hers. "Falling in love?"

She nodded. "Ever since you brought me that Symphony bar. Or maybe ever since I saw your legs under my frog bathrobe. But, I've tried not to."

"I think since you knocked the stupid cigarette out of my mouth."

She grimaced. "Good, 'cause I'd do it again."

"I hope so."

The kiss began as a tender exploration—their first intimacy with the love-word between them. The night was building up new mugginess, and the fire did nothing to cool their bodies. Abby melted in his arms and spread closer to him the way warm honey might slide down a spoon before it dropped onto his tongue. She fit perfectly, torso to thigh, curve to angle. Every nerve in his body begged for her touch. He pulled the hem of her soft, blue, buttoned blouse from her jeans and burrowed his fingers past the denim waistband to the swell of her bottom.

Malleable, tantalizing, her skin pebbled with little goose bumps as he kneaded it, bringing heat and more hardness to his body.

"Slow down, cowboy, or we'll waste my fire."

He let her go, reluctantly. She straightened and handed

him a set of saddle bags. "Dig out the marshmallows and the thermos; I'll find us two sticks. You can't have a fire without toasting marshmallows.

"Lord, Abby, you're going to kill me with sugar overdose. What's in the thermos?"

Her slightly evil grin didn't hide the smoky glaze in her eyes. "Schnapps. The goal is to make you sluggish, so I can keep a step ahead of you. You scare me."

"I do not."

"Oh," she said, her smile not dimming a bit, "but you do."

"Is it because you're religious, Abby?" His question was half-serious. "The kids helping at church all the time. Prayers before meals. Don't get me wrong, I love that about you. But is that why I scare you?"

"Yes." She looked down. "No." Her smile turned shy. "My dad was religious and big on propriety. I have some of that, but I'm not quite as fanatic. My faith is important to me. I'd never have made it through these years without it. But, propriety isn't my issue with you. I can't get past the plain old hormones. That's what scares me."

"Hallelujah for hormones." Relief made him laugh. "I have a plan for dealing with those."

Chapter Twenty-Two

ABBY LICKED THE last bit of marshmallow from her fingers and pretended not to stalk Gray with her eyes as he worked on his upper lip with swipes of his tongue tip. She forced her eyes to the tree line where Bijou and Jackson stood tied to sturdy limbs, their saddles on the ground, their muffled grazing sounds comforting in the dark.

Gucci should have been one of the horses stomping and snorting, and pain sliced through her at the knowledge her beloved stallion would never be tethered in this spot again. But Gray was here, and his presence was the first thing to even approach filling the hole torn in her heart.

Turning back to the campfire, she closed her eyes. She loved the heat on her face—the ultra-hot flush from the flames. The heat was intensified tonight, in every secret spot of her body. Gray's presence owned her awareness, along with the cricket songs and the pounding of her pulse in her ears.

"You look cold." His voice startled her, banishing the last thoughts of horses and losses.

A laugh spilled from her lips. "That's ridiculous."

"It's not. I say you're shivering." He unfolded his powerful legs, pushed to a stand, and Abby's stomach moved into a rocking samba of excitement as he strode to stand over her. "I can see you shaking from here."

"You need glasses."

"No, I need something much different."

He knelt in front of her. Her stomach dipped; her breathing accelerated.

"I think my plan to slow you down has backfired." She swallowed. "You need to work off some of this sugar high."

He placed four fingers between her breasts and pushed with gentle, steady pressure until she lay on her back, her head just off the quilt. Walking his hands up either side of her body, he crept forward until he was suspended over her, balanced on his hands and toes.

"Good idea." He lowered his body, and his hot breath, sweet with a lingering scent of the schnapps, swept her face. She sucked it into her lungs like the smoke of a drug.

His biceps contracted then straightened. A perfect push-up. "One," he said.

"Oh, jeez." Her breath escaped like steam from a valve.

His arm muscles bunched—down and up again. "Two."

The third time, his torso whispered against hers, prickling like static electricity. "Three."

Next he brushed her full body, breast to thigh. Blood pounded to her core. "Four."

"Who does push-ups anymore?" The words squeaked past her larynx.

"I do. Five."

The campfire's heat jumped from the pit to Abby's body, and she fought to keep from pulling him onto her to end the teasing.

"Six."

"Oh. Gray." She closed her eyes as throbbing settled between her thighs and radiated until it pounded behind her navel.

She thought she'd been ready for him, but she'd never imagined anything like this. Push-ups. Just—*push-ups*. She'd never think of them the same way again.

"Seven."

Soft lips touched her forehead. Foreheads weren't supposed to have this many nerve endings.

"Eight."

She reached around and grabbed hold of his biceps. She arched her back, and when he came down again, her pelvis grazed his with a slick shot of current.

"Nine." His lips found her nose, and she whimpered.

"Ten." Lip to lip. Wet, lingering, he pressed against her for several seconds before pushing up. He hadn't even broken a sweat, and when she forced herself to open her eyes his were riveted on her, a dreamy, opaque, cousin-of-blue color like new steel.

"Eleven."

"How many can you do?"

"As many as you want. Twelve."

"How many can you really do?"

His full weight came to rest atop the length of her. "Tonight? Only twelve."

She forced her heavy limbs around him. His lips sealed against hers, and his tongue, thick, hot, and strong, swept deep into the recesses of her mouth. A long, mutual groan sent liquid rushing to the spot where they fit flawlessly in the age-old, hard-to-soft, male and female puzzle.

Sibilant wind in pine tops formed background music, and everything else outside their entwined bodies disappeared. The sensuous weight of fingers in her hair set her to quivering. The pulsing of warm lips against hers changed pressure from soft to firm and back like they were coaxing music from an instrument. Scrabbling her fingers at Gray's lower back, she dug against his shirt until it bunched beneath her fingers and led her to skin.

"Yessss," she murmured into his mouth.

"Oh, Abby, sweetheart, you taste so good."

He erased every bit of nervousness, and there'd been plenty to erase. Despite her easy answer to his question earlier, she'd thought long and hard about heading down this path with him. Her well-meaning father had indeed drummed the sin of this unmarried act into her head, and Abby had passed the same morals on to Kim. But Abby was not fifteen. She was thirty-seven. Married once. Long past ignorance about safety, and tired of worrying about taboos she knew heaven didn't care about at her age.

With her ankles hooked around his thighs, she pushed the last of her guilt away and locked his body to hers.

They rocked as one until Gray braced his knees on either side of her hips and with one powerful surge flipped their positions. When she lay draped over his body like cling wrap, he cupped her face between his strong palms.

He kissed just beneath her jaw, twisted his head, and trailed his lips to the hollow of her throat. Goose bumps played witness to his thrilling skill.

"I told you you were shivering." The words singed her skin like falling sparks.

"I guess you weren't crazy." Her eyes closed.

With determined dexterity, his hand delved between them, and he loosened three buttons of her shirt, then twisted his wrist to find her breast. "So sweet," he said against her lips.

He performed pure and simple magic. Through cool satin his clever fingers rolled her sensitive skin between his thumb and forefinger, turning first one nipple then the second into throbbing peaks. After he'd kissed her thoroughly, tugging her bottom lip over and over with painful gentleness, he pushed her torso up, leaving her straddling him as he turned his attention to the remainder of her buttons. The fabric parted, baring her stomach and lacy bra. Before she could lie back down, his abs contracted and he sat, pushing her backward.

"You are exquisite."

"You almost make me believe that."

"By the time we're done, there'll be no 'almost,' Abby, I promise."

His lips charted a damp path across her belly. He worked open the button on her jeans, lowered the zipper and spread her fly so he could claim the skin below her navel, too. With moves bordering on reverent he worked back up her body, cupped one breast and bent to kiss her through the fabric of her bra. Right through the satin he worried the pebble of skin, laving until the material was so wet and hot she could no longer tell there was anything between her and his mouth. She grasped his head to her.

He chuckled, blew on the wet spot, and sent chills like little luge-riders down the mound of her breast into her body.

If she'd ever thought you had to be naked to make love, the indescribable pleasure of unrelenting wetness against her skin left that belief tattered like a white surrender flag.

"Are you done fooling around?" She whimpered.

"Do you want me to be?"

"No. Yes."

"Make up your mind, sweetheart," he teased. "Shall I come or shall I go?"

"What you shall do is stop throwing my bad puns back in my face." She groaned again, then wriggled from beneath him and knelt, grabbed for his T-shirt hem and scrunched the green fabric up his torso. With the grace of a bullfighter, she slicked the shirt off his body and lost her breath in a whoosh. His firm pecs and a perfect fan of dark hair greeted her at eye level.

"Lord in heaven. Now I remember why you're so good at push-ups."

She burrowed into his chest hair, its softness sending tingling heat down her arms. He peeled her blouse from her shoulders like the skin of an exotic fruit, and once it had joined his shirt, he attempted to pull her close.

"Unh, unh." She escaped and sank in front of him, pressing her lips to the dusting of hair beneath his navel. The trail beckoned her to his waistband and was just enough to tickle her upper lip as she worked downward. His button slipped through its buttonhole at the command of her fingers, and she unzipped his Levi's to match her.

"I haven't done this in a very long time."

"I have to tell you, love," emotion rasped the tone of his voice to gravel, "I can't tell."

She outlined him through his denim fly and his shape grew easier to trace with each pass of her finger. His muscles clenched.

"Abby," he groaned. "You're killing me." He tried to catch her hand, but she resisted, relishing a power she'd never known she could have over a man.

"Stop fussing," she murmured. "Turn about is fair play."

She gripped the sides of his thighs, and, before she could think about her boldness, kissed him through the fabric. His choked swallow heightened her excitement.

"Look here, you," he said, parroting her earlier question. "Are you done fooling around?"

A joyous chuckle escaped her as she shuddered in pleasure. "I am if you are."

"Oh, I am."

In three seconds her bra disappeared, her jeans were shimmying down her hips, and her laughter mingling with groans as she fought with his Levi's. Socks followed and they sank together onto the ground, the thick blanket protecting them from beneath, and the crackling fire warming them from the side.

His tongue sparred with hers, slippery and breathtaking. She roamed his skin with her hands, shoulder blades to hard glutes, allowing him to pull on her hips until she fit against the hard ridge she'd been tracing moments before.

"I want you." Conviction filled her voice.

"Wait, wait," he whispered. "I'm not callous, Abby, I have protection."

"I knew you would."

"Trusting little cowgirl." He kissed her and fumbled for his pants. A few seconds later she'd helped him hurry, and he was back in her arms.

"Oh, man, who knew that could be sexy?" His hard sigh sent high voltage to every one of Abby's nerve endings.

"I think you could stand on one foot, hold an umbrella and make a stupid face and you'd be sexy right now," she laughed.

"Have I told you how amazing you are? How turned on I am?"

"You don't need words, mister . . . ohhhh!" A zing of deep pleasure rocked her as Gray slipped one hand between them and stroked deep into her warm core. Her head fell away from him and he kissed her throat.

"Yeah," he breathed. "So sweet. Come on, love, come with me now."

It had been a long time, but Abby didn't feel one instant of discomfort as Gray arched and slid into her. Satisfying fullness, erotic stretching, an arrow-pierce of souls connecting, all overwhelmed her and, for long seconds, he lay still within her.

He moved first. It took a shivery moment of shared smiles and speechless trial-and-error to learn from each other and find the universe's most timeless motion, but once its rhythm gathered, the blanket, the fire, and the woods fell away again. Sparks and sensation built until Abby's hitched breathing matched Gray's. Perfect feeling grew, and she tried to hang on to the wave crest, to ride it until Gray was ready, but her limbs quivered and her body shook. His every movement was too intimate for her to control. Behind her eyelids, colors began to swirl.

"Gray . . ." she began helplessly, only to be shocked by his voice.

"Oh Abby, girl, it's now. Now, love."

The light behind her eyes synced with the blazing campfire, and they rocked together, then called out together, then were lifted higher by every coordinated thrust. For one glorious moment she had a coherent thought—that although she knew she couldn't live in this state of hyper-climax forever, she wanted to try more than she'd ever wanted anything in her life.

The wave crashed, and wondrous relief hit her right along with hot tears. He collapsed against her, his weight keeping her grounded and safe. A happy sob caught in her throat.

"Hey, silly, don't cry." His tender voice whispered through his breathing.

"Then don't make love like that." She wasn't crying hard, but tears coursed from the corners of her eyes. Rough thumb strokes wiped them away, leaving her feeling ridiculously cherished.

"Sorry. I'll work on it." He shifted within her one last time, and they both moaned.

"Yeah, so will I. I didn't make you cry at all."

"How do you know, you haven't looked at me."

She opened her eyes and grinned. His pale gaze blazed into her, fevered and bright. "Nope, no tears."

"No, but, god, you look beautiful."

She didn't know how to return the compliment, or tell him he'd been right, that she believed him. She was a glowing wood sprite, a fairy nymph, a woodland goddess.

"Scootch over." He shifted with her, making her laugh at the awkwardness of trying to move while connected.

He flipped one end of the blanket over them and let them settle apart, draping his leg over her thighs and gathering her close. The hard ground wouldn't allow them to lie there for long, but at that moment the quilt was as good as ten down mattresses, and Gray's sweet, sexy breath settled into a satisfied cadence against her hair. Money problems, beloved stallions, snooping media, and the insanity of celebrity were relegated to little sealed compartments in her brain. The compartments weren't locked, but they were guarded by the shivery foot soldiers of lovemaking's aftermath. Gray's mouth settled on hers one more time, and she wished she believed the army was strong enough to withstand anything.

Chapter Twenty-Three

"ANY REGRETS THIS morning?" His voice, roughened from abbreviated sleep, tickled her neck. Abby stood at the counter, beating eggs for scrambling, and grinned. An open window let in the perfume of peonies and wildflowers. Perking coffee added its stimulating dark spice. Her bare feet on the linoleum felt almost as good as Gray's fingers on her skin.

"None. Guilt maybe. Kim gave me a fairly hairy eyeball when I tucked her in at 3 a.m. She knows."

"She doesn't *know* anything. Even if she does, there are things adults who've been married before can do that kids can't. It's that simple."

"I was a virgin when I married Jack. I . . ." An embarrassed giggle eked its way free. "Now, why would I tell you that?"

"Dunno. Do you think it'll affect me wanting to marry you?"

She spun, splattering beaten egg onto the floor. "Marry?"

Gray took her wooden spoon, set it aside, gripped her cheeks, and stared earnestly into her eyes. "Would it be such an unreasonable thing to talk about? I mean, not like we'd do it tomorrow . . ."

"Gray . . . I . . ." Her heart flopped in complete arrhythmia, yet she couldn't deny the forbidden excitement that filtered through her along with the shock.

He kissed her eyelids, her brows, her cheek, and her earlobe. "We're good for each other. At least, you are for me—more than you could ever know. I could learn to be good for you."

"Stop it. You're already good for me." She might not have admitted it a week ago, but it was the truth now. At least, on an emotional level.

"Things would be better for both of us. Aside from the fact that I'm completely crazy about you, I could make a better home for Dawson, and we could make things easier for you and Kim."

For the first time her blood chilled. *Make it easier.* That's what Jack's parents had always said. She pulled away, wounded, angry, and embarrassed. "What makes you think I need anyone to make things easier?"

"Come on, Abby, don't." His voice didn't change. No condescension or pity tinged it. "You know how much I admire you. I don't think for a second you need me—

look what you've accomplished here in the past eleven years. But as honest as we are with each other, you still hide a lot. Things are tight, you struggle. A lot of people struggle."

"It doesn't mean I can't take care of myself or my daughter."

"Nobody says you can't."

"Oh, yes they do. They have." She spun on him, not wanting him to know what a failure she'd felt like the past three weeks, but unable to keep her fears from him any longer. Tears threatened, barely kept at bay. "Jack's parents have scrutinized me for years. They threatened to take Kim right after Jack died, because they knew then how much debt I was in. Not that they can threaten to take her anymore, but they will say 'I told you so' any chance they get. They've never forgiven me for raising their only grandchild on a shoestring."

"Is that what this is about? Proving yourself to people who just don't matter?"

"It's habit," she said dully. "If they think it, others think it."

"Nobody thinks it. What they all think is that you'll sacrifice anything for your family." He lifted her chin gently. "How did you pay for the well? Abby?" His voice was soft but hit her like a bludgeon.

A tiny sob broke free. She didn't want to say the words out loud. She missed Gucci so much it made her feel guilty, because she'd lost more important things in her life before than a stupid horse. She pulled away from him, anguished.

"Gucci wasn't really just out in the pasture, and you weren't giving him the night off last night, were you?" Shocked, Abby flinched as each word pierced her heart. "He's gone, isn't he?"

"How could you know that? Why would you think I'd sell . . ." She couldn't finish. Her gaze fell from his.

"I'm slow sometimes, but I'm not blind. I'm so sorry, honey. My point is, you don't have to keep this stuff a secret from me. I have a good shoulder for leaning on. And let's just say, for argument's sake, that you and I were to do something drastic one day." His smile turned impish. "Wouldn't it be a nice extra that you wouldn't have to worry about finances?"

Despite her embarrassment, Abby leaned against his chest and let him hold her while her few tears spent themselves. "I hate that I can't keep things up. I can't even keep a stupid job . . ."

"What about your job?"

She groaned and pushed away from him. "You mean you don't know about that, too? The job at the architectural firm is ending. My boss is disbanding the company. Bye-bye twenty bucks an hour. For two weeks I've been pounding the pavement, but nobody will have me."

Gray snorted in laughter. "All the more reason for *me* to take you. I'll have you. Kind of like I had you last night."

"Yes. You did. And if I hadn't taken you just as thoroughly, I'd be slugging you for that chauvinistic remark, you arrogant jerk."

"Abby." His voice, muffled in her hair, contained a

smile. "We've been good like this since the first minute we met. Sparring with you is like being on vacation. Tell me we can stay together when I'm done with this tour. That we can talk about the future and maybe a new farm where you can keep all your horses and just work with them—not have to pound the pavement."

At that moment his vision had a powerful draw. "I wasn't lying about starting to fall in love with you." She trembled at the import of her words. "But I'm not *staying* with anyone, even you, in order to be rescued."

She hadn't meant the words to sound so harsh and for an instant a wounded look crossed Gray's face making Abby feel cold. But he sighed and nodded.

"I get that. But would you *share* yourself with someone in order to do the rescuing?"

She stared at him, marveling that he'd salvaged what could have been a colossal meltdown. She stepped back to the stove, putting her fork back to stir the eggs. Her heart pounded. "I don't know, maybe we should talk."

"Just where were you until all hours this morning, young lady?" Kim's voice in the doorway made Abby and Gray spin in unison.

Her daughter wore a pair of khaki short shorts and a cherry-red crop top tied at the midriff. Hidden in a thin smile was the glint of wounded anger.

"Hey, Kim." Gray answered first. "We found a good spot for a campfire and got to talking."

"Yup." Abby nodded. "We weren't worried about you guys. I'm sorry, sweetie, we just lost track of the time."

Kim smiled at Gray and avoided Abby's eyes. "Last time I tried the 'lost track of time' line, I got a lecture."

"What?" Abby asked, suddenly annoyed with her daughter's snit.

"Because you aren't a grown-up. Age has privilege." Gray smiled, too, but wounded surprise lit Kim's eyes. He'd already mentioned the dad-word last night. Having him speak like a parent must have felt like salt in a cut. Still, he softened the blow with his usual suave. "Aw, Kimmy, it was no big deal, and we came back safe and sound. And now, we've got some party planning to do. I hear we're having guests and presents and everything." He made a bug-eyed face, and Kim, partially appeased, copied him.

"Sylvia and Ed," she agreed. "And Mrs. Baxter and her family."

"It sounds great. So let's get hopping."

The morning passed in a happy blur of chores and birthday secrets. Gray mowed the lawn. Dawson tackled garden raking. Kim worked two horses. Abby cleaned. It would have been drudgery except for the fantasy family surrounding her, making every task a joyous circus. Gray added to the chaos in her heart by flirting at every opportunity. By the time she'd lost count of his cheeky lines of innuendo and stolen kisses, he had her so turned on she was certain it showed like sun in the darkroom.

She was unsuccessfully diluting her libido with ice tea and devising a way to get out alone with Gray again that night, when she heard the slam of car doors. Roscoe, cooling himself in the piano alcove, gave a low bark, followed moments later by a rap on the front door. Since it hadn't been used in years, Abby opened it cautiously and didn't stop Roscoe from leaping against the screen.

Some watchdog, Abby thought as the door opened and the dog waded happily into the group. To her shock, she came face-to-face with the fastidious Chris Boyle. He pulled off a pair of aviator sunglasses and smiled. "Hello, again, Mrs. Stadtler."

A hefty black man sporting neat cornrows and a bright yellow Guinness Stout T-shirt, squatted at the bottom of the porch steps letting Roscoe wiggle around him in greeting. "Hey, there. How are ya pooch?"

A slender, handsome man stood beside him in worn jeans and a black T-shirt, sporting a neat, brown mustache and goatee, and hair pulled into a thick pony tail. He smiled, his eyes tossing golden sparks her way.

"You must be Abby." His leisurely voice didn't match the dynamic fire in his gaze, but the combination was oddly comforting. "I'm Alfred Jackson," he said. "Most people just call me Spark. I'm sorry to surprise you like this."

Her thoughts wheeled like startled bats. Spark kicked backward without looking and connected his heel with the wide expanse of Squatting Guinness-Man's thigh. He grunted and hoisted his two-hundred-fifty-plus pounds to a stand.

"Hey, Abby." His mouth grinned and his voice boomed. "I'm Miles Dixon."

"I . . . this . . . ohmygosh, *surprise* is an understatement." She struggled to keep her gaze direct, as Chris Boyle, his smile never dimming, nodded in sympathy.

"I hope you'll forgive us. We kind of wanted to surprise our boy since it's his birthday. I'm sure you understand. He was so eager to come back here we wanted to make sure he plans to return to us." Beneath the smile was a veiled accusation.

"I have no doubt he does." Abby challenged him with a pointed gaze.

"What the hell is this?" Gray strode around the front corner of the house.

"Yo! There's the man!" Miles called as Gray marched toward the trio. They engulfed him in back slaps and rough embraces, their greetings spiced liberally with language that would have made her father call for their salvation. Gray untangled himself and came for her. When his hand closed on hers, warmth and reassurance finally returned her confidence.

"You've met Chris before, but what do you think of these idiots?"

She donned her best manners and smiled, unsure why she wasn't happier to have met them. "Miles, Spark, wonderful to meet you. Chris?" She held out her hand. "Good to meet the mastermind again."

"He ain't no mastermind, Miz Abby." Miles popped the manager on one elegant shoulder. "He's just got us to follow his ass around and make him *look* like a genius."

Abby had to laugh. The humor was as genuine as the twinkle in Miles's charcoal eyes.

"You look right at home, Covey." Spark eyed Gray,

fresh from his stint with the lawnmower, the toes of his old running shoes stained a bright green.

"This is a great place," Gray said without hesitation. "You've already met the dog. Got a cat, some kids, a couple of chickens, horses, chores. And, of course, Abby."

"I hope you'll come in and stay a while." Abby rested her eyes on Spark, which kept her from choking on the words. His easy demeanor was genuine, too, but she didn't believe for a minute they'd come just to celebrate Gray's birthday.

"That's too good an offer to pass up, thank you," Chris said.

Abby's heart sank, but there was no taking the invitation back.

THEY'D BE LEAVING soon. She told herself repeatedly that peace would return at least for the night when Chris Boyle took his two charges back to the hotel. The bad news was they were all returning for the party tomorrow. Abby took a fortifying breath and let herself into the house. Gray had stayed in the barn with the kids and sweet Colossus Miles who, it turned out, was as big an animal lover as Abby. She amended her thoughts. Miles and Spark would be joys to have at Gray's birthday. It was Chris who was medicine show barker, televangelist, and Donald Trump in one overly well-groomed package.

Not that Gray could see it. In the fifteen minutes Abby had been able to get Gray alone, he'd been the one to press her. Why was she upset? What had happened? The only thing she'd been able to do was spill Elliott's accusation.

"All he wants to do is test Chris's motives," she'd told him. "If Chris isn't doing what Elliott thinks he is, there'll be no harm. Chris will just ignore the picture."

To her relief Gray had not been angry. He'd only laughed and pulled her close. "Sweetheart, can't you see what Elliott's trying to do? Putting a wedge between Chris and me would be the ultimate revenge. I've known Chris ten years longer than I've known Elliott, and he's captained this boat with barely a glitch. I can't mess with that kind of success, Abby. We won't be sending any pictures."

He was right. She headed for the refrigerator and some icy water. She had no cause to believe Elliott St. Vincent over the man who'd brought Gray to global adoration. Gray loved Chris. She loved Gray. Her loyalty needed to lie with him.

A streak of orange and a plaintive yowl stopped her. Bird halted by her legs and raised an indignant head. *Me-owwwwl*. This was his reaction to strangers invading his space—the reaction he'd never had to Gray. She squatted, ran a hand over his back, and then heard the voices.

"Do what you have to do to get him away from this flea-bitten dump." Chris didn't hear her sneak to the living room doorway. He stood beside Spark in the alcove with vitriol polluting his satin voice. "She's a gold-digger. She'll sink him faster than the iceberg sank the Titanic."

Abby's legs buckled with hurt and anger. She gripped the door jamb with all the strength in her fingers.

"That isn't fair, Chris. We can warn him not to cancel

any more concerts, but we don't know Abby. She seems like a wonderful woman. I think she's good for him." Tears pricked her eyes. As much as she'd grown to detest Chris, she'd fallen head-over-teakettle for Spark. God bless him.

"No! Don't you see how she's manipulating him? Using his boy? Damn it, Spark, she's playing us for all we're worth. He'll give up touring for her, and, what? Mow her lawn for the rest of his life? She's damn fine-looking, I sure don't blame him for wanting a piece of that for a while, but he's not a one-lawn kind of man. And I can't promise I could get him back to where he is now once he's tired of playing Farmer in the Dell."

"You can't run his personal life. He's an adult."

"I've always run his life. He'd go gallivanting around the globe singing to Alzheimer's patients if he didn't have me. I'll do what needs to be done to make sure I keep running his life."

Abby didn't dare stay to hear more. She stumbled backward, nauseated and shaking. To her face, Chris had oozed smooth charm. Smooth like Lex Luthor, she realized. But she had to face the fact, too, that no matter how distasteful a man he was, Chris could very well believe he had Gray's best interests at heart. She scooped Bird from the kitchen and carried him to the back stoop. She didn't know why the big cat allowed her to hold him like a stuffed toy, but he did. And he purred when the first of her tears plopped onto his orange head.

Elliott had written out instructions for her in case she decided to help him with his sting. All she had to do was create a header that made it look like her e-mail came from an anonymous photographer. A simple message, "I've found your boy. He's in Minnesota. Contact me if you want me to keep his whereabouts a secret," was all Elliott claimed it would take. Chris would grab the chance to spin the picture his own way.

She couldn't do it.

She had to do it.

She should tell Gray what Chris had said, give him another chance, but he'd been adamant he wouldn't play Elliott's game. If Elliott was wrong, Gray would never know the picture had been sent. But, if Chris was manipulating Gray's career at any cost, and if he planned to keep her away from the man she was growing to love . . . She had to risk helping Elliott.

Late that night, with her finger poised over the send key, she told herself it was only a small experiment. If her perfect picture of Gray and his son did get printed, the public would see them in a wonderful, warm light. Still, a swell of bile rose in her throat, and she couldn't shake the feeling that if she sent her potentially damning cargo off into cyberspace, she'd be starting a launch sequence to disaster.

Chapter Twenty-Four

"Wow, IS THAT my cake?" Gray entered the kitchen and caught Abby around the shoulders, giving a squeeze that earned them a lazy smile from Sylvia.

"And Kim's." Sylvia cuffed at Gray's fingers when he reached for a slick of frosting. "You have to share, even if you could eat it all yourself."

"I could." He shook his hand and bestowed an unabashed hug on Sylvia. "It looks incredible."

Sylvia had a delectable talent with cakes. This one was decorated with a guitar, outlined in icing and filled in with the exact colors of Gray's blue Ovation. The guitar was surrounded by feminine flowers, and Gray's and Kim's names.

"I came to tell you all everyone's looking for you girls." Gray lifted a finger as if to try another steal, but Sylvia narrowed her eyes and he grinned.

"More like looking for the cake," Sylvia scolded.

He waggled his brows.

Abby patted his side then wiggled her fingers, laughing as he doubled over, basking in the familiarity. "Go away now." She pushed at him. "The cake will be there soon enough."

"Mean, mean woman." He kissed her, right in front of Sylvia, and left.

A rush of warmth flushed Abby's cheeks, and she covered her face in her hands, giggling. When she looked up, Sylvia chuckled. "Oh, Syl, what do you think? Is he perfect-gentleman enough?"

"I sure hope not." Sylvia lifted a knife and pretended to wipe it on a towel.

"What?" Abby sputtered.

"You're kids; you like each other." Sylvia fixed her with a wise eye. "There wouldn't be much to keep up the interest if he were a perfect gentleman."

Abby's mouth dropped. The aloof old faker. All at once, the source of perpetual light between Sylvia and Ed became a lot clearer.

"That singer makes you happier than you've been in a while, and that makes us happy. All right, then." Just that succinctly she was done with the mushy stuff. "Let's go party a little bit. You bring the cake out for me."

A full-on stampede greeted them as Abby set the cake in the middle of the picnic table. She produced three boxes of birthday candles, and while she speared forty-five of them into the frosting she considered the unlikely mix of guests. Spark's wife Lindsey had flown in, as had Misty Donahue. Karla had been in nirvana talking music with Gray and Spark. Her husband, Roger, had struck up a conversation with Chris, and Ed viewed the hubbub with a bottle of beer and an eagle eye. He might have looked like the forgotten patriarch of a rowdy family, but his sharp, vigilant gaze showed he wasn't missing a trick.

Abby lit every single candle, and, fueled by laughter, the party broke into a raucous, out-of-tune rendition of "Happy Birthday" that left Abby's eyes streaming.

"For a group of singers, that was the worst performance I've ever heard," Ed said for her.

"We're on vacation," Spark replied. "No busman's holiday."

"Okay." Gray held up his hand. "Mine isn't the only birthday today, as you all know. Kimmy? Front and center!"

Star-struck, Kim hopped up next to Gray, her eyes fiery with excitement. Spark handed Gray his guitar. Misty, beside Kim, winked and nodded.

"Yo, sixteen candles!" Miles clapped his hands, and Ed stepped in with matches.

"He knows how to put on a show, doesn't he?" Abby startled at the voice in her ear.

Chris had kept a low profile all afternoon, for which she'd been grateful. She half-feared he was slick enough to have figured out the e-mail plot. He had to have received the photo.

"He's good with people, if that's what you mean."

"Oh, my dear Abby." His laugh was robust and confident. "That's putting it very mildly, as you'll learn if you endeavor to stay with him for any length of time."

"Excuse me?" She turned just enough to eye his profile. "*Endeavor* to stay with him? Are you suggesting something, Mr. Boyle?"

"Of course not. I'd like you to go into this with your eyes open, however. For your sake. I love Gray like family—we all do. But we know him. He talks about you as the new woman in his life. But, my dear, you aren't the first new woman by a long shot."

"I'd be a hermit with my head in the sand if I didn't know that."

"Then you also know it's possible to get hurt if you play in his circle."

"You don't want me with him." Abby faced him. "I don't know why, since you don't know me. But let me tell you, Mr. Boyle. Chris." She impaled him with a frank stare. "I'm not looking for anything from him, and he knows it. I love my home, and although I'm deeply attracted to Gray, we don't know yet if our lives will ever mesh. We just want the chance to find out. You might consider, if this works out, although I'm not his first woman, I might be his last."

If Chris hadn't stared just a nanosecond too long, and if the crease beside his handsome mouth hadn't twitched and deepened an extra millimeter, Abby might have believed his next words. "I have nothing against you, Abby, but that isn't the first time I've heard that line either. I care more than you can imagine about Gray, so in truth my job is to protect both of you. I just want you to take care." He walked away without another word.

"Of all the . . ." She stared at the grass, welding her lips tight to keep her thoughts inside. She pounded clenched fists on her thighs. *Egotistical, condescending jerks.*

A guitar chord lifted her from her angry reverie. Kim, mesmerized, stood with moony eyes trained on Gray, while he and Misty launched into a lilting version of "Happy Birthday"—Marilyn Monroe–slow if not sexy. How the heck "Happy Birthday" could spellbind a yard full of adults Abby had no clue, but it did. Misty's phenomenal, sultry alto swirled with Gray's crooning baritone, thick and musically caloric—like slow-churned ice cream for the ears. When they finished, Abby was lost in his voice and his eyes. She wanted nothing more than to whisk him away and turn him into her own private dessert.

"Happy day my birthday twin," Gray said.

"Oh, thank you. That was beautiful." Kim whispered in near reverence, but Gray didn't allow the mood to grow. He raised his palm for a high-five, and Kim's grin blossomed like a summer crescent moon. "Blow out your candles, Kimmy, then we can eat cake. Then we get presents!"

"All *right!*" Kim made short work of the sixteen candles and bent to the task of cutting.

"Hey, gorgeous." Gray's arm encircled her from behind, and he nuzzled her earlobe.

"Hey . . ." She spun in his arms. "I kind of wish it were my birthday. That song . . ."

"Mmm, liked it, did you?"

"Uh, yeah, Gray . . . duh." She rolled her eyes in her best teenager imitation.

"You don't need a birthday for me to sing sexy to you."

"Oh, and I've learned that, too. You spoil me—and to think I wasn't even a fan at first."

He set his forehead against hers. "Why do you think I fell so hard for you? I had to win your love without the fame or the glitz—they never impressed you."

"Still don't," she whispered.

"Won't it be fun when this is an every-year event?" Gray nuzzled her ear again, and Abby slapped his shoulder.

"Don't get cocky just 'cause it's your birthday. I never said I'd marry you."

"But you might."

A thrill of excitement darted around her insides like a trapped firefly. "I might."

Half an hour later, the evening had donned the best of summer with a gentle breeze and hazy, seven o'clock light filtering through rustling leaves. Karla stood in front of the guests, who'd assembled like theater-goers in lawn chairs and blankets on the grass. Gray gave her a thumbs-up. He liked Karla Baxter—especially after talking with her for quite a while earlier. She exuded not just effervescence but a genuine honesty that invited friendship.

"I thought it would be awkward coming to a party for a famous singer," she began. "Turns out Gray Covey's just a regular guy, which is, I think, what he'd like all of us small-towners to know.

"I've been spending a lot of time arm-twisting today, and I'm thrilled that Gray told me I can make an official announcement. He's agreed not only to help convince the powers that be to hold our annual music camp in three weeks, but he's volunteered to participate—right after the last concert of his tour. He'll teach some classes and help organize the Kabbagestock concert. What do you think?"

Gray shrugged away the whoops and thanks, and avoided looking at Chris, who had heard nothing of this venture. He wasn't sure himself why he'd agreed, except that, while playing for arena-sized crowds was exhilarating, those crowds weren't changing his standings on the charts or feeding his creativity. They also didn't stop the panic inside every time he realized there were no plans, no dreams, for when he could no longer sell out a concert.

Karla's music camp represented a project so different it terrified him. He hadn't been adrenaline-pumping, go-for-broke, it-might-fail-but-what-the-hell scared and excited in a long, long time. From the chair next to his, Abby crinkled her nose. "You're so cool," she whispered. His heart careened into his chest wall.

Her delicate feminine scent was ingrained in him. The memory of her body intertwined with his wouldn't leave him. Like a randy teenager, all he could fantasize about was riding off again with her and reprising the most amazing lovemaking of his life.

More unbelievably, she wanted him for no other reason than love. He'd never trusted that in any woman before. His connection with Abby felt soul-deep. He'd rushed the gate with talk of marriage, but he was as certain of his desire to stay with her as he was of needing his next breath.

"Hey." A stroke on the back of his hand sent a shiver

up his arm. "They're talking to you. "It's gift time, singer-man." She grinned. "You and Kim get up there."

"Ours first!" Kim crowed, beating Gray to the front. Several wrapped packages appeared, and surprise emotion clogged Gray's throat when she handed them to him. He hadn't gotten simple, old-fashioned birthday gifts since his mother had gotten sick. The boxes contained treasures. A soft, blue silk shirt from Abby and Kim, a very mother-like sweater from Sylvia, and a custom-printed sweatshirt from Ed: "Don't bother the Goddess."

"You're a fun guy, Ethel." He thumped the old man on the back, more at home than he'd been in five years.

"Yup, and you're definitely more fun than *I've* had in a long time." He turned to Kim. "Okay, young lady, age went before beauty, that's for sure. Close your eyes."

Kim clapped like a five-year-old. Ed and Dawson disappeared around the side of the house. Gray's stomach did anticipatory high-dives and flips. "Eyes closed? Promise?"

"Yes! Yes!"

A moment later the pair reappeared, carrying Ed's birchwood trunk, three-feet-by-four-feet, with a hinged lid, and a hand-rubbed polish. Affixed to the top was a huge pink bow. Gray tapped Kim's shoulder. "Okay, you can look."

For long seconds Kim stared, her brows knitted as she assessed the box. Gray grinned and stole a glance at Abby, who had two palms over her mouth in happy surprise.

"Your mama says you been looking at the fancy tack

trunks in your catalogues for years," Ed said. "I stole a look-see and decided I could do just as well. Gray and Dawson, here, helped pick out the wood. You go ahead and open 'er up. See if it'll do."

Little mewing squeals emanated from Kim as she sank to her knees. "Ed, su-weeet! It's gorgeous, just gorgeous!"

Gray knew exactly what the inside of the box looked like, with a metal stand bolted to one end for holding a saddle, and a removable, partitioned tray over the top for holding small items. His pulse pounded like a piston as he waited for Kim to lift the lid.

She froze as if she'd been hit with a Taser. When she did move it was to swivel her head and stare at her mother, but Abby only shrugged. Kim's eyes found Ed's, then Gray's.

"No way." Her eyes began to glisten. "No way no way no *way!*" She delved into the new trunk and hoisted the dressage saddle Gray and Ed had placed there hours before. "Is this from you?" Her voice bordered on the hysterical.

"Dawson and me."

"This is unbelievable. Mom! Look. It's my County dressage saddle."

Abby, too, had frozen in place, but unlike Kim, she no longer smiled. Her eyes registered shock and her voice grated with a twinge of irritation. "That's wonderful, Kim."

She didn't look at him. Kim set the saddle back on its rack and launched herself at Gray with arms spread. He had no time to deflect her embrace.

"Thank you, Gray, oh thank you."

Her slender arms tightened, and he let her cling. She was too hopped-up on excitement to make anything of the hug. She gave a last huge squeeze and jumped to where Dawson stood on the fringe of the group. Before he could escape, she'd thrown her arms around him, too.

"Hey." Immediately pink-faced, he unhappily withstood the attack.

Neither Ed nor Sylvia escaped the wild thank-you, either.

Abby still looked two flashes short of angry. Gray approached her chair and squatted, forcing her to look at him. The sparkle of laughter from moments before was lost.

"It's too much, Gray."

"It's all right. It's a special birthday. We can talk about it later."

"Oh yes, we can and we will."

He relaxed. He could win her over. Besides, his final surprise would soften her for good. Dawson slipped away and Gray's heart went back to beating double time. He grasped Abby's hand and pulled her reluctant frame out of the chair. Her mouth had already lost its pinched look.

"This was quite a birthday, Mr. Covey." She offered a grudging smile.

"It's not quite over. There's one more present. For the birthday girl's mom."

He could tell by looking at her she didn't want to be excited. But she was. "Oh?" She pulled back to stare. "Do I even want to know?"

He spun her in place and put his hands over her eyes. "I bought back a piece of your heart." He kissed her ear. "And, selfishly, what I hope is a long future of nighttime horseback rides." He'd had a better speech planned, but the mood of the party didn't warrant grand words. With a peek over Abby's head, he confirmed Dawson was in sight leading a head-tossing Gucci from the barn. Kissing Abby lightly one more time, he drew his hands away.

Her shoulders hunched, and her hands flew to her mouth. "How? What?" Further words dissolved into choked sobs.

"You can't live without him. I don't want you to live without him."

She spun on him with tears in her eyes, and the collective oohing from their gathered friends turned into clapping and cheering. But there was no joy behind Abby's tears. "You!" She cried, her hands trembling. "How dare you?"

Chapter Twenty-Five

She might as well have crushed him with a mace.

"Abby, I . . . ."

She held up her hand. Without speaking, she headed toward her horse. Stricken by the reaction, Gray could hear her sob across the yard as she threw her arms around the stallion's cresty, bay neck.

"I think you got her, dog." Miles slapped him on the back.

His stomach churned, the joy he'd been savoring curdled in his gut. "I guess so." Swallowing back acid, he watched in despair.

"You got Gucci back! How did you do it?" Kim hopped to his side and kept hopping in place. He'd have given part of his soul to have had Abby react that way.

"Ed found the people who bought him," he said dully. "He called them for me and since they had another prospect I didn't have to pay that much more to get him back."

"Are you okay?"

He squirmed under her perceptiveness. "Yeah, I'm not sure your mom knows what to think. Go be my spy, would you? And make sure she's okay?"

He waited several excruciating minutes before gathering the courage to approach her. She stood with her hands buried in Gucci's long mane speaking to Lindsey and Misty. Gray beseeched them with his eyes, and they excused themselves.

"Are you still angry with me?"

"Oh, yeah." Her voice came with frightening seriousness.

"For goodness' sake, why? Abby . . ."

"Stop, Gray. If you don't understand why, then I did a very poor job of making myself clear during this relationship."

"You don't want me paying bills for you. I get that. These are gifts, Abby."

"They're gifts I cannot possibly compete with."

"Since when are presents about competition? Good lord, I . . ."

"That saddle was the desire of her heart, and you handed it to her on a silver platter. I was making her work for it."

"And she has worked for it. She's a great kid, and you've given her an incredible work ethic—she didn't expect it. She's beyond excited, and you would have given it to her in a heartbeat if you could have."

"But I couldn't."

"She doesn't care."

"But I care. And Gucci . . ."

"I was very lucky. I know you don't want me butting in, but can't you see this isn't help? You said you'd let me show you I'm not just passing through your life, well, this is what happens when someone who loves you simply wants to do something nice. I wasn't trying to buy your love. Why would I ever think I had to? My heart broke when I found out you had to sell him, Abby. I wanted him back, too."

"But the decision was mine, and I'd made it. You had no right to unmake it and bring back all the pain it had involved."

"Pain? For the love of . . . Forgive me for wanting to make you happy, Abby." Anger slowly overtook the hurt in his heart. Strong resiliency was one thing. Stubborn pride was another. He admired her desire to make it on her own—he loved her for it. But this was ridiculous.

"Look." She lowered her eyes. "You did make me happy. I admit that now he's back, I won't be sending him away. But I'd like to pay you back for him over time."

Her words slashed through his heart as cleanly as a fencer's foil. "I don't want . . ."

"I know. I know your heart was true in all of this. But it's a fundamental issue you don't seem to understand. It's no big deal to you that you have money, but I don't want it. What you need to do is find something worthy to spend it on. Don't make me your charity, Gray. I loved you for being you."

Loved? "I don't even know what to say."

"I know you don't."

Gravel crunched in the driveway by the house, and both he and Abby looked to the red, mid-sized Ford rolling to a stop. When the driver emerged, Gray knew his day had disintegrated beyond salvation. "What is he doing here?"

After swiveling his head like a periscope scanning for the enemy, Elliott locked his sights on Gray and broke into a loose-limbed trot. "Take it easy, Gray. Just hear me out."

Before either could say a word, Chris materialized like Merlin between them, purple-faced, his eyes almost invisible behind a murderous squint. "What the fuck are you doing here?"

Elliott hefted a folded tabloid newspaper and held it beside his temple, wagging it for emphasis. "I have something Gray and Abby need to see. You," the corners of his mouth rose as he turned to Chris, "have already seen it."

"You little prick. Coming here was stupid."

"We'll see who's stupid, not to mention the prick, in a minute."

Gray took the proffered newspaper. Abby's gaze held something very close to terror, as she looked with him at the picture printed beneath a banner headline: Gray Covey's Secret Uncovered." He vaguely heard her ask Dawson and Kim to take Gucci back to his stall, but he couldn't have said whether they obeyed since his stomach was deciding whether to collapse on itself or send its birthday-food contents hurtling. He'd seen the photo before, too. In Abby's darkroom.

"What is this?" Elliott's boot could have been planted

across Gray's throat in a dark alley for all the sound that came out of it.

"It's a sting. It's time to stop and smell the rat, Gray."

"How did you get this?" Anger churned in his gut, but it didn't translate to his voice. A sick, terrifying thought pounded at his brain as he turned to Abby. "How did he get the picture?"

"I didn't." Elliott stepped to Abby. "I've never seen the picture before."

"St. Vincent!" Chris made up for Gray's lack of voice. "I think it's time for you to leave."

"You'd like that wouldn't you?" Elliott's calm baffled Gray. He bore the assurance of a man who'd fixed the fight and knew he couldn't lose. "Then your singer would never find out you're the one submitting all the pictures to national rags.

"That is the biggest cockamamie load of bull."

For the span of a heartbeat Gray glanced at his manager, and then his senses returned. "What the hell's wrong with you, Elliott? You've been trying to make money off of our friendship and now you're using Abby and Chris? He's right. Get out of here."

"No." Abby's tremulous voice stopped him.

He frowned. "Abby, don't. You don't understand."

"I understand perfectly. Because I sent the picture."

If the ground had opened up and swallowed the entire place, Gray wouldn't have been more stunned. "Excuse me?"

"I sent it, Gray. You know it's mine. But I put the false name on my outgoing e-mail and sent the photo to Chris. Elliott's telling the truth."

Gray's stomach went into a free fall where the only landing spot was the hard reality of something awful. Spark and Miles now stood within earshot. Miles looked ready to eat someone. Spark, in rare outward anger, looked ready to hand him the fork and knife.

"You wouldn't. I said I didn't want any part of that scheme."

"And you have no idea how guilty I feel. But you refused to see the truth."

"This isn't all." Elliott's voice, the only calm thing in the whole bizarre scene, cut through Gray's churning thoughts. "The picture appeared this afternoon, so there's been enough time for reporters to start making their ways here. The copy I had Abby send with the picture reported you were *somewhere* in Minnesota. Somehow," his eyes shot scathing darts Chris, "that got changed specifically to Kennison Falls. This place will be crawling with media within twelve hours.

"You lying scumbag." His manager's face now flamed red.

"So, then, you're calling Abby a lying scumbag too?"

"She knows what's in this for her if Gray stays on top."

"That's enough!" Gray's anger finally erupted. He spun on Chris, knuckles tight, muscles straining like slingshot bands about to be loosed. "You'd better tell me right now what's going on. I've trusted you with my life, almost literally on occasion."

"And look where you are because of it."

"Then you owe me the truth. *Have* you been screwing with me? Is it you making this tour a spectacle?"

"Ask him, Gray," Elliott interrupted. "About Jillian Harper and how that one's backfiring on him. And how he told the people at your mother's nursing home he was me." Elliott remained the only calm person in the group. "I never sent my pictures anywhere, and I know my files were accessed at least three times when I wasn't online."

"You have no proof I did those things."

"Aside from my word, which we all know is worth a chewed wad of gum at the moment, I figured out a way to catch a thief." Elliott looked from Gray to Spark to Miles. "I figured if we could manufacture a newsworthy picture and put it in Chris's hands, he'd bite."

Gray didn't like one bit where he was headed. "If you're blowing smoke up our asses for revenge, Elliott . . ."

"The only revenge I'm after is to kick your sorry ass for never once considering I wouldn't do what you've accused me of doing."

The first nudging of shame wormed its way into Gray's heart. Elliott was right—he had believed the worst of him from the start. Because Chris had convinced him of the worst.

"Why did you drag her into this?" Gray barely glanced at Abby.

"I had to beg her." Elliott said, with sincerity only long friendship allowed Gray to see. "But now Abby can attest that she's the only one who had access to this picture. And she didn't send it to the paper either."

Abby's touch on his bicep begged him to look at her, but his mouth filled with bile and cotton. Why hadn't she told him? Forced him to listen? No other betrayal in his life had hurt so much. When he did face her, pallor had sapped her skin of all summer color.

"When did you decide you couldn't trust me so you had to go behind my back?"

"This was never an issue of trust," she whispered. "Elliott did beg me, but I had no intention of helping him until last night, when Chris made the decision for me." A visible tremor shook her. "He said he would do anything to keep you in the public eye. Then he called me a gold-digger one too many times."

Gray stared at his bristling manager.

"This has gotten beyond ridiculous." Chris's tone branded them all dimwitted underlings for whom he'd lost patience. "Gray, we've always used publicity to keep your name in front of your fans. The recent stories and rumors that make you look like an unwitting victim can't be bought. They're too good to pass up as PR opportunities."

"You jeopardized someone's career and reputation and almost ruined a friendship for the sake of record sales and manufactured public sympathy? How did you ever get the idea I wanted that kind of fame? How long have you believed you could use me like some sort of chess piece in my own life?"

"You've been a pawn in your own career since you sold your first record." Chris made no attempt at conciliatory speech. "How the hell do you think you got to the top? You'd be nowhere without my ideas."

Sucker punched and bruised in every inch of his heart, Gray faced his manager somberly. "You know what? I've changed my mind. I think it's you I'm telling to leave."

Abby, numb and lost, stared at a Gray Covey she didn't recognize. She'd moved to full-fledged hatred of Chris, but the words still socked her in the gut.

"Get your head out of your ass, Gray. Don't be ridiculous." His manager made to slap his back but Gray twisted away. "What?" Chris stared in disbelief. "Are you firing me?"

"No. I'm not stupid enough to make another snap life decision. I'm just asking you to get away from me until any of this makes even a little sense. I don't know whether to murder you in your sleep or sue you from here to Jupiter."

Chris didn't even blink. "Good idea. You think and we'll talk when you've got your perspective back. You're letting a loser photographer and a gold-digging woman trying to keep her farm from crumbling around her, color your emotions."

Fury boiled over in Abby's stomach. "You pompous, conceited . . . How dare . . ."

She took an involuntary step, but strong hands grasped her from behind, and Spark whispered in her ear. "Don't, Abby. Let it be, darlin'."

She allowed him to hold her back but didn't hold her words. "Now I'm the one telling you to leave." Her jaw ached with tension. "Whatever Gray decides to do, you are not welcome on my farm, Mr. Boyle."

Chris pinched the bridge of his nose and huffed in disbelief. He opened his mouth, shut it, and turned away. "You and your wife will have to find your own way back to the hotel, Jackson, unless you're ready to leave now."

"We'll be fine." Spark was the only one whose voice and demeanor remained unchanged. Even Elliott looked like the pipsqueak who'd started a fight and been forgotten during the pummeling.

Abby scanned the groups still chatting and eating cake in the yard. By some miracle, no one seemed aware of the bomb that had detonated two hundred feet away. With cold that originated bone-deep, she turned back to Gray. "I'm sorry." She wanted to reach for him, but the ice in his eyes stopped her. "We were trying to help."

"Help?" Gray took a pointed step back from her. "You used me every bit as much as Chris did."

"Hey, that's not fair," Elliott said. "Take it out on me. I twisted her arm."

"I trusted her."

"You can still trust me." Tears stung the back of her lids, and she fought them angrily. "Or do you think Chris is right? I've been doing all this to make money off of you?"

"Yeah, that's it, Abby. I've suspected you all along. I faked it convincingly night before last to get my way with you, didn't I? Damn, I'm as good as I think I am."

"Oh, that was cruel." She held her tears to a slow leak.

"Gray. Man, I think it's time for you to stop talking, all right?" Spark laid his hand on Gray's forearm. "You're in shock. So am I. Don't say something you'll regret."

Gray listened and ran a hand through his hair—hair Abby had combed and woven through her fingers, and wanted to touch now even though her insides were in physical pain. How could she still want him so badly when it was obviously impossible between them?

"Right," he said. "It's probably best I leave, too, before I do say anything else." His empty eyes made her stomach flip then hit bottom like a dive gone horribly wrong. "I'll put my things together and go to a hotel."

Incredulity was all that was left to power her speech. "You're running away? Is this where your son gets it?"

He stared as if he couldn't believe she'd used that weapon. "I'm sparing everyone potential ugliness, Abby. We obviously can't talk tonight. I'll come back in the morning and settle our plans. I still have Winnipeg, St. Paul, and Richmond left on the tour schedule. I promised Kim a backstage tour when I'm here. I won't renege on that."

"And Karla?" Abby shot back, hurt and desperate. She didn't want him to leave. It wasn't fair of him to leave.

"She can trust me, too."

Everyone could trust him. Except her. She turned away, every nerve quivering in pain. "Fine. I'll let you explain it to the kids and say your good-byes whenever you're ready."

She was saved from stultifying awkwardness when Elliott touched her on the arm as Gray headed for the house. "I'm sorry, Abby. I truly am."

"It was my decision." She stared at the ground, seeing nothing.

"You were brave. I didn't expect him to take it out on you."

"He took it out on you for almost a month. If we're lucky, you'll have your friendship back."

"Don't pretend to be kind," he said. "This sucks, and

you're angry and hurt. That doesn't mean you're weak. I don't think you like to be weak."

She couldn't speak.

"I owe you a lot." His mustache rose. "I know what you've risked for me."

"I did it for him." She wiped an eye. "Not that it matters."

"It matters. I . . ." He dug into an inner vest pocket and pulled out a tri-folded piece of paper. ". . . have something for you. Don't get the idea it's any kind of payment. I started this long before I asked for your help."

"What?" She wiped her other eye.

"Your pictures. The ones at the restaurant in town."

"What about them?"

"I asked around. Everyone knows those photos; everyone loves them. And everyone seems to know where there's another. A friend here, a random business there. You gave them away."

Her mind tried to find his meaning, but she was too exhausted. "I used them as Christmas gifts and thank-you gifts. Sometimes it was all I had—"

"That's not the point. The point is, several people actually said they'd love to have an Abby Stadtler in their house or their office. 'An Abby Stadtler.' Do you know what that means?"

"No." She shook her head and wiped two more drops from her eyes.

"You could sell your work. I told you I do more than take pictures of famous people. I have a little-known interest in collecting art, and I know a few people in the legitimate photography business." He handed her the paper. "It's a letter from a dealer. He wants to see your work, Abby. He wants to talk to you about a number of projects. All I did was show him a picture of a picture and tell him you were one of the most talented photographers I've seen in a long time."

Her head spun. "I don't know what to say."

The world looked a little fuzzier than it was supposed to when Elliott grabbed her forearms and gripped. Her knees turned to Slinkies and the next thing she knew her cheek was hugging his vest.

"Whoa, whoa. You okay?" He peered at her. "I didn't mean for that to happen."

"I'm sorry." She pushed herself away, the momentary dizziness clearing. "I'm overwhelmed. I can't believe you did this. I can't . . . th-thank you enough. But I have to think about this? Please? So much is happening right now."

She didn't want to think about it all. She wanted to run screaming into her darkroom and lock the door.

"Of course you do. The information is all in the letter. You call him whenever you're ready. There's no hurry."

She gave him an impulsive hug, and when she released him and turned, Sylvia had materialized at her side. Elliott turned her over to the older woman with a nod, and Abby dissolved in her arms.

"There, now, Abby. Kim told me. Come, we'll sit together."

Sylvia's mothering couldn't stop the night from proceeding on its course of self-destruction. Nobody believed the lame story Gray and Spark concocted about spending the night working on a new song, except maybe Karla and her family who said their good-byes none the wiser. Everyone else knew something was wrong. Sylvia doggedly headed the clean-up with Kim and Lindsey. Ed and Dawson fed the horses. Miles, Spark, and Misty kept Gray huddled in heavy discussion. Elliott disappeared like a boy who'd poked a mountain lion.

Like a prisoner on suicide watch, Abby endured streams of inane chatter. It would have driven her crazy had her brain not been too numb to feel.

Finally, Gray went upstairs and packed.

The next she knew, Gray, Spark, Misty, Lindsey, and a sobered Miles stood by Gray's rental car. They all hugged a bemused Kim and wished her a happy birthday. Gray shook Ed's hand. He thanked Sylvia for a perfect cake. He stood in front of Abby. "I'll see you in the morning," he said.

That was it. If it was possible for a body to be taken over by aliens, Gray was living proof. He led Dawson several steps away. Their unheard exchange ended with Dawson shrugging off his father's hand on his shoulder and stalking toward the house. Abby prayed for him to follow the volatile boy, as he'd been doing more often when the teen went into his hormonal tantrums.

Instead, he glanced one sad time in her direction. And he left her.

Chapter Twenty-Six

THEY MADE A sullen parade trudging across the driveway to the Loon Feather the next afternoon. None of the four said a word when the café door jangled and Lester's ecstatic wolf whistle filled the air. Dawson pressed his face against the cage.

"Howdy Stranger." He wiggled a finger at Cotton.

The little white bird bounced like a bobble-head doll. "How, how . . . deee." Dawson abandoned his gloominess with a huge grin. Abby forced a smile, wanting to be ecstatic. "How, how, deee, stray . . ." Abby stole a look at Gray, but his expression remained impervious even to Cotton.

"Hey, you guys!" Karla met them with a smile. "Survived the party? Noon rush is over, I think you'll have plenty of privacy."

Abby accepted a hug, and when Gray took his, it wasn't jealousy but hurt that welled within her. He'd been civil to her all morning, friendly even, but he hadn't so much as picked up her hand. She couldn't believe this was the man she'd let herself make love to just three nights ago, and that a mere twenty-four hours ago they'd been teasing about marriage.

But Karla suspected nothing. She thought this was Gray's treat before he left for Winnipeg and had no clue that he'd refused to stay at the farm, using the "what if the paparazzi followed me" excuse.

Kim followed Gray to the booth, and nobody fussed when she slipped in beside him. Abby slid in across from them. Dawson remained with the cockatiels.

"He'll teach that stupid bird to talk yet," Kim said.

"Looking like it," Gray replied.

Kim stared from him to Abby and set her face more firmly into the scowl she'd worn all day. The uncomfortable quiet only broke when Dawson rejoined them.

"Goofy bird. She can almost do it."

"Impressive."

"Good job."

Gray and Abby spoke simultaneously and looked as if two monks had broken a vow of silence. Dawson glared just as Kim had. "That's it, you two. What's going on?"

"What do you mean?" Gray asked.

"We might be kids, but we have eyes." Dawson narrowed his. "You didn't go work on any song with Spark last night. You're hardly speaking to Abby. We deserve to know what the problem is."

"Sit down, Son." Gray's tone gave Dawson no room for

argument, and the boy slid next to Abby. "You're right. A few things are changing."

"Changing?" Concern bloomed in Kim's eyes. "How?"

"It's time for me and Dawson to go back home."

"Home?" Dawson added his surprise. "You aren't done touring yet."

"Ten days, three gigs. And I'd like you to come."

"I don't think so."

"Okay, let me rephrase. You are coming."

"Gray, I . . ." Stupefaction cut off Abby's words. Was he was so angry at her he was willing to abandon all his efforts on his son's behalf?

Karla interrupted by coming to take their orders and forcing them to don pleasant faces until she was finished.

"Now answer *my* question," Dawson demanded when she'd gone. "You two were all over each other yesterday."

"That's inappropriate," Gray admonished, but his son ignored him.

"Elliott showed up, Chris left. In my book that's good. What happened to you?"

"It was before that." Bitterness tinged Gray's voice. "The question really is what happened when Gucci showed up? Right Abby?"

How dare he turn the challenge around in front of the kids? This wasn't their business. "I'm willing to discuss that, Gray. You've shut any conversation down by being blind and stubborn about Elliott and Chris."

"Aha," Dawson said, reminding Abby just how perceptive and older-than-his-age he could be. "Chris."

"Chris is the one who's been sending the pictures." Gray's voice held no emotion, just angry fact.

"All the pictures? Like the one of Grandma?"

"Yes. But, it seems Abby joined the subterfuge by sending in that latest picture of you and me."

"Mom, how could you?" Kim joined her hero by adopting his shock and disappointment.

"Way to go, Abby!" Dawson grinned at her.

With all her heart, she wanted to laugh, because their children were hilarious. Instead, Gray's words cut her to the quick.

"Yup. Way to go, Abby," he continued. "Because, ironically, your part in this little sting will have a big, nasty side-effect. Your peaceful life is finally going to be shattered. And that," he looked at Dawson, "is why we have to leave. If I'm not here, the press won't stay around."

"Fine. You go. They won't care if I'm here."

"Oh, yes they will. As long as you're here, they know I'll be back." His voice turned cajoling. "Besides, I've got need of some fresh ideas for the music, and I want your input. The best thing is for you to keep sitting in with the sound guys at the concerts."

Abby's stomach scrabbled toward her throat. Gray had just regressed to Day One and become the over-eager, neophyte father expecting his son to thrill at the chances offered. Had he forgotten every lesson he'd learned the past month?

Dawson's eyes shot sparks hot enough to set the gingham tablecloth on fire. "Jeez, Dad, are you on crack? You're doing it again, blowing everything because of your stupid career. You've had, like, eight girlfriends since Mom left you, and you let them all just go. You didn't care, you didn't even try. Until Abby. She's the best, you told me so."

Abby's heart lurched. Gray had talked to Dawson about her?

"I'm not going anywhere with you. Take your stupid, big, famous mixing software and, I don't know, stick it up Chris's butt."

"Dawson, enough."

"I'm leaving."

"Sit down." Gray ordered.

"I'll see you at home. Have a great lunch."

Gray started to stand, but Kim was in his way, and Abby reached across to touch him for the first time.

"Don't, Gray. It'll just make a scene."

"Whoa, hey there Dawson."

Abby looked up at the sound of Elliott's voice. The three other tables of people paid little attention as Dawson brushed past the photographer with a miserable, wookie-like grunt. Lester let loose with "Colonel Bogey" and was echoed by a faint "How, how . . . deee, stray . . ." The first tears dripped from her eyes.

"You're like bad food, St. Vincent." Gray stared blankly at Elliott, but his voice held none of its previous venom.

"Yeah, and you'll get over me just like you get over a gut ache. Hey, Abby."

"Elliott." She wanted to be angry that Gray seemed less peeved at him than at her. But the things that were angering and not angering her today had her believing up was down.

"I came to warn you, you have about three minutes before the first ten photographers in town bribe Dewey Mitchell into telling them where you might be."

"Oooh." Abby balled her fists and pounded them in frustration against the ridge of her eye sockets. "What did I ever do to Dewey that he has it in for me? I thought we were friends."

"You probably didn't marry him." Elliott gave a jovial shrug.

"Would you like to know why?" Abby narrowed her eyes, still damp from tears of moments earlier. "He's a stupid boy. I'm surrounded by stupid boys."

"And I'm surrounded by stupid grown-ups." Kim, who'd watched the exchange with disdain, spoke with unexpected vehemence. She followed Dawson's example and stood, pushing Elliott aside to do it. "Dawson is right."

Abby let her go, as well. Kim didn't need to see any more unpleasantness. Lester chose "Andy Griffith" for her as she slapped her way through the Loon's front door. The instant its bell quit dinging, Karla swung in with her tray of food. She stopped short and stared at the new configuration of people at the booth.

"I'm confused," she said with a grin.

"You have no idea from confused," Abby muttered.

"Whoever's here, eat up. I've got three burgers and a chef's salad and I'm not taking them back."

The doorbell tinkled again and Lester whistled. "Karla? You'll never guess what we heard." Gladdie Hanson's voice easily drowned out "Colonel Bogey." Two seconds later, the

Sisters stood in front of Gray and gawped. "It *was* you."

It shocked Abby to see the two old town gossips bright-eyed as fawns and at a loss for words.

"I was me?" Gray laughed and plastered on another cheerful face. "Well, whoever I am now, it's a pleasure to meet you. You all keep this town running if I understand."

He stunned with his charm, as always.

"Well—" Gladdie didn't gush, but she pinkened. "If you aren't just as nice as they say. Abigail, have you taken up with this one like the rumors have it?"

"No, Gladdie, we're just friends. Gray is Dawson's father."

"Imagine that." Claudia touched her own cheek, then brushed at the hair over her ear. "I actually heard something true on *Entertainment Tonight*." Claudia laughed.

The staid and stoic Sisters of Kennison Falls watched *ET*? Could the day get any more surreal?

"I'm sorry your peaceful town is being plastered all over the media," Gray said. "I tried to keep it quiet until Dawson and I left."

"Leave? That's too bad. Abby likes having Dawson here. A man around the place." Gladdie assessed Gray with a kindly eye. "You'd probably like it, too, if you gave it a chance. We hear you have a show up in the cities this weekend."

"We don't go to those rock concerts anymore," Claudia added. "But if we did, we'd go to yours."

"No, we wouldn't, because you won't ride on the freeway." Gladdie dismissed her sister. She leaned forward as if confiding a secret to Gray. "She won't ride in anything that goes fast."

Despite everything, a smile twitched at the corners of Gray's mouth. "I think, perhaps, you're a wise woman."

"I used to," she said cheerily. "Had a friend killed in a big crash one time, too many years ago to count. I've just taken life slow and easy since then; it's too short to hurry through."

Abby stared. How had she never known this?

"Good advice, Miss Claudia," Gray said.

"I can't wait to tell my grandkids I met you." Claudia took the handshake he offered and Gladdie did likewise.

"Same for me. You take care now."

They left with aplomb and seated themselves at their usual table.

"Damn, why can't all my fans be like those two?" Gray mumbled.

"No lie," Elliott said.

"Are you still here?" Gray glowered at him.

"I'm trying one last time to protect your sorry butt. You two need to get out of this place before . . . well, shit. Never mind." "Andy Griffith" filtered through the café.

Four men in jeans and various combinations of casual sport coats and pocketed photographers' vests entered the Loon and gazed around the room like a four-headed dragon, each neck swiveling to take in a different section of the café.

"Stay put, Gray," Karla said. "I'll see what they want."

"Lie if you have to," Elliott said.

Gray hunkered into the corner of the booth, rubbing his dull eyes, looking like a man giving up. Abby wanted to forgive him everything at that moment, but she couldn't touch him. His recoil would hurt too much.

"May I help you, gentlemen?" Karla asked as Elliott sank into the spot Kim had vacated.

"Yes, ma'am. We've learned that Gray Covey is staying somewhere in the area. We just saw his son coming from the café here and hope, perhaps, you can help us."

"Gray Covey, the singer?" Karla's voice held the perfect amount of incredulity. "I'd love to meet him. You said his son was here? Who's his son?"

"Dawson Covey, ma'am."

"I don't know a Dawson Covey. I've met a Dawson Cooper . . . He works for an older couple several miles out of town. I think your information was about a different Dawson."

For the first time, Gray sought Abby's eyes. The briefest flash of light between them acknowledged the memory, then the light dimmed again.

"Do you mind if we sit for some coffee?" another man asked. "Maybe we can figure out some other place to look."

"Ummm . . . of course." Karla's bravado wavered.

Elliott peered around the banquette and blew out a sigh of frustration. "One of them's Kyle Rodriguez. He works for the *Inquiry*; he's not even an independent. Damn, Gray, you're big news."

"Ducky."

"I'll grab your coffee, guys, but you aren't going to find

any famous singers in Kennison Falls." Karla laughed. "Faribault north of here is where somebody of Gray's caliber would stay."

"Been there, ma'am." The voice belonging to Kyle Rodriquez was suave. Abby shivered. If they'd seen Dawson, they'd seen Kim. The scenario got worse and worse. "All signs point to a local resident putting him up."

"I don't think so." Karla's voice remained adamant.

Abby's heart sank. Gray couldn't even leave through the back door because they'd be spotted crossing to the kitchen.

"Say, excuse me . . ." Abby, Gray, and Elliott shared a look of shock at Claudia's voice, calling above the chatter. "You aren't talking about that famous singer there, are you? That one with the color for a name?"

Oh no, please don't, Claudia, please don't. I know you're excited, but . . . Abby despaired. She didn't know what would happen if the men discovered Gray. It wasn't him she worried about, but the kids and the town. She couldn't be responsible for them getting thrown into a spotlight and their personal problems dragged through the tabloids—especially Dawson. His tough young male emotions were fragile.

"Gray Covey, yes ma'am," Rodriguez said, interest evident in his voice.

"We met him this morning."

"You did?"

"Yes, sir. I drove into Faribault to get some yarn, you know, and there he was, bold as brass sitting in the coffee shop where we stopped."

Abby pressed a hand to her mouth. Gray's lips hung parted but motionless. Elliott's eyes widened like a northern pike's.

"When was that, ma'am?"

"What would you say, Gladdie? An hour ago? We came straight here. Nice fellow."

"An hour? That's all?" Rodriguez asked. Abby could already hear the scraping of chair legs, and her heart beat in a furious, hopeful rhythm.

The group of paparazzi managed to cajole a location out of the Sisters, and Abby, Gray, and Elliott stayed bunkered in the booth until Karla appeared, grinning.

"Gone," she said. "All four. Out of here like prospectors to the Yukon."

"Karla, I could kiss you. Let me out, St. Vincent."

Abby slid out, too, and when Gray was free of the seat he nearly sprinted to the table where Gladdie and Claudia sipped coffee as if nothing out of the ordinary had happened.

"I'm giving each of you a huge kiss and hug whether you want it or not." He embraced Claudia from behind.

"Watch it, isn't that sexual harassment or whatever they call it?" Gladdie asked.

Abby finally broke out laughing. She'd thought she'd known these women—slow, gossipy, old-fashioned. Here was proof eavesdropping had a positive effect—like the good side of nuclear power. And that you never knew the true depth of anybody.

"You saved my life." Gray hugged Gladdie next.

"We take care of our own."

"I'm sorry you had to tell lies for us." Abby offered her own small hugs. "Claudia you've never driven to Faribault in your life."

"But I've always wanted to." Pleasure oozed from her. "This was a fantasy trip."

"Heck," Gladdie smiled like an embarrassed imp. "The Lord will forgive us some little white lies used to save someone's life. Like those nuns in *The Sound of Music*."

Gray laughed, too. The Sisters seemed to have worked a little magic.

"Well, Captain von Trapp here thanks you," Elliott interrupted. "But he and Maria have to hightail it over the mountains to Switzerland. Come on, Gray, you got a reprieve, but they aren't the only mercenaries looking for you."

"When did you get to be my master and commander?" Gray's words held no animosity.

"Since I overthrew your old regime. Until you find a new boss, I'm the best inside source you have."

Gray looked at him for just a moment, then stuck out his hand. "Okay."

Abby followed them through the kitchen and out to the car. A twisted knot of relief and jealousy roiled in her gut. They'd gotten away, Chris had been exposed, Gray was on the verge of making peace with an old friend. But she hadn't done anything Elliott hadn't done—and not a single word of reconciliation was offered to her the entire drive back to the farm.

Chapter Twenty-Seven

THE BAND'S FOUL luck returned with a vengeance. Misty contracted laryngitis fifteen hours before show time in Winnipeg. Miles and Wick, who'd never disagreed in their lives, blew up over a technical issue involving a broken amplifier. Spark broke two strings onstage, and Micky popped a snare. Dawson, forced into accompanying the band in spite of full-on arguing and foot-dragging, was barely civil. The fans cheered as wildly as ever, but it only galled everyone with proof Chris was right: disaster sold. By the time the Lunatics returned to Minnesota for their St. Paul concert, Gray felt like they'd all walked a hundred miles uphill, on ice, with heaters in their shoes.

Things didn't start auspiciously in Minnesota. His bandmates had quit sniping at each other, but in addition to a light array that had come out of the truck smashed, Chris had shown up briefly, putting everyone on edge.

"I thought we were friends, Chris. How can you ask why I'm upset?"

"Friendship is all well and good, Gray." Chris had bitten off his words with steel teeth Gray had never noticed before. "But this has always been about business. You wouldn't be in this filled arena without the excitement I generated."

He'd generated? As if no talent was involved at all. Gray didn't know whether he was angrier at Chris for the vile backstabbing, or at himself for having been blind to what so many people had tried to tell him.

Spark called it a rape. Everyone had been friends with Chris—he'd represented them all. But the extent of his sensationalistic PR dealings was just starting to get unearthed. Spark and, to everyone's surprise, Elliott turned into de-facto leaders, but the whole band was wounded.

To make matters worse, he'd lost Abby, too. Anger still coiled in his gut when he thought how she'd used him against his wishes. He wanted to talk to her, work it out, but she wouldn't answer his calls.

The only bright spot in any of it was watching Dawson forget his anger when he sat at the mixer console with Corky. He still blamed Gray for the demise of the relationship with Abby, and he was angry Gray hadn't yet dealt with the private-school issue, but when the sound checks began passion took over.

Now, preparing to take the stage at the Excel Center, Miles clapped Gray on the shoulder. "You doing okay? About ready?"

He shook himself and focused on his bandmates. The

arena was sold out, and they'd learned a frantic scalping business had gone on outside, far more than usual. Rumors that Gray had been spending time in the state were fueling hyper-interest. Once again, it flew in the face of his anger with Chris, but at least it made for a lively audience.

"Sorry." He set his game face firmly in place. "I'm ready. Did you find everyone?"

"Got 'em all directly stage right," Spark nodded. "Kim is ecstatic. Ed brought ear plugs and said to tell you he's wearing your sweatshirt."

Gray couldn't help but laugh even while his heart broke at the thought of losing Ed and Sylvia right along with Abby. And Kim. Dang her little hormonal hide. "Ed Mertz is downright mean," he said.

"Two minutes." Spark's announcement was the signal for adrenaline to start pumping.

The onstage lights were down. Only the glowing indicators on amplifiers, electric pianos, and sound pedals lit the way. The unique odor of electricity, metal, wood, and hot lights filtered through him, familiar as oxygen. All six bandmates slapped his palms as they headed one-by-one to the stage, leaving him to wait. His heart rate steadily accelerated until it stopped dead for just that second before he was assured of The Sound. He never believed it would come, and it always did. Tonight it was a tsunami of cheering, screeching, and stomping as the band struck the first chords of Gray's new opening song.

Shrugging the tension out of his shoulders, he inhaled a full breath and sprinted up the stage stairs. With precision timing he let the music lead him to dark center stage. Stepping to his mic, he pulled a guitar strap over his head. White hot light blazed in his face and everything but the stage, the band, and the screaming disappeared. Even as the words to his first song flowed like life's breath from his mouth, and he acted the part everyone came to see, he strained to look stage right and pierce the overwhelming light. Of all the fanatic, chanting people in the arena, there was only one he wanted to see.

ABBY'S BREATH HUNG suspended in her throat when she caught sight of him, a shadowy form slipping onto the stage, visible only to those in the rows closest to him. He moved with lithe grace—the lion at his home watering hole. Kim's fingers tightened around Abby's bicep like a clamp, each intake of her breath sounding like a sob.

"Forever," she managed to say. "My gosh, he's singing it."

Abby recognized the song. He'd sung it at her piano, saying he never performed it live. Now he sang it for her daughter. She glanced at Ed and Sylvia to her right, unable to believe they'd come. Spark had brought the set of new tickets that morning and offered two of them to the Mertzes. The sight of Ed in a dapper gray sport coat with her stupid Barn Goddess sweatshirt underneath it was a sight she'd never imagined in her craziest dreams. Sylvia looked properly pained for a woman past seventy at a rock concert, yet her eyes shone with anticipation.

The band hit a crescendo, and when three spotlights

fired at once onto the man she loved, the man she *had* loved, she gasped. Kim screeched. Ed whistled. Sylvia grinned.

And the rest of the crowd erupted.

Wavy-haired, long-limbed, sure-handed. Lord, oh lord, he was beautiful. He usually wore a sequined blazer over a bright, matching T-shirt. Tonight he was magnificent in solid red with fitted black pants that flared over sexy, Beatle-y boots. Fascination overtook her as Gray leaned into the microphone and swayed his hips into the rhythm of the joyful backbeat. She scanned the band and thrilled to the little leaps of excitement flittering through her at the sight of Spark, finessing his guitar, and Miles, setting his beat onto an assortment of African bongos with sure hands, and Misty swaying in a gorgeous beaded dress of olive green.

Abby had a hard time seeing the performers. She tried to feel the fan worship, see Gray as the others in the arena saw him, but what she saw was his thick hair and knew, intimately, that it was heavy as velvet. She saw his fingers nursing chords along the neck of his guitar and knew how they could coax little moans from her throat.

The sadness slammed her. Ninety-into-a-brick-wall pain, deep and sorrowful, pulled a gasp and a sob from her throat, while Gray continued his siren song.

"Oh, Mom," Kim moaned in her ear, startling her. She turned to see tears streaming down her daughter's face. "I love him sooooo much."

Abby closed her eyes. The melodrama was too over-the-top, yet she wanted to weep right along. "I know you do, sweetheart." She kissed Kim's head. "I know you do."

THE ST. PAUL Hotel was known for its ritzy elegance, and there was no lack of glitz or elegance in the small ballroom where Gray and his band met with the local movers and shakers who'd paid mega-bucks for the chance to clasp hands and have pictures taken with him. But in spite of the hoity-toity attendees, the after-party was infused with laughter and joking camaraderie.

Kim and Dawson had greeted each other like separated twins, and Abby hadn't given her adopted son any choice in the huge hug she'd bestowed on him. Ed had gotten to shake hands with the mayor of St. Paul and was suitably impressed. He had no end of admirers of the sweatshirt and delighted in telling its story to anyone who'd listen. Sylvia had struck up a down-home conversation with a state representative's wife, and, as with the Sisters, Abby could only marvel at the depth she'd never guessed existed in her neighbors.

The ballroom looked like an elegant saloon girl, decked out in finery, surrounded by food and admirers. It smelled like beer and roast beef. It sounded like a midway. Abby wanted to hate it, but she couldn't.

"Hey, beautiful." Spark surprised her by handing her a glass of club soda with a lime, while she stood in a corner, watching Gray sign autographs and schmooze the St. Paul dignitaries. "I've been watching, and this has been your drink of choice tonight. Are you a teetotaler, Abby Stadtler?"

She laughed. "Hey, handsome. No, of course not. I just have to drive home."

"That's a long way. You should take Gray up on his offer to stay here."

"I have animals waiting, Spark. And Ed and Sylvia don't want to stay."

"Chris Boyle was cruel to you the other day." He changed subjects in a surprise right turn.

She shrugged. The subject of Chris Boyle made her furious; it was better to keep her mouth shut.

"I'm sorry," he continued. "But there is something you should know."

"What's that?" She smiled wistfully. Spark was a gem of a man.

"I've known Gray since we were eighteen-year-old kids with more dreams than sense. He's been through the standard rock crap—we all have. Booze and drugs, a few affairs."

"If you're his new PR guy, you should give it up." Abby laughed, a touch grimly.

Spark rolled out his lazy smile in return. "Gray Covey was never destined to become a Keith Richards or a Kurt Cobain. He's always been too ethical to end up a drugged-out rocker. He and Ariel had to get married, but he gave it a good go. Would you believe he never cheated on her? I don't know if she believes that to this day, but it's true. Chris couldn't stand it—Gray wasn't any fun at all at parties, he used to say. He did everything in his power to put Gray in compromising situations Ariel might walk in on, or hear about."

"Why the history lesson?" Abby didn't know if she wanted any more information. It was already too painful to think about Gray ignoring her from across the room.

"The point is, I've never seen Gray like he's been the past month with you. Serious to God, darlin', he's a different man. When he caught sight of you in the audience tonight? The show took on a whole new feeling. He sang like Sinatra, and we played like the London Symphony. Chris saw the change before any of us. He didn't like you on principle, Abby, any more than he liked Ariel. In an odd way, it wasn't personal."

She rose up on the toes of her one pair of strappy party shoes and placed a soft kiss where Spark's mustache met his beard. Her clothing left her feeling conspicuous, a softly flared black crepe skirt that stopped four inches above her knees, a snug, white T-shirt covered in pearlescent sequins, and a multi-colored vest she'd always loved. She'd had no intention of wearing anything sparkly tonight—but Kim had dressed her and brooked no argument. She'd even done Abby's hair—an hour with hot rollers and a curling iron—and, admittedly, it alone felt beautiful, falling in long bronze-hued curls around her face.

Unfortunately, the only ones who noticed didn't count.

"You're a wonderful man, Alfred Jackson."

"I know." He returned the gentle peck. "Give him time, okay?"

She sighed, searching the festive room and the excited faces. "I heard he's still trying to placate Ron Revers. He wants a public apology now."

"That's true. Gray really could come out on top, but

it's another sleeping-with-the-devil kind of thing. This is a harsh business sometimes."

"That's why I don't think time is my problem." Abby smiled sadly. "The devils never stop coming. Ron Revers is not the first, and he won't be the last. It's too much for me."

"Makes me sad, darlin'."

"Yeah. It does me, too."

Gray didn't ignore her all night. He told her she looked stunning. He introduced her to friends. But she knew Gray Covey now, and she knew how gifted he was at interacting with his fans. She'd been relegated, if not to fan status, then to that of someone who needed impressing—handling. They were full-circle, back to the moment she'd laid eyes on him at her barn door, trying to impress her enough to woo his son away from her. He'd done it—impressed her. With his earnestness, his chivalry. His stupid song . . .

The song. He'd always promised to sing it to her when he'd finished it. He hadn't even sung it tonight. It seemed he was keeping his promises to everyone but her.

She couldn't make it to the end of the party. Spark brokered a compromise that allowed Kim to stay overnight in Misty's room as well as allowed Dawson to skip the last concert in Richmond. Gray didn't fight him, Abby guessed, because he was having little luck with Ariel. She expected Dawson back in England in two weeks to start school.

He was no longer Abby's concern. Dawson could

come home with Kim and stay through music camp, but then the boy had no choice but to spend his last week in L.A. He'd leave Abby's life, right along with his father.

"Gray?" She interrupted him reluctantly to tell him she was leaving, her heart unbearably sad. "I have to get Ed and Sylvia home—it's late for them. But the kids can stay. Elliott will bring them home in the morning. I think he's a nice guy. I'm glad he's been exonerated."

"Yes. I . . . I am, too. But you're leaving?" The first honest emotion she'd seen burned through his practiced smile. "You have to go?"

It was her cue to say yes, but she couldn't get the word out. Knowing the pressure behind her sinuses would only be relieved by tears, she nodded instead.

"I'll see you in a week, then, when I come back for the camp and to get Dawson."

Swallowing hard, she pressed a wistful kiss on his cheek and left, Ed and Sylvia in tow. A little too much like Cinderella from the ball, except both strappy sandals stayed firmly on her feet.

Chapter Twenty-Eight

THICK, VISCOUS AIR had turned the afternoon into a sauna when Abby reached home and poured herself out of her car. The small sense of relief over finding a job at the tiny office supply store in town was overshadowed by frustration that a whole week's new salary wouldn't fix the dead air-conditioning in her car. Smearing her hair back from where it clung to her forehead in damp clumps, she looked for signs of life from the kids.

She hoped they were in better moods than when she'd left that morning.

Not that she could blame Dawson for being plain angry with his parents. Neither Gray nor the mysterious Ariel seemed able to converse like adults and reach any positive outcome. When Dawson had received an e-mail confirmation that his flight to England had been booked, he'd called his father in a rage. All Gray had done was say he'd fly back with him and work things out face-to-face. Dawson's two-day temper tantrum even had Roscoe avoiding him.

Kim's anger was more mysterious. Something had happened the night of the concert, and she refused to talk about it. Abby sighed. Dealing with one teenager was difficult. Dealing with two was like navigating a minefield on a rhinoceros.

She reached the back door, and Roscoe crawled from a cool spot under the granary, his tail wagging half-speed in the heat. "Hello my gorgeous boy." Abby accepted a welcome-home kiss, and he ambled back to his dug-out.

Across the field a bank of dirty, silver-gray clouds boiled low on the horizon. Above them, the sky glowed sickly olive green. A niggle of concern edged into her mixed pot of emotions. The heat, the color of the sky, the odor of ozone and overripe grass spelled tornado watch. She changed her mind and called Roscoe into the house. Once inside, she called for the kids. Silence answered.

Switching on the kitchen radio she heard only music, no warnings. Dawson and Kim had to be in the barn, and Kim knew enough to keep an eye on the weather. Abby headed for her room, punching the TV remote en route.

The work-out clothes she donned were blessedly cool—a pair of microfiber blue short-shorts Gray had once hinted she should wear everywhere, and a pink tank top. Twisting her thick, soggy hair behind her head, she stuffed two chop-sticky spikes through the knot to keep it off her neck. After slipping on a pair of ancient tennis shoes, she returned to the living room in time to hear the special weather report she'd feared.

Listening to the counties on the watch list, Abby tied her shoes and spied her camera on the end table next to her chair. The sight caused a fresh wave of sorrow. She couldn't think of taking pictures without thinking of the darkroom. She couldn't think of the darkroom without memories of Gray's kiss.

Nor could she forget he was directly responsible for putting photography back in her life.

But it all broke her heart afresh every time a memory surfaced.

The TV meteorologist reached Faribault County, and Abby sighed. If there was going to be a thunderstorm, she'd put the horses in the barn to avoid hail and thunder. If there was going to be a tornado, their chances were better outside, where they wouldn't get trapped in a falling building. A frisson of nervousness traced through her stomach.

The sky had deepened to a thrashing-ocean green, and the clouds now appeared close enough to touch when Abby headed for the barn in search of Kim and Dawson. Instead of the kids, she was shocked to find Ed bent over Kim's new tack trunk.

"Hello young one," he said. "Success?"

"I got the job at Brenda's."

"That okay?"

"It'll have to be for now." She loved Ed—so blunt yet so non-judgmental. "What's happening? Where are the kids?"

"Dunno." He looked up. "I figured they were inside."

"No. Did they go riding?"

"I think all the four-leggers are here. I came to fix that bad hinge on this trunk, and I found a few nails to pound along the way. One of the stall doors was hanging kinda poorly."

"Oh, Ed, I don't pay you enough for you to keep bailing me out."

"You don't pay me nothing, missy, and you better not ever try." He harrumphed when she kissed his craggy cheek.

"I love you, Ed. So, where are my wayward children? There's a tornado watch."

Fifteen minutes later, they'd searched every inch of the barn and pastures. All horses were accounted for. All tack was in place. Still, Abby didn't panic until she went back up to Kim's room and found several drawers ransacked and her daughter's teddy bear and pillow missing. A search of Dawson's room also turned up a missing pillow as well as no sign of his laptop.

"Oh, dear God, Ed. He's done it again. He's run away and taken Kim with him."

"Those crazy kids. Did they leave a note?"

No note, no messages on her computer, nothing could be found. At last, Ed picked up the phone and dialed his wife. When he smiled, Abby realized just how terrified she'd been.

"Sylvia says she left you a voice message about an hour ago."

"Oh my gosh, how stupid of me." Abby lifted the cordless off its base and heard the beeps indicating a new message. "I never checked."

"Hi Abby," the message said. "Just thought I'd tell you your two crazy kids are sneaking around up here with backpacks and pillows. They're hunkered down in the new tool shed out back now, and I figure I'll let Ed go talk to 'em when he gets back from your place."

Relief filtered through her even as frustration boiled. She was going to strangle that boy to within an inch of his life.

"I'll go up. Wanna come along?"

"You know what? You give 'em what for, send them back, and I'll finish the job."

He grinned with the kind of relish only a trusted older person could pull off and left Abby to monitor the weather and the phone. He'd been gone just long enough to walk home, when Abby heard the faint but gut-wrenching warble of a civil defense siren. She'd never liked the undulating moans of those alarms, and this time her kids were in harm's way. She waited impatiently for Ed to call with news they were safe. She jumped when the phone rang.

"Ed?"

"Abby?" His voice was too quick, too clipped. "Abby, them kids aren't here. Sylvie says she saw them go into the shed an hour ago and never saw them come out. But they're gone."

"Noooo." She wailed to match the sirens. "Ed, please, check your basement. Check the extra rooms. Maybe they got nervous about the weather and are hiding until it blows over."

Kim and Dawson weren't anywhere at the Mertzes'.

As the winds increased with each passing minute, and as the TV and radio confirmed there were three tornados on the ground within ten miles of Kennison Falls, Abby dissolved into unadulterated hysteria.

She called 911, and the dispatcher promised that even though all emergency vehicles were out and the children weren't considered missing if they'd only been gone an hour or two, police would keep an eye open for two teenagers exposed to the storm. She knew she had to call Gray. He'd be rightfully furious if anything happened and he hadn't been told. She imagined her own anger in the reverse situation.

The wind howled like Halloween. In the ugly, eerie dimness, tree branches whipped all the way to the ground. Her fingers trembled as she dialed the number Gray had given her. The one Kim had used to call about Gucci.

Tears clogged her throat. How could she have ignored the unbelievable lengths Gray must have gone to in order to get her horse back? *Oh, how come you don't answer?* She got the voice-mail message: "Hey, you've reached Gray's phone. Sorry it's not really me. Leave your message and number and I'll call you back." His voice brought tears. The wind's howl turned to an official roar.

"Gray! It's Abby. I need you to call me. Kim and Dawson have run off in the middle of a tornado warning. It's about six o'clock." She sobbed, feeling like a fool—she who prided herself on being the rock in a crisis. "We can't find them and you need to know . . . I'm sorry." She was just blathering. "Please call back."

She hung up. She redialed two more times. And then she remembered the piece of paper Spark had handed her before she'd left the party three nights ago. She jumped for her purse on the counter and dug frantically until she found her wallet. There. Spark's cell phone number. She tried to still the violent quivering in her hands as she pressed the numbers. A small branch flew past her window.

"Hello?"

Abby sobbed with relief. "Spark? Spark, it's Abby."

"Darlin'? Wha . . . wrong?" The line was static-filled and broken.

"I need to find Gray. He's not answering his phone."

"Calm down . . . went to . . . mother's. Now tell . . . what's happen . . . Dawson?"

"Y . . . yes," Abby struggled to stay calm. "He and Kim have run off, and we're in the middle of a huge storm. T . . . tornadoes just miles away. Gray . . ." She knew from the dead air she'd lost the call. She dialed again, but there was no response. Cell phone, land line, everything was gone.

A crash resounded from outside, and Abby screeched. A horrifying noise, like a jet about to land where it shouldn't, roared toward her, and she called Roscoe desperately. He came. She called Bird, and even he came. Two slinking, shivery mounds of helpless fur. She grabbed them both to her and hunkered next to the innermost hallway wall. Bird growled. Roscoe leaned into her, licking her neck, as nervous as she was—Dorothy and Toto.

"Please Lord. Please Lord. Please Lord." She chanted

the litany hoping God could read the rest of her prayer from her head. "Please, please, please . . ." The air smelled like ozone and smoke. She chanted until the jet flew straight over her head.

THE AFTERMATH WAS pristine sunshine and glistening leaves like the movie *Twister*. Abby stood in her yard, shaking but alive, and Roscoe wagged his tail as if he'd protected her all along. Bird disappeared, no longer needing her. A disaster of twisted branches and leaves carpeted the lawn, and the rickety corncrib, as well as the garage roof, were no more. Her wildflowers lay sprawled flat like drunken party goers. Her heart wouldn't leave her throat as she forced away images of what might have happened to her daughter and Dawson.

She sprinted to the barn, praying she'd missed the children somehow. Three-fourths of the shingles were gone, and her old silo was ground into rubble, but the barn was intact, the hay was safe, and all the horses, although agitated, were fine. But all her searching and desperate calling turned up no sign of the kids.

She dashed back up the driveway and past her house, panic fueling her strides. It took her and Roscoe five minutes of mud-slogging before she saw from a distance that Ed and Sylvia's house still stood. Panting with her first spark of relief, she reached the top of the road, and a sob broke from her throat. Sylvia's gorgeous lawn and flower beds looked like ground zero for a monster-truck rally. The small arena Ed had built for Kimmy when she'd been a little girl lay in a pick-up-sticks mess. She spotted her beloved neighbors, moving robotically through their shredded yard.

"Abby!" Sylvia met her half-way across the muddy expanse. "You're all right. Thank the Lord." The older woman gathered her into a fierce embrace.

"And you, too. Did the kids?" she asked, her heart wild in her chest.

Sylvia's sad, gray headshake sent Abby's stomach into her toes as fresh horror built. No, she thought. No, they couldn't be lost, not today, it would be too cruel. "Tomorrow is July twenty-fifth," she said, her whisper strangled.

Eleven years to the day since the accident.

"We'll find them." Sylvia wept, stroking her hair. "We'll find them, honey."

After another scouring of the Mertzes' house, shed, and grounds turned up no sign of Kim or Dawson, they abandoned their houses and headed for town in Ed's truck.

What greeted them was horror.

Only a fourth of beautiful Kennison Falls remained. The town's residents filled the streets, milling like zombies, some sobbing, some sorting through the debris of a hundred bomb blasts. Twisted streetlamps littered the road, and the tatters of Independence Day flags lay in desecrated heaps. The year-old water tower was a tall amputated stump, and not a single old maple stood along Main Street.

Sylvia stared, ghost-faced. Ed's rounded, old knuckles protruded skeletally as he gripped his wheel. Abby buried

her head between her knees, her stomach heaving in disbelief and panic, and Sylvia stroked her back with a heavy
motion. "They're all right, honey. They're all right."

By dark everyone knew about the missing teens, and
the town's numbness was wearing off. As far as anyone
could tell, Kim and Dawson were the only two humans
unaccounted for. The toll on businesses, vehicles, vener-
able old trees, and landscaping was much higher. Dewey's
station was gone, the little library and its wonderful lions
were gone, ten homes had been flattened. And, worst of
all, the Loon Feather was a shell. The kitchen stood intact,
three-and-a-half dining room walls remained, and several fragments of the huge mural remained, but half the
roof had collapsed, along with the front entrance. There
was no sign of her photos. No trace of Lester and Cotton's
cage. Even while she fought the horrifying knowledge
that she was on the verge of losing another child, Abby
wept for the stupid birds.

When it was too dark to continue searching, Karla
tried to talk her into coming home with her, but Abby
insisted on returning with Ed and Sylvia in case the children found their way back. Once she made sure her animals were safe and fed, and Sylvia had ensconced her on
the couch with a thick handmade quilt and a gallon of
tea, Abby finally allowed herself to bawl in earnest. After
there were no more tears left, she didn't feel better, but Ed
stopped keeping vigil.

The pounding irritated her through the fog of a fitful
sleep. She didn't realize it was the door until the sharp,
electronic bong of the doorbell frightened her awake.

"Kimmy???" She threw off the quilt and yanked the front door open with no care for caution.

Her breath caught. Gray stood on the porch, his eyes a wild mix of grief and concern. "Abby, Abby, thank God. You weren't at your house, and I panicked."

She launched into his embrace with renewed sobs, and he held her until he could loosen her arms enough to set her feet back on the ground. "Honey," he said in her ear, "I'll hold you all night, but the neighbors are watching."

She pulled away and let Ed and Sylvia swarm Gray as if he were a long lost son.

"I tried to call. I'm so sorry," Abby told him.

"I was already on my way here." He held her on the couch, stroking her hair, imparting strength. "I had to come back, Abby, I couldn't let things end like that between us. I didn't get your message or Spark's until I landed."

"You—you were coming back?"

"Shhh. Yes. Don't worry about that now. Let's find the kids." His grim face didn't hold any promises, but his huge, calm presence gave her the ability to dig for hope.

Gray nearly lost his composure, however, when he saw Main Street. Even at six in the morning it wasn't deserted. Neighbors shared news, discussing the seven-mile path of the storm. Local media news crews already poked cameras and microphones in front of as many residents as would talk. Gray kept a low profile, choking back emotion as he walked through the rubble of downtown of Kennison Falls.

Kim and Dawson remained the only two missing people. Sooner rather than later the reporters would pounce on Gray's missing son. Abby dreaded this, but couldn't even begin to contemplate keeping Gray's name out of the media anymore. Nothing mattered. Nothing except her daughter and the boy who'd become her own surrogate son.

Over a hundred volunteers showed up at seven to form search teams. Parties combed the park and trails for signs of the kids. Police interviewed residents and drivers outside of town. Classmates called every person Kim remotely knew to see if they'd heard from her.

By nine o'clock, Abby, flabbergasted by the support but ten days' worth of tired, stood beside Gray in the center of Main Street weeping in front of the tattoo parlor. It was one of a dozen businesses relatively unscathed, and all she knew was that she'd let Kim have three tattoos and get a giant kangaroo herself if her daughter would just turn up alive and well.

"Yo! Abby! Gray! Y'all look lost, man!"

Abby spun. Down the leaf-and-branch-strewn street marched Miles flanked by Spark, Lindsey, Misty, Micky. And Elliott.

"We couldn't let you face this alone." Micky reached Gray first and dragged him into an embrace. "Wick and Max will be here this afternoon. There were storms in L.A. last night, too."

Lindsey and Misty swarmed Abby like sisters. Spark gifted everyone with his incredible, unwavering calm. And nobody blamed her for the loss of the children.

She did that all by herself.

The horrible memories of the date grew stronger as

the day wore on. Abby put one foot in front the other, numb, terrified, silent. Clinging to Gray, helpless except to let the town's countless angels coordinate the search for her children, she stood with him in front of the library in a rare moment alone. He gathered her close with both arms, rubbing as if warming her. Her first tears of the day fell.

"I know, I know," he crooned. "It's going to be okay."

"It's not, though." She burrowed into his hold, unable to avoid telling him any longer. "This is it. This is the date it all happened."

"What?"

"The accident." The words whispered past her lips.

"Today?" His incredulity was all-encompassing. "Oh, God, Abby, no. It can't be."

"I can't do it. I can't live through it again." Sobs wracked her, but Gray startled her by pushing her an arm's-length away.

"That is *not* what's going to happen this time." Harsh lines of promise etched his beautiful face. "We are going to find them. Do you hear me? We'll find them."

We. She wanted to believe his words. Wanted to believe in the *we*. She pushed back into his arms and tried.

Wicks and Max arrived as promised and were eagerly adopted by a team based in the park. Miles set his substantial frame to helping dig through rubble and dilapidation. Micky, Spark, and the women drifted to wherever they were needed. And Elliott, no camera in sight, attached himself to Gray and Abby—a self-appointed bodyguard, keeping unwanted questioners at bay.

Inevitably, the media closed in, and with them swarmed the paparazzi. In one of the day's very few positives, Abby discovered another wonderful thing about her town. Once the residents of Kennison Falls found out the rag photographers were gunning for Gray or Abby, it didn't take any police force to keep the intruders at bay. The tattered town adopted Gray immediately and thoroughly, and between the stoic citizens and Elliott, no outsiders got within fifty yards of the singer they'd finally found.

Just before three o'clock, Abby, grimy and exhausted, stood with Spark in front of the Loon Feather for the twentieth time that day, unable to resist a pull to the spot. The millionth and millionth-and-first tears of the day coursed from her eyes for her children, her birds, her haven in town. Gray, Elliott, and Ed were across the street, talking to Dewey. Disaster made for strange bedfellows.

"Gray told me about this place," Spark said. "He says it's where he fell in love with this little town."

"It's heartbreaking. Did he tell you about the cockatiels?"

Spark nodded. "Yeah. Dawson teaching the one to talk."

"I can't bear . . ." The words wedged in her throat, and for the briefest moment full silence reigned. Not a single shout or crash from a thrown piece of debris marred the quiet. Then she heard it. She strained, listening, and her heart threw itself against her ribcage. "Spark? Did you hear something?" Faint, muffled, it came again.

The "Colonel Bogey March."

"Gray!!!" she shrieked, scrambling toward the wreckage of the café. "Gray! Here!!"

Thirty seconds later, fifteen people piled into the debris, and Spark shushed them all frantically, his calm shattered for the first time.

"Lester?" Abby cried. "Lester sing to me, sweetie. Cotton?"

She listened a long—a very long—moment until a wolf whistle emanated from beneath a pile of countertop. With a heave from three strong men, including Gray, Dewey, and gentle, gorgeous Miles, a space in the hollow of a wall cupboard opened up, and there, safe and sound, sat the cage no one had expected to see again. Lester flapped and squawked, then burst into "Andy Griffith." Cotton bobbled her head up and down, up and down, up and down.

Miles let fly a whoop that made Cotton shriek. "They's the famous birds! Dog, this is a good sign. A *good* sign."

Abby smiled and pressed her face against the cage, eyes streaming, momentarily relieved. "Good boy. Good girl," she cooed.

"How-dee stray. How-dee stray. How-dee stray-jer." A shock through her heart sent Abby stumbling backward. Gray caught her, his arms circling her torso. "How-dee stray-jer."

"What's she saying?" Spark asked.

"Howdy stranger." Abby's voice shook. "She only says that for one person. Gray? Oh please, Lord. Gray??" Her body and her vocal chords shook with a violent tremor.

"He's got to be here." Gray pushed aside several large hunks of lumber and two tables, and found a large piece of linoleum countertop braced against a door. "Where does this lead?"

"How-dee stray-jer."

"The basement!" Abby joined him, her thoughts frantic. Miles and Dewey heaved the heavy counter out of the way. Gray yanked the door open to find the staircase crisscrossed with two-by-fours.

"Dawson? Kim?" He shouted into the blackness, the quaver threading through his voice giving away every bit of his fear and hope.

"Dad?"

"Mom?"

Abby's knees buckled.

They were trapped beneath the collapsed section of the café's floor, and the only injury was to Kim's foot. It took fifteen precious minutes to clear the stairwell, but when Gray and Abby reached the basement, Dawson scurried out of a hole secured by rescue workers, into the waiting arms of his father. Abby rejoiced for Gray as his son clung like a six-year-old.

"How did you two get here?" Gray stroked Dawson's head over and over.

"Old Mister Jirek." Dawson's words were muffled in Gray's shirt. "He was going to town to pick up his wife and get her home before the storm. We hitched a ride and told him we were meeting you."

"I'm gonna ground you for life, buster," Gray's voice quavered with emotion.

"Here in the U.S.?" Dawson lifted his head, and the band members at the top of the stairs burst into laughter.

"Let's get Kimmy out, and then I'll deal with you." He kissed Dawson's hair twice more, unashamedly and finally let him go. He peered into the man-made escape hole, next to a burly firefighter. "Hey you," he called. "Your foot hurts, huh?"

"I think it's broken. I tripped running down the stairs. Was there really a tornado?"

"Indeed there was. But it doesn't matter anymore. Now we can fix everything."

Abby marveled at the warmth and humor in Gray's voice. There were mercenaries across town scheming for a way to steal his picture and associate it with this disaster. He should have been useless and self-centered, but he was a hero. He took care of details. He'd set aside his personal problems. He could speak like a father to a girl who needed comfort in a crisis. He could lead a family. He was so much more than his money and his wealth. Where had her head been all these weeks thinking selfishly of herself?

"Is my mom here?"

"She sure is."

Gray let the fireman go into the rubble and pull Kim to safety, but he took her immediately from the rescuer and cradled her in his arms. She held his neck, burying her face in his T-shirt until they reached Abby, and he set her down, making sure she was steady on her good foot.

"Mommy!"

Abby grabbed her in a hold that she never intended

to let go. Kim wept, but Abby had shed her last tear for a while. When all four stood at the bottom of the stairs, Gray wrapped his arms around them all. "Kimmy, you couldn't mean more to me if you were my own daughter, and losing you would have hurt as much as losing Dawson. And you . . ." He spread his hand over Dawson's head. "We were frantic. If you ever do such a boneheaded—"

"No." Kim's small voice cut him off. "It's n-not his fault. I ran away and he tried to s-stop me. Then he wouldn't let me go alone."

"You?" Abby held her, confused. "Why?"

"Because, I didn't want Gray to be right. He told me the night of the concert I was confusing needing someone strong, like a father, with being in love. I-I felt so stupid and, and mad." She stuttered, burying her face deeper into Abby's arms.

"You aren't stupid, sweetheart."

"I re-remember a-all the times I needed help. With the clar-clarinet and Gucci and here. I knew you'd co-come. The best times are when you act li-like a dad." She reached to Gray, and clung to his neck as he lifted her into strong arms. Abby found she had more tears after all.

"It isn't safe down here. Let's get you up to the EMTs, huh? Can I carry you?"

She nodded against his shirt. Abby put her arm securely around Dawson and sought Gray's eyes. "Can we really fix everything?" she asked.

The pale blue of his irises shone in the dim basement light. "I guess that's up to us."

Chapter Twenty-Nine

"No. Now MORE than ever I don't think you should cancel it." Gray stood at the front of Kennison Falls's makeshift city council room in the drafty basement of the Lutheran Church. He faced the exhausted mayor and five city council members. Behind him crowded a good portion of the town's residents, and beside him stood Elliott along with Karla, narrow tear tracks forming mini deltas on her dusty cheeks.

"It's fine, Gray." Karla's rounded shoulders slumped. "I understand why there's no way we can hold the camp. There's no time. Now there's definitely no money."

Gray stroked her hand. It was temporarily fragile, like everyone in the room. "I'd like to make a proposal."

"By all means, Mr. Covey, we need as many ideas as we can get at the moment." Sam Baker, the fireplug-shaped mayor of the devastated town, looked far older than his fifty-four years and way past bone-weary. Considering the paparazzi force had done nothing to ease his considerable burdens, Sam had been surprisingly welcoming to Gray.

It didn't hurt that the Lunatics had also become Kennison Falls adopted sons, continuing to dig in and dig out with as much fervor as the locals even after all souls were accounted for.

"If we've learned anything in this country it's that one thing we all need after a disaster is joy to take our minds off the pain." Gray kept his voice solemn. "Music camp will be that joy. And my band and I would like to help."

Elliott gave Gray a supportive pat on the back and took over. "If we find a suitable venue for an expanded . . . Kabbagestock?" He scowled at Karla. "Really?" Titters floated through the room, welcome sounds from the exhausted residents. "Gray would like to perform a benefit concert and donate the proceeds to the town. Meanwhile, if we can get basic safety clean-up done and get those businesses that are able back up and running, I'll personally work on promoting those businesses and the concert, in a respectful way. It could be good for the whole town."

For several seconds silence hung in the room. Gray swallowed bittersweet emotions. It should have been Chris standing by his side. Instead, lawyers were scrambling to make sure Chris had no access to Gray's assets until final decisions were made. Chris out. Elliott in? The world had been blown off its moorings by more than a Midwestern twister.

"That's a pretty generous offer I hafta say, Mr. Covey."

"Gray."

"Thank you. Gray it is."

"What about security?" a councilman identified by hand-written sign as Daniel Hopka asked in concern.

"I have a large staff of road personnel, and I'll donate their time for whatever help you need. I'm not good at coordinating rebuilding efforts, but I can help organize a music camp." Gray self-consciously rubbed his skin, scratchy with dust-laced scruff.

"We all love Mrs. Baxter's music camp. It's been a tradition here for fifteen years." Sam Baker looked down his short line of council members. Each nodded.

"To say we appreciate your help would be understating our feelings." Councilwoman Ann Gunderson, her eyes bright, her words eager, was the only one who'd shown signs of being a fan. Gray smiled back at her. The town would get used to him. If he wanted to stay, he had to be more than a celebrity curiosity.

"I've grown to love quite a few people in Kennison Falls. I want to help."

"Oh, Gray," Karla faced him, tears streaming into her smile. "I don't know what to say."

"Don't say anything. Give me a hug, and let's get to work."

Two hours after the council meeting, Gray leaned against Abby's living room door jamb, and she smiled from the sofa. Stretched out with her tousled head cradled in Abby's lap, Kim slept like a comatose patient. Her left foot, swathed in several inches of flesh-colored Ace bandage, was propped on two pillows—badly sprained, but not broken. Bird lay curled against her good leg, purring like a lawnmower.

"I swore I was going to wring their necks," Abby said softly, "but I can't bring myself to be angry."

"I know the feeling, believe me."

His tired gaze settled on the recliner across the room where his son, his safe son, was heaped in a much less elegant state of slumber beneath a thick quilt. Roscoe snoozed in front of him.

Dust and filth still covered Gray hair to shoes, exhaustion encroached on every body part, and unspoken words hovered precariously between him and Abby. But with his family—what he desperately wanted to be his family—gathered secure and safe within his sight, a soul-deep contentment was doing a great job staving off full exhaustion.

While Abby extricated herself slowly from pillow duty, Gray took in every movement and detail. Grime smeared her face, her blue shorts hiked up past the swell of her inner thigh, and her white, zippered hoodie was striped like zebra skin. She stood, and her waistband rode down exposing the soft skin of her waist. Her gorgeous bottom popped toward him when she bent to smooth Kim's hair.

His body buzzed with the thrill of being near her again. His tired, besotted male brain ogled her without guilt. Sylvia and Ed were tucked into their house with promises that tomorrow there'd be a willing crew to help sort out their yard. The Lunatics were ensconced at a hotel in Faribault. The kids slept. She faced him, and for a moment they stared as if each waited for permission.

Gray moved first, crossing the room to gather her tightly, aching with weariness and, given the circumstances, inappropriate desire.

"Did I ever tell you how glad I was to see you this morning?" she asked.

"Did I ever tell you how glad I was that you were safe?"

"I need to say something, Gray. I'm sorry. I'm so sorry I betrayed you, and it was a betrayal no matter how well-intentioned."

"No. I understand. I do. I'm glad you did it."

"It won't happen again. It wasn't like me."

"It was exactly like you. Fighting for me like you fight for everything you care about."

She tilted her head up, but he didn't let her gaze linger. He craved the taste of her mouth like an addict craved heroine, and, with a starving, searching kiss, he covered her lips. The bold surge of her tongue parted his lips, gentle suction pulled shards of pleasure from deep in his body. She was rare, wonderful wine he'd gone years without tasting.

"We're good at this," he whispered when they parted, reluctantly.

She set her forehead against his lips. "We're good at a lot of things. We were good today, but I don't know what it means."

"I've figured out what it means for me. When I got it through my stubborn head you sent that picture against my wishes to save me, I came back. I want to change my life with you. I want you to *be* my life."

"So serious." Her eyes shone the way they had the first

time he'd looked at her, but behind the teasing mask they held the same, familiar doubts. When he squeezed her fingers her gaze slipped sideways.

"I'm not taking this lightly." He turned her cheek back. "You told me you didn't want to be my charity. You've never been a charity case, Abby. But you were right when you told me to find something worthwhile to do with my money. Dawson told me I was so rich I could afford to cure Alzheimer's." His laugh was self-deprecating. "Well, I can't, but I can help."

"Yes. You could."

"Chris wasn't—isn't—a philanthropic man." Anger and sorrow pricked at his heart in equal parts, as he realized he was already thinking of Chris Boyle in the past tense. "I was raised by my manager to be a selfish businessman, and I didn't realize it."

"There isn't a selfish bone in your body." She rubbed her hand against his chest. "I heard you at that council meeting. I know how generous you are with Kim and Dawson and me."

Just like that, they reached the heart of the problem between them. Gray drew his breath deep, fortifying his resolve. Praying—as he'd been doing all day.

"Chris always said I didn't have time to waste on philanthropic projects like an Alzheimer's foundation. He would never have stood for the benefit concert. He turned things just like it down left and right, but I never paid any attention. It's being with you that's shown me why my life has had so little meaning."

"Stop." Her blush was beautiful beneath the dirt smudges. "I know I'm prideful, wanting to make things work all by myself, asking for help from no one but God. Why do you think I was so angry about Gucci? About the saddle? I want to do it all myself. I really have been living in fear of losing Kim, losing everything, for so long."

"Did Jack's parents really threaten to take Kim from you?"

"They took me to family court. Tried to prove I couldn't provide proper schooling, or clothing, or adequate food and shelter. They didn't like that I'd married their son in the first place, and they semi-blamed me for his death. They put the fear in me for quite a few years."

"I was selfish, even when you first told me that. I thought it was hyperbole, and I just wanted what I wanted, even though I wanted it for good-intentioned reasons. I'm sorry."

"You don't have to be sorry. I don't know how to change the fact that it's still impossible to think about letting go of my independence."

"But is it independence, Abby? Or have you simply learned to keep people away so you don't lose them again? You let people tell you how strong you are, but do you let people tell you it's okay, even after twelve years, to be scared or sad? To need help? Are you sure you aren't that drowning woman who faithfully believes God's going to rescue her, but doesn't recognize the rescue when it comes?"

He didn't realize at first she'd started to cry. When

he recognized the shimmy in her shoulders as silent sobbing, his heart fell to his stomach. "Abby, I didn't mean
to—"

"I know that joke." The soft skin beneath her eyes glistened. "When the woman dies and gets to heaven and
asks God why he didn't save her, he says, 'I sent you a
boat and a helicopter, what more did you want?' I know
the whole town recognized you as part of the helicopter
crew who'd arrived to save them today, Gray. They know
how to accept help, why is it so hard for me?"

"You're tough, but you're wounded. You lost most of a
family and were threatened with having what was left of
it taken away, too. Kim might be safe with you now, but
why should you risk finding another family just to risk
starting the losing process again? I get it."

"And yet, I almost did lose it."

"We both almost did. And I can't guarantee nothing
bad will ever happen. But I can help you stop living in
fear. Dawson isn't Will, but he fills a hole, and you love
him. I'm not Jack but I can love you like an obsessed man.
C'mon Abby, get into my rowboat."

A small smile, nervous but genuine, slipped onto her
lips. "Maybe I'm just afraid of how big the rowboat is."

"It's true. I can afford a big rowboat. But that could
be fun. We could sell this place and buy you the farm of
your dreams."

She stiffened in his arms, as he'd expected. "Oh, Gray,
that's just it. I'm not ready for that." The clouds in her
eyes darkened with her endearing, stubborn pride. He
held her tighter. She was new at this, but he was ready

this time. With a flourish in his voice he played his ace.

"I said we *could*, I didn't say we should. Besides, you're a woman of means yourself now. You can buy your own boat. Elliott told me about the dealer who wants to see your photos. And there is the picture I sent to the record label's art department. They like it."

"You what?" She shook her head in wonder. "Oh, Gray, I don't know how I feel about either of those things. Nothing is guaranteed even if I don't stop you from helping me."

"The point is something *will* come of it if you choose to work at it. You know that's true, because you know you're good enough. And if you don't know it, I'll spend the rest of my life convincing you. Maybe you think this boat of mine is too close to being an ocean liner, but what if God isn't rescuing you, Abby? What if He's finally giving this drifting ocean liner a lifeboat?"

"I don't believe that for a second."

"Just believe it for a nanosecond, and we'll build from there."

This time her smile morphed into a laugh. "You're a fine salesman, Mr. Covey. I'm not sure it's all as easy as you seem to think it is."

"Oh, love, I don't think for one second this is easy. But it is easi*er* with two. And together, if we can rebuild a town, we can certainly remodel a farm. We can keep the name but we could give old Jumbawumba Ranch a makeover with our stamp on it."

"Stop dissing my name." She let herself melt against him, losing her tenseness, letting the storm in her eyes pass.

"Jambalaya," he kissed her. "Jujuwonky." He kissed her again. "Jabbywickets."

"Gray?"

"Yes, Abby?"

"Stick to the push-ups." She snaked one long, lovely leg around his thighs and slid it up to his rear. Fire licked at his belly. Every ounce of fatigue drained away.

"It's a new day," he mumbled against her lips, nipping, reaching around her hips, lifting until both her legs wrapped him like cotton candy spinning onto its cone.

"We're good at new days." She kissed him. "Can we just have a few of those for me to get used to? Please will you and your rowboat be patient?"

"I'm patient," he promised. "You'll get impatient with my patience."

She giggled, and her breath went through him like shock therapy, making the hair on his arms, legs, nape, and crown stand on end. Healing him.

"I never told you, but I have a camping mattress I think will fit perfectly in this little darkroom." She squeezed her legs around his hips.

"If we make it out of the shower . . ."

"Eeeewww." A voice hoarse with sleep made Abby freeze in his arms.

She buried her head in his shoulder and groaned, then slowly unwrapped her legs and slid her feet to the ground. "I was just going to ask if you thought the little demon children heard us."

"You two are revolting." Dawson stretched and

shifted, peering at them with half a face showing from beneath the blanket.

"Good, then we're practicing proper parenting techniques." Abby touched Gray's cheek and turned with calm toward his son. As always, he marveled at her innate skill with him.

Dawson, with brows furrowed, looked like a gopher poking out of his hole. "My mom would have yelled at me for hearing what you guys just said. Kind of the no-sex-I'm-British thing. This is why I want to stay here. It's more, I dunno, real." He scowled. "Even if it's really disturbing."

"Think how wonderfully disturbed he'd be if you'd been his mother all along." Gray couldn't help himself. He was too immersed in his dream to be politically correct. "No offense to your real mother."

Dawson shrugged, unconcerned. Abby batted him with a firm hand.

"You need to be kinder to Ariel. She isn't a horrible mother, or you'd never have left your son in her care. And he's a good kid—look what he did for Kim."

"I'm right here," Dawson mumbled. "My ears work."

"You still want to stay?" Abby asked him.

Gray's heart pumped nervousness into his system. The thought of duking it out with Ariel was still a weak spot for him, but before he could counsel caution, Abby and Dawson were negotiating.

"You know I do."

"Well, you should know I want you to stay, too. I'd

love you to go to school here, get your driver's license, play baseball. I'm not your mother, Dawson, but I love you anyway. I'll help your dad negotiate with your mom if you promise to understand there are probably just as many rules here as there were in England."

"Abby, I . . ." Gray looked from Abby to his son, still not certain this promise was a good idea. He had no idea if Ariel would allow this without a fight.

"I'll do rules." Dawson dropped the blanket and changed from timid gopher to scrappy wolverine. "Dad. I just want to stay here. With you."

What the hell could he say to that? With a sigh he realized Ariel didn't hold every single good card in the deck. "I want you to stay, Son. Very much."

Abby turned her bright aquamarine eyes on him with joy. "That's all it takes from you, Gray. You are a master of public relations. You need to turn some of your charm on Ariel and let the animosity go. Don't treat her like an enemy. She has to be an ally. If you do that, I think she'll fall all over herself letting him stay here for the school year. I do."

"Yeah, Dad. Be nice to her instead of being a jerk."

Now the kid had gone from wolverine to pathetic, begging spaniel. For the barest instant his words and Abby's stung. Then he laughed out loud. Abby was right—as right about him as he'd been about her. Lord, how they needed each other.

"Fine," he said, staring deep into Abby's smiling eyes, talking to Dawson. "I'll banish the jerk. I'll make it work for you to stay. Now, is that all or will you go back to sleep now, so we can shower and go to bed?"

"Oh, *man*!" Dawson threw the quilt over his head and disappeared.

"Goodnight, Dawson," Abby called, laughing. Silence. She lifted her lips to Gray's ear. "I'm impressed, Mr. White Knight. You seem to have saved the day again."

The compliment burrowed deep into his heart, as he led her out of the room. He'd told her he had patience—he'd lied.

Patience had never been his strong suit.

Chapter Thirty

MAX YASGUR HAD nothing on Chuck Tupy when it came to land contribution for a music festival. Music reverberated across Chuck's farmland adjacent to the state park. No rain, no naked hippies, no smashed guitars—but this had Woodstock beat hands-down.

Abby swiveled her head trying to burn Kabbagestock images into her mind. An ocean of bodies undulated like tropical waves over a beach of blankets spread edge-to-edge. Kids, parents, and grandparents stood, sat, stomped, clapped, whistled, and called, all united temporarily over the same music. Teens who'd escaped security hung like monkeys from surrounding trees, toddlers and grandpas alike danced across what, days before, had been a Guernsey pasture.

Gray and his band struck the last chord of what had started as Beethoven's Fifth Symphony. A pulse-destroying cymbal crash carried into the crowd to be swallowed by eight-thousand cheers. Part of Gray's unique claim to fame was playing, at each show, a classical music piece. He could coax symphonic sounds from his band while he showed off his early training with a variety of musical instruments. But then he would slowly ratchet up the tempo and let his musicians rock out on Beethoven, Mozart, Tchaikovsky.

Rock's Rachmaninoff.

Kennison Falls kids who'd never known classical music could be cool cheered like crazed soccer fans. The oldest residents, dutifully showing solidarity by being there, stared glassy-eyed at the corruption of sacrosanct classics.

Abby turned to Karla and threw her arms around her friend in a triumphant embrace. To say the camp, held for three days before the concert, had been a success would have been like saying the tornado had caused a little damage.

"My gosh, he's amazing," Karla hollered as the crashing chords wound down.

Abby looked to the stage and caught the full force of Gray's smile. Her heart banged in her chest like a bongo out of sync. More than amazing. He was weak-in-the-joints sexy. No spangles adorned him today, just his thousand-dollar jeans encasing his long legs, a well-fitted, black T-shirt, bearing pictures of the Beatles from the *White Album*, and his scuffed Nikes.

Abby raised her camera, twisting the telephoto lens to close in on the sweat-curled ends of his shaggy hair and the embroidered guitar strap straining across his shoulders. She'd already exposed three rolls of film in ninety minutes trying to preserve the hot motion in still photos.

She didn't care if he ever wore a sequin again—this plain, body-hugging look got her blood pumping fast and hot. Or was it the sexy voice? Or the depth of his skill? Or the way he managed to make his gaze sear into her until every other person in the wild crowd disappeared?

She swung her lens away from him and focused on her daughter, who, along with three of her best friends, hovered stage-left, giggling like hyenas on banned substances. They'd been christened "Lunatic-ettes," and given the status of official band go-fers by Spark. Seeing Kim over-the-moon rather than moony-eyed was an indescribable relief.

"I guess we've done enough damage to the classics, what do you think?" Gray called when the song ended. "How about something nobody has ever heard before? Would you let me debut a new song here at Kabbagestock?"

The crowd's raucous approval continued, and Gray found Abby's eyes once more. After working with him side-by-side for the week, and falling more deeply in love with his amazing spirit and drive, she'd come to believe she could read his emotions. This time she sensed an unusual nervousness in his eyes, and she formed a silent question with her brows.

"This is a collaboration with my son, Dawson, who helped with the arrangement." Abby glanced behind the crowd, knowing Dawson was with the sound techs. "It's a little bit of a new sound for us. See what you think."

She hadn't heard the tune in six weeks, but it was as familiar as if it played on the radio ten times a day.

"A storm-eyed girl took my hand one day . . ."

The music soared, and an unusual, hard edge drove the chorus, even though it was a soft love song. The melody poured over Abby like thunderstorms and sunshine. His promise to her kept in a song. Her song.

She made no attempt to hide her tears. She'd never wanted to live in someone's shadow again, but she remembered what Gray had told her the day after the tornado. "If you don't believe you're good enough, I'll spend the rest of my life convincing you."

Without a doubt, she knew he would.

When he finished, the crowd surged to its feet. At first she didn't hear the low chant rumbling beneath the applause. Then it burst into clarity—sending heat and chills, embarrassment and pride dancing through her body.

Ab-by! Ab-by! Ab-by! Kim and the Lunatic-ettes revved the crowd like circus barkers.

"Ladies and gentlemen, if you haven't guessed, that song goes out to Kennison Falls's very own Abby Stadtler. Abby, I think you need to come up and take a bow."

Mortified, she shook her head. The song had made an unequivocal-enough statement. She'd shout "I love you" back at him this minute, but no way was she ready for front-and-center.

Placing the microphone in its stand, Gray grazed the crowd with his hot-ice eyes and urged them with a "come-on" wiggle of his fingers, garnering more roaring encouragement. When she shook her head again, fighting a trill of excitement and a knot of fear the size of Micky's bass drum, Gray cupped his hands around imaginary oars and made a rowing motion.

The ball was hers to play. Then, like a last-chance angel offsetting the devil of doubt, Ed appeared at her side. "Go on up there, Abigail. I think he's got something for you."

"I . . . but . . . What if . . . ?"

"Nobody can answer the 'what ifs,' honey. But if you're waiting for someone to promise it'll be all right, then fine, I promise it'll be all right."

"You do? Ed?"

He pressed a kiss on her forehead. "It'll be like having James Bond for a son-in-law."

Son-in-law? She stared at him as if he'd escaped his padded cell, but he only shooed her toward the stage.

Next thing she knew, Gray reached for her hand. The happiness in his eyes pulled like a tractor beam. When she stood in front of the crowd—in front of him—an unexpected calm descended, and the drumming of fear in her stomach subsided. The surroundings blurred. The man did not. Wasn't that the key? That, for them, the crowd would always be there, but in the background?

Gray pulled his Les Paul's strap over his head and handed the guitar to Spark. Without preamble he sank to one knee. The crowd went berserk.

Unamplified, his voice carried to her alone. "I once thought Fate had it in for me. Turns out, I'm her favorite child. The proof is you, Abby. I told you I want you to be the rest of my life. Like it or not, I'm here to prove it in front of all these people. I'd like to be your future, too. Will you marry me?"

He held a gold circlet between his thumb and forefinger, and for a moment her fingers trembled over her mouth, waiting for disbelief to dissipate. Finally, she reached for the ring, and their fingers collided. She yanked on his hand to make him stand.

"Yes," she whispered, laughter diluting her tears. "I think my rowboat just came in."

He hauled her into his arms. Just before she closed her eyes, she caught his thumbs-up to Spark onstage and Elliott offstage. Sound from the wild crowd enveloped her.

And the whole world watched as she kissed him.

About the Author

LIZBETH SELVIG lives in Minnesota with her cradle-robbing husband and a border collie that inspired the character Dug "Squirrel!" the Dog in the Disney movie *Up*. After working as a journalist and editor and raising an equine veterinarian daughter and a talented musician son, Liz entered and won RWA's Golden Heart°contest in 2010 with her contemporary romance, *The Rancher and the Rock Star*. In her spare time, she loves to hike, quilt, read, horseback ride, and play with her nearly twenty four-legged grandchildren. You can connect with her on Facebook, Twitter, or her Website: www.lizbethselvig.com.